MASTERPIECE

A NOVEL BY

CHARTER ROAD

TATE PUBLISHING & *Enterprises*

Published by Tate Publishing & Enterprises, LLC
127 E. Trade Center Terrace | Mustang, Oklahoma 73064 USA
1.888.361.9473 | www.tatepublishing.com

Tate Publishing is committed to excellence in the publishing industry. The company reflects the philosophy established by the founders, based on Psalm 68:11,
"The Lord gave the word and great was the company of those who published it."

Cover design by Amber Gulilat
Interior design by Nathan Harmony

Published in the United States of America

ISBN: 978-1-61739-733-2
1. Fiction / Christian / Fantasy
2. Fiction / Christian / Romance
11.05.09

This book is dedicated to my beloved, Lord and Savior, Jesus Christ. He is the road that leads to eternal life.

Special thanks to Chappy, "The Chance," Brandon Chappell, and Phyllis Baines for all their help and encouraging words in the preparation of this book.

A thick fog shrouded the dark, bloated clouds over London, casting a gloomy ambience over the city. The temperature was slowly dropping, and the first sign of winter snowfall would soon appear. It was another normal day in the busy metropolis, like so many others that had come and gone. People were browsing through stores, catching buses to cross town, or enjoying lunch at a nearby café. Outside dining customers were often serenaded by the cooing of pigeons waddling around the tables, searching for a midday meal.

In the distance, Big Ben could be heard faithfully announcing the noon hour. Shortly before the twelfth chime, the sound of whistling wind blew into an inconspicuous place at the far end of the Ritz Mall, a classy shopping center catering primarily to the rich. On the heels of the wind appeared a blue energy sphere that shone like a radiant star. Within the core of these magnificent particles of light materialized a young Irish chap named Rane Rivers and his British wife, Haley. She had transported the two of them to the mall using a teleportation device that looked much like a silver pocket watch.

Haley was a bonny lassie with long, curly, red hair that framed her bright green eyes and flawless, cream-colored skin. On her left cheekbone was a tiny, heart-shaped beauty mark. She had a gentle nature about her and a keen eye for detail. Her girlish humor and zeal for life made her fun to hang out with.

Rane was quite attractive. He had striking, teal blue eyes that often drew attention away from the other features on his lightly freckled face. His short, wavy, blond hair topped a firm body that stood six feet tall. He had a wounded heart that often made him disagreeable to be around, but, still, deep down inside, there was a lovable, little boy yearning to come out.

Haley peered guardedly through the veil of light into the shopping complex, making sure no one was around to see them. When she didn't spot anyone in the immediate area, she looked toward the other end of the mall and saw several shoppers standing motionless like posed mannequins in front of a display window. She giggled at their statuesque appearance and then pressed her thumb on top of a small, crystal button located on the right side of the teleportation device. All at once a portal opened up, allowing her to enter the vicinity of the mall. Racing against time, she grabbed her spouse by the hand and tried to pull him through the electrical outlet before the twenty-second window closed. Much to her surprise, he broke free from her grip, surmounted with sheer panic by all the purple and blue energy ribbons blocking the passageway.

Haley extended a friendly hand toward her trembling husband, who was slowly backing away from her. "Don't be afraid. Everything will be all right."

Rane widened his eyes at the high voltage that was impeding their way of escape and took another step backward. He was so scared of being electrocuted that, when his wife recaptured his hand, he started shouting hysterically in an uneducated hodgepodge of British and Irish dialect, "No, let go o'me, lassie!"

Tightening her grasp on his hand, Haley slipped the silver pocket watch into her ski jacket pocket and said consolingly, "I promise, love, you won't be hurt."

Doubting the idea that he could safely pass through the hazardous energy field without being killed, Rane bellowed, "Are ye crazy? We can't go through there. We'll be ripped apart!"

Haley saw the portal closing fast and knew she had to do something. With lightning speed, she used a judo technique on her husband and flipped him through the opening.

Caught off guard by the unexpected maneuver, Rane shrieked with fright, tumbling head-over-heels onto the polished, mall floor.

Haley cringed guiltily when Rane's head slammed against the side of the wall and hurried over to see if he was all right. She had barely made it through the outlet herself before the time portal vanished in a twinkling of an eye. After making sure they were now moving at the same speed as the other patrons in the mall, she leaned over at the waist and said to her husband, "Are you okay, your highness?"

Badly shaken up from the fall, Rane wobbled his dazed head and then looked up at his wife. When her face went out of focus, he crossed his eyes and placed his quivering hand to the side of his temple, groaning miserably, "Ooh, my aching head."

Haley gripped his forearm with both hands, tugging hard until she got him to his feet. "Uh, sorry about that, I guess I don't know my own strength."

Rane still wasn't fully cognizant of what he was doing prior to the fall, until a picture of high voltage flashed through his mind. Disturbed over what he saw, he glanced over where the time portal used to be and then diligently inspected his body for any signs of impairment. Not seeing anything wrong with himself, he sought corroboration from his wife. "I'm not dead, am I?"

Haley struggled to keep a straight face, not wanting him to know she was laughing inside at his ludicrous question. "No."

Rane didn't believe her and felt for a pulse on the side of his neck. When he didn't feel a throb, he protruded his eyes worriedly and said, "I think me heart stopped beating."

Haley giggled under her breath at him fretting over nothing and then tried to come up with a way to take his mind off himself. After spotting a twelve-foot Christmas tree through the giant picture window behind them, she redirected his attention toward the open square by saying, "Don't you think that's a bonny tree?"

Rane glanced indifferently out the window at the large, silver, Christmas balls hanging on the noble fir branches and answered in a voice of exasperation, "What! I might be having a heart attack an' all ye can think about is some daft tree?"

Haley flashed her straight, pearly-white teeth at him and said almost laughing, "You're not having a heart attack, your highness. If you were, you would have difficulty telling me about it."

Flustered by the way she kept addressing him, Rane made a sharp tug on the snug waist of his faded blue jeans and said, "Would ye quit calling me 'yer highness?' Ye talk t'me as if I'm somebody important."

She peered into his piercing, bluish-green eyes as if she could see right through him and whispered ardently, "You'll always be a king in my eyes, Rane. I'm just so glad I finally found you. I've been looking for you for over a year. I've missed you terribly. Where have you been?"

Shocked that she knew his name, Rane cocked an eyebrow and carefully looked her over, thinking in the back of his mind that she was drop-dead gorgeous. "Where have I been?"

Haley tidied her green cashmere sweater and replied, "Yes. Remember, we got into a fight on our anniversary, an' you walked out on me."

Rane touched the tender lump on the right side of his head and winced from the pain. *Walked out on ye?*

"Why didn't you come back, love? Haven't you missed me?"

"Missed ye? How come ye seem t'know me, but I dunno ye?"

Haley hooked several strands of hair behind her left ear, giggling flirtatiously. "Stop teasing me, Rane. You know who I am. I'm Haley McConaley Rivers, your wife."

Rane stared unrecognizably at her facial features for a long moment and then shook his head with certainty. "Honest, lassie, I've never seen ye before in me life."

She noted his serious expression. "You mean this whole act isn't a charade? You really don't know who I am?"

Rane eyeballed her good looks a second time. "No. Should I?"

Haley called to mind some of the childish pranks she and her husband used to play on each other and gave him a suspicious smirk. *Oh no you don't, Rane Rivers. You played this little memory loss trick on me once before. I'm not falling for it again.*

She diverted her interest out the window when she caught sight of two green parrots landing on top of the Christmas tree. Wishing she had romance back in her own life, she watched them nuzzle their beaks and sighed hopefully. "Aw, the love birds look happy."

Rane forced himself to glimpse at the birds she was talking about and then made an uninterested face at his wife. "Why did ye bring me here anyway? An' how in d'world did ye get me from my house t'the mall in less than ten seconds?"

Haley was still entertaining romantic thoughts and didn't answer. She seemed to be miles away as she envisioned her own husband caressing his ample lips against hers.

Noticing her lack of interest in what he was saying, Rane tapped his wife on the shoulder and queried, "Miss McConaley, are ye listening t'me? What magic trick did ye use t'zap me here?"

Batting her eyelids rapidly as if waking up out of a dream, Haley turned toward him, drawing her eyes onto his mouth. "Huh?"

Feeling like he wasn't getting through to her, the tension in Rane's voice mounted as he pointed his thumb in the direction where the time portal used to be. "How did ye do that?'"

Haley roamed her desiring eyes over every inch of his freckly face, finding his boyish charm seductively appealing. "I'm sorry. What did you say?"

Although Rane was bothered by the way she was gawking at him, he tried not to let it show. "I said, 'How did ye do that?'"

She answered naively, "How did I do what?"

Highly peeved over her lackadaisical attitude, Rane yanked on the collar of his black wool sweater and replied, "Ye know what. One moment I'm lying in me bed on my twenty-first birthday, thinking about this weird dream I had, an' ye suddenly popped into d'room an' scared me half t'death. Then, with a wink o'yer eye, ye grab me by d'hand an' whoosh, d'next thing I know I'm here at d'mall."

He suddenly became aware of his attire and got more upset. "Wait a minute. I was wearing briefs an' a blue undershirt. How did these clothes get on me?"

Dying to know what he saw while asleep, Haley overlooked everything else he said and asked, "What were you dreaming about?"

Rane sighed heavily from all the stress he had been through and began recounting the strange images he had seen in his sleep. "I, uh, dreamed I was a luminous star in heaven."

"How did you know the star was you?"

Rane made an uptight face at her for being nosy. "'Twasn't hard t'figure out: my name was on it."

She waited for him to say something further, and when he didn't, she decided to satisfy her own curiosity by picking his brain. "So what happened then?"

He lowered his brow, struggling to recall every detail of the dream. "I turned into a British king—seated on a throne amongst an innumerable amount of other kings. We were joyfully singing a love song out o' d'Bible like it was a hymnbook or something. I've never heard a choir harmonize so flawlessly like that before."

"Do you remember the song you were singing?"

He considered the lyrics and replied, "I believe it was John three sixteen."

Haley thought about the passage of God's love, and a delighted smile spread across her face. "That sounds like a wonderful dream."

Bored with his surroundings, Rane leaned over the edge of the wood railing and peered down below at the numerous shoppers bustling about on the bottom floor. "'Twas, till we…"

Rane promptly corrected his slip of tongue to protect his ego. "I mean… some of 'em closed d'book on God an' started singing a different tune."

Still hanging on his every word, Haley interrupted his vague recount to ask, "So these kings stopped letting the love of Jesus orchestrate their heart?"

Not quite sure what she meant, Rane shrugged his shoulders. "I guess."

Haley leaned beside him on the railing and asked, "After they lost sight of the King's love, where did they go?"

Convicted from some of the things he saw in the vision, Rane chewed on the skin around his thumbnail, something he routinely did whenever he felt uneasy or afraid. "They drifted backwards into a time warp."

Upon hearing the metaphorical pictures he described, Haley called to mind a warning in the Bible in Hebrews chapter two verse one, about heeding the truths you hear, lest they slip or drift away, and immediately afterwards mused, *To forget your identity in the King would be like having amnesia.*

Totally intrigued with this phenomenon, she pumped Rane for more information about his dream. "What made you believe they went into a time warp?"

Rane made it quite clear that he was getting tired of all her third degree. "What are ye, a detective or something?"

Uncertain why she was smiling at him, he gave her a strange look before sharing the answer. "They're royal clothes had changed into a knaves,' an' each person was imprisoned inside a timepiece. Since they were standing on d'opposite side of d'secondhand an' d'midnight hour never changed, it didn't take a genius t'figure out they weren't moving forwards in life."

Haley visualized herself standing on the reverse side of a clock and thought, *He's right. From their point of view, they would see the hand of time moving backwards.*

While continuing to unveil his dream, Rane started cracking his knuckles, another one of the nervous habits he had picked up over the years. "I saw so many universal clocks an' watches floating out in the twilight zone with people trapped inside 'em, I couldn't count 'em all."

With a far away gaze in his eyes, Rane said, "What I can't figure out is, why d'Jack o' Hearts?"

Haley perceived what the imagery meant but didn't let on to her husband. "They were all dressed up like a Jack of Hearts, huh?"

Rane nodded his head briskly. "Aye, like on an English playing card. They looked absolutely ridiculous in those sixteenth-century clothes."

After he had finished laughing at their unusual attire, he rubbed his clean-shaven chin a couple of times and said spookily, "I gotta tell ye, 'twas really creepy hearing all those knaves talk in backwards speech like a tape recording playing in reverse. They just kept standing there like a bunch o'gumbies watching d'secondhand on their timepiece move counterclockwise, shouting, 'Emit, emit, emit!' 'Tis like they had nothing better t'do than waste precious time."

Interpreting that the twilight zone represented an outer space of imagination just beyond ethical limits, and that *emit* was simply *time* spoken backwards, Haley took off in the middle of all his uncertainties and headed down the corridor.

Rane promptly chased after her, still recalling the things he saw. "Come t'think of it, I thought I saw me imprisoned inside a timepiece that looked a lot like d'clock tower in London. An' I had an open Bible in me left hand, but every time I turned d'page, it would turn back to d'same one."

His thoughts abruptly came back to the present when he noticed the perceptive look on her face. "Ye know what d'dream means. Don't ye?"

She glanced uneasily at the dubious gleam in his eye and sped up her stride.

Rane was practically running to keep up with her. When she finally stopped in front of a display window, he reiterated his question. "Ye do. Don't ye?"

Knowing he wouldn't like the translation, Haley deliberately didn't answer. She just stood there in front of the showcase, gazing through the glass window at a replica of the Imperial State Crown, which was resting on top of a scarlet velvet pillow.

Rane glanced apathetically at the simulated gems embedded in the crown and readdressed his question as if she didn't hear him the second time. "Don't ye?"

Haley avoided eye contact with him while playing with the silver chain around her neck. "Yes. God has given me the gift of interpretation."

Dying to hear the explanation of his dream, Rane propped his hand on the glass case and leaned closer to her face. "So why was I dressed up like a Jack o' Hearts?"

Secretly wishing he would drop the subject, Haley swallowed uncomfortably and remained silent.

When several moments passed without getting any feedback, Rane got upset and raised the tone of his voice. "Are ye listening t'me, Miss McConaley? I want t'know why every time I turned this particular page in d'Bible, it would turn back to d'same one?"

She slowly turned her head in her husband's direction and said repentantly, "We've been on baby steps too long, Rane. How can we ever expect to enjoy the fullness of the crown if we're not willing to grow up spiritually?"

Affronted by her statement from a heart filled with pride, Rane took a fleeting glance at her two-inch heel, brown leather boots and said, "What do ye mean baby steps? I'm grown up. I read me Bible at least once a month. That's a hopping pot more'n most me age. I know I haven't been t'church in a while, but I never forget t'mail in me tithes an' offerings."

He tweaked his nose and added, "An' what's it t'ye anyway? I don't even know who ye are."

Haley stepped closer when he went back to feeling the lump on his head. Having doubts about her previous guesswork, she peered into his bluish-green eyes, thinking, *Maybe he's not pretending after all. Maybe the blow to his head when he fell caused him to lose some of his memory.*

Rane felt nervous about her luscious lips being that close to his mouth, so he pulled his head back and queried, "What are ye doing?"

Haley answered in a passionate, soft tone, "Rane, look at me."

Rane bugged his eyes at her and replied, "How can I not look at ye with ye that close t'me Irish face?"

She ignored his sarcasm and went on to ask, "You really don't remember me?"

Rane smelled fresh peppermint on her breath as he meticulously scrutinized her visage. Although he had no spark of recognition of who she was, he secretly thought she was quite sexy. "If I do, it escapes me for d'moment."

Haley bit her lower lip while thinking of a way to jar his memory. "All right, I'll just have to prove it to you."

She then puckered up her lips and started whistling a tune into the air, sending a covert message to the teleportation device in her jacket.

Rane wondered what she was up to, until he saw a tiny, silver robot, about the size of a playing card, peeking at him from inside her coat pocket. Jumping to the conclusions that it was an alien, he shrunk back in alarm and started squealing loudly.

The shiny bot with thin lips and a round nose the size of a small BB, widened his big, baby blue eyes at his inventor, snickering in his cutesy, Irish voice, "Whiz Kid, ye funny guy."

Haley immediately tried to quiet her husband's hysteria by speaking in a soft tone. "Rane, calm down; Reddy won't hurt you."

Rane got himself under control and then frowned at the bot for laughing at him. The trauma to his heart could clearly be heard in his voice as he said to his wife, "What is that thing?"

She giggled at Reddy for winking his right eye at her husband. "It is a nanobot."

Rane curiously studied the bot's composition, paying close attention to its coiled, glittery golden hair, made out of soft metal fibers, and the belly button overlaid with white diamond specks. "A nano what?"

Haley twisted one of the loose curls on Reddy's bangs to make it tighter as she answered, "A nanobot. He's a particle communicator."

"Like I even know what that means," he grumbled under his breath.

Haley let go of the coil on the bot's head and started tickling his round tummy. "Isn't he cute? He has an Irish brogue just like you."

Ill at ease that the bot was actually laughing as she tickled it, Rane opened his mouth to speak and quickly closed it, forgetting what he was going to say.

Haley smiled widely at her husband. "Would you like to hold him?"

Rane put up both hands in strong protest and took a couple of steps backward. "Not on yer life. Ye keep that thingamabob away from me."

Feeling a need to defend the nanobot, Haley said, "Thingamabob? Reddy's not a thingamabob. You gave him to me as a wedding gift. Don't tell me you don't remember making Reddy either?"

Keeping his distance, Rane vigilantly eyed the bot's rounded, silver cheeks and long skinny arms. It was quite clear in the tone of his voice that he didn't believe a word of it. "I made that gizmo, eh?"

"Uh-huh."

"All by meself?"

"That's right."

Rane shook his head at her disclosure. "Go on, lassie, I think this genius would have remembered making Little Silver."

Reddy waved his teensy, metallic fingers at Rane and said, "Hi, Whiz Kid."

Haley sniggered at the bot's high-pitched greeting and then noticed the confused expression on her husband's face as he looked over at her. "What's wrong?"

"Whiz Kid?"

Haley answered with a smile. "Reddy always calls geniuses Whiz Kids. He's such a fun little toot."

Rane smacked his forehead with his palm, thinking aloud, "I got t'quit watching scary pictures before I go t'bed at night. What a nightmare I'm having."

He took his hand down from his face when he saw her zipping the bot up in her coat pocket. "Are ye going t'tell me why ye brought me here t'the mall?"

Haley nodded and pointed toward the picture window. "See that giant Christmas tree out in the open square?"

Rane glanced out the window and replied, "Aye."

"God wants us there at precisely two o'clock."

Roused with curiosity, Rane put his next question flatly. "Why?"

"I'm not sure. He hasn't told me the reason yet."

Rane looked at her like she was a complete idiot. "Yeah right, an' I think ye've been tippin' d'applejack bottle a little too much, lassie."

He rudely fanned his hand in front of her face and said, "Now off ye go, cheerio."

Haley peered sadly into his eyes while laying her hand to his cheek. "Please, Rane. Don't turn me away. Try to remember our love."

Rane pushed her hand down from his face and said coldly, "Look, lassie, if this Irishman ever loved ye, 'tis long forgotten."

Haley felt the pain of his rejection pierce her heart like a sharp blade as she watched him walk away. She squeezed her eyes shut, causing several teardrops to stream down her cheeks.

Rane pushed open one of the glass doors and went outside the mall. The thick fog that had been there since early morning had finally lifted, giving him clear visibility of an old pub across the street. Desiring some hot tea, he decided to go there and dodged the heavy traffic to get to the other side.

Haley tearfully spied on Rane through the picture window inside the mall. She wasn't about to let him walk out of her life a second time and tailed him like a protective bodyguard.

It wasn't long before Haley caught up with Rane and found him staring at a huge poster from the outside window of a seedy, Irish tavern called Lucky Spirits Pub. She eyed the two leprechauns and the three, green four-leaf clovers painted on the front of the grey building and decided to sneak up on her husband. After quietly stepping over a broken beer bottle on the sidewalk, she wiped the tears out of her eyes and then peered over his shoulder. "What are you looking at, your highness?"

Hearing a familiar voice, Rane turned his head to see who it was. The instant he saw his wife, he made a troublesome face and whined, "Oh no, not ye again; I thought I got rid o' d'likes o'ye."

Haley gave him a friendly grin and afterward eyeballed the picture of the shiny, red sports car on the poster. "I didn't know you liked the Panthera Sports Coupe."

His eyes lit up like two Christmas bulbs while promptly replying with a great deal of fervor, "Aye, ain't she a bonny car?"

Admiring the green-eyed panther lying on top of the hood of the vehicle, she replied, "Yes."

Rane dug into the candy bag inside his coat pocket and pulled out a handful of orange and cherry jellybeans. After picking out an orange one, he popped it into his mouth and began sucking on it like it was some sort of emotional pacifier. He then offered some of the candy in his hand to his wife. "Do ye want one?"

Haley selected one of the colored beans and placed it on her tongue. "Mmm, the cherry ones are my favorite."

While taking in a breath of fresh, winter air, she heard the carol *God Rest Ye Merry Gentleman* playing over the loud speaker at the mall. Enjoying the gaiety of the moment, she said, "Rane, did I ever tell you that Christmas is my favorite time of year?"

He gave her an annoyed look, crossing his arms. "An' just how could ye have tol' me that when I just met ye?"

Although it bothered her that he couldn't remember who she was, Haley's cheery disposition remained unchanged. "You know why I like it so much?"

"No. Why?" Rane asked, as if anything she said mattered.

"People are always jollier at Christmas…"

She paused briefly to stare at her spouse's grumpy visage and went on to say, "At least they used to be."

Rane tried to look the picture of innocence as he queried out of foolish pride, "Are ye insinuating I'm not jolly? Well, I don't need d'likes o'ye t'tell me I'm not happy when I'm happy. I should know whether I'm happy or not. I'm happy, so don't tell me I'm not happy when I'm happy."

Haley put on her black wool gloves and giggled at him. "You're just a happy Chappy kind of guy, huh?"

Upon hearing the pet name she called him, Rane queried, "I know I'm going t'regret this for asking, but what's a Chappy?"

She glanced over at an Englishman going into the tavern before replying, "Chappy's a little nickname I call you since your middle name is Chap."

A dubious glint shot through his eyes. "How did ye know me middle name was Chap?"

Haley smiled and commenced dancing around her husband. "I told you, I'm your wife. You'll remember when you get your memory back."

Dumbfounded by the happiness she possessed, Rane thought, *Nobody's that jolly, not even Santy Claus. She must be high on something.*

Haley spread her arms out to the side, spun around on the toe of her right boot, and giggled girlishly. "Dance with me, Rane. It's fun."

With a panicky look on his face, he glanced up and down the street and said, "Dance in public? Are ye daft? People will think I'm a kook."

She continued sniggering. "So let them."

Rane made a quick tug on the collar of his black turtleneck sweater like the wool hairs were aggravating his neck. "No. People will laugh at us."

"That's okay. Maybe they could use a good laugh."

Not wanting to draw any public attention, Rane disrupted Haley's ballet by pinning her swaying arms to her side. Looking her square in the eyes, he said, "No more dancing. I want some answers, Miss McConaley."

Haley's green eyes sparkled like two emerald jewels as she stared longingly at her husband's discontented face. "Please, call me Haley."

Feeling uneasy by her apparent infatuation with him, Rane let her go and started cracking his knuckles. "Why are ye staring at me like that, lassie?"

With her nostalgic eyes still glued on his, Haley moistened her plump, cherry-colored lips by giving them a quick lick of her tongue and answered, "I'm just glad you're finally dreaming about me again."

Unsure what she was talking about, Rane slicked back his crimped, flaxen hair and asked, "Why would I be dreaming about ye?"

Yearning to hold her husband in her arms, Haley's voice filled with intense emotion. "'Cause the best dreams are the ones we share together."

"So ye think I'm dreaming about ye, dreaming about me?"

Haley hummed some of the carol she was listening to earlier before answering, "That's right."

Presuming she was completely off her rocker, Rane rolled his eyes, griping under his breath, "Why is it I always seem t'attract d'weird ones? I must be d'most unluckiest gumby in d'world."

Rane put his focus back on the picture of the car and noticed the fine print at the bottom of the poster. "Hey, it says they're giving away one o' these cars in a drawing for Christmas."

"Really?"

He nodded, putting a handful of jellybeans into his mouth. His cheeks were so full of candy he could hardly speak. "I sure would love t'win it. Ye should see d'bomber I drive."

Haley sniggered. "I have. Most of it is held together with duct tape."

He stared bewilderedly at her face. "I'm not even going t'ask ye how ye knew that."

Haley's eyes glimmered with excitement as she suggested, "Rane, why don't you go inside an' enter the contest?"

Rane livened up somewhat at the thought of winning the car. "Why not? I might just get lucky."

Haley made it quite clear she detested his superstitious belief in chance. "Get lucky?"

She was a firm believer that all their blessed steps were encoded before the day they were ever born, basing her belief from the truth written in Psalm 37:23 and Psalm 139:16; Jeremiah 1:5; and Matthew 6:10. But she also knew they had a free will. If they chose not to put their faith in God, they could go off course and miss out on seeing the masterpiece He had intended for their life.

Haley followed Rane into the noisy, crowded pub and noticed there was standing room only. All the mahogany parlor chairs at the twelve tables were taken, including the barstools up at the bar. Celtic music was playing over the airways, a sweet medley of flutes, fiddles, uilleann pipes, piano, and guitar. The patrons were busy drinking alcoholic beverages while watching a rugby match on a small telly, mounted from the ceiling at the far end of the bar. They didn't seem to be bothered at all that the air reeked with cigar and tobacco smoke.

Haley bobbed her head while dancing in place to the Irish music. Feeling a strong desire to share her jubilant mood, she waved at the customers like she was their best buddy and said loudly, "Hi, everyone, merry Christmas. If you have some free time ..."

She pointed several times at the top of her husband's head and said further, "Come by and wish my birthday boy a happy birthday, okay?"

A few patrons gave Rane a disinterested look and went right back to watching television.

Rane frowned at his wife for drawing attention to him. "Would ye quit it! I don't want those blokes coming over here."

Haley didn't understand her husband's shyness toward strangers, for she had been raised to be friendly to everyone. "But if we keep our heart locked up in a box, what good is it?"

Rane shook an uncaring head and leaned his elbow on the mahogany countertop. Checking out the area behind the bar, he noted the numerous bottles of imported liquor and the clean, beer glasses overturned on the glass shelves. While scoping out the tavern for the location of the forms, he spotted a couple of Irishmen playing draw poker at a corner table in the back of the room. Pointing discreetly in the direction of the two men, he whispered to Haley, "Look, lassie, they're playing for money."

Haley despised the greedy spirit behind gambling and couldn't wait to leave. Her husband, on the other hand, didn't seem to be bothered by it at all. In fact, he rushed over to where the two men were wagering and started nosily observing their card game.

Haley tagged after him and tried to deter him from the table by pulling on his arm. "Come on, Rane, let's go find the forms."

Rane elbowed her grip off his arm and retained his strong fixation on the game. "In a minute. I want t'see who wins first."

Determined to get through to him, Haley gently gripped his chin with her gloved hand and turned his head in her direction. "The one who wins is the one who doesn't gamble."

Rane jerked his jaw free from her grasp and said grumpily, "Would ye stop? Ye act like we're really married."

She got nose to nose with him and firmly declared, "We are."

He raised his voice in defiance. "We are not!"

Rustie, one of the two Irishman playing cards at the table, stroked the coarse hairs on his red beard while listening in on their little spat. He was a stocky chap in his mid-forties with freckled skin and strawberry-blond hair. He was biased about women speaking their mind and made no qualms about it by the way he narrowed his sky blue eyes at Haley.

Martel, the other gambler at the table, was a gaunt gentleman in his early seventies. He had sparse, gray hair, grayish blue eyes, and badly wrinkled skin. With nothing better to do with his retirement, he came down to the pub every afternoon just to hang out with his friend Rustie.

Rustie took a long drag off the cigarette in his hand and rudely blew the smoke into Haley's face. He was tired of hearing her nag Rane and took it upon himself to scold her. "Leave him be, girlie. Let him be a man, why don't ye… or he'll be nothing more than a whipped pup."

Repulsed over the stench of the secondhand smoke, Haley laid her gloved hand in front of her nose and started coughing.

Rane wasn't a bit concerned about his wife's misery. He was too wrapped up in pride over the idea of being humbled by a female. "Whipped by a lassie—that'll be d'day."

Martel peeked at the five cards in his hand and then squinted recognizably at Haley. "I thought ye looked familiar."

Rane looked over at Haley, who had just finished coughing, and asked in a voice of surprise, "Ye know him?"

Martel took it upon himself to answer for her. "Aye, she was in here last week telling everybody about this Jesus of hers."

Rane was amazed at Haley's boldness in sharing her faith and questioned it aloud. "She did?"

"Aye, d'way she talked about him, ye'd think he was d'greatest treasure in d'world."

Taking a short puff off his cigarette, Rustie eyeballed Haley's good looks and said, "I remember ye now."

While stripping her black gloves off her hands, Haley smiled warmly at both Irishmen and said, "The King's offer of love still stands, gentlemen."

Rustie tapped the ashes off the end of his cigarette, placing the butt on the edge of the ashtray. He flipped over the King of Hearts face card, which he had discarded from his hand, and snickered roguishly, "Go on, lassie, I don't need yer King. Why I can buy love for a pot o'gold."

He elbowed his gambling partner on the arm, chuckling, "Right, Martel?"

Martel gulped down a shot of Irish whiskey before speaking up for his friend. "That's right. Rustie here is a very wealthy man."

Haley stuffed her gloves back inside her coat pockets while observing a huge oil painting hanging on the wall directly above the table. After frowning distastefully at the picture of two leprechauns gambling over a pot of gold, she said, "The only gold required is your faith, gentlemen."

Preferring to thumb his nose at her proposal, Rustie's uppity attitude remained. "My faith's in me doubloons, lassie. I don't need a savior."

Haley's eyes drifted momentarily toward the amber flames burning inside a stone fireplace, located along the same wall only a few feet away. She sat down at the table next to Rustie and said in a gentle, concerned voice, "When your pot of gold suddenly disappears, sir, what will save you then?"

Martel licked the cracked, dry skin inside the corner of his mouth and snickered playfully, "I guess she tol' ye, eh, Rustie."

Rustie was so enraged that a woman had made him look foolish in front of his comrade that his face turned beet red. With his fierce eyes bulging like a bullfrog, he reached down into the hidden pouch inside his brown leather boot and pulled out a combat bowie knife. Straight away he stabbed the pointed end of the steel blade through the eyes on the King of Hearts and grabbed Rane by the forearm, whispering crossly, "Ye let yer lassie talk t'me like that again, boy, an' I'll cut out her tongue. Do I make meself clear?"

Terrified by his threat, Rane's eyes grew wide at the razor-sharp, curved edge on the knife as Rustie yanked it out of the table. Swallowing hard as if he had a huge marble stuck in his throat, he rapidly nodded his head and answered, "Aye."

Rustie hid his knife back inside his boot. He then gave Haley another odious sneer and went back to concentrating on his cards.

After mulling over his hand, he not only called his opponent's bet but raised the wager considerably.

Martel was stunned at the large stake he had placed in the pot. Afraid of risking all the money he had to live on for the month, he took another gander at his poker hand. Losing confidence in his three kings, he wiped the sweat off his brow and gulped down another shot of whiskey, hoping it would numb his fears. Feeling the hard liquor burning down the back of his throat, he hissed, exposing his rotten teeth. He lustfully eyed the huge money pot in the center of the table and checked his hand again. Unable to trust the three kings to give him the spoils, he folded his hand by laying his cards face up on the table. "Too rich for my blood, mate."

Rustie exposed his five cards by dropping them face up on the table. Gloating over his bluff, he snickered impishly, "Read 'em an' weep, pops. All I had was three lousy jacks."

Rane was surprised at how easily the old Irishman had been tricked into conceding defeat and questioned it under his breath. "He had the king's hand an' folded it?"

Bitter over losing his money, Martel pursed his wrinkled lips at the victor and then stormed out of the pub.

Haley got tired of all the gambling egotism and went and sat at the bar.

Rustie greedily collected the purse off the table and stuffed it inside his wallet. While picking up the cards off the table, he glanced up at Rane and asked, "Do ye want t'play, laddie?"

Rane's anxieties about gambling for money were clearly evidenced by the insecure look in his eyes. The more he thought about wagering, the faster he cracked his knuckles. He was scared he might fall into the same fate as his mother, who was so addicted to the high she felt in gambling that all her friends called her an "adrenaline junkie."

Although Rane had been taught by his mother to play high-stakes poker at the early age of five, he never played for money again after the night she walked out of his life. However, he had to admit the craving was still there, and he carried the cards she gave him everywhere he went. They were slightly worn and faded after fifteen years, but he couldn't bring himself to part with them.

Rustie took several, short puffs off his cigarette and thumped the ashes onto the scuffed, hardwood floor. After laying the butt on the edge of the ashtray, he exhaled a cloud of smoke out of his lungs and proceeded to shuffle the cards. "Do ye fancy draw poker, laddie? Or would ye like t'play a wee game o'black jack?"

Rane's heart sped up as he eyed the wagering leprechauns in the painting on the wall. He was afraid Rustie might call him a sissy boy if he didn't gamble and quickly thought up an excuse not to play. "I'm, uh, a little short on cash right now, chum. Maybe next time."

He hurried away from the table before the Irishman had a chance to say anything else and joined his wife up at the bar.

Haley noticed her husband was a little on edge as he leaned his elbows on the mahogany countertop. Rane gave her a subtle glimpse out of the corner of his eye and afterward called out to a stout, auburn-haired Irishwoman, who was busy filling a stein full of beer from the tap behind the bar. "Barmaid, where do I find d'entry forms for d'drawing?"

Rane became offended after the freckled-faced woman deliberately turned her back on him without saying a word. Acting immature, he smacked his hand on top of the counter and said, "If ye're trying me patience, lassie, ye're doing a good job of it."

Haley tried to keep peace by whispering to her husband, "Maybe she didn't hear you. Ask her again."

Rane pouted his lips as he glared at the back of the waitress's head. "She heard me all right."

He reached over the countertop and rudely tugged on the barmaid's apron string. "Lassie, I say, 'Where do I find d'entry forms?'"

Bothered by Rane's disrespect, the woman whirled around and scolded, "Pish tush, laddie, didn't yer mum ever teach ye any manners?"

The barmaid took one of the entry slips out of her apron pocket and handed it to him. "Anything else, yer majesty?"

Rane was so upset over the way she addressed him that he walked off without showing good manners.

The barmaid hollered out to him from behind the bar, "Ye're welcome, laddie, an' d'name's Maggie."

Feeling convicted by the Irishwoman's chiding, Rane turned back around and forced himself to give homage. "Thanks, Maggie."

The barmaid raised a proud chin as he walked away, whispering to herself, "So there is a king in there after all."

Hoping to get away from the noisy crowd cheering on the rugby match, Rane found a remote table in the back of the room and saw Rustie leaving out the side door. He secretly spied on him through the window until he disappeared out of view. He then sat down in the chair closest to the casement and started filling out the form.

Haley crept up on her husband by treading softly along the wood floor. Seeing him scribble his name down on the entry blank, she rested her hand on his shoulder and queried, "Rane, do you expect to win?"

Rane flinched slightly from her unexpected touch and looked up at her interested face. After taking a moment to consider what she said, he replied, "Not really."

Haley dragged one of the parlor chairs out from under the table and sat down next to her husband. "Then why waste time filling out the ticket?"

He stared at her stupidly. "Aye, good point."

Haley felt the bot squirming around in her coat and unzipped her pocket. She gave him a disapproving frown, and he immediately settled down.

Rane scratched out his name on the paper. "Who needs a fancy sports car anyway? Having a hoppin' pot o'money seems like a sin."

"You can't help anybody poor. An' besides, having a lot of money isn't a sin. It is the love of money that corrupts."

He reached into his coat pocket and pulled out the pack of playing cards his mother had given him when he was a little boy. "I say I'm better off without it. I'd probably just gamble it all away."

Disappointed in his pessimistic attitude, Haley crossed her long, slender legs and queried, "Why expect the worst?"

Irritated by her inquiry, Rane threw his pen down on the table and replied, "'Cause I've always had d'worst. Are ye happy now?"

She put a caring hand on his wrist and queried softly, "What happened to you, Rane? You never liked to talk about your childhood."

He slumped back in his chair, sighing heavily before revealing the nightmare he had locked away inside his heart. "If ye must know me life story, I was abandoned by me mum when I was about six an' a half years old."

She raised her gentle voice out of deep concern. "Why?"

He thought about his mother's gambling addiction, which presided over everything else in her life, including him, and snapped, "I'd rather not talk about that if ye don't mind!"

Rane removed his coat and put it around the back of his chair. "Anyway, after she dumped me, I managed t'survive by stealing food an' whatever else I needed. I couldn't tell ye how many times scavengers beat me up an' took away me clothes."

"I'm sorry, Rane. I had no idea."

The more Rane thought about his nightmarish past, the madder he got. With a demented look in his eyes, he crushed the entry form in his hand and said, "Ye're sorry. Do ye know how humiliating it is t'be stripped bum naked on d'street?"

"No."

"Or how it feels t'live down in a stinky sewer fighting off disgusting rats?"

Horrified that he had to endure such unpleasant memories, Haley cupped her hand over her mouth and gasped, "Rats?"

Rane's hardened heart was not moved by her empathy. He just stood to his feet, threw the wadded ball of paper into the corner of the room, and kept on complaining. "Aye, rats. I was so hungry once, I ate one of d'nasty boogers."

Haley pursed her lips with disgust. "Ugh!"

Feeling remorseful for some of his actions, he parked himself back on his chair and said, "I didn't want t'steal. I tried begging for food but people would shoo me away. It made me wonder where d'love of Christ was, till I met a man named Caleb Rivers."

He gazed off into space, going deeper into the past. "I was nearly dead from malnutrition when he found me in an impoverished area in d'outskirts o'London. He literally saved me life."

"I'm glad he took you off the streets an' adopted you, Rane."

Rane lowered his brow in question of her statement. "How did ye know I was adopted?"

"I told you, I'm your . . . "

He rudely cut her off, pointing a stern finger at her nose. "Don't say it."

She waited until he withdrew his hand from her face before asking, "So you lived with your dad in Ireland?"

Sentimental thoughts welled up in his mind as he reached inside his coat for more candy. "Aye, at his huge estate."

Rane carefully emptied the fistful of jellybeans onto the table. "Caleb was a very wealthy man. Shortly after I came t'live with him, he tol' me about Jesus an' asked me if I had ever accepted him into me heart."

"Had you?"

"Aye, Emma had led me to d'Lord when I was only six years old."

"Who's Emma?"

Rane picked up one of the cherry jellybeans off the table and tossed it into his mouth. "Emma was me Irish nanny. She taught me how t'speak Gaelic an' some other language that escapes me for d'moment. She was really smart."

Haley smiled and replied, "Smart, huh?"

He nodded. "She took care o'me while my mum danced in a nightclub show in Vegas. My mum didn't care much for her Christian religion, but she was d'only one who would watch me that late at night. In fact, my nanny was d'only person mum allowed me t'be around. I lived a very secluded life."

"You weren't allowed to play with other children?"

Rane shook his head. "No."

Seeing the sad look on his face, Haley decided it would be best to change the subject. "When was the last time you saw Caleb?"

Rane chewed fast on the candied bean in order to swallow it before giving his answer. "I saw him right before I moved back t'London."

"Why did you come back here?"

Rane reflected on his earlier years and felt an overwhelming sense of grief. He struggled hard to choke back the sorrow, but it could be easily heard in his voice. "I . . . I needed t'get away after Caleb died."

To hide the tears welling up in his eyes, Rane looked out the window toward heaven and said prayerfully under his breath, "I know he's with ye now, Lord, but I sure miss him."

Reddy, who was programmed to respond to human emotions analytically, overheard him and whispered to himself in a caring tone of voice, "Aw, Whiz Kid."

Believing he could cheer him up with a simple hug, the bot sprung out of Haley's pocket, landed on the table, and headed toward his inventor.

Hoping to avoid pandemonium in the bar, Haley scooped the bot up in her hand before anyone had a chance to see him and stuffed him down inside her coat pocket.

Reddy popped his head back up, whispering in a desperate tone, "But Whiz Kid needs me, Haley."

She shoved his tiny head back down in her pocket, whispering sternly, "No, he doesn't."

Completely oblivious that his wife was wrestling with the bot to keep him concealed inside her coat, Rane turned back around and wiped a tear out of the corner of his eye. "I dunno why Caleb put up with me. All I did was make his life hell."

Haley swatted her pocket to let the bot know she meant business while grinning nervously at her husband. "Uuuuh, why-why would you think that?"

He removed the playing cards out of the laminated box and began shuffling them on the table. "'Cause I dropped out o'school t'run d'streets with a rowdy bunch."

"Oh," she replied and then took another peek in her pocket to make sure the bot was lying low.

Rane stopped mixing up the cards and gazed vacantly at the colored jellybeans lying on the table in front of him. Thinking back on his former alcohol and cocaine addiction, he said, "I was always coming home drunk or high on crack."

He blinked rapidly to fight back the tears of regret. "What I couldn't understand was how Caleb could still love me through it anyway."

"He sounds like a remarkable man."

While thinking warmheartedly about Caleb, Rane froze his movements. "Aye, that he was. Right before he died of ole age, he read me a verse out o' d'Bible an' said, 'Rane, never forget God made ye t'be a masterpiece, something special that no one else could be.'"

Haley eyed her coat pocket, thinking, *Ooooh, so that's why you put the song inside the timepiece.*

"Anyway, after he died, I took a few household keepsakes t'remember him by an' then signed over d'entire estate t'Pastor Flannigan. He was a good friend of Caleb's an' promised t'turn d'place into a Christian orphanage for homeless boys."

Haley smiled favorably at his generosity. "I bet Caleb would have liked that."

Rane forced a slight grin on his face and went back to separating the face cards from the deck. "I believe he would."

"Rane, whatever happened to your real dad?"

He accidentally dropped the Queen of Hearts playing card on his lap. "I don't remember much about him. He died when I was a wee laddie."

Haley watched him retrieve the card he had dropped. "Did you ever try to find your mum again?"

His disposition turned unpleasant at the mention of his mother. After slamming the rest of the cards down on the table, he pursed his lips at his wife and snapped bitterly, "Now why in hell would I want t'do that?"

Haley countered his offensive tongue with a gentle rebuke. "'Cause you need to forgive her so you can go on with a new page in your life."

With a vengeful fixation in his eyes, Rane tore the Queen of Hearts card into teeny-weeny pieces and threw them behind his shoulder. "No! I'll never forgive her for what she did t'me."

Haley gazed at the aloof expression in her husband's eyes. The broken pieces of the Queen of Hearts brought back a painful memory from her past.

Rane didn't like the way she was staring at him and started nervously cracking his knuckles. He knew something was bothering her by the pool of tears glistening in her eyes but didn't know how to respond in love. Feeling fearful about the situation, he broke eye contact with her and queried, "Don't ye have somewhere else t'go, lassie?"

Haley forced herself to grin, wiping a tear trickling down her cheek. "No, looks like you're stuck with me."

Rane eyed the Jack of Hearts playing card on the table and said, "Great, now I got two shadows following me around."

Haley propped her elbow on the table to support her tired head. "You still don't believe I'm your wife. Do you?"

Rane got up out of his chair. "I dunno, lassie, for all I know ye could be some lunatic off d'street."

Looking thirstily at the bar, he said, "I'm going t'get a spot o'tea. Do ye want any?"

He watched her shake her head at his offer and then headed toward the bar.

A few moments later Rane returned to the table carrying a stein full of steaming-hot, Irish tea. Without uttering a word, he sat down and gazed out the window at the first fall of winter snow. When he grew tired of seeing the snowflakes drifting through the air, he placed his large beaker down on the table. He then picked up the London newspaper that the former patron had left on the table and began reading the headline aloud. "Kidnapper Gets D'upper Hand."

Haley gripped the top of the newspaper and pulled it down from his face. "Hey, Chappy..."

With an uptight expression on his face, Rane pried her hand off the paper, picked up his stein by the handle, and asked, "What?"

Haley's emerald eyes danced with excitement as she drew her nose closer to his face. "I've got a great idea."

Rane blew a couple of breaths on his scalding tea to cool it off while dreading the worst. *Oh please no.*

Haley watched him take a careful slurp of his hot brew and said, "Why don't we ask the patrons to join us in singing some Christmas carols to Jesus?"

Taken aback by her suggestion to sing in a public bar, Rane swallowed the tea down the wrong pipe and started hacking and coughing.

Patting him on the back as he coughed, she queried, "Doesn't that sound like fun?"

Straining not to cough, Rane slammed his beaker down on the table and replied in a raspy voice, "I hope ye're joking."

Rane reached into his rear pocket, pulled out several napkins he had picked up from the bar, and then wiped the drooled tea off his chin.

Still in high spirits, Haley broadened her smile. "I think it is a great idea. Don't you?"

Rane glanced uneasily around the room at all the grumpy faces peering in his direction. Intimidated by the way they were looking at him, he tossed the damp napkins aside and hid his face behind the newspaper. "Uh, maybe later."

"Okey-dokey," she replied in a sprightly voice.

While quietly reading one of the articles, Rane commented in an upset tone, "I don't believe it."

Haley nosily peeked over his shoulder to see the paper. "What?"

Keeping his eyes glued on the editorial, he answered, "Some crazy fool tried t'kidnap a wee lassie over at d'Ritz Mall. What's d'world coming to?"

Reddy poked his head out of Haley's coat pocket and imitated his inventor's articulation in a squeaky voice. "What's d'world coming to?"

Haley quieted the bot by placing her index finger against her lips.

Reddy imitated her hand signal, whispering to himself, "Shush."

As soon as Reddy sunk back down in her pocket, Haley asked about the write-up. "You said he tried to kidnap her?"

Rane promptly rescanned the highlights of the article before answering, "Aye, it says some undercover detective lady was in d'area an' foiled his plans."

"Good for her," she said gaily.

He looked up from the newspaper and turned a critical tongue. "What do ye mean, 'Good for her'? She let d'gumby get away."

Haley leaned back in her chair, sighing disappointedly. "Oh that's too bad."

Rane's face flushed beet red with thoughts of revenge as he brooded over the mistreatment of an innocent child. "I wished I'd been there t'catch him. I would have kicked that 'Napper right in his goolies. Then he could have spent d'rest ov his life singing soprano in her majesty's pleasure."

Feeling too warm from the high temperature in the bar, Haley removed her black ski jacket and put it around the back of her chair. After stroking the fluffy, gray and white synthetic fur around the hood, she said, "With all the violence on the streets today, I'm sure glad our children will have a protective daddy like you to look after them."

Rane laughed at the thought of raising kids. "Go on, I ain't going t'be no daddy."

Staring uncomfortably at her husband, Haley started fondling her sterling silver, heart-shaped locket attached to the silver chain around her neck.

Rane eyeballed her anxious expression and laid the newspaper down on the table. "Why are ye looking at me like that, lassie?"

Not sure how he was going to handle the news she was about to tell him, Haley bit her lower lip, answering shyly, "Um ... I ... I was going to tell you last Christmas, but I never got the chance."

Rane picked up his stein, sniffing the enticing aroma of the spiced tea. "Tell me what?"

Haley squirmed restlessly in her seat. "That I ... um ... that I ..."

Rane swiped his index finger across his nostrils, growing impatient from his wife's reluctancy in giving him a straight answer. "Go on . . . spit it out."

Haley squeezed her locket tightly in her hand while watching him sip his tea. "That I was . . . "

Taking it upon himself to give her a helping hand, Reddy hopped up on the table and happily announced her little secret. "Pregnant."

Shocked after hearing the news, Rane unintentionally spit his tea at the tiny bot and swallowed the remains down the wrong pipe. While turning red in the face from hacking up the brew, he managed to safely set his stein back on the table.

Now that the cat was out of the bag, Haley lost her restive tongue and began scolding the tea-drenched bot for disclosing the information. "Reddy, how could you?"

Reddy dove under the pile of newspapers to avoid being seen by the onlooking customers and answered in a rushed, contrite voice, "I'm sorry, Haley, I'm sorry. I thought ye wanted him t'know."

After Rane finished clearing the fluid out of his throat, he turned his traumatized eyes onto his wife's and hollered, "Pregnant?"

Rane's loud announcement caused a momentary silence in the bar. Seeing the customers staring nosily in his direction, he huddled closer and whispered, "Ye think I got ye pregnant?"

Haley put a confident look on her face. "Yes, shortly after we were married."

He pursed his lips. "Would ye stop pretending like ye're my wife."

Reddy secretly spied on them from underneath the newspapers and inadvertently caught sight of the napkins lying on the table. Desiring to clean the tea off his face, he slowly reached out, being vigilant not to be seen, and snatched one of the paper cloths.

Still acting self-assured, Haley held out her ring finger toward her husband. "I have the wedding ring to prove it."

Rane grabbed her hand and carefully examined the sparkling white diamond mounted to the silver band on her finger. After getting an eyeful, he looked up at her, snickering, "Where did ye get this, lassie? Out of a Cracker Jack box?"

Reddy, who had just finished cleaning the tea off his body, placed his hand on his belly and chuckled goofily, "Cracker Jack box, ye crack me up."

Haley was insulted by her husband's belittling remark and hastily retracted her ring finger to her heart. "No. We picked it out together at Fabishes Jewelry Store. The ring means a lot to me, even if I did have to pay for it myself."

Rane put on an arrogant visage. "Is that so?"

He picked up the rest of the napkins lying next to him and started wiping up the tea he had spurted on the table. "Well, I got a newsflash for ye, lassie. I don't love ye."

Haley closed her heart to his words like an un-blossomed rose, for she longed to hear him say how much he loved her. Fighting a strong urge to cry, she looked down at her diamond ring and began twisting the silver band back and forth. "That's only 'cause you've forgotten who I am."

The leanness of mercy in Rane's soul was quite evident when he rolled his uncaring eyes, tossed the damp napkins aside, and went back to reading the paper. "Lassies."

Haley's tears trickled onto her wedding ring. Just when things seemed the worst, she recalled something God had said through the Prophet Jeremiah: "My people have forgotten me days without number."

Experiencing the sadness firsthand, Haley thought how grieved the Holy Spirit must have felt at that moment. She knew God cherished every second his children spent with him.

Reddy's hair turned sparkly blue, responding systematically to the emotion Haley was projecting. After dropping the napkin in his hand, he leaped off the table and landed on her lap. He laid his cheek against her stomach and gave her a comforting hug. "Aw, Haley, don't cry. I love ye."

Haley smiled emptily at the bot's affection. After all, his love wasn't real. He was only a robot programmed to say it. She could clearly see why God had given mankind a free will to love him, or it wouldn't mean anything.

While Haley was putting the bot back into her coat pocket, she wished for God to help her husband remember how to love her again. The very next moment, she heard Jesus's gentle voice in a British tongue, touching her heart with his truth. *Haley, I love you. I will never leave you nor forsake you.*

A joyful smile spread across her face at her Lord's promise of eternal love. She knew he meant it. His love for her would never grow cold. It was a priceless gem. Jesus was the one person who would always be faithful in keeping his vows. He had given her his Holy Spirit as a guarantee, a symbolic ring of their eternal union together.

Haley gazed at the light shimmering inside the diamond on her ring, thinking how grateful she was to God for turning her heart of coal into a precious jewel. She looked over at Rane, who was quietly reading the paper as if she didn't exist. She sighed wearisomely at the thought of being ignored and decided to use some memorabilia to try and wake up his memory. After unhooking the clasp on her necklace, she removed the silver chain from around her neck, opened the heart-shaped locket, and tapped her husband on the left shoulder. "Rane, I have something for you."

Rane turned to the next page in the newspaper and replied uninterestedly, "More bad luck no doubt."

She glanced fondly at the two motion pictures inside the ornament in her hand and said, "No, pictures of our baby, Faith Patience Rivers."

Rane kept his focus on the paper while referencing her statement in a skeptical tongue. "Oh sure, an' I suppose we had twins too."

Haley pretended to be serious as she dangled the locket in front of his face. "No, triplets."

Rane widened his fretful eyes at the thought of caring for three kids and snatched the necklace out of her hand. "No way."

Haley couldn't resist a few sniggers at her husband's uneasiness as he laid the newspaper down on the table. "I was kidding about the triplets."

Rane peeked inside the locket and saw two pictures of the infant. He chuckled favorably at the clip on the right where the baby was blowing bubbles out of her mouth. "She's a cute little thing. I love d'pink bow on her headband."

Haley smiled at the picture of her daughter's happy face. "She's four months old. Isn't she adorable?"

"Aye, that she is."

He took his eyes off the locket and looked back at his wife. "Where is yer baby?"

"With my mum. She begged me to let her take care of her for a couple of days while I took some time off to be with you. If I know my mum, by now, she's probably spoiling her rotten."

Rane scooped up the rest of the jellybeans off the table and crammed them all into his mouth. With his right cheek jammed full of candy, he commented distortedly, "I don't blame her. If she was my daughter, I would."

Haley pointed at the crystal lever on the side of the locket. "Rane, push that button an' the picture on the right will change."

Intrigued, Rane crunched on the candy in his mouth while pressing the switch. Right away the motion clip changed to a picture of himself chasing Haley around the Christmas tree at the Ritz Mall. Shocked by what he saw, he choked down the masticated sugar in his mouth and said, "That looks like me."

Recapturing a precious moment from the past, Haley's face beamed with joy. "It is one of my favorite pictures. My mum took it a few days before we were married."

Rane had misgivings about her testimony and wasted no time handing her back the locket. "Go on, ye know those pictures are fake."

She hooked the silver necklace back around her neck and said innocently, "I don't know what you mean."

Curious what was going on, Reddy snuck out of the pocket and climbed back up on the table.

Rane snickered at his wife before saying, "Ye didn't have t'go through all this trouble just t'get a date with me, lassie. Ye're quite a looker an' ye obviously love Jesus. I'd go out with ye. Although I am a bit ole fashioned. I prefer t'do d'asking."

Haley grinned from ear to ear and then gave her husband a quick peck on the cheek. "I would love a date with you, your highness."

Rane wiped her lip print off his face. "What did ye do that for?"

"You needed a smoochie."

Without getting up out of his seat, Rane scooted his chair a little to the right and gently scolded, "Listen, lassie, when d'king's ready for a smoochie, he'll let ye know."

He picked up the newspaper and hid his face behind it.

Haley giggled under her breath at his childish antics until she sighted a write-up about time travel on the back of the newspaper. She instantly thought about her husband's research and pushed the paper down from his mug. "Oh by the way, how is your new particle solution coming?"

Rane gave her a dense look and asked, "My what?"

She scooted her chair closer to his as she answered, "Your particle solution in quantum physics. You are a physical scientist."

He chuckled at the thought of being intelligent. "A physical scientist?"

Confused why he was laughing at her, Haley's tone turned serious. "What's so funny about that?"

Keeping an arrogant attitude, he stifled his mirth to answer, "I don't even know what participle resolution an' quazio physics means."

Reddy rested his tiny hand on the side of his inventor's beaker, snickering to himself, "Whiz Kid, ye funny guy, that's particle solution an' quantum physics."

Rane eyed the bot out of the corner of his eye and said to Haley, "Why does d'little fella have his hand raised?"

She leaned forward to speak sweet-spiritedly to the bot. "'Cause you want t'tell him what the words mean, huh, Reddy?"

Reddy lowered his hand, eagerly nodding his head. "Quantum physics means . . . "

Rane rudely interrupted the bot's explanation with a sharp rebuke. "Never ye mind. Ye just stand there an' shush."

Reddy pouted his lips as if he was going to cry. "Okay, Whiz Kid. I shush."

Rane noticed the bot's fiber optics were turning glittery blue. "What's up with his hair?"

Haley gently stroked the sparkly hairs on the bot's head. "Whenever Reddy simulates a sad feeling his hair turns blue."

Still feeling like Haley was trying to con him, he cracked a confident smirk out of the corner of his mouth and said, "I believe I just found a loophole in yer story, lassie."

She watched him gulp down the rest of his tea as she queried, "What do you mean?"

He sat his stein back on the table and answered, "I couldn't have built that bot."

"Why not?"

He motioned his index finger toward Reddy, whose blue hair had just turned back to its original color of blond. "That's white diamond chips in his belly button, an' he's obviously made out of pure silver."

With a droll grin on his face, Reddy looked down at his round tummy, patting it a couple of times. "Little Silver, that's me."

Haley saw a bus boy heading in their general direction and swiftly covered the bot with the newspaper. "So?"

Rane got nose to nose with his wife as he replied, "As ye can clearly see, I'm a pauper. Where did I get d'money?"

She promptly corrected his character defamation. "Your highness, you got the chips for his belly button from the diamond ring your mother gave you, an' you used Caleb's silver utensils to make the rest."

Rane sat back in his chair with his arms crossed, steaming mad. The mere mention of his mother set off his Irish temper. "Go on, lassie, 'tis hard t'picture me mum giving me anything but a heartache."

Reddy crawled out from underneath the newspapers and asked, "Can I come out now?"

Rane looked around for the bus boy and saw him clearing a table nearby. Relieved that he hadn't seen the bot, he proceeded to admonish Reddy in a barely audible voice. "Ye're already out. Now get back under there before I pop ye on yer bum."

Reddy probed the spanking warning, surmising it might cause him a bit of discomfort. "No spank, I be good. I'll crawl back under d'paper, an' ye won't even know I'm here."

Rane whispered to his wife, "Knowing Reddy, that should last all of about ten seconds."

Reddy spied on his inventor from underneath the papers and saw him popping jellybeans into his mouth. "Whiz Kid, can I have a jellybean?"

Rane flicked his middle finger at the newspaper and whispered, "What happened to 'ye won't even know I'm here'?"

He got up out of his seat with his empty mug in hand and said to Haley, "I'm going t'get another cup o'tea."

"I'll take one!" Reddy said in a muffled voice from underneath the pile of papers.

Rane pressed his fist firmly against the newspaper. "Maybe ye'd like a knuckle sandwich t'go with it."

Reddy guffawed at Rane as if he was a slapstick comedian. "A knuckle sandwich, Whiz Kid, ye funny guy."

Haley giggled at the bot's monkey business as her husband headed toward the bar.

CHAPTER 5

Not five minutes later, Rane returned to his seat cradling a fresh beaker of hot, Irish tea between his palms. He placed the stein down on the table and reseated himself in his chair. While waiting for his brew to cool off a bit, he separated the classified ads from the pile of newspapers, making sure he didn't expose the bot hiding underneath.

Haley glanced at the help-wanted section he was looking over and asked, "Why do you need a job?"

He answered sarcastically, "It seems I have a nasty habit. I like t'eat."

Rane skimmed through the advertisements, reading the ads aloud. "Let's see now… car dealers, detailers, engineers, jack of all trades, sales, teachers."

Haley overlaid his jumbled speech by asking in a smart-alecky tone, "Is there one in there for a physical scientist?"

He took a breather from reading the paper to counter her cheeky remark. "Har-har."

"I'm serious. You were on the verge of discovering a particle solution for accelerated space travel. What did you do with the blueprints?"

Rane chuckled doubtfully. "Me? Come up with a particle solution for space travel? What a joke."

"It is no joke, Rane. Reddy was one of your very first tests. I admit he has a few bugs in him, but you were going to work those out."

Listening in on their conversation from underneath the newspapers, Reddy hollered out in a shrill, fretful voice, "Bugs? I got bugs?"

Rane took a quick glimpse around the room to see if anyone had overheard the bot and then lowered his head toward the paper, whispering tetchily, "Ye are d'bug. Now shush!"

Haley could tell her husband's patience with Reddy was wearing thin, so she put him back in her pocket. "Rane, I'm telling you the truth. You're a genius."

Not being able to see himself in such a prestigious light, Rane chuckled a bit before replying, "I hate t'burst yer bubble, lassie, but this Einstein couldn't even hold down a simple job like working in d'sewer."

The disillusionment could clearly be seen on Haley's face as she queried, "You took a job in the sewer?"

"I did, till I got fired yesterday."

Haley was a bit confused after hearing his confession and tried to piece things together. *He left his research for a job in the sewer? Rane would never do that. He must have lost his memory prior to the mall. I wonder what happened to him.*

Not sure what to do next, she sighed in frustration and said, "Rane, maybe you should see a doctor."

He brushed off the idea with a firm lift of his hand. "Oh no, nobody's going t'play around inside my head."

"You want your memory back, don't you?"

"There's nothing wrong with me memory."

She crossed her arms and said, "All right, then tell me what you were doing last Christmas?"

Rane narrowed his eyes in deep thought and answered foggily, "I was, uh, I was, um ... I know I was doing something. What was it?"

Haley cut in on his vacant thoughts. "You don't remember. Do you?"

Feeling fearful that he couldn't come up with an answer, Rane's hands began to tremble. "I-I ... I do, it-it, it escapes me for d'moment that's all."

"Then chase it down."

Choked up with fright, Rane raised his voice to almost a shout. "I can't!"

She glanced at the patrons staring nosily in her direction and then whistled another tune to send a clandestine message to the bot.

Rane gaped at her, uncertain what prompted her musical aspiration.

Choosing to keep her secrecy for the moment, Haley merely smiled at him and then slipped her hand inside her coat pocket. After pulling out the silver timepiece, she handed it to him and whispered, "You made this teleportation device. Try an' remember."

He meticulously examined the luminous, six-pointed, baby blue star embedded in the silver lid on the pocket watch. Not recalling anything about it, he opened the timepiece and heard a beautiful melody playing inside. At that precise moment, two teeny holograms appeared on top of the crystal that protected the time indicator in the lower portion of the watch. "Hey, that's us. Dressed up like a British king an' queen."

"Yes," she replied as if hoping their royal attire would help him wake up to the truth.

Rane was so captivated by the joyful sound of the music that he started humming the tune as if he had heard it before. "What is that song?"

With a peaceful gleam in her eyes, she thought about how God had created all of his children to do good works and whispered fervently, "It is called 'Masterpiece.' Isn't it beautiful?"

He answered in a voice of admiration, "Aye, that it is."

After the ballad had finished playing, Rane's projected kingly image inside the watch faced his queen with love in his eyes, took her by the hands, and began reciting a passage of scripture out of the book of Ephesians, chapter two, verse ten. "We are his workmanship created in Christ Jesus for good works ..."

Upon hearing the royal words, Rane was awestruck. "'Tis d'same verse Caleb read t'me."

Hearing more of the audio, he quieted himself to listen. "Which God prepared beforehand that we should walk in 'em."

Rane repeated the passage as if he was waking up out of a trance. "We are his workmanship."

Being overzealous to clarify the poetic meaning of the word "workmanship," Haley spoke up and said, "His masterpiece."

Rane considered his unhappy life and sighed woefully. "Then why do so many of us die a copy?"

"Simple, human pride says, 'We don't need the King's hand. With a stroke of luck, we can paint our own pictures through life.'"

Rane immediately thought about some of the depressing, counterfeit pictures he had painted himself into and nodded his head. "Aye, I can think of some pretty hellacious ones at that."

He examined the rest of the watch and saw the engraving on the inside of the silver lid. Curious what it said, he read it aloud. "I'll always have time for ye."

"You had those words etched in the timepiece before you gave it to me."

Although he had no memory of the heartfelt affection, he played along by saying, "O'course, I'm a serious romantic."

Rane barely got the words out of his mouth when he felt the watch quivering in his hand. Frightened by the sensation of it changing its molecular structure, he shrieked and dropped the bot on the table. He watched Reddy pick himself up and then said to his wife, "Lassie, ye mean t'tell me that bot can manipulate his molecular structure and turn into a watch?"

"You mean a teleportation device."

Reddy batted his long, black eyelashes and said with a smile, "Whiz Kid is a serious romantic, huh, Haley?"

Haley was tickled by what the bot said and threw her head back, laughing. "Yes. He's a serious romantic."

CHAPTER 6

Rane picked up the one-eyed Jack of Hearts playing card off the table and at once thought about the costume he was wearing in his dream. "Lassie, what did d'jack's clothing symbolize in my dream?"

Haley eyed the card in his hand and replied, "Regressing backwards in status."

Rane grabbed a big handful of jellybeans out of the plastic bag inside his coat and stuffed them all into his mouth. His cheeks were so full, some of the candy almost slipped out as he spoke. "I kinda figured that."

Keeping one eye on the bot to make sure he stayed out of mischief, Haley said, "Now you see why it is so important that we spend time with our Heavenly Father every day so he can polish our speech."

Although Rane was pretty sure he knew what she meant, he still asked for clarity. "Polish our speech?"

Referencing the divine speech of God, Haley took her small Bible out of her coat pocket and scrolled through the pages. "You know, let the King retrain our mind to think the way he thinks. Then the devil won't be able to use our carnal tongue to kick us around anymore. You can't fool him. He knows what true royalty sounds like. Haven't you ever seen the movie *My Fair Lady*?"

Rane laid the Jack of Hearts card down on the table before asking stupidly, "Is that a horror picture?"

Reddy placed his hands behind his back, snickering goofily, "Horror picture."

Displeased with her husband's answer, Haley said, "The only horror picture would be to wake up an' find out you lived your life as a guttersnipe an' didn't have to."

Rane swallowed the candy in his mouth and then licked the sugar off his lips. "Ye mean we can actually live a portion of our lives differently than what God intended by being in d'wrong frame o'mind?"

She held up the open Bible in front of her face. "Sure, that's why the devil tries to keep us away from our royal mirror. He knows the eyes are a gateway to the soul an' doesn't want us to wake up to who we really are in Christ."

Haley lowered the book and was pleased to see the interest in her husband's eyes. "He knows that if we find out we're really blessed kings, we'll start expecting the best to happen instead of the worst. Then he won't be able to devour our dreams like a plague of stripping locusts devouring a good crop."

Reddy squeezed his right eye shut at the one-eyed Jack of Hearts on the table and scolded, "Ye naughty winker, shame on ye, back in yer box."

He picked up the playing card and slid it back into the card box.

Rane sat restlessly in his chair, the question of his own loss of memory troubling him greatly. "Haley, t'think ye're cursed when ye're really blessed, isn't that kind of like having amnesia?"

Haley stuffed her Bible back into her coat pocket and then picked up the bot. "Oh definitely, our speech would be a dead give away."

Rane suddenly had a flashback of the twilight zone he saw in his sleep. "Is that why I was talking backwards in my dream? 'Cause I'm not awake t'who I really am in d'King?"

Haley put the bot into her pocket and nodded her head. "Kind of like a cat squeaking in the tongue of a mouse, wouldn't you say?"

Rane eyed his dark shadow on the wall and held up his hand in gesture for her to quit talking. "Okay, okay, I get d'ugly picture."

She picked up the King of Hearts playing card off the table and laid it beside the other three kings. "God dealt us a kings hand, Rane, an' all the jacks in the world can't beat it."

Losing interest in what she was saying, Rane queried, "What time is it?"

Haley reached inside her pocket, whistling the tune that would draw the timepiece.

Rane gave her a funny look and said, "Lassie, that's a weird habit ye got there."

She giggled at his statement and then handed him the teleportation device out of her coat pocket.

Rane opened the timepiece to check the time and accidentally pushed the crystal button on the right side of the watch. Seeing a green light flicking inside, he got a little anxious and said, "Hey, lassie … "

She leaned toward him. "Yes?"

"What's d'flashing green light mean?"

Haley eyed the blinking light while spontaneously massaging the front of her long, slender neck. "You turned on the particle communicator."

"What's that do?"

She took her hand down from her neck and pointed at the empty counter window to the right of the crystal in the lower portion of the watch. "The device is now monitoring your sound wave energy."

Rane cracked a partial smile and said, "'Tis monitoring me?"

"Uh-huh. The light actually stops flickering an' turns red if you speak any negative words."

He made a baffled face and queried, "How does it know t'do that?"

She replied wittily, "The energy being released into the atmosphere. The sound waves are either positive or negative, depending upon the force dominating our hearts. To resonate with sound energy other than God's love is not only harmful to our bodies but to the world around us."

Haley got up out of her chair and started putting on her ski jacket.

Rane watched her zip up the front of her coat. "Where are ye going?"

Haley pushed the chair she was sitting in back under the table. "I have a quick errand to run. I'll meet you over by the tree."

Rane stuffed the rest of the cards back into the plastic-coated box. "Why are we going again?"

"God hasn't told me yet. I guess we'll find out when we get there."

He waited until she went out the side door before snickering under his breath. "Find out when we get there. I ain't going, Christmas tree indeed. Who does she think I am, Santy Claus?"

The instant Rane spewed the negative words out of his mouth, the flashing, green light on the side of the watch turned red. Straightaway the miniature queen inside the timepiece vanished as his kingly appearance regressed back to a knaves. Overcome with anxiety, his heart rate and breathing quickened. "Why did Haley disappear when my image changed?"

He peeked into the round crystal at the bottom of the watch and added, "D'time changed, too. 'Tis now midnight, an' d'secondhand is moving counterclockwise. I must have accidentally pressed d'wrong button."

Rane frantically pushed the knob on the side of the watch, hoping to switch it back to the way it was before. All at once he saw the words "time warp" flashing red like a beacon across the center of the crystal. Widening his eyes with panic, he chastised himself by calling his brain stupid. "Now ye're in for it, gumby. Ye broke d'thing."

Hearing the Big Ben gonging the second hour, he felt a sick feeling in his stomach for not showing up at the tree. Fidgeting restlessly in his chair, he picked up the newspaper off the table and began rereading the kidnapping article to take his mind off his troubles.

Thirty minutes after the clock chime, Haley came hurrying into the tavern from the main entrance. Seeing the serious expression on her face, Rane muttered under his breath, "I'm in trouble."

Haley walked up to her husband, who had just jumped up out of his seat with a guilty look on his face, and said earnestly, "What happened, Rane? You didn't show up."

Scared to admit his guilt, he hid the watch behind his back.

Haley knew he was hiding the timepiece from her and gently coaxed him to divulge the truth. "What's wrong?"

With fear brimming in his eyes, he took a step backwards and said self-protectively, "Nothing's wrong."

"Don't be afraid, love. You can tell me."

When he refused to answer, Haley held out her hand for the timepiece, and he hesitantly placed it on her palm. Noting the image change inside the watch, she looked up at him and said sadly, "You didn't believe me. That's why you didn't come."

Not wanting to be held accountable for his actions, Rane shrugged like it was no big deal.

CHAPTER 7

Meanwhile, earlier, outside the Ritz Mall in the open square, Bob and Edith Chandler, and their six-year-old daughter Mary Kay, were strolling down the sidewalk admiring all the beautiful decorations.

Edith looked over at the twelve-foot Christmas tree and recognized a handsome, young Irishman sitting on a cast iron garden bench only a few feet away. He was wearing a sixteenth-century costume like the Jack of Diamonds on an English playing card and had a snobbish air about him as if royal blood coursed through his veins. She couldn't resist a slight snicker at his appearance and wondered why the fellow was staring at her like he, too, knew who she was. Her deep train of thought was abruptly interrupted when her daughter tugged on the sleeve of her mink coat.

"Mommy, can I go play by the Christmas tree?" asked Mary Kay.

Edith repositioned the gray beret on her daughter's head and said affectionately, "Ask Daddy."

Mary Kay wrapped her arms tightly around Bob's middle. "Can I, Daddy, please?"

Bob smiled at the hopeful look in his daughter's eyes. "Sure, sweetie, go ahead."

Mary Kay handed him her rainbow-haired dolly she called Babs and said, "Keep your eye on my baby. Don't let anybody take her, okay?"

Bob shut his left eye while holding Babs in front of his nose. "Don't worry. I got my eye on her."

May Kay giggled, "Daddy, you're being silly."

Without further ado, she happily squealed all the way over to the tree.

Bob snickered at the doll in his hand, thinking how ridiculous he must have looked a moment ago. He then gazed up at the snow falling from the gray sky. The fresh powder was so lacy and soft, it dissolved the instant it touched his warm face. Feeling childishly giddy, he opened his mouth wide and tried to catch one of the snowflakes on his tongue. "Edith, did you ever find out who paid for our trip to London?"

She kept a watchful eye on her daughter as she replied, "It was probably your dad. He's been trying to get us to take a vacation for years."

Bob nodded to agree and then started wiping snow off the top of his bald head.

Edith looked over at the costumed man on the garden bench and said, "Bob, look."

"What?"

Edith gestured her head to get him to look in that direction and replied, "The young man over there, dressed up like Lucky Jack."

Bob turned around and was shocked to see a famous gambler out of his past. "If I didn't know better, I'd swear that was Lucky Jack's ghost come back to haunt me."

Edith sniggered at his overactive imagination. "Oh, Bob, I think your conscience is still bothering you."

He cleared his throat and answered croakily, "I don't know what you're talking about."

"Yes, you do. You still feel guilty about cheating Lucky Jack out of a million dollars."

Gloating over a dark victory that happened over eighteen years before, he replied, "No, I don't. I'm glad I did it. He just would have bought more diamonds with it."

"Glad?" she replied upsettingly.

"That was our briefcase full of money that he won at the poker table, Edith."

"And I told you to stop gambling away our money."

"Instead of complaining, you should be thanking me."

"For what?"

"It was my sheer genius that got our money back after I paid Kathryn ten thousand to switch briefcases on him."

"You had his fiancée do it?" she queried with a look of disgust.

He used the tip of his ring finger to wipe some spittle out of the corner of his mouth and then put on a sneaky grin. "Yeah, she took one of the hotel keys, snuck into his hotel room, and switched briefcases. It's a good thing she didn't know what was inside the case, or she would have stolen the money herself."

"What did she think was in it?"

"Insurance documents."

"You didn't get away with it though."

"How was I to know he was an electronics wizard? Jack never told anybody."

Thinking back on what happened that night inside their hotel room, Edith giggled, "I'll never forget the look on your face when you opened your briefcase and that surveillance eyeball flew out of there."

He smiled at her recount. "That was pretty funny, huh?"

She sniggered some more. "You tried to swat it with the newspaper, but it flew out the window."

"Yeah, I wouldn't even have known what it was if Lucky Jack hadn't called our hotel room and told me."

Edith stopped laughing and gazed up at the snowflakes falling from the sky. "Bob, did you believe those stories in the tabloids about Lucky Jack having ESP?"

He nodded. "Nobody's that lucky. He always knew exactly when to hold and when to fold his cards."

Edith took her mini-camera out of her purse and said, "Bob, I want to get a picture of me and Lucky Jack. Go ask him if it's okay."

Bob eyed the red coronet on top of the man's shoulder-length, blond wig and replied, "No."

Edith saw other people secretly admiring the Jack's costume too and said, "Come on, Bob, it's not every day you see someone dressed up like a celebrity. And you've got to admit, he looks exactly like him."

Bob nodded and shouted toward the stranger. "Hey, Jack, my wife wants you to pose with her for a picture!"

The tall, thin Irishman Bob called Jack slowly got off the bench. After straightening his frock with a sharp tug on the hem, he ambled toward them.

"Oh good, he's coming over here," Edith said in an excited voice.

The mysterious gentleman, who looked to be about twenty-six, walked up to the Chandlers and gave them a bewitching, enchanting smile as if he knew everything about them.

Mary Kay was curious about who the stranger was and followed him over to her parents.

Bob handed Babs to his little girl while chuckling at the man's costume. "You're starting trick or treat a little late this year, aren't you, pal?"

Ignoring the wisecrack, the Jack stroked his musketeer-style, blond mustache and said in an Irish accent, "Allow me t'give ye one o'me calling cards."

He used a sleight of hand and made it look like he pulled a Jack of Diamonds playing card out of thin air.

Bob took the plastic-coated card from him and was surprised to see the magician's face on the Jack of Diamonds. After staring curiously at the wink in his right eye, he lowered his gaze onto the business name printed across the bottom of the card and thought, *Jack's Masterpieces? That was Lucky Jack's gallery.*

He looked up at the impersonator's face and mused further, *That can't be him. Lucky Jack died about fifteen years ago.*

Jack interrupted his rumination by saying, "I see ye're a gambling man, sir."

Bob grinned at the idea of someone recognizing his fame. "Yeah, I'm a high roller. You've seen me play on TV?"

"No. I could tell by d'way ye eyed d'card."

Edith glanced at the playing card in her husband's hand and then drew her attention onto the sparkling white diamonds on the Irishman's fingers. "Your rings are beautiful."

He admired the large gems on his fingers as he replied, "Aye."

Showing off more of his magical arts, Jack rested the rim of another Jack of Diamonds playing card on the tip of his index finger and twirled it. As the card spun faster and faster on its own, he swished his nimble fingers around it like an expert magician and spoke out an incantation to alter its form. "Abracadabra! Pres-to!"

He stopped the card on a dime to show his captive audience that it had changed into the Jack of Hearts.

Dazzled by his showmanship, Edith gaped at the face card in the man's hand and said, "Say, that's a pretty neat trick."

Mary Kay looked up at Edith and queried, "Mommy, is he a magician?"

Edith nodded at her daughter and then put her concentration back on the performer, hoping to see another one of his card tricks. "He sure is, honey."

Jack once more swirled his hand around the card and said, "Abracadabra!"

When the card suddenly vanished before her very eyes, Edith applauded his magic act. "How did you do that?"

Jack blew on his palm and made it look like sparkling gold dust spewed into the air. "I used a bit o'pixie magic."

He had no sooner spoken his enchanted words when he lost control of his body and started involuntarily twitching his head to the left. Speaking in a mechanical tone, he reiterated, "Destroy pictures that exalt themselves against d'knowledge o' God. Destroy pictures that exalt themselves against d'knowledge o' God. Destroy pictures that exalt themselves against d'knowledge o' God."

Amused by the Irishman's anomalous behavior, Mary Kay pointed at him and giggled. "Look, Daddy, the magician man is acting like a robot."

Bob gaped intriguingly at the stranger's mechanical paroxysm. Unsure what to do, he looked over at a couple of rubberneckers passing by and then whispered into his wife's ear, "What's wrong with him? Why does he keep repeating himself?"

Edith studied the man intently and whispered back, "I think he's having a seizure."

While watching the magician jerk his head uncontrollably, Bob stuffed the card he had given him into his overcoat pocket. "Those are not spasms, Edith. Anyone can see he has a demon."

She shook her head at him for poking fun at the Irishman. "You've been watching way too many horror pictures lately, Bob. Everywhere we go you think you're seeing imaginary demons."

"I do not."

She glanced over at several people gawking at the Jack as they walked past him on the sidewalk. "You do too."

Acting like his old self again, the Irishman said, "Sorry about that, folks. I dunno what came over me."

Edith noticed his coronet had fallen off his head and picked it up out of the snow. Handing it to the Irishman, she queried, "Are you okay?"

He put the crown back on his head and answered sprightly, "Couldn't be better."

Jack looked down at Mary Kay and then said to Edith, "Would ye like me t'perform more magic for ye by making yer daughter disappear?"

"You can do that?" Edith queried in a voice of surprise.

He nodded and replied, "'Tis a simple trick. Here, I'll show ye."

Conjuring up the spirit of magic, Jack waved his hand around Mary Kay's head and said loudly, "Abracadabra, disappear!"

When nothing happened, Edith stood dumbfounded. "She didn't vanish."

With a naughty glint in his eyes, the Jack replied, "She will. An' all it will take is a wink of an eye."

Thinking the man to be a bit psychotic, Bob pushed the magician back from his daughter and asked in a demanding tone, "Who are you?"

Jack reached underneath the collar on his smock and pulled out his lucky talisman that was attached to a thin, gold chain around his neck. The shiny, gold amulet he prized so highly looked like an inverted pyramid of letters arranged to spell out the magic word 'Abracadabera.' One fewer letter appeared in each line until only the "a" remained to form the highest point of the triangle. After giving them a sly grin and a quick wink of his right eye, he replied, "Lucky Jack."

Edith saw the wind blow the man's hair back, exposing a ruby, diamond-shaped earring pierced through his left earlobe. She knew the real gambler used to wear an earring exactly like it and gasped in fright. "You're Lucky Jack?"

Jack quickly covered up his lobe with some of the blond hairs on his wig and then gave them another crafty smirk. "I tol' ye I'd get even with ye one day for stealing my money. Who do ye think sent ye d'free trip?"

Bob didn't sound too sure of himself as he spoke to his wife. "He's lying. Lucky Jack committed suicide about fifteen years ago. It was in all the papers."

Edith whispered fretfully into her husband's ear, "Then how did he get Lucky Jack's good luck charm? And how did he know about the money?"

Bob replied in an anxious, rushed voice, "I-I don't know. Let's-let's just get out of here."

Jack snickered under his breath while watching the Chandler family make a hasty retreat in the opposite direction. Pleased with himself for all the havoc he'd caused, he walked over to the cast iron bench he was previously sitting on, wiped off the snow, and sat back down.

The Chandlers strolled down the sidewalk, not saying a word to each other for several minutes.

Bob noticed it had finally stopped snowing as he followed his wife into a souvenir shop. Not interested in all the little trinkets, he took Jack's card out his overcoat pocket and stared at the holographic image of the Big Ben on the back. Showing it to his wife, he said, "Edith, look at this clock mirror. Why do you suppose the time is set for midnight?"

After eyeing the hands on the clock, Edith took a quick glimpse out the store window and saw Jack still sitting on the bench. Making a joke about him, she whispered to her husband, "Maybe he's really a king in disguise. You know—the stroke of midnight thing—like when Cinderella's appearance changed in the fairytale."

Bob frowned at his wife for sniggering at him and then put his focus back on the card. He didn't see anything out of the ordinary at first until he started moving the card back and forth. Suddenly, the images inside the hologram became visible.

"What is it?" Edith queried, noting the apprehensive gaze in his eyes.

Bob slowly looked up at her with his mouth gaped wide open. "Jack's reflection is trapped on the other side of the clock, and there are three green locusts attached to the spikes on his red coronet."

Skeptical of his story, Edith snatched the card out of his hand and peered into the hologram. When the image of the Jack suddenly appeared inside the Big Ben, she widened her eyes in shock and said, "You're right. The green locusts have eyes like a crocodile's and a tail like a scorpion's."

"I don't claim to be no genius, Edith, but I think those winged insects are supposed to symbolize a bunch of demons."

Edith put the card in her coat pocket, giggling under her breath, "You and your demons. It is nothing but a magic card."

She purchased a thimble with a picture of the Big Ben on it and followed her husband and daughter out of the store. "Bob, I have to go to the bathroom. Would you please keep an eye on Mary Kay until I get back?"

"All right."

Bob got tired of waiting on his wife and started pacing back and forth. Feeling a little congested, he took Mary Kay into a nearby shop and bought himself a cup of peppermint-flavored cappuccino. While taking a sip of his coffee, he saw a rugby match on the telly and started watching it. He was so absorbed in the game he didn't know his daughter had wandered outside.

Edith finally returned and saw her husband stepping out of the coffee shop after purchasing a second cup of cappuccino. She slipped the handle on her purse over her arm and then put her hands inside her pockets. Feeling the card in her right pocket, she pulled it out and said, "Oh I forgot I put this in there."

He took a slurp of his coffee and replied, "Throw it in the trash."

"I will. I just want to take one last look at the hologram."

She shifted the card around until the hidden images appeared inside the clock mirror. Horrified by what she saw, she gasped almost breathlessly. "No."

Bob couldn't help but notice the anxiety in his wife's eyes. "What's wrong?"

Edith was preoccupied with looking around for her daughter and didn't answer right away. When she didn't see her or Jack in the open square, she queried uneasily, "Bob, where's Mary Kay?"

Bob took another sip of his cappuccino and glanced around the immediate area. "She was with me in the store just a few minutes ago."

All at once the panic welling up inside Edith's heart came pouring out. "What? Weren't you watching her?"

Feeling intimidated by the aggressive tone of her voice, Bob cringed fearfully. "Of course I was watching her."

Edith flushed red with anger as she shouted into her husband's face, "Then where is she?"

"Uh, she-she's probably playing over by the tree," he stammered. "Why? What's the matter? Why are you so upset?"

Edith heatedly stuffed the card into her husband's hand. "Lucky Jack is after our daughter."

Deeply concerned for his child's safety, Bob queried, "What do you mean?"

"Look in the hologram on the back of the card."

Bob peered into the Big Ben to see what his wife was talking about and saw a picture of Lucky Jack holding his little girl's hand. Frightened by what he saw, his face turned pale as a ghost. "How did he do that?"

Edith gave her husband an angry look. "I don't know, but you better hope for your sake that nothing has happened to my baby."

Without further ado, she darted toward the Christmas tree.

Bob threw his plastic coffee cup into the garbage can and hurried after his wife.

Combing the area around the tree with a desperate look on her face, Edith shouted to the top of her lungs, "Mary Kay! Mary Kay!"

Unable to find her daughter anywhere, Edith's fretting intensified. Looking toward her husband, she sobbed, "Bob, she's not here."

Trying not to panic, he blinked his eyes rapidly and said. "She's got to be around here somewhere."

Searching, with her husband, among the numerous people walking about, Edith called out to her daughter once more. "Mary Kay!"

"Mary Kay!" Bob hollered reiteratively.

When Bob looked over and saw Jack reseating himself on the garden bench, he stormed up to him and said accusingly, "What did you do with my daughter?"

Jack stroked his mustache, giving him an insolent grin. "Is she worth a million pounds t'ye?"

Bob pointed a stern finger at the magician's face. "So help me if you've touched one hair on my little girl's head, I swear I'll kill you."

Jack lifted a proud chin and said, "Beware o'me magical powers, Bob-oh. Raise that finger at me again, an' I'll turn ye into a grasshopper right where ye stand."

Bob formed his hand into a fist and snarled, "Why you ..."

Edith pushed down his arm of defense and said, "Leave him alone, Bob. He obviously doesn't have her. We're just wasting time. We need to go find Mary Kay."

Bob could see how worried Edith was and decided to comply for her sake. "You're right, honey."

Just as they walked away, Jack heard an Irishwoman's voice coming through the receiver inside the earring in his left earlobe. "Jack, I need ye back at d'gallery. D'three British Intelligence agents investigating my sister's death want t'meet with me at six thirty. I smell a rat. They're definitely up t'something."

After fifteen minutes of searching frantically for her daughter throughout various stores in the open square, Edith began to lose hope. Tears of sorrow streamed down her face as she called out, "Mary Kay, Mary Kay, where are you?"

When Bob saw his wife weeping heavily, he put a comforting arm around her and said, "Don't worry, Edith, we'll find her."

Edith took a lace handkerchief out of her purse and wiped her dripping nose. Sniveling piteously, she said, "Bob, I'm so scared. Do you suppose that magician really made her disappear?"

Although Bob's heart was overcome with concern, he tried to act as if he had everything under control. "No. She probably just wandered off into one of the toy stores."

He patted his coat pockets. "I must have left my cell phone back at the hotel. I'm going to that store over there and call the police. You wait here by the tree in case she comes back, okay?"

Edith stopped weeping momentarily to respond to her husband's request. "All right, Bob."

On his way back from the store, Bob glanced over at the bench and noticed the Jack was gone. Curious where he went, he walked up to a tall, slender, forty-year-old Irishwoman, who was now sitting in Jack's place, and asked. "Who are you?"

The woman with short, strawberry-blond hair pushed her dark sunglasses further up the bridge on her nose and replied in her Irish accent, "Jillian Finney, sir."

Bob tried not to let it show that he was highly repulsed by all the hideous scars on her face. "Where is the young Irish kid that was sitting here?"

She licked her slightly chapped lips and queried, "Beg y'pardon?"

Speaking to her as if she were dense, he replied, "Lucky Jack. He was here a minute ago. Where is he?"

Presupposing he was daft by his outlandish statement, she giggled. "Yer eyes must be playing tricks on ye, ole chap. Lucky Jack died quite some time ago."

He coughed impatiently. "The police will find him."

Bob started to walk away and then turned back around to ask the Irishwoman another question. "Hey, lady, you didn't happen to see a little girl with long blond hair running around here anywhere, have you?"

Jillian brushed some fragments of snow off the sleeve of her gray wool coat and shook her head. "No, sir."

He looked up at the dark clouds and started to ask her why she was wearing sunglasses. Feeling like it wasn't that important, he pressed on with the conversation at hand. "If you do, let me know. I'll make it worth your while."

She nodded her head slightly and said, "Aye, sir."

Bob returned to his wife and found her holding her daughter's dolly in her arms. He gently caressed his wife's hand, and she slowly looked up at him with tears glistening in her eyes. "Bob, I found Babs under the tree. Mary Kay would never go off and leave her baby. Something bad must have happened to her." With that, she broke down in tears.

Bob embraced his distraught wife in his arms and allowed her to cry heavily upon his shoulder. He couldn't help feeling remorseful that he had left his baby all alone and wondered if he'd ever see her again. He knew he was the one responsible for his little girl's disappearance and wanted to remove the guilt from his mind. If only there was a way he could go back in time before he winked his eye at his daughter's well-being. The more he thought nostalgically about leaving his most prized possession to the winds of chance, the more the flashbacks haunted his soul. *"Daddy, make sure you keep your eye on my baby. Don't let nobody take her, okay?"*

Back at the tavern, Rane was staring at his wife like he didn't know what to do next. He knew she was upset with him for not showing up at the Christmas tree.

Haley reset the meter on the watch and noted the time was twenty minutes before three. She then closed the lid and put the timepiece back into her coat pocket. Hating the tension between them, she queried, "Don't you have anything to say, Rane?"

Rane started nervously cracking his knuckles. "So I didn't come… nothing happened. I dunno what ye're so upset about. No harm was done, right?"

When she kept on staring at him, Rane crossed his arms and said pompously, "All right, fine, tell me what was so important that I had t'be there."

Her voice was un-condemning and soft upon reply. "I needed your help in apprehending the kidnapper—the man who went after that little girl."

"What little girl?"

"The one you read about in the paper."

Rane eyed the newspaper on the table and retorted skeptically, "No. I don't believe ye."

"I'm afraid it is true."

Shaking his head in denial, he plopped himself on the seat of the chair and picked up the paper. Staring at the caption on the kidnapper, he said, "But that can't be. I read that some detective lady rescued her."

Haley opened the inside of her jacket and pulled out her black leather wallet from a hidden pocket. After opening the single-folded case, she showed him her picture identification and law enforcement badge and stated unhurriedly, "I was the detective you read about in the paper, Rane."

Taken aback after seeing the silver, star-shaped badge with a United Kingdom crown resting on the top spike, he lowered the paper onto his lap and gasped. "What? Ye're d'detective?"

She made a sympathetic face on his behalf and put her badge away. "I am."

Rane squeezed his eyes shut in a futile attempt to restrain the tears of regret. The repercussions for his defiant behavior buffeted his mind as he whimpered under his breath, "Oh, God, please tell me d'kidnapper didn't get away because o'me."

After several moments of feeling sorry for himself, he wiped his tears on his sleeves and laid the newspaper down on the table. While putting on his navy blue jacket, he thought of something that didn't make sense. "Wait a minute, if ye just rescued her, how did d'story get printed in d'paper already?"

Haley picked up the write-up off the table and answered, "This is Saturday's paper."

"Saturday's paper?" he queried confusedly.

She pointed toward the upper, right-corner on the front page. "Yes. Look at the date, today is only Friday."

Rane took the newspaper out of her hand and read the date aloud. “Saturday, December 22, 2018.”

He looked up at his wife and asked, “But how can that be?”

Haley sat down in the chair beside him, whispering mysteriously, “I told you, Rane. You’re dreaming about me.”

Rane rolled his eyes at her ridiculous story and then checked the time on the clock behind the bar. Clinging to a shred of hope, he blurted out, “Maybe ’tis not too late; d’kidnapper might still be in d’area.”

Rane tossed the paper aside and zipped up the front of his coat. With a look of desperation, he huddled closer to his wife to whisper in private and said, “I’ve got t’find him, Haley. What did he look like? D’article didn’t say.”

While drawing from her astute memory, Haley whispered back, “He was a bald man, in his mid-fifties I’d say. He had small, grayish blue eyes, an’ one could tell he was from a wealthy background by the clothes he wore.”

Totally engrossed in what she was saying, Rane asked, “What was he wearing?”

“He had on a gray wool suit under a black overcoat an’ a purple, silk scarf wrapped around his neck.”

Before she had a chance to say anything further, Rane jumped up out of his seat and boldly declared, “I’m going t’find that ’Napper if it is d’last thing I do.”

Just as he turned around to leave the tavern, Haley spoke up and said, “Rane, wait!”

He spun around and asked impatiently, “What?”

Haley answered him in a secretive tone. “There was something else.”

Filled with curiosity, Rane leaned toward her with his ear cocked. “Aye?”

She looked about the tavern to make sure no one was close enough to overhear her and then whispered, “The kidnapper had a Band-aid wrapped around his left earlobe.”

Rane creased his brow while considering the possibility that the man might have cut himself shaving and then left out the side door, heading for the mall.

After he had gone, Haley picked up the newspaper and went into the ladies restroom. After tossing the paper into the trash, she made doubly sure that she was alone. She then opened the lid on the teleportation device and whispered her new coordinates into the tiny speaker inside. "Ritz Mall Christmas Tree."

She pushed the particle acceleration button on the side of the watch and instantly disappeared.

Rane's panting warm breath pierced the cold air as he dashed all the way to the Ritz Mall. When he didn't find anyone in the shopping complex that fit the description Haley had given him, he walked over to the Christmas tree, feeling an overwhelming sense of despair. Fluttering his eyelids from the heavy fall of snow, he gazed up at the cloudy sky and started weeping to God. "'Tis my fault d'kidnapper got away, Lord. I'm t'blame for this. If he winds up hurting some wee babe, I couldn't live with meself."

Haley suddenly materialized next to her husband and put a comforting hand on his shoulder. "Everything's going to be all right, love. You'll see."

Snowed under with guilt, he shrugged off her hand as if she had some sort of contagious disease and blubbered bitterly, "Get away from me! Ever since I've met ye, I've had nothing but more bad luck."

He took off running, stumbling on the wet snow, to a secluded place outside the mall. He wept heavily until his eyes were almost swollen shut and then once more cried out to God. "If only I could

go back in time before I winked me eye at sin. If I had obeyed ye, Father, this wouldn't have happened. I promise I'll do what ye asked me, Lord. I'll even forgive me mum. Please, just give yer laddie another chance. I don't want t'get into heaven an' see yer masterpiece flash before me eyes, only t'find out I settled for a copy."

Haley reappeared in front of her husband and said tenderly, "Jesus loves you, Rane, an' wants you to come back to him."

Rane used the collar on his turtleneck sweater to wipe the dampness off his face and then managed a feeble grin. "I know he does."

Haley checked the time on her pocket watch and then noticed it had stopped snowing. "Chappy, help me to apprehend the kidnapper."

Rane shivered from an unexpected gust of chilly wind. "But what if we can't find him, Haley?"

She noted the look of concern in his eyes and answered assuredly, "God will help us."

His voice perked up somewhat after hearing her positive feedback and drew off what she shared with him at the gallery. "Aye, after all, we got d'winning hand, right?"

She nodded her head with certainty and put the timepiece away in her coat pocket.

Rane checked his pockets. "Ye got any paper?"

"For what?"

"T'write down d'clues we get."

Haley took a small notepad and black ink pen out of another hidden pocket inside her jacket and then gave them to her husband.

Rane flipped over the purple cover on the tablet and said in a raring-to-go voice, "Okay, let's get to it. Where should we start looking?"

She pulled her black gloves out of her coat pockets and glanced toward the busy street. "I surmise the art gallery."

He lowered his eyebrows over his bluish-green eyes and queried inquisitively, "Art gallery? Ye think d'bloke might be an artist or something?"

"Possibly."

"What makes ye think that?"

Haley took a book of matches out of her coat pocket and handed them to him. "I saw the suspect toss these into the trashcan when I was tailing him."

Rane stared interestedly at the picture of three playing cards arranged like a fan on the front of the matches. Positioned from left to right were the Jack of Diamonds, Jack of Spades, and the Jack of Clubs. After noticing one of the suites was not in the original group, he looked up at his wife and said in a bemused tone, "D'Jack o' Hearts is missing?"

She watched him draw his eyes back onto the matches as she answered, "I know. I was wondering about that myself."

Rane read aloud the business name on the matches. "Jack's Masterpieces."

She nodded, putting on her gloves. "That was Lucky Jack's gallery. If I'm not mistaken, it closed down to the general public years ago. I didn't know they had reopened it again. Did you?"

Rane opened the flap on the matches and discovered there were only two sticks left inside. "No. Do ye remember what street 'tis on?"

Haley took the book of matches from him and replied, "Great Britain. It is about a mile from here."

Still feeling guilty over his previous actions, Rane thought of the child he read about in the newspaper and asked curiously, "So how did ye know what d'wee lassie looked like?"

She dropped the matches inside her coat pocket. "God flashed a picture of Mary Kay in my mind while I was waiting in line at the store. She was playing with her dolly by the Christmas tree, an' I understood someone was planning to kidnap her."

"So where is she?"

"After I rescued her from our suspect, I took her to the security office at the far end of the mall until they could locate her mum. I then called the dispatcher to make sure her parents had called the police. When I found out they had, I came back to the tavern to see what happened to you."

"Oh," he replied remorsefully.

Haley heard her cell phone ringing and answered the call. "Hello. Oh good, they found them. Okay, I'll be right there."

She hung up the phone and began to explain to her husband what was going on. "That was mall security. The police finally located the little girl's parents. I'm going over there to see if I can find out anything."

"I'm coming with ye."

CHAPTER 11

On their way back to the Ritz Mall, Haley sucked the cool, fresh air deep into her lungs, thinking how pretty the red bows looked that were tied around the black poles on the six street lamps outside the main entrance of the shopping center. She rubbed her gloved hands together and noticed the daylight was disappearing. "I was talking to Mary Kay about Jesus, an' she confided in me that a friend of hers at school had led her to the Lord about a week ago."

Rane took the candy bag out of his pocket and emptied the rest of the jellybeans into his mouth. "A wee lass led her to d'Lord?"

She grinned and nodded. "But Mary Kay's afraid to tell her parents because they're atheists."

He threw the empty bag into the trashcan as they walked past it. "Oh that's too bad."

Rane and Haley approached the Christmas tree in the open square and spotted a couple of British policemen talking with the Chandlers.

Haley recognized the two uniformed bobbies and hurried over to them to see what she could find out. "Hi, fellows."

Officer Peter tipped the brim of his black helmet to acknowledge her presence and continued writing down the Chandler's report.

Todd, Peter's partner, gaped at the female sleuth with a suspicious gleam in his eyes. "Hi, Haley, what's homicide doing here?"

She opened her mouth to answer but then got distracted when she saw Mr. Chandler.

Seeing that the detective was more engrossed with Bob than with him, Todd tried to get her attention off him by waving his hand in front of her face. "Earth to Haley, come in."

Haley came out of her trancelike state and apologized for her rudeness. "I'm sorry, Todd. What were you saying?"

"I said, 'What's homicide doing here?'"

Before answering his question, Haley looked around to see where her husband went and saw him on the other side of the tree talking to Mary Kay. "Oh just checking things out."

Todd repositioned the armhole on his bulletproof vest, which was hidden underneath his white shirt and green, reflective jacket, and chuckled playfully, "Still believe God helps you solve all your cases, huh?"

Haley brushed her red bangs to the side of her forehead and replied in a blissful tone, "Uh-huh."

Peter stopped writing for a moment to comment on what his partner said. "Maybe you should ask God to help you, Todd. She's been decorated with honor twice in the presence of her majesty."

Todd sneered at his partner for making fun of him and then stared enviously at the gumshoe. "How did you really crack that last murder case, Haley? Not even Sherlock himself could have figured that one out. The queen even said so herself."

Haley suddenly felt a quivering sensation in her coat pocket and knew Reddy was shape-shifting himself back into his original form.

She tried not to giggle at the bot as he whispered through her pocket in his cutesy, Irish voice, "God helped us, eh, Haley?"

Haley grinned at Todd's jealous face and answered, "I told you, God helped me."

Officer Peter smiled at her answer and then put all his attention back on Bob's testimony. "I'm a little confused, Mr. Chandler. Your daughter told us the kidnapper looked like you, but yet you and your wife claim he looked like Lucky Jack."

Edith saw Mary Kay heading in her direction as she replied, "Officer, my daughter tends to make up stories from time to time. All kids do."

Todd chuckled naughtily. "Sounds like you're both making up stories to me."

Bob was offended by the officer's remark. "What do you mean we're both making up stories?"

"Come on, Mr. Chandler, you honestly expect us to believe the man who tried to kidnap your daughter looked like Lucky Jack?"

Mary Kay was eager to help and said, "Ask Haley. She saw him."

Not knowing the detective had been on the scene, Peter turned a puzzled face in her direction. "What's she talking about, Haley?"

Feeling uncomfortable about giving a testimony she wasn't quite sure of herself, Haley promptly replied, "Uh, gentlemen, can I speak to you privately for a moment?"

Todd answered back willingly, "Sure."

Haley led the two policemen away from the Chandlers and confessed, "I hate to pull rank on you, fellows, but I called my dad earlier, an' he said I could take over this case."

Peter became highly suspicious of her motive as he put his writing pen into his jacket pocket. "Why would homicide be interested in a simple kidnapping?"

Todd crossed his arms and said, "Yeah."

In an act of secrecy, Haley slid her hand down inside her coat pocket and pulled up the book of matches. With her fingers cupped around the evidence, she took another peek at the name of the establishment and then let the matches fall back into her pocket. "We believe it might be directly connected with another murder case."

Although it bothered him that she used her father's "chief of police" influence to get her way, Peter shrugged it off as if he didn't care. "Go ahead. It is just one less thing for us to do. Right, Todd?"

"That's right."

Haley watched her fellow officers walk away and then went back over to where her husband and the Chandlers were standing.

Edith spoke teary-eyed to Haley. "My daughter tells me you're the one who rescued her."

Mary Kay looked up at Haley and swiftly nodded her head. "She is, Mommy."

Haley smiled favorably at the child as she hugged her dolly and then answered Edith's question. "Yes, ma'am."

"I want to thank you for what you did."

"All the thanks belong to God. He's the one who sent me to help her."

Bob frowned at the detective for redirecting his wife's gratitude to a God he didn't believe in.

Edith wiped her nose on her handkerchief and said tearfully to Haley, "But still, you had to risk your life to save my baby."

Haley gave the woman a short, comforting hug and said, "I was happy to do it."

Feeling ill at ease about paying homage to the detective, Bob decided to turn the tables. "What are you thanking her for, Edith? It's her job. It's what she gets paid to do. If she was any good at it, she wouldn't have let the kidnapper get away."

Knowing it was partially his fault the man got away, Rane passed his wife an understanding look.

Edith was so ashamed of her husband's rudeness, she groaned miserably under her breath, "Oh, Bob."

Peering around the vicinity for the kidnapper at large, Bob exposed his thoughts of vengeance. "When I get my hands on that Jack, he'll regret the day he was ever born."

Rane's curiosity aroused the instant he heard Bob mention the kidnapper's name. Hoping to get some clues that would help him and Haley solve the case, he readied his pen and notepad and queried, "Sir, if ye don't mind me asking, what did Jack look like?"

Bob smacked himself on the stomach when he heard it growling and said, "He looked like a demon."

A naughty grin gradually spread across Rane's face as he queried, "An' just how would ye know that, sir? Have ye ever seen one before?"

Affronted by his arrogant attitude, Bob replied in a condescending tone, "Yes. As a matter of fact I have."

Edith jumped in on the conversation to give Rane a more detailed description. "No. The man didn't look like a demon. He looked exactly like Lucky Jack."

Rane scribbled the information down on the notepad and chuckled doubtfully, "*The* Lucky Jack? Get serious. D'bloke's dead."

Bob came to his wife's aid by saying, "I know that sounds crazy, but she's telling you the truth. He even wore the same diamond rings and talisman as Lucky Jack."

Edith pinched her left earlobe and said, "And the same ruby, diamond-shaped earring. I saw it when the wind blew his hair back."

Confused after hearing more of her testimony, Rane whispered to his wife, "I thought ye said d'kidnapper was an old codger with a bald head."

Haley inconspicuously eyed Mr. Chandler's visage before answering in a subdued tone of voice, "He was."

Suddenly remembering the item Jack had given her husband, Edith's eyes filled with anticipation. "Wait, I can prove it to you. He gave us one of his calling cards with his picture on it."

She turned toward her husband and said, "Bob, show it to them."

Without even looking at it, Bob took the card out of his overcoat pocket and handed it to the detective.

Haley noted the face on the Jack of Diamonds and then showed it to her husband. "It looks like Lucky Jack all right."

She flipped the playing card over to see what was on the back.

The second she did, Bob pointed toward it and said in an excitable voice, "You want proof, there's a picture of the kidnapper with my daughter inside that Big Ben hologram on the back of the card."

Stunned by his statement, Haley looked up at Bob and queried, "Are you serious?"

"Yeah, look inside the clock mirror."

Haley nudged her husband in the side when he started snickering under his breath. Trying to keep a straight face herself, she said to Bob, "Sir, there's nothing on the back of this card."

Bob snatched the card out of her hand. "There is too."

After discovering she was telling the truth, he scratched the top of his bald head like he was confused and said, "I swear to you, me and my wife saw them, huh, Edith?"

Edith nodded her head. "The Jack had three winged locusts on his coronet, and each green insect had eyes like a crocodile's and a tail like a scorpion's."

Reddy had been secretly eavesdropping on their conversation from inside Haley's coat pocket. Upon hearing Edith's description of the locusts, he made a repulsed face and quivered his tiny body, whining in a shrill voice, "Ugh! Gross! Is that what my bugs look like?"

Haley shook her pocket to let the bot know she wanted him to keep quiet and then said humbly to Bob, "I'm not doubting your word, sir. I'm sure you saw what you said."

Bob held the Jack of Diamonds up in the air as he replied, "My wife thinks this is some sort of magic card."

Haley noticed the sky was completely dark now as she queried, "Why do you say that?"

He glanced over at Edith before answering, "Because the kidnapper was a magician, just like the real Lucky Jack. He could make things appear and disappear out of nowhere. Everything about him was weird."

Edith put in her two cents. "Bob's right. He acted really strange, and his Irish brogue changed at one point to sound robotic."

Having doubts about the Chandlers' witness, Rane stuffed the notepad and pen into his coat pocket. "What do ye mean 'robotic'?"

Bob answered sharply, "He sounded like there was someone else in there with him, okay, pal? Why make us tell you this again? You cops have our report."

Haley held out her palm and asked politely, "Mr. Chandler, do you mind if we keep the card?"

Bob gave it to her as he replied, "No, go ahead. I was going to throw it in the trash anyway."

Haley placed the playing card inside her coat pocket for safekeeping and said to Edith, "Ma'am, may we speak with you privately for a moment?"

Edith glanced uneasily at her husband before answering, "Yes."

"Make it quick," Bob grumbled. "I'm hungry."

Rane and Edith followed Haley until they were safely out of Bob's hearing range.

"Mrs. Chandler, the man who kidnapped your daughter didn't look like Lucky Jack," Haley said gravely.

Edith made a bewildered expression and queried, "He didn't?"

Haley slowly shook her head at Edith. "No."

"Then what did he look like?"

Not confident of how the woman was going to react to her side of the story, Haley bit her lower lip, hesitating to reply. "Um . . . I don't quite know how to tell you this."

"Tell me what?"

Haley pushed some of her curly, red hair behind her ear and heaved a huge sigh of dread. "I guess I should start at the beginning. Mrs. Chandler, after I received the tip-off from God that your daughter was going to be kidnapped, I waited until the perpetrator moved on her."

"And?"

"I tailed them both to the bus stop, wondering why your daughter acted like she knew who he was."

Rane queried in a voice of complete surprise, "She knew d'kidnapper?"

Haley nodded her head to answer her husband's inquiry and continued telling Edith her story. "I finally approached the gentleman, an' your daughter swore he was ..."

When she was reluctant to answer, Edith's curiosity aroused, causing the tone of her voice to sound anxious and pushy. "Swore he was who?"

Rane crowded closer to his wife, eager to hear what she was going to say next.

Haley could feel her spouse breathing down her neck as she answered, "Her dad."

Rane's eyes grew wide. "He did?"

Taken aback by her answer, Edith glanced over at her husband. "The kidnapper looked like Bob?"

Reddy, too, was stunned by the news and popped his head out of Haley's pocket. "He did?"

Haley shoved the bot's head back inside her pocket, sighing in relief that no one saw him.

Mary Kay, who had tagged after them, nodded her head fast and said, "He did, Mommy. The detective's not lying. He looked and talked exactly like Daddy."

Edith combed her fingers through the back of her daughter's long blond hair and said in a soothing tone, "I believe you, honey. Now go back over there with Daddy until Mommy's done talking."

Mary Kay repositioned the gray beret on her head and replied, "Okay, Mommy."

Without hesitation, she merrily skipped over to her dad.

Edith shivered from a gust of cold wind and continued chatting with Haley. "So what did you do after my daughter told you he was her dad?"

Haley brushed some of her windblown hair out of her eyes and answered, "I asked the man to show me some identification."

"Did he?"

"Yes, surprisingly it checked out."

"Then how did you know he wasn't Bob?"

"Your little girl pointed at the Band-aid wrapped around his left earlobe an' asked him why he was wearing it."

Confused by her statement, Edith was slow upon giving her reply. "A Band-aid? Bob isn't wearing a Band-aid."

"Your daughter's statement definitely drew my suspicion, so I asked her where her mum was. That way I could be certain that the gentleman was in fact her dad."

"What did d'kidnapper do then?" Rane asked pryingly.

"He pushed me on the ground an' fled the mall. I would have chased after him, but I couldn't risk leaving Mary Kay all alone. He might have been a decoy. So I called my dad down at the police station an' told him what happened. He alerted the patrol unit in the area, but they couldn't find him."

Still beating himself up for his past mistake, Rane lowered his head and mumbled guiltily under his breath, "Maybe if this gumby had been there t'help ye, d'kidnapper wouldn't have got away."

Feeling the chill in the air, Edith clasped her hands together and peered around the open square. "It frightens me to think there's some stranger out there who looks exactly like Bob."

Haley referenced the woman's testimony by asking, "Mrs. Chandler, do you have any idea why this man would want to take your daughter?"

Edith glanced in the direction of her husband. Afraid what he might do if he found out she told them, she hesitated to answer.

Haley placed a gentle hand on the woman's shoulder and begged persistently, "Please, Edith. Help us to find him."

Terrified that the kidnapper might come back after her daughter, Edith decided to spill the beans on what her husband had done. "You promise you won't tell Bob I told you?"

Rane and Haley both nodded their head to agree.

Edith huddled closer to them and whispered, "About eighteen years ago, my husband played a poker game with Lucky Jack in Las Vegas and wound up losing one million dollars. He devised a plan to switch briefcases on him and got our money back. When Lucky Jack found out about it, he called our hotel room and swore to Bob that he would get revenge on him one day."

Tired of waiting on his wife, Mr. Chandler hollered out in a whining tone, "Come on, Edith. I want to get something to eat."

All at once Haley heard her cell phone ringing again and took it out of her coat pocket. She spoke to the calling party on the phone while trailing Rane and Edith back over to Bob. After hanging up her phone, she said, "Mr. Chandler, the police department is sending out Detective Calvin Aimes. He will put you an' your family in protective custody for twenty-four hours."

Deeply concerned for his daughter's safety, Bob picked up Mary Kay as he queried, "Protective custody? You think the kidnapper might try it again?"

Knowing how scared the Chandlers were, Haley stared at them with compassion in her eyes and nodded her head. "They usually do. That is why it is important that you don't let Mary Kay out of your sight, not even for a second."

Edith readily agreed. "We won't. We promise."

Haley turned on the high-powered camera feature on her cell phone and held up the view screen. "I'll have to take a snapshot of your faces for Calvin. He'll need to know what you look like."

"Okay," Edith replied.

Haley took their photo and then typed a short text message to Calvin. "Where will you be dining?"

Edith pointed at a fancy restaurant down the way a piece and replied, "At Prestigious Choices."

Haley included the location of the eatery in the text and then sent the message and the picture to Detective Aimes through her private Internet service at the police department. Once she had finished that, she put her cell phone back into her coat pocket and said to Bob and Edith, "I want you to stay at the restaurant until Calvin arrives. He should be there in about a half hour. When he gets there, make sure he shows you his badge an' driver's license."

Still upset over being duped by the Jack, Bob replied in a sarcastic tongue, "You can count on it."

Rane noted the anxious look in Edith's eyes as she watched several men pass by. Sensing her uneasiness stemmed from the kidnapper at large, he gave her a pat on the back and said reassuringly, "No worries, lady. Jesus is on d'case. He'll help us find him."

Bob was hugely offended and shouted at Rane. "Keep your God! We're atheists."

He grabbed his wife by the hand and stormed off down the sidewalk.

Allowing his carnal thoughts to rule him from being weak in faith, Rane hollered back in a disrespectful tone, "We intend to, gumby!"

Still snorting like an angry boar, Bob turned around and shouted, "If you're supposed to epitomize what the love of Jesus looks like, you can keep your Christianity!"

Haley gave her husband a sad look as the Chandlers walked away.

Rane didn't want to be held accountable for his actions, so he spoke to his wife as if she was a bother. "What?"

"We need to pray for them."

He raised a harsh voice. "Why should I pray for d'likes of him? He insulted me."

Feeling grieved in her heart over his insolence, Haley answered tearfully, "Bob's right, Rane. We're supposed to be a reflection of the King's love."

Feeling convicted by her merciful heart, Rane lowered his head and said in a barely audible tone, "I know."

The very next moment Rane thought he heard the Holy Spirit leading him to repent for calling Bob stupid. Hating the idea of humbling himself, his heart sped up.

Uncertain why her husband was standing rigid with his eyes bulged, Haley asked, "Rane, is something wrong? You look pale as a ghost."

Not wanting to bury the hatchet between him and Mr. Chandler, Rane deceived himself into believing the request was only a figment of his imagination. "For a moment there, I thought I heard d'King telling me t'go ask Bob's forgiveness. Isn't that crazy?" he chuckled.

"No. I'm sure you heard right."

Disliking her answer, Rane quit laughing and pouted his lips. "What do ye mean, 'I'm sure ye heard right'?"

"Well I know the devil wouldn't ask you to do it."

Rane crossed his arms and said in defiance, "No. I'm not going t'apologize."

Seeing the pride in his eyes, Haley pulled her small Bible out of her coat pocket and opened it to the book of James 1:22–25. She held the page containing the scriptures in front of his face like a mirror and declared passionately, "Ooh, look at that gorgeous reflection."

Rane pushed the book down from his mug and queried, "What are ye doing?"

With an innocent smile on her face, Haley pointed at the passage of light and replied, "Showing you your humble heart in the King."

Rane thrust his chest out like a proud peacock and said pompously, "I don't need ye t'show it t'me. I know what it says."

When he turned his back on her to mope, Haley stared at the back of his head and decided it would be a good idea to read the verses aloud. "But be doers of the word, an' not hearers only…"

Rane spun around and showed her his lack of patience. "Yeesh! I tol' ye I didn't want ye t'read it t'me."

She smiled at him and kept on reading. "Deceiving yourselves. For if anyone is a hearer of the word an' not a doer, he is like a man observing his natural face in a mirror; for he observes himself, goes away, an' immediately forgets what kind of man he was. But he who looks into the perfect law of liberty an' continues in it, an' is not a forgetful hearer but a doer of the work, this one will be blessed in what he does."

Torn between humility and self-pride, Rane clasped his fingers on top of his head and started pacing back and forth. After mulling over the degradation in the back of his mind, he felt an overwhelming sense of anxiety and threw his hands up in the air. "I can't do it! I can't! I got me pride."

Haley closed the Bible and put it back into her coat pocket. "An' pride is exactly what God intends to strip us of. You want your crown back, don't you?"

Rane thought about the splendor of the crown and slowly nodded his head. "Aye, I do indeed."

She smiled at him and said, "Then love is the only way."

Just when Rane thought he had enough nerve to do the right thing, he suddenly panicked and allowed his imaginary fears to overcome him. "No. I can't do it . . . I can't. 'Tis too humiliating. He'll-he'll think I'm a gumby."

Haley wasted no time in reassuring him that everything would be all right. "You can, Rane. Just take a step of faith."

Rane peered in the direction of the Prestigious Choices restaurant, swallowing uneasily at the thought of demeaning himself to Bob. "But he's going t'laugh at me."

She caressed his cheek with her gloved hand and said to be helpful, "Chappy, why don't you do what I do?"

"What's that?"

She took her hand down from his face and replied, "Try not to let your left hand know what your right hand is doing. That always works for me."

Rane sighed at the expectant look in her green eyes. He knew the Holy Spirit was leading him to do the right thing. "All right, I'll do it. 'Tis d'only way I'm ever going t'have any peace."

He lowered his head and slowly sauntered down the sidewalk. While dreading his apology to Bob, he started whining under his breath to God. "Please, Jesus, don't make me do this. 'Tis so degrading. Can't I just send d'bloke a postcard or something?"

Fifteen minutes passed before Haley saw Rane heading back in her direction. As he walked up to her, she queried in a hopeful voice, "Did you apologize?"

He nodded. "Aye, I finally worked up enough kingly courage. I can't say 'twas easy."

"Did Bob accept your apology?"

Rane made a perturbed face and replied, "No. I even offered t'pay for d'bloke's meal, but he threw me quid right in me face an' then ordered me a piece o' humble pie."

Feeling a strong impulse to giggle at his last comment, Haley quickly slapped her hand over her mouth. "I'm sorry he did that to you."

"Oh I can tell ye feel sorry for me by all d'snickers on yer breath."

Reddy leaned his elbows on the edge of Haley's coat pocket, snorting chuckles through his nose. "Snickers on yer breath, that's funny."

Rane chuckled a smidgen at the bot for being comical and then carried on with his conversation with his wife. "Ye know I was actually tempted t'take him up on his offer for pie."

"You were?"

"Sure, I was craving something sweet."

"Speaking of something sweet…"

Haley reached her hand inside her left, coat pocket and pulled out a red canister shaped like a heart. She smiled widely at her husband's handsome face and started singing, "Happy birthday to you, happy birthday to you, happy birthday, dear Chappy, Happy Birthday to you."

Reddy watched her give the gift to Rane and then made his wishes known too. "Happy birthday, Chappy."

Rane grinned from ear to ear at the gift she gave him. "Ye guys actually got me something?"

Delighted at his happy response, Haley giggled faintly. "Sure. That was the errand I had to run. Open it."

Rane took the lid off the tin and saw a heart-shaped sandwich inside. Drawing the container close to his nose, he sniffed the aroma inside the white bread and said in a craving tone, "Mmm, smells like peanut butter an' jelly, my favorite."

Pleased that he liked her birthday gift, she nodded her head and replied, "It is. I even had the clerk cut off the ends."

He ripped the heart-shaped sandwich down the middle and then stuffed one half of it into his mouth. "Why?"

Haley used her index finger to brush a breadcrumb off the corner of his mouth. "To let you know that my love for you will never end."

Doubting her sincerity from being dumped by all the women he ever cared about, Rane threw the other half of the sandwich into the trash and wiped the crumbs off his hands. "Never end, eh?"

Knowing it was her half of the heart that he had mentally tossed away, she gave him a sad look and replied in a barely audible tone, "Not real love anyway."

Feeling uncomfortable with the topic of their conversation, Rane choked down the food in his mouth and shifted his concentration onto his surroundings. While pondering the overwhelming odds of finding their suspect, he said, "Haley, London's a big city. How are we ever going t'find d'kidnapper? He could be disguised as anyone. 'Twill be like looking for a needle in a haystack."

She shrugged off his pessimism by keeping a confident stance. "Not really, we just have to compile the clues."

The bot nodded his head at her words and picked up his tiny magnifying glass from off the bottom of her pocket. With a firm grip on the black handle, he held the round glass in front of his right eye and said playfully, "Haley, can I play Sherlock this time?"

Haley smiled at the bot's cute face and nodded her head. "All right, but stay out of sight, okay?"

Reddy shouted jubilantly into the air, "Oh goodie!" and then ducked down in her pocket.

Rane took his pen and notepad out of his jacket and said to his wife, "But we don't even know what d'bloke really looks like."

She sighed off his negativity and gave an optimistic reply. "Well, I do know one thing for sure. The perpetrator was wearing a Band-aid around his left earlobe. The question is…why was he or she wearing it?"

Following Haley down to the bus stop, which was located on the west side of the mall, Rane wrinkled his brow and asked, "Ye said he or she. Ye think d'kidnapper might be a lady?"

Working undercover, she quickly scanned the earlobes on the group of people waiting for the bus to arrive. "Probably not, but the kidnapper was disguised, so I'm not ruling out the possibility. Also, considering there were only two sticks left in the book of matches an' that the suspect smelt like nicotine, I would say he or she is a smoker."

Making sure he could see what he was about to write, Rane stood under the security lights at the bus stop as he flipped over the cover on his spiral notebook. While scribbling down the clues on the paper, he spoke one aloud. "Jack might be a bald lady in disguise."

All at once a funny idea shot through his mind. "Hey, I just thought o'something."

She took a couple steps closer to him and asked, "What's that?"

"If d'kidnapper's a lassie, wouldn't she be called a Jack-ee?" Rane queried and then chuckled at his dry humor.

When she didn't laugh at his joke, he nervously cleared his throat and put the notepad and pen into his coat pocket.

Haley observed the heavy, Friday afternoon traffic on the main street as she pondered the clues aloud. "How could the kidnapper look an' sound like Bob one moment an' then like Lucky Jack the next?"

Thinking she was talking to him, Rane interrupted her private meditation to give a slow and unsure response. "D'Chandlers did say he was a magician."

Haley took the card Bob had given her out of her coat pocket and looked at it again. "If he is, he's quite good at it. The two suspects don't look anything alike. An' if Lucky Jack's dead, who was the man trying to kidnap Mary Kay?"

Rane shrugged his shoulders to indicate he hadn't a clue and then remembered something Edith told them about the magician. "Was d'bald chap wearing a lucky charm?"

She put the card back in her pocket and replied, "I didn't see one, but it could have been hidden underneath his shirt."

He started to crack his knuckles and stopped when he eyed the ring finger on his right hand. "What about d'diamonds Edith mentioned earlier? Was he wearing any?"

Drawing off her astute memory, Haley stood silent for a moment. "No, but he could have removed them."

"So why didn't he remove d'Band-aid? 'twas a dead giveaway."

While giving it more thought, she bit down on her lower lip and then said under her breath, “Unless he was covering up a pierced hole in his lobe.”

Haley took her cell phone out of her coat pocket and said, “I’m going to call the file clerk down at the police department an’ see if there were any charges ever filed against Lucky Jack.”

“Oh good. Hopefully they’ll come up with something.”

She nodded to agree and called the number at the station. Soon as the file clerk saw her name on her private cell phone, she said, “Hi, Haley.”

“Hi, Margaree, can you do me a big favor?”

“Just name it.”

Before giving her reply, Haley took the book of matches out of her coat pocket and stared at the picture of the three Jacks. “Could you check an’ see if anyone ever filed a police report against Lucky Jack?”

“The dead gambler?”

“Yes.”

She sighed heavily at the amount of work involved. “Okay, but it may take awhile.”

“Thanks, Magaree. You’re a peach. I owe you one.”

Seeing their means of transportation pull up in the loading zone, Rane tugged on his wife’s arm and said, “Haley, d’bus is here.”

Being a spur-of-the-moment person, Haley looked down the street at all the snow on the sidewalk and replied, “I’ve decided to jog over instead.”

He made a repulsive face at her suggestion and pointed his thumb at his chest. “What? Ye expect me t’run?”

She tousled his blond hair with her fingertips. “Sure. It is not far, an’ the exercise will be good for us.”

Rane smoothed his hair back the way it was and quickly thought up an excuse not to run. “But ’tis dark outside. How do ye expect me t’see where I’m going?”

She giggled softly at his reaction. "That won't work, Chappy. We're downtown. There's plenty of street lamps an' bright lights."

Without further ado, Haley took off running down the sidewalk as if she was doing the fifty-yard dash. "Race you there."

Rane groaned deeply under his breath and then chased after her. When he almost slipped a couple times on the snow, he shouted from behind her, "Would ye slow down? I'm not a jack rabbit!"

Haley stopped along the sidewalk by a nearby park to let her husband catch his breath. "I can't believe you're winded already, love. We only ran a few blocks."

Shocked by her remark, Rane coughed several more times and said puffing, "Only a few blocks, eh? I-I felt like … like I just ran ten miles."

All at once they heard a drunk singing an old Irish ditty off-key while digging through the trashcan. "Me Irish eyes are crying, for me lassie's gone away."

The redheaded Irishman in his late fifties stumbled about with a bottle of whiskey in his hand. Hearing Rane and Haley talking, he quit singing and staggered over to them with his bulldog heeling beside him. Nosily verbalizing his slurred speech, he said in high spirits, "Top o' d'evening t'ye. Me name's Jake."

Rane turned up his nose, wheezing at the nauseating stench of stale whiskey on the man's breath. "What are ye trying t'do, mate, kill me? I just barely got me wind back as it was."

The Irishman chuckled at Rane and then started pinching his nose while impersonating the sound of a car horn. "Honk, honk, honk."

Rane smacked the man's hand off his beak. "Would ye quit it! I don't want d'thing bigger than it already is."

The Irishman bent over and patted his pooch on the head. "This is Butchie. He's a champion, he is, not afraid of anything. Lucky Jack's ghost came back t'haunt me a minute ago, an' he bit him right on d'leg, he did."

Rane exchanged a brief, surprised look with his wife before asking the drunk, "Lucky Jack's ghost?"

While nobody was watching, Reddy secretly waved at the dog, whispering, "Hi, Butchie."

Jake looked around the park to make sure no one was around and then said to Rane, "Aye, d'stingy bloke swore he'd get even with me one day for stealing some of his chips off d'poker table. Serves him right, though, for not buying me a bottle o'whiskey. A chap gets thirsty, ye know."

Haley spoke up to make a point. "Sir, the man you saw could have been just someone masquerading as Lucky Jack."

Straining to see her face through blurry eyes, the Irishman rubbed his chin, which was inundated with a huge crop of red, coarse whiskers, and replied, "Nah, 'twas him all right."

Rane snickered in his wife's ear, "Seeing ghosts. Is he drunk or what?"

Jake took a big swig from his bottle. "That ghostie will walk with a gimp d'rest of his life, he will."

Still believing Jake saw a man and not a ghost, Haley asked inquisitively, "Sir, exactly where was Lucky Jack when your dog bit him on the leg?"

Jake pointed over to one of the streetlamps near a park bench and replied, "Right over there."

He then pulled a Jack of Clubs out of his dirty trench coat pocket and handed it to Haley. "He said this was one of his calling cards."

While she was busy examining the card, Jake put his arm around Rane's neck and started joking with him. "I got a little, green elf hidden in me coat pocket. I carry him around with me for luck."

Rane motioned his head toward his wife as he whispered to the drunk in an overdramatic voice, "If he's anything like d'silver one in her pocket, ye're in big trouble, chum."

The Irishman laughed at Rane's remark as if it was the funniest thing in the world. "Big trouble, chum."

He then moseyed on down the street with his bulldog, singing, "Me Irish eyes are crying, for me lassie's gone away."

Haley made sure Jake was well out of the area before handing the evidence to the bot. "Reddy, scan these cards an' the matches an' tell me if you find two prints alike. Exclude me an' Rane's, okay?"

Picking up on the secrecy in the quiet tone of her voice, the bot peered through his magnifying glass at the items she gave him and whispered back, "Okey-dokey, Haley. Sherlock is on d'case."

Watching the bot scan both sides of the cards with a beam of light shooting out of each eye, Rane said in a voice of astonishment, "He can actually do that?"

She giggled at his reaction. "Yes."

Reddy finished scanning the items and handed them back to her. "No two prints alike, Haley."

Stumped by his findings, she muttered her thoughts aloud. "But that can't be. If it was the same suspect then his fingerprints should be on all the evidence."

Rane took the matches out of her hand and looked at the faces of the three Jacks. "That's true."

After placing the two cards in her coat pocket, Haley headed toward the lamppost, whistling another tune into the air.

Rane put the book of matches into his jacket and tagged after her, saying, "Ye're quite a musical lassie, ain't ye?"

She smiled at his comment, huddling closer to explain. "That's how I secretly contact Reddy."

Like a bulb turning on inside his head, Rane replied, "Ooh."

Haley pulled a small, silver flashlight out of her pocket and said, "The different melodies lets Reddy know what device I want him to change into."

Rane stared in amazement at the shiny object in her hand. "So what happens if someone was t'walk by an' whistle one of those tunes?"

While answering his question, she turned on the flashlight and swept the beam of light across the snow. "Nothing. Reddy's translator is programmed to respond only to our sound waves."

Rane watched her shine the light on the snow and queried nosily, "What are ye looking for?"

Haley kept her fixation on the ground as she replied, "Blood."

"Why?"

She looked up at his face long enough to say, "Jake said his dog bit the suspect on the leg, right?"

"Aye."

"Then we should be able to get a blood sample on him."

Enlightened after hearing her motive, he said, "Hey, ye're right, we should."

Not finding anything in the snow, Haley shined the flashlight up ahead and said commandingly, "Reddy, scan the area for blood."

Right away a shaft of baby blue light shot through the circular glass on the end of the flashlight and started scanning the grounds. Once Reddy had completed his search, he disclosed his findings in a deep, British voice. "No trace of blood was found, Detective."

Wondering why the radical transformation in the robot's character, Rane didn't hesitate to ask, "What happened t'Little Silver's voice?"

Haley turned off the flashlight and put it back into her pocket. "It changes whenever Reddy's molecular structure is altered from his original form."

"He sounded so serious, like some British Intelligence Agent. I liked him better d'way he was."

Haley peered into her husband's teal blue eyes and then indirectly shared her sentiment with him by referencing the bot. "Yes. I prefer the fun-loving Irish boy too."

When Rane looked up at the sky and started whistling coolly, Haley knew he understood what she meant.

Pressing on with her investigation, she looked around the area. "I'm surprised Reddy didn't find any blood."

Rane blew his warm breath on his hands to warm them up and queried, "So what do ye think is going on?"

Haley bit her lower lip, pondering heavily on the clues. "I'm not sure."

Rane sat down on the bench and started scribbling down the clues Jake gave them. While listening to a car pass by on the street, he asked, "So tell me, Detective, what do ye do for fun when ye're not out chasing bad guys or taking care of yer baby?"

Haley joined him on the bench. "I spend time with God."

Her green eyes lit up with delight as she thought about some of the intimate conversations she had with the Holy Spirit, her best friend in the whole world. "He's fun to be with an' has a great sense of humor."

Rane gave her a dense look. "He does?"

She smiled, nodding her head. "Uh-huh. Ask him to show you that part of him sometime."

Haley put her thoughts back on the case and stood back up. "Well, we better get going."

He sighed wearily at the thought of more running and got up off the bench. "Okay."

Rane was relieved when they finally arrived at the gallery. While listening to himself puff hard from his long run, he silently read the name on the neon sign on the front of the building. *Jack's Masterpieces? Why does this place look so familiar?*

The very next moment he had a flashback of himself inside the gallery. He was only six and a half years old at the time and was still in the custody of his Irish mother, Kathryn.

"Mummy, why are ye crying? What's d'matter?" Young Rane queried worriedly as he watched the tears trickling down his mother's slightly freckled face.

Kathryn wiped the tears off her cheeks with a quick sweep of her hands. "Rane, sometimes bad things happen 'cause o'bad choices."

Not quite sure what she was talking about or why she took him into the gallery in the first place, he glanced up at one of the leprechaun paintings hanging on the wall. "Bad things?"

Kathryn got quiet as they walked down the main corridor of the building. When she saw an open door that read "Private. Keep Out," she stopped abruptly and knelt down beside her son. After handing him a new deck of playing cards, which she had taken out of her pants pocket, she said tearfully, "I love ye, baby."

Young Rane put a comforting hand to her cheek and said, "I love ye too, Mummy. Don't cry. Everything will be all right."

Kathryn took his small hand down from her cheek and affectionately kissed his palm. She then let go of his hand and started crying harder. "Promise me something…"

Sensing something bad was about to happen by the way she was acting, his response sounded anxious. "What?"

"That ye'll never forget me."

He smiled favorably at his mother's pretty face and said, "I won't forget ye."

Kathryn pulled the five-carat diamond engagement ring off her finger that Lucky Jack had given to her and placed it in her son's hand. "I want ye t'have this, for luck."

All at once Jillian Finney appeared in the doorway to the private room and started throwing accusations at Kathryn. "Did ye honestly think ye could keep d'boy hidden from me forever, lassie?"

Frightened by the strange woman's malevolent expression, young Rane quickly hid the gifts his mother had given him in his back pockets and queried in a shaky voice, "Mummy, who is this lady?"

Kathryn stood to face Jillian. With a pool of tears glistening in her sea blue eyes, she entreated, "Please, I'm tired of running from Lucky Jack's ghost, tired of being scared of things that aren't really there. I want me life back, so I came t'pay ye what I owed him."

"Then I guess ye get t'keep that pretty, wee head on yer shoulders after all."

Jillian pulled on a few strands of Kathryn's hair and said in a pretentious voice, "I see ye cut yer blond hair an' died it black… clever girl."

Kathryn lowered her head shamefully and several teardrops escaped out of her eyes and splashed onto the marble floor.

Jillian held a cold stare on her for several moments. "Why did ye take off with d'child? Lucky Jack won d'laddie fair an' square."

With tears cascading down her cheeks, Kathryn slowly looked up at the woman and sobbed, "I couldn't give up my baby, so I ran."

"Ye double-crossed Lucky Jack an' cheated him out of his inheritance. That boy brought more joy t'him than ye ever did. My brother would still be alive today if it weren't for ye."

The woman's accusing tone caused more uneasiness to fill young Rane's heart as he looked up at his mother. "What's she talking about, Mummy?"

Kathryn chose not to answer her son.

Jillian glared at Kathryn and handed her a Jack of Diamonds playing card.

Kathryn looked uncertainly at Lucky Jack's profile that was on the face of the Jack of Diamonds and the name of his gallery printed across the bottom. "What is this for?"

Jillian gave her a wicked smirk and replied, "'Tis a calling card from yer ex-lover. He left ye a message on d'back."

Kathryn turned over the card and peered into the Big Ben hologram like the one Bob had seen. The second she saw the reflection of Lucky Jack holding onto young Rane's hand, she screamed in a shrill voice, "Noooo, he can't have my baby. He's mine."

Jillian grabbed Rane by the hand and said hatefully, "Lucky Jack loved ye, an' ye broke his heart. Now 'tis yer turn t'suffer."

Young Rane's heart sped up with anxiety as the strange woman held a firm grip on his palm. "Mummy, what's going on?"

Kathryn's lips began to quiver as more tears of guilt streamed down her pale face. Feeling helpless to save her child, she started bawling. "Please don't take my baby away from me. I'll pay Lucky Jack back d'money somehow."

Jillian's pitiless heart remained unchanged. "All d'money in d'world won't buy back my brother's life. If ye so much as step one foot back in London, Jack's ghost will finish d'job he started."

Feeling a need to defend his mother from the woman's hostility, young Rane kicked Jillian hard on the right shin. "Leave her alone, ye evil witch!"

Overcome with pain, Jillian clutched both hands around her leg, shrieking loudly, "Ow!"

Gnashing her teeth, she hobbled toward the boy and snarled, "Ugh! I'm going t'kill ye for that, ye little brat!"

Kathryn stepped in front of her son to protect him and whimpered pleadingly, "Please, Jill, don't hurt him."

With pursed lips, Jillian scowled at young Rane who was peeking at her from behind his mother. "I'll let him live for me brother's sake, not yers."

Kathryn put the playing card Jillian had given her in her pants pocket and managed to tearfully choke out an appreciative responsive. "Thank ye."

She fought back the hysteria as she knelt down to hug her beloved son one last time. "Please, Rane, don't hurt her anymore. Be a good laddie, for Mummy."

After she had finished embracing him, young Rane stared uncertainly at her sad face. "Tell me what's wrong, Mummy? Maybe I can help ye."

When she just stood up and walked away without saying a word, he knew he would never see her again. He broke down and started crying noisily. "Mummy, come back. Please, Mummy, I'm scared."

The second he tried to run after his mother, Jillian grabbed him by the scruff of his neck. "Shut yer gob, laddie, ye belong t'yer dad now."

Horrified by her announcement, he tried wriggling out of her tight grip. "My mummy said me daddy's dead. Now let me go!"

Jillian gave the boy a smug look and queried, "Didn't yer mum ever tell ye she gambled ye away t'yer dad for a mere six million pounds?"

With snot running out of his nose and his face drenched with tears, young Rane shook his head at her cruel words and blubbered, "No, ye're lying. She wouldn't do that. She loves me."

"Ask her for yerself, laddie."

Overhearing their conversation, Kathryn went back to weeping profusely out of a guilty conscience and hurried toward the emergency exit at the end of the corridor.

Right before she left the building, young Rane hollered after her in a voice of anguish, "Mummy, tell her that isn't true!"

Haunted by his distressing voice, Kathryn cupped her hands over her ears and ran through the door.

As the door slammed closed, her son's blood-curdling screams were left behind. "*Mummy!*"

Concerned about the dead stare in her husband's eyes, Haley shook his arm and queried, "Rane, are you all right?"

Jarred into the present by the shaking of his body, he replied fuzzily, "Huh? What?"

"I said, 'Are you all right?'"

Still in a daze, he pushed the heel of his hand against his temple and nodded his head.

Haley looked around the grounds and spotted an old, black Cadillac parked across the street. Pointing it out to her husband, she said, "Rane, look at the license plate on that car over there."

He fixed his eyes on the bumper of the car and then read the information on the plate aloud. "JACK777."

Rane turned toward his wife and queried, "Ye think that's d'kidnapper's car?"

She nodded and then took another check around the area. "Keep an eye out. I'm going to go over an' have a look."

"Okay."

Haley darted across the street and then nosily peeked through the car window to see what was inside. When she had finished her search, she ran back to her husband and said, "I saw a book of matches on the front seat like the one the suspect threw away. The driver is definitely a smoker. There were piles of cigarette butts in the ashtray. I'll run a license plate check on the vehicle later."

Reddy suddenly popped up out of her pocket with his magnifying glass held in front of his right eye and said, "Haley, I ran d'fingerprint check through d'security network."

She kept her ear glued on what he had to say while she and Rane strolled up the path to the main entrance. "What did you find out?"

The bot lowered the round glass from his eye to answer, "D'fingerprints belong t'Jake an' d'Chandlers."

Upon hearing the report, Haley appeared to be a bit confused. "But what about the kidnapper's prints?"

Trying to be helpful, Rane spoke up and said, "Maybe he was wearing gloves."

"No. The man I saw wasn't wearing gloves, an' Edith testified that the kidnapper had rings on all his fingers."

He chewed on the skin on the side of his thumb and replied, "Oh that's right."

Reddy peered through his magnifying glass at his silver fingertips and offered his opinion whether they wanted it or not. "Maybe d'kidnapper didn't have any prints like me."

Rane frowned at the bot's suggestion as he and his wife approached the double glass doors.

Haley opened the gallery door by pulling on the silver handle. Before going inside, she looked down at the bot and whispered, "All right, Reddy, be quiet as a mouse, okay?"

"Okey-dokey, Haley. I be so quiet ye won't even know I'm here."

Rane snickered to himself. "That should last about ten seconds."

Rane followed Haley into the gallery and leisurely wandered about the foyer, looking for clues. While viewing all the luxurious décor, they saw two limestone pillars standing proud on opposite sides of the room and three rubber plants in stainless steel planters over by the front desk. In the center of the lobby was a huge three-tier fountain made out of white marble. Mounted and seated on opposite sides of the bottom tier were twin statues of leprechauns, holding a pot of fool's gold. Toward the back wall sat a Queen Anne sofa and a couple of matching chairs. These rare antique pieces had cherry wood frames with white upholstery. A polished coffee table complemented the love seat with its exquisite design. It was cluttered with a variety of outdated poker publications and fame and fortune magazines. The periodicals headlined articles about the infamous Lucky Jack and were laminated to protect them from damage. Underneath the furniture was a cream-colored area rug with a red-diamond pattern. Everything in the vestibule screamed extravagant spending, right down to the cream marble floor.

Haley unenthusiastically trailed Rane over to the leprechaun fountain and watched him gaze at the clean water cascading down the top tier. While he was enjoying the peaceful sound of the stream, he peered into the bottom basin and saw a huge pile of British coins. Desperate for his luck to change for the better, he extended a beggar's hand to his wife and said, "Lassie, give me two pence. I want t'make a wish."

Reddy overheard him and readily adopted the idea. After grinning at the loose change glistening in the water, he personified the same penniless character as his inventor by asking for a handout. "I want t'make a wish, too, Haley. Can I have a penny?"

With a disgusted look on her face, she slapped both their hands and answered, "No!"

Rane jiggled his hand toward her and said persistently, "Come on, lassie, I'll give it back t'ye."

Insulted that her husband would actually ask her to support him in the practice of divination, she stomped her right foot on the floor the way she usually did when she got upset and said rebukingly in his face, "No! I will not grieve the heart of the Holy Spirit by seeking my fortune from the fountain of Gad, Meni, or any other lucky god for that matter."

He propped his hand on top of the marble head on one of the leprechaun figurines and replied naively, "Gad an' Meni? Who are they?"

She pushed Reddy down in her pocket to keep him hidden from a couple who had just walked by on their way out of the gallery and then eyed the elf statue that her husband was leaning on. "False gods of fortune that some of our Lord's people left Him to worship."

Reacting to her affirmation, Rane instantly retracted his hand from the sculpture as if it were a poisionous snake, shrieking under his breath, "Yigh!"

He wiped his palm across the front of his sweater as if it had been tarnished from touching the image.

Haley resisted the temptation to laugh at what he was doing and, instead, told him where he could find the information. "They're mentioned in Isaiah, chapter sixty-five verse eleven."

Rane put his mind back on the case and inadvertently caught sight of Carol, a young, British clerk typing on her keyboard from behind the ticket counter. He grabbed his wife by the hand and pulled her over to her to see if they could find out anything.

Carol stopped typing when she saw the couple approach the desk. Trying to make a sale, she put on a pleasant smile. "Good afternoon. Would you folks like to take the tour?"

Uncertain what she was talking about, Rane leaned on the rose marble countertop and answered shyly, "Oh, uh . . . "

Seeing he had a loss for words, Haley came to her husband's aid by saying, "No, but would you mind if we look around?"

She smiled. "Sure, if you buy a ticket."

Rane huddled closer to his wife, whispering in her ear, "Maybe she'll let us if ye show her yer badge."

Haley whispered back, "I don't have a search warrant."

"Oh."

Haley read the woman's name tag before asking, "Carol, are those magazines on the coffee table about Lucky Jack?"

She nodded. "The articles boast about how he took down the top gamblers in the world, winning poker tournaments in prestigious casinos in places like Monte Carlo, Las Vegas, Hong Kong, Singapore, and Atlantis."

"Do you mind if we browse through the magazines?"

Carol formed her pale pink lips into a smirk. "Not without a ticket."

Haley exchanged a brief let-down look with her husband and then decided to drill the clerk to find some answers. "I heard the gallery had closed some time ago. When did it reopen again?"

"About a couple months ago."

"How much is the art tour?"

Rane was afraid he didn't have enough money to pay for both tickets, so he spoke up before Carol had a chance to answer. "Can ye give us a moment t'think about it?"

"All right," she answered politely and went right back to typing.

Rane pulled his brown leather billfold out of his rear pocket. He then turned his back on the girls to secretly check the amount of money he had stashed inside.

Haley sniggered in her heart at his secrecy and then looked around the general area, hoping to find a clue. After several moments of quietly observing the huge mirror covering the wall behind the clerk's desk, she saw a hologram appear within the glass. Excited about her new discovery, she tapped her husband on the arm and motioned her head in that direction. "Rane, look, it is an army of Lucky Jack clones, dressed up like a Jack of Diamonds."

Rane made sure Carol wasn't watching and then stretched his neck to get a better look at the reflection of the famous gambler. After watching the vast number of replicas marching single file down a road that led to a huge mountain of sparkling white diamonds, he whistled under his breath and said, "There must be millions of him."

Haley paid close attention to the appearance of the Jacks. "Yeah, they all look exactly like him."

He shoved his wallet back inside his pocket and snickered into his wife's ear, "Talk about being in love with yer face."

Haley secretly admired the beautiful, Imperial State crown resting on top of the pile of diamonds and then put her attention back on the knaves. "Rane, why do you suppose the Jacks are carrying a primeval axe in their left hand?"

He shrugged. "I dunno."

Haley spoke up to get the desk clerk's attention. "Excuse me, miss."

"Yes?"

"Did you see a man come in here dressed up like Lucky Jack?"

Carol giggled. "No. I think I would remember that."

Haley lowered the tone of her voice to speak privately with her husband. "Now remember, Rane, anyone who smells like nicotine an' has an earring or a Band-aid on his or her left earlobe is a possible suspect."

Rane watched Carol hook her hair behind her ears and whispered to his wife, "Looks like we can scratch d'clerk off d'list. Her lobes are clean."

Haley took a fleeting look at the clerk's earlobes and then stared back at the mirror. All at once she felt Reddy scurrying up her pant leg with his tiny magnifying glass in his mouth. She scooped him up in her palm and cupped the other hand over the top of him to conceal him from the clerk's view. Wondering what he had been up to, she looked around for a place to slip away. "Rane, I'll be back in a minute."

Assuming she was going to the bathroom, he replied, "Sure, take yer time."

Haley carried the bot to a secluded spot down the hall. After taking one last look to make sure no one was coming, she began her interrogation. "Reddy, where have you been?"

Acting bashful, the bot twirled one of his glittery golden curls around his index finger and replied, "Ye promise ye won't get mad, Haley?"

She nodded her head. "I promise."

Analyzing the possibility that she might get mad anyway, Reddy sat down on the edge of her palm and started defending himself. "I was just covering our tracks. I was only gone for a moment."

Dreading the worst by the way he was acting, Haley's next line of questioning came out slow and cynical. "Reddy, what did you do?"

He lowered his head out of guilt and then gradually looked up at her face. "I altered my molecular structure an' penetrated d'security system."

Haley stared toward the camera in the entranceway, whining in a distressed tone, "Oh no, please tell me you didn't tamper with their surveillance equipment, Reddy."

Reddy blinked his eyes innocently at her troubled face. "I had t'stop d'cameras from videotaping us, Haley."

He held up his magnifying glass in front of his right eye and said in a playful tone, "We're working undercover, right?"

She glanced at the picture on the security monitor and asked, "So what video is that?"

Reddy squirmed uneasily in her hand. "Footage from yesterday."

She moved her palm closer to her chin, whispering at the bot in a taxing voice, "An' just where did you get the idea to loop the film?"

Seeing the displeasure written all over her face, Reddy started whining like that would make everything all right. "I saw 'em do it in one o'yer detective shows, Haley."

"You were watching *Gumshoe* on the telly?"

He nodded. "Please don't be mad at me."

Haley gave the bot a couple of pats on his head to quiet his fretfulness and heaved a tiresome sigh. "Well, I suppose there's no harm done, unless of course Carol looks over at the monitor."

"Why would that be a problem, Haley?"

Haley pointed in the general direction of the clerk, giggling, "Carol is typing on the keyboard, Reddy, but the monitor shows her talking on the phone."

Realizing he had made a huge mistake, Reddy shoved his palms underneath his bum and said coyly, "No spank."

Haley kept on sniggering at the bot's ridiculous antics. "Reddy, I don't know why you keep playing that little charade. No one has ever spanked you."

She stifled her giggling and deposited the bot into her pocket. While looking down at his childlike face, she gave him another gentle rebuke for misbehaving. "From now on, you make sure you stay in there an' keep out of sight."

Happy to be forgiven, he brightened his countenance with a big grin. "Okey-dokey, I be so quiet ye won't even know I'm here."

Haley waited until the bot ducked down in her pocket and then hurried back to the front desk.

By the time Haley got back to the ticket counter, she discovered the hologram was no longer playing. Dying to know more about it, she interrupted the conversation between Rane and the clerk by asking, "Excuse me, Miss ..."

Carol heaved a niggling sigh at her. "Yes?"

"The hologram quit playing. How often does it run?"

Carol took a haphazard glance at the mirror on the wall and then replied in a cultured articulation, "Twice every hour. If you want to see more, you'll have to take the tour."

Haley gazed at the mirror as if the hologram was going to miraculously come back on at any moment. She then looked back at the desk clerk and asked, "Could you tell me why all the card soldiers were carrying an axe instead of a sword?"

Carol shook her head and pressed on with her typing.

Upon seeing the disappointed expression on his wife's face, Rane said, "Carol, how much are d'tickets?"

Retracting her hands from the keypad, the clerk replied, "Thirty pounds, sir."

Shocked after hearing the price, Rane whistled and said, "Thirty pounds? Why so much?"

Hoping to persuade Rane into taking the tour, Carol wasted no time in giving him a sales pitch. "I know it sounds a bit pricey, but trust me it is well worth it. The artwork is absolutely stunning, an' the virtual reality programs are unlike anything you've ever seen."

He motioned his head toward the mirror behind the desk. "Are all d'holograms as good as that one?"

"Uh-huh."

Rane reached into his back pocket and pulled out his wallet. "Ye're not just saying that t'get me t'buy a ticket are ye, Carol?"

With a deceitful grin on her face, the clerk fluffed the back of her short, sandy blond hair. "No, sir."

Carol took a quick glance at the clock on the wall, noting the time was after five thirty. "If you're going to take the tour, you better hurry. The last one starts in about twenty minutes."

Anxious to snoop around inside the gallery, Rane opened his billfold and fished out a hundred-pound note. After sighing sadly at the last bit of money he had in the whole world, he looked up at the clerk and said, "All right, Carol, I'll take a couple o'tickets."

After she gave him his tickets, Rane put the change of forty pounds into his wallet and stuffed it into his rear pocket. While spying on what the clerk was typing on her screen, he saw a man's portfolio and assumed she was searching the Web for romance. Snickering at the thought, he said, "Lassie, take me advice, computer dating is a waste o'time."

"Why? Have you ever been out on a computer date before?"

He shrugged his shoulders as if his life was common knowledge. "Aye, a hoppin' pot o'times."

Haley was shocked that her husband had dated other girls before and raised a jealous voice. "You have?"

Caught off guard by her unexpected change in character, Rane wrinkled his brow and replied, "Aye, what's wrong with that?"

Haley crossed her arms and pouted her lips. "You never tol' me about them. When was this?"

"When I lived in Ireland with Caleb."

Upon hearing his answer, Haley stared down at the countertop, thinking out loud, "Oh, before you met me."

Rane called to mind the bad dating experiences and said, "'Twas a waste o'time though."

"Why?"

"'Cause all d'lassies that lousy, computer-dating service matched me up with were fakes."

She put on a self-righteous air by saying, "You could have saved yourself a lot of heartache if you would have just asked God to pick your dream girl."

Acting dense, Rane cracked his knuckles and queried, "If she's of d'same faith, why would he care?"

Haley rolled her eyes at his warped way of thinking. "He picked Adam's bride, didn't he?"

Carol cut in on their little argument. "Sir, why did you think the girls you went out with were fakes?"

Rane speculated in the back of his mind why the clerk had a sudden interest in his computer dating but decided not to question her about it. "'Cause they dumped me after they found out what was in me wallet."

Carol leaned toward Rane's charming face and said flirtatiously, "Maybe it is time you went out on a real computer date."

Haley was secretly hoping her husband would honor her by telling the woman he was married. When he failed to meet her expectations, she lost her temper and stomped the heel of her boot on his foot.

Feeling excruciating pain, Rane simultaneously dropped his ticket on the floor and bellowed to the top of his lungs, "Ow!"

Haley responded to his misery in an uncaring, lofty voice. "Oh I'm sorry. Did I step on your toes?"

Hobbling around on one foot, he answered maddeningly, "Ye know that ye did."

Haley suddenly felt remorseful for her rancorous actions. "Oh dear, I seem to have let jealousy get the better of me."

While trying to put his weight back on his sore foot, Rane said short-temperedly, "No kidding."

She extended a caring hand toward him. "I'm sorry, Rane. I shouldn't have done that."

Rane refused to accept her humble apology. "Ye're sorry? Ye're not d'one with a broken foot."

Carol, who had been standing there, watching them, queried curiously, "Are you two married?"

Rane replied in a put upon tone, "Ye'd think so, wouldn't ye?"

"Of course we're married," Haley replied with assurance.

He got up in her face and said in his defense, "We are not."

"We are too. I became Mrs. Rane Rivers on December twenty-fourth, twenty sixteen. We were married at the Liberty Church in London. You can call my dad down at the police station where I work an' have him verify it if you would like."

She took her credentials out of her inside pocket and showed it to Carol.

After seeing her shiny, silver badge, Carol was sure Rane was lying and slapped him hard on the right cheek. "Why, you pig!"

"Ouch!" Rane bellowed, caressing his hurting cheek. "What did ye do that for?"

Carol replied in a high-strung voice, "You let me flirt with you while your wife is standing right next to you? Have you no shame?"

She looked him over with a face of vengeance and said further, "Why they ought to castrate men like you."

Rubbing the sting out of his throbbing cheek, Rane pouted his lips at Haley like a spoiled child and declared, "She's not my wife."

Carol regained her composure and respectfully made her apologies to Haley for her unbecoming behavior. "Sorry about that, ma'am. I didn't know he was your husband. He's not wearing a wedding band."

Bending down to pick up his ticket off the floor, Rane grumbled under his breath, "I dunno what she's apologizing t'her for. I'm d'one with d'bruised cheek."

"Where do we go for the tour?" Haley asked Carol.

Carol pointed eastward toward the long hallway and replied, "Go all the way down to the end of the corridor until you get to the double doors ..."

The clerk lowered her hand to the countertop and said further, "Then wait for the escort to come out ... Merry Christmas, Detective."

Haley smiled and replied cordially, "Merry Christmas."

Without further ado, she headed in the route the clerk indicated.

Rane shook his head at the clerk and then hurried down the corridor to catch up with Haley. When his wife kept on walking as if he wasn't even there, he blocked her path by stepping in front of her and asked meekly, "Aren't ye going t'talk t'me?"

Haley stared at him with a hurt look in her eyes. "Sure, what do you want to talk about?"

"Come on, Haley. I was just flattered that Carol thought I was attractive that's all. Is there a crime in that?"

Although Haley was wondering how he could be so insensitive knowing how she felt about him, she managed to choke out a tearful reply. "Is there?"

When she took off down the hall again, Rane ran after her and asked, "Ye weren't really jealous, were ye?"

Haley stopped walking, crossed her arms, and turned away without answering.

Rane inconspicuously peeked around the side of her head. Seeing tears dripping down her cheeks and her countenance tensing up with sorrow, he whispered under his breath, "Ye were jealous."

Not knowing what to do, he pulled a blue bandanna out of his back pocket and handed it to her.

Haley used the large handkerchief he gave her to wipe the dampness off her face. "I don't know why you're acting so surprised. My heart is not made of stone, you know. It can break."

"Ye mean ye really like me?" he asked in a voice of alarm.

Haley sniffled, nodding her head. "I think you're wonderful."

He brushed off her compliment by making a sarcastic remark about her stomping on his foot. "Oh sure, I could just feel d'love back there."

Haley's teary, green eyes locked on his as she voiced her true feelings for her husband. "I love you, Chappy, an' that's the truth."

Unable to trust the sincerity in her words from being hoodwinked by other women, including his own mother, a sea of negative emotions began to stir in his heart. "Ye love me?"

Haley spread a warm smile across her face and intensified the passion in the tone of her voice. "With all my heart."

He reflected back on the heart-shaped sandwich she gave him and raised a cynical voice. "Hah! Ye don't even know me."

She gazed with adoration at the features on his handsome visage. "I'd know you anywhere, Chappy. I memorized every part of you. From the ten, tiny freckles on your face to the green, four-leaf clover tattooed on your left buttocks."

Highly embarrassed that she knew the naked truth, Rane widened his eyes and then made a quick turn of his head in the general direction of his derriere. "Ye know about that?"

Haley giggled softly at his modest reaction. "Yes."

He lowered his eyebrows in a bamboozled state and asked, "But I've never tol' anyone. How could ye possibly know that?"

She took a fleeting look at the crowd of tourists gathered by the double doors and then answered, "I know a lot about you."

Rane peered into her admiring eyes and queried guardedly, "Like what?"

"Like your favorite sandwich is peanut butter an' jelly."

He cracked an arrogant smirk out of the corner of his mouth. "That didn't take a lot o'detective work t'figure out. I tol' ye that earlier."

Haley quickly thought up another clever answer. "Okay, how about, um, you love to watch scary pictures."

Rane gave her a perturbed look and started cracking his knuckles. "Ye heard me say that too."

She pushed up her jacket sleeves like she meant business and sped up her answers. "Your favorite color is red; you read a fantasy book called *Bugby* four times; when you were a little boy you had a pitbull named Pumpkin, an'—"

Squeamish that she knew so many intimate details of his private life, he sharply interrupted her exposé. "Hey, how are ye doing this trick?"

To silence his anxieties, Haley pressed her three middle fingers against his lips and said dotingly, "It is not a trick, your highness. I'm your queen, the one God picked to love you."

Out of spite, he squeezed her fingers and pulled them down from his mouth. "Go on, lassie. Yer talk of love don't mean anything t'me. I'm on t'yer little scam. Ye can have me last forty pounds. I'll gladly give it t'ye."

While trying to wriggle her fingers out of his tight grip, she whimpered, "Let go. You're hurting me."

He pursed his angry lips and pushed her hand away.

Choked up with tears from his harsh actions, Haley cuddled her sore fingers. "I'm sorry that some woman broke your heart, Rane."

Rane immediately became defensive. "An' just what makes ye think that?"

Haley stuffed his bandanna back into his hand and replied, "Hurting people hurt people."

Rane was speechless as he watched his wife stroll over to join the other tourists waiting outside the double doors. Not wanting to see her sad face, he turned his back on her and leaned his head against the wall. While wondering how she could possibly know so much about him, he suddenly had a flashback of them quarrelling at their flat in London. It was on Christmas Eve, a year after they were first married.

"Rane, please don't go," Haley pleaded as her husband removed his blue undershirts from his top, dresser drawer. "God can help us work out our problems if we just let him."

Pretending not to see the sorrow in her eyes, Rane turned a cold shoulder on her advice by carrying his shirts over to the black luggage lying open on their king-size bed.

Feeling shut out of his heart, Haley started crying. "Please, you're my Chappy. I love you. I can't think of my life without you."

Reddy added his own sentiments while taking his inventor's shirts out of the suitcase as fast as he was putting them in. "Aye, Whiz Kid, we can't think of our life without ye."

Rane walked back over to his dresser, grabbed all his balled, black socks out of the second drawer and then peered emptily out the window at the falling snow. Insensitive to the emotional abuse it would cause his wife, he said, "Forget us, Haley. Yer dad was right. We were too young t'get married."

Feeling unsettled at the thought of going through life forgotten by her husband, she rebuked him sharply. "That isn't the problem with our marriage, an' you know it. You won't let me get close to you."

Rane tossed the armful of socks he was carrying into the luggage on the bed and said in his defense, "That's not true."

Haley sniffed her nose and used the back of her hand to wipe away a teardrop trickling down the beauty mark on her left cheekbone. "Then why do you keep secrets from me?"

Unsure of himself, he stared in the direction of Reddy, who was busy pitching the socks back into the dresser drawer, and replied, "I... I don't keep secrets from ye."

She gripped her husband's chin and steered it back in her direction. "You wouldn't let me see your birth certificate or our marriage application before you turned it in? I don't even know who your real parents are."

Rane pushed her hand off his jaw and replied uncaringly, "Is that important?"

Highly upset by his cavalier attitude, Haley raised her voice at him and said, "Is that important? What's the matter with you?"

He grabbed his glass jar of jellybeans off the nightstand beside the bed and snapped at her. "Nothing is d'matter with me!"

"Then why do you get angry at me every time I ask you a question about your mum?"

Rane gnashed his teeth at the mention of his mother and angrily threw the candy jar into his suitcase. He then pushed Reddy off the edge of the bag, causing the bot to do a belly flop on the bed, and slammed the lid closed. Without saying another word, he grabbed the handle on the suitcase and stormed out of the room.

Hoping to soften his heart by telling him she was pregnant, Haley chased after him into the living room. "Rane, please don't do this. It is our anniversary, an' God gave us a special gift this year."

He stared at the beautifully wrapped packages under their lighted Christmas tree and then said to be cruel, "I don't want it."

Grief-stricken by his rejection, Haley picked up her Bible off the lamp table beside her and removed the Queen of Hearts playing card she was using as a book marker. Holding the card toward him, she recalled the endearment that meant so much to her. "But you said, you loved me, an' that I'd always be your queen. Remember what you said the day we got married."

Giving his wife a cold stare, Rane removed his silver wedding band from his ring finger and slammed it down on the table. He then snatched the queen of hearts card out of her hand, tore it up into tiny pieces, and tossed them on the hardwood floor like the romantic sentiment meant nothing to him. "I don't want t'remember anymore."

Haley felt as if it was her own heart he had tossed away. With quivering lips, she stared painfully at the remnants on the floor. She was so upset she found it difficult to speak for several moments. Her grief seemed to be more than she could bear as she broke down in a heart wrenching sob. "How could you do that? We vowed before God that we would love each other always."

Rane unfeelingly watched the tears stream down her face and then opened the front door.

Haley held the Bible toward him and sobbed, "God told us to love one another. How can you just walk away from your first love?"

He swallowed uncomfortably at the thought of turning his back on God and then stormed out the door into the fall of snow.

All at once the double doors opened, and a British tour guide stepped out into the hallway to greet the ticket holders. After closing the doors behind her, the woman said in a loud, nimble voice, "Good afternoon, ladies an' gentlemen. Welcome to Jack's Masterpieces, the only virtual reality gallery in the world. My name is Prosperity, an' I will be your escort for the next hour. Once you're allowed inside the viewing room, please refrain from any roughhousing, eating or smoking, or taking any photographs."

Just as Rane walked up to join Haley and the other tourists, he was rudely bumped into by Richard, Walter, and Carter, three American preppies running up to take the tour at the last minute.

Perceiving they were troublemakers, Prosperity gave the vacationing students a perturbed glance and then continued talking informatively to the group. "All the artwork in the gallery was masterfully engineered by a brilliant artist named Artur Jack Finney."

After hearing the artist's name, Rane was sparked with a hint of recognition and whispered under his breath, "Artur Jack Finney?"

Prosperity went on to say, "He was known to hide secret things about himself in his artwork, but I don't think anyone was ever able to figure out exactly what the symbolism meant."

To make sure he had heard the man's name correctly, Rane raised his hand to get verification.

Prosperity acknowledged him by saying, "Yes. You have a question?"

Rane put his hand down before replying. "Aye, did ye say his name was Artur Jack Finney?"

Richard, one of the three preppies, was envious of Rane's good looks and spoke insultingly about him behind his back. "Duh!"

In answer of Rane's question, Prosperity replied, "That's correct, sir. Lucky Jack's real name was Artur Jack Finney."

Upon hearing what he believed to be bad news, Rane looked like his heart had just sunk into his stomach. Not wanting Haley to know what he was doing, he ducked behind another tourist before secretly removing a faded snapshot from his billfold. It was a picture of his real dad that his mother had given him when he was very young. His father was only eighteen at the time and still living in Ireland. He was dressed up in a brown tweed suit. He bore a remarkable resemblance to Lucky Jack, except he had short blond hair and no mustache.

After Rane had finished staring at the photo, he flipped it over and silently read the inscription on the back, "To my beloved Kathryn, forever yours, Artur Jack Finney."

He queezed his eyes shut and thought painfully, *No, it can't be true.*

Haley snuck up behind her husband to see what he was hiding and saw him staring unhappily at the photo in his hand. "Rane, is something wrong?"

Startled by her voice, he stashed the photo and his wallet inside his coat pocket and answered shakily, "Uh… wrong? No, there-there's nothing wrong."

Although Rane was emotionally distracted by a dark secret haunting him from the past, he didn't let it stop him from hearing what the tour guide was presently saying.

"Artur was born in nineteen seventy-six an' tragically died in two thousand three when he committed suicide."

Rane's mouth gaped open in shock after hearing the tour guide's disclosure. He knew about the infamous Lucky Jack from his pictures in the casinos, but he had never heard how he died. Anxious to know what drove him over the edge, he spoke up. "Prosperity, he was so young. Why did he kill himself?"

Prosperity stared off into space as she replied, "No one knows for sure. Artur just walked into the gallery at midnight on Christmas Eve, set a picture of his ex-fiancée on fire, an' then shot himself in the temple."

Richard eyed the *Fortune* magazine he had rolled up in his hands and exposed some things he had read about Artur to the group. "Yeah, the dude must have been out of his mind. He had everything to live for and kills himself over some lousy showgirl."

Prosperity recognized the laminated periodical Richard was holding in his hands and raised her voice upsettingly. "Did you take that magazine off the coffee table in the lobby?"

Richard tossed the publication across the floor. "What magazine?"

Carter and Walter chuckled under their breath at their friend's quick thinking.

Prosperity pursed her lips to indicate she was displeased with them and then saw Carol running up to get the periodical. Rane and Haley took advantage of the short disruption and walked among the tourists discreetly eyeing their earlobes.

Carol picked up the magazine off the floor and said, "I'm sorry, Prosperity. I didn't see him take it."

"That's all right. He should have known better."

Carol hit Richard over the head with the periodical and walked away.

Although the white diamond post in Richard's left earlobe wasn't red or diamond-shaped, Haley felt they should check him out anyway. Drawing her husband's attention to it, she clandestinely darted her green eyes in the preppy's direction and pinched her left lobe.

Rane got her undercover message and followed her over to Richard. Being careful not to be seen or heard, he silently sniffed the back of the preppy's head for any cigarette smoke. Not smelling anything but cheap cologne, he looked over at his wife and shook his head.

Haley didn't see anyone else in the group wearing an earring or a Band-aid, so she raised her hand into the air to ask the tour guide another question.

Prosperity motioned her hand in her general direction and said, "Yes?"

Haley lowered her hand. "What was the name of Artur's fiancée?"

Prosperity eyed Rane biting on the skin around his thumbnail before replying, "I think it was Katie or Kathryn, something like that."

Haley accidentally startled her husband into yanking his thumb out of his mouth when she nudged her elbow against his side. "Rane ..."

Afraid she might have figured something out about his past, Rane blinked his eyes worriedly at his wife and whispered, "What?"

Endeavoring to keep her conversation with her husband private, Haley cupped her hand to the side of her mouth, whispering, "This might be a clue, write down the woman's name, okay?"

Rane nodded his head while secretly sighing in relief that he wasn't found out.

Haley waited for her husband to fish his pen and small notepad out of his coat pocket and then continued her line of questioning at the tour guide. "Prosperity, who discovered the body?"

"Jillian, Artur's younger sister."

"What was she doing here?"

Wondering why she was asking so many questions, Prosperity suspiciously eyeballed the sleuth before answering, "She merely stopped by the gallery looking for her brother an' smelt the smoke. Luckily she was able to save the Locust 52257 from being destroyed."

Recalling the Chandler's testimony regarding the mysterious insects, Haley lowered her eyebrows into a befuddled expression. "The Locust 52257?"

Prosperity nodded her head a touch. "The mainframe that runs all the programs in the gallery."

Needing more information to help them find their suspect, Haley pressed on with her interrogation by asking, "Prosperity, did Artur create the hologram behind the ticket counter?"

Prosperity peered unemotionally into the detective's meddling eyes. "Yes. He masterfully engineered 'The Battle of Armaggedon' right before he died."

"Why did he name the piece that?"

Anxious to hear her reply, Rane stopped jotting down the clues and looked up at the escort to hear what her answer was going to be.

"Lucky Jack's biggest dream was to be the king of diamonds."

Enlightened by the information she provided, Haley thought, *Ooh, so that's why the Jacks were carrying an axe instead of a sword.*

Richard pushed his way to the front of the group, knocking several people out of the way. "Did his dream come true?"

She raised her brow at him for being rude to the other tourists and then responded in a superior tone. "No. He had his heart set on the Hope Diamond, the largest gem in the world, but the British owner wouldn't sell it to him, not for any amount of money."

"Why not?" Richard asked.

Prosperity's presumptuous attitude remained constant as she checked the bob of hair on top of her head. "To quote the proprietor's words to the late Mister Finney, 'It is a gem fit for a king, an' you don't have royal blood.'"

"So what did Artur do?" Haley asked nosily.

The tour guide raised her chin into the air, sniggering a little. "He told him to keep his lousy diamond an' boasted that Jacks are better."

Quickly turning serious, the tour guide said, "Now if you'll hand me your tickets, we'll begin our tour... unless of course you would like to spend all your tour time on questions."

A hefty American glowered at Richard and Haley and said, "No, we wouldn't."

Once Prosperity had collected all the stubs off the tickets, she opened the double doors and led the group inside a huge ballroom.

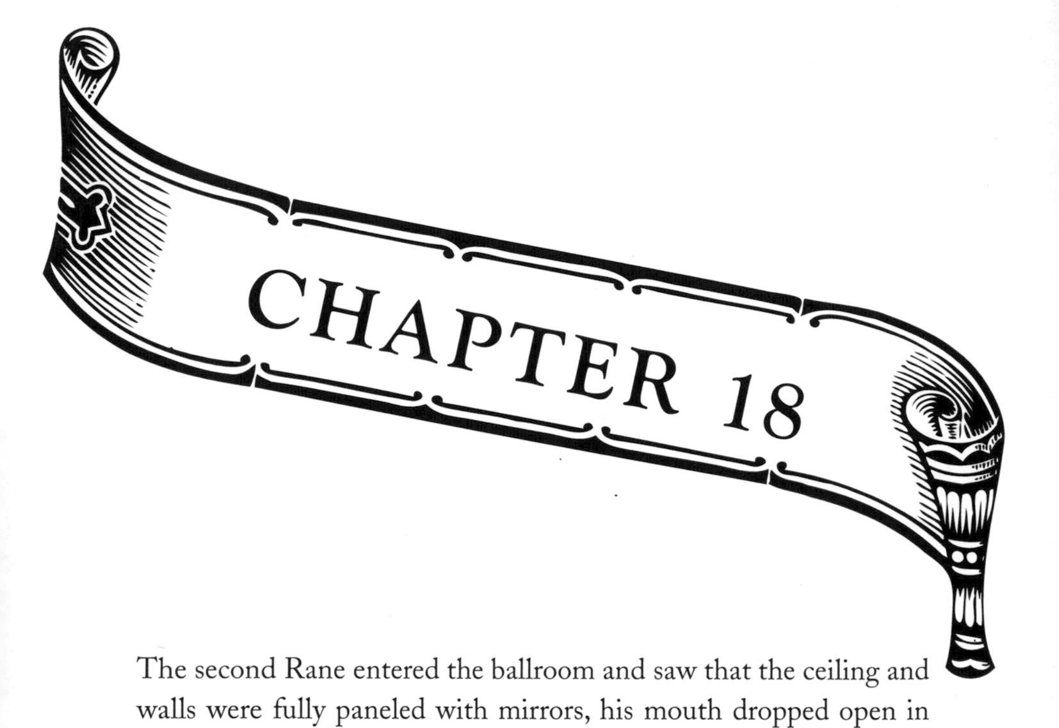

The second Rane entered the ballroom and saw that the ceiling and walls were fully paneled with mirrors, his mouth dropped open in astonishment. "Whoa!"

Haley whirled her head about the room and said in a voice of wonder, "It is like we just stepped inside a sphere of glass, huh, Chappy?"

Prosperity spoke up and said, "The simulated mirrors are actually a protective energy shield to keep tourists out of the holograms. The one you're about to see should be coming on at any moment."

She had no sooner finished talking when the hologram began to play.

Rane gaped in awe at the different reflections now appearing inside the fake mirrors. He was blown away by the advanced technology that went into constructing all the holographic pictures. "Absolutely remarkable. Gamblers, cocktail waitresses, roulette wheels, slot machines, blackjack tables. There's even a huge, decorated Christmas tree over by d'bar. If I didn't know better I'd swear I was peering into a real casino in Vegas."

Haley, too, was enthralled by how authentic the virtual images looked. Piveting her head in all directions, she readily agreed. "The artwork is magnificent."

Rane stuffed his notepad and pen into his coat pocket. "Aye, I can actually hear d'gamblers talking at d'poker tables."

Haley tapped her husband on the shoulder and pointed up at the reflection inside the sheet of glass on the ceiling. "Rane, look at that chandelier. It looks so real."

Rane shifted his gaze upward. "It sure does."

Prosperity drew the attention of the tourists by announcing, "This particular hologram is Artur's most famous achievement in virtual reality. He called it *Wrapped up in Luck*. Incidentally, this is a replica of the casino in Vegas where he first appeared as the legendary Lucky Jack."

Fascinated by the commentary, Rane unconsciously cracked the knuckles on both hands, muttering to himself, "Ye don't say."

The tour guide pointed at the virtual images inside the replicated mirror while continuing to enlighten the tourists. "As you can clearly see, all the gamblers in the simulation are dressed up like Lucky Jack. It was Artur's way of keeping his memory alive."

Richard eyed one of the gamblers anteing several white diamonds into the gem pot on the poker table. The sight of the precious stones jarred his memory into recalling something he had read about in *Fortune Magazine*. "Prosperity…"

She looked over at him. "Yes?"

"I read that Lucky Jack hid his good luck charm and all his diamonds in the gallery the night of his death. Is that true?"

Prosperity shook her head. "No. Jillian an' the police combed every inch of this establishment an' never found a trace of his talisman or the diamonds."

Haley eyed the class ring Richard was wearing on his hand and said to the tour guide, "What about the diamond rings he wore on his fingers?"

"They couldn't find them either. Whatever Lucky Jack did with all his diamonds, one will never know. He took that secret to his grave."

Rane pointed at the lifelike casino inside the mirror in front of him and queried, "Prosperity, why do these holograms look so real?"

The tour guide folded her arms, answering his question intelligently. "'Cause the Locust 52257's mainframe is controlling the environment—its microprocessor is a highly sophisticated, independent, neural stimulator system. There is not another protype like it anywhere in the world."

Rane looked at her stupidly, for her explanation went right over his head. "How believable are these holograms?"

Prosperity peered into his concerned eyes and said strangely, "They're as real as you believe them to be, Rane. In fact, Aileen, Artur's older sister, actually thought the Locust 52257 was secretly producing images to manipulate her with fear. She even closed down the gallery, thinking she was having a nervous breakdown."

Slightly shaken over what she said, Rane asked, "But how could a machine know how t'do that?"

"Artur programmed the computer to analyze an' respond to human behavior systematically."

The tour guide's answer made Haley think about the bot inside her coat pocket. *That's strange. It sounds like the same technology used on Reddy.*

Showing off his intellect, Carter downplayed Prosperity's tutelage by stating, "That's not surprising. The computer's neural net was programmed by human intellect. Of course the genetic communication would be faulty."

Prosperity frowned at his response and then continued to enlighten the group. "Aileen tried fixing the Locust 52257's neural net, but unfortunately she died in a car accident before finishing the project."

Horrified by the news, Rane widened his teal blue eyes and gasped. "What happened?"

"According to the police report, she lost control of her vehicle an' hit head-on with another car."

Rane wrinkled his brow, making a bewildered face. "I don't remember reading about that in d'paper. When was this?"

"About a couple of weeks ago. She called the police department shortly before the accident, screaming about some swarm of locusts covering her windshield."

Reddy whispered fretfully from inside Haley's pocket, "She had bugs, too, an' they killed her?"

Haley lowered her head, whispering at her pocket, "Reddy, be quiet. I want to hear this."

Prosperity lifted some fallen strands of her light brown hair and stuffed them back inside the bob on her head. "The police followed up on her call but found no sign of an insect anywhere in the wreckage."

Like a sponge, Rane soaked up everything she said. "What do ye think really happened t'her?"

Prosperity's perceptive eyes roamed over to Haley's face. "I'm no detective ..."

She shifted her focus right back on Rane as she finished answering his question. "But I think Aileen actually believed a holographic image could kill her."

Slightly on edge, Richard whispered to Carter, "She's lying. An imaginary picture can't kill you. She's just trying to scare us."

Prosperity looked about the room and noticed the fretful stare in some of the tourists' eyes. Trying to ease their minds, she giggled. "No. I was only joking. It was just a hoax. Aileen's death was merely an accident."

Not seeing a change in the tourists' expression, Prosperity quickly turned serious. "No, really, Jillian ran a diagnostic check on the computer's neural net, an' it was functioning perfectly."

"Then why did Aileen see all those insects?" Carter queried suspiciously.

"Aileen suffered from narcolepsy and had taken several amphetamines the day of the accident. The drug must have caused her eyes to play tricks on her, that's all."

Appeased by her answer, Carter replied in a tone of concession, "Oh."

After Prosperity had finshed easing everyone's mind about Aileen's unbelievable demise, she continued on with her oration. "Artur was hailed by the public as the luckiest man in the world. Rightly so, for he was the richest one too."

The stocky American, who was standing on the other side of Prosperity, rested his forearms on his protruding belly that was roughly the size of a basketball. "I heard virtual reality videos (VRVs) are being released for sale to the public. Is that true?"

"Yes. As more people get the microchips implanted underneath their skin, the holographic videos will be commonplace."

"The VRVs are designed to work with a microchip?"

"Yes, but in order to operate the programs, you'll have to purchase one of the newer cell phones that are compatible with the chip. The entire cost, including the microchip, will run you about a thousand pounds."

"How does it work? Richard asked curiously.

"According to Jillian, you just insert one of the miniature virtual reality disks into the compartment on the back of the phone an' then dial the serial number on your microchip. The satellite overhead will connect your chip to the virtual reality network an' the system will take over after that."

Haley acted like she was deep in thought about something else as she commented quietly, "Let a system control your mind? That sounds scary."

Prosperity looked around the room and asked, "Would anyone like to experience this hologram firsthand?"

She saw several hands go up, including Rane's.

Haley was grieved that her husband would actually volunteer and whispered in his ear, "Put your hand down."

Rane deliberately tuned out his wife's request when he saw the tour guide pointing at him.

"You, the gentlemen in the black turtleneck sweater," said Prosperity. "Do you believe in luck?"

He lowered his hand and queried, "Why?"

She took her eyes off Rane for a brief moment to grin at the greedy gamblers inside the hologram. "You can't reflect something you don't believe in, now can you?"

Still allowing his mind to be ruled by superstitious beliefs, which he had learned from his mother and former friends in Ireland, Rane shrugged and answered coolly, "Sure, I believe a guy can get lucky."

Prosperity smiled at his answer. "Then we'll let you go."

Filled with excitement, he pointed his thumb at his chest and said to the crowd, "Hey, she picked me. No one has ever picked me before. I think my luck is changing."

Jealous that he didn't get chosen, Richard sneered at Rane.

Prosperity spoke to the computer as if it were in the room. "Locust 52257, need access entry into hologram 30914, deactivate energy shield."

After hearing the humming noise of electricity power down, she said to Rane, "All right. You can safely enter the hologram now."

Rane was a little nervous about entering a computer-generated environment. He had never done anything like this before. Looking over at his wife, he swallowed hard and queried, "Aren't ye going t'wish me luck?"

Hoping to change his mind, Haley grabbed her husband by the hand and whispered fervently, "Chappy, Jesus don't want you wrapped up in the superstious belief in magic or chance."

He made a dense face at his wife and whispered back, "What's wrong with a bit o'luck? It can't hurt anything."

Haley couldn't believe how fast he had reverted back to his old, gullible way of thinking. She was so upset about it that she started speaking in a rushed tongue. "Wake up, Rane. Your life is not founded upon a fluke or a wheel of fortune. You're not lucky one moment an' unlucky the next. You're already blessed with every spiritual blessing in heaven. God has your whole life already written out for you. Just ask him to read you the pages."

The tour guide raised her voice to break up their little huddle. "Go on, Rane."

Just as he reached out his hands toward the mirror, Haley whispered her final words of warning from the wisdom in Proverbs 23:5. "Chappy, don't put your trust in money, for it can make itself wings an' fly away."

He lowered his hands to his sides and asked, "Fly away? How?"

Haley considered her husband's research as she replied, "New technology comes out every day. It doesn't matter if you're a big tycoon in oil. If someone figures out a better way for us to travel, then that oil won't be worth a dime."

Although Prosperity was losing patience with him, she didn't let it show in the tone of her voice. "Rane, are you ready?"

Rane glanced over at the tour guide and then looked back at his wife. Seeing she was still upset, he tried to reassure her by responding in a lackadaisical attitude. "Nothing bad is going t'happen, Haley, ye'll see."

"Please don't do it, Rane. If you turn your back on the King's advice, the devil will come at you like a devouring locust."

Longing for the seductive glamour of the casino, Rane thumbed his nose at her counsel and deprived his heart of the truth. "I just want t'have a bit o'fun, that's all."

When she turned away from him without saying anything more, Rane shook his head at her and then stepped toward the artificial mirror with his hands held out in front of him. Believing he was going to hit head-on into the glass, he flinched frightfully. The second he touched the hologram field, he felt a negative energy wave enter his body, causing it to resonate for about five seconds. Feeling woozy from its effect, he clasped his hands to the sides of his head and groaned, "Whoa!"

After the sapped, disoriented sensation lifted from Rane's head, he realized he was now standing inside the virtual casino. Peering around the room at all the risktakers gambling away their money, he chuckled happily, "I don't believe it. I actually made it."

Desiring to share the paranormal experience with Haley, he turned around. After discovering the mirror he went through had been replaced by a backward-revolving door, he gnawed fretfully on the skin around his thumbnail, thinking, *What's this doing here? Where is everybody?*

Hoping to find the tour group on the other side of the revolving door, Rane dashed outside and found himself in the middle of the street at night on the main strip in Las Vegas. Totally confused about what was happening to him, he looked around at all the neon lights and then down at the road, noticing it was paved entirely with jumbo-sized face cards of the Jack of Diamonds. "What's going on here?"

He peered upward at the twilight sky and heard a horn honk behind him and an Irishman's voice shouting, "Get out o'me way, Jack!"

Rane spun around to see who honked the horn and was surprised to see Lucky Jack sitting behind the wheel of a cherry-red Panthera sports coupe. Mesmerized by the fantasy, he patted the hood on the car and said, "I don't believe it. D'virtual images are so real I actually believe I can feel 'em."

The notorious gambler, who was in his prime of twenty-one, had a lit cigarette in one hand and a bottle of applejack in the other. "Get yer dirty hands off me sportie, laddie!"

Rane withdrew his hands from the vehicle and humbly apologized. "Oh, sorry."

Lucky Jack made a sweeping motion with his cigarette hand and said, "Now get out o'me way. I'm in a hurry."

Rane was curious how a picture could be talking to him and went around to the driver's side of the car. While gaping at Lucky Jack's annoyed face, he thought about the conversation he had earlier with Prosperity.

"How believable are these holograms?"

"They're as real as you believe them to be, Rane."

Seeing the befuddled expression in Rane's eyes, Lucky Jack took a quick swig from his bottle of brandy before asking, "Are ye lost or something?"

Rane answered as if his mind was in a fog. "Lost?"

Lucky Jack angrily tossed his smoldering cigarette out the car window. "I said, 'Get out o'me way!'"

Tired of being mistreated, Rane shook his fist at the young driver and snarled, "I'm going to, gumby."

Quick to offend, Lucky Jack's eyes filled with vengeance. "Gumby? I'll show ye who's a gumby."

Without hesitation, he picked up his semi-automatic weapon off the seat next to him and opened fire at Rane's feet.

Frightened by all the sparks flying off the pavement in front of him, Rane squealed hysterically while jumping around as if his boots were on fire. "Yeeeiiigh!"

Lucky Jack was actually enjoying his rival's misery. He took another swig from his bottle of brandy and chuckled tauntingly, "Hop, grasshopper, hop."

A virtual image of a young woman walked up and saw the snickering gunman shooting at Rane. Afraid of being hit by one of the bullets, she ducked behind a parked car, shouting frantically into the air, "Help! Somebody call the police!"

Exhausted from running around in circles, Rane tripped over his own feet and fell onto the pavement, badly scraping the top of his left hand. Seeing the blood dripping from the fresh wound, he yanked his blue bandanna out of his back pocket and heard the driver yelling at him.

"Do you feel lucky, Jack?"

Rane looked over to see what he meant and was horrified to see Jack's gun aimed at his head. Although the picture wasn't real, he believed the weapon could harm him. Shutting his eyes tightly to avoid seeing the end, he started whimpering to God. "Oh, Lord, please don't let him kill me. If ye let me live, I promise I'll try t'quit calling people gumbies."

Just as Jack pulled back the trigger, he heard a police siren coming up from the far end of the street. Hoping to avoid a jail sentence, the gunman stashed the weapon under his seat and sped off down the boulevard.

Hearing the driver squeal his tires around the corner, Rane slowly opened his eyes and heaved a sigh of relief. "Oh good, he's gone."

Just then, a middle-aged, American couple ran out into the street and helped Rane to his feet.

The man eyed the drops of blood on the street and said, "We called the police when we saw that you were in trouble. Are you all right, son?"

Rane cringed while using his handkerchief to dab the blood off the top of his hand. "Aye, I'm okay."

"That's a nasty cut, boy," said the gentleman's wife. "You want us to take you to a doctor?"

Hoping to stop the laceration from bleeding any further, Rane answered her question while using his teeth to tie up the handkerchief around his hand. "No. I'm all right."

The woman gave Rane a sympathetic look and then thumbed her nose in the gunman's direction. "Don't worry, son, his day will come. I always say, 'You reap exactly what you sow.'"

Ruminating on how his offensive tongue almost got him killed, Rane spoke in a low-key voice. "That's for sure."

The man, along with his wife, accompanied Rane over to the sidewalk and asked, "Son, if you don't mind my asking, why are you dressed up like Lucky Jack?"

"Lucky Jack?" Rane queried in a voice of complete surprise and then quickly checked his clothing.

After realizing the man was telling him the truth, Rane looked up at the couple's interested faces and chuckled out of nervous tension, "I am dressed up like him, how about that."

While trying to conjure up an explanation for his unusual dress attire, Rane chewed on the skin around his thumbnail. "I'm wearing these clothes because … um … "

Finally coming up with an answer, he lowered his thumb from his mouth and said, "For a joke."

Certain he wasn't on the level the woman lifted her chin and replied, "Oh."

Eyeing the man's wristwatch on his arm, Rane queried out of curiosity, "Sir, what time is it?"

The gentleman checked the time and answered, "It's midnight."

Rane appeared to be lost in thought as he whispered to himself, "Midnight? It can't be."

He touched the bearded area on his face and discovered he had a twelve o'clock shadow. "How did these whiskers get here?"

Closely observing Rane's abnormal behavior, the man adjusted his black horn-rimmed glasses on his nose and queried, "Are you sure you're all right, young fella? You look lost."

Rane again repeated the word as if his mind was in a fog. "Lost?"

Hearing a police siren only a few feet away, Rane anxiously looked around for a way of escape and shook the couple's hand. "Thanks for all yer help. Cheerio!"

Without further ado, he disappeared into the throng of spectators who had gathered to see what the uproar was about.

Unsure where Rane went, the gentleman peered around the busy street and hollered into the crowd, "Son, come back! Don't you want to file a complaint?"

The man's words fell onto deaf ears for Rane had dashed back inside the simulated casino, hoping to find a familiar face from the tour group. While staring at the revolving door, he called out, "Haley? Prosperity? Carter? Walter? Anybody? I'll even settle for help from Richard."

After searching the entire casino, without any success of finding them, he lowered his head in hopelessness. Not knowing what else to do, he just roamed around the casino. As he passed by one of the gambling tables, he felt someone tap him on the right shoulder and turned around to see who it was.

"Would you like to try your luck at blackjack, sir?" asked Tom, a young American dealer, standing behind a blackjack table.

Rane eyed the other customed players sitting at the table and then sat down on the padded bar stool. "It seems I got time t'kill."

Tom signaled for the cocktail waitress to come over to the table and then noticed the bandanna tied around Rane's palm. "What happened to your hand?"

Rane eyed the blood seeping through the handkerchief and acted as if it was no big deal. "Oh, 'tis nothing but a wee scratch."

While the cocktrail waitress was taking Rane's order for a drink, one of the gamblers at the table put his arm around her waist. Hugely offended, she picked up the man's well drink and dumped it on top of his head. "Dirty Jack, you touch me again and it will be the last thing you ever do."

Dirty Jack used the inside of his cloak to wipe the booze off his face and then responded to the cocktail waitress's threat by speaking discourteously, "Men aren't blind, girlie. If ye want t'be treated like a lady, start dressing up like one."

Rane watched the waitress leave in a huff and suddenly heard a bell ringing, and the tinkling sound of silver dollars falling into the coin hopper. Wondering what all the excitement was about, he turned around and saw a flashing red light on top of one of the slot machines.

The Jack who had just won was hopping up and down, shouting into the air, "Yahoo! I won d'jackpot."

Jealous of his good fortune, Rane muttered under his breath, "Why that lucky devil."

Overhearing his comment, Dirty Jack showed him the virtual reality video in his hand. The cover on the plastic case had a graphic of three phantom locusts like the ones Bob had seen. "I'm lucky too. I won this at d'poker table today. 'Tis called Alien Space Invaders. I can't wait t'see d'special effects."

Rane turned up his lip at the picture on the case and then suddenly heard a noisy chirping sound. Looking up at Dirty Jack to see if he had heard it too, he saw a horde of green locusts leaping about on the man's head. Horrified by their hideous appearance, he said under his breath, "If I were ye, chum, I'd throw that video away. Ye got too many invaders already."

Tom was tired of waiting on Rane to ante and smacked the table to get his attention. "Hey, buddy, are you in or not?"

"Oh, uh, I'm in," he replied cloudily.

He took the last bit of money out of his wallet and laid it down on the blackjack table. The dealer promptly exchanged Rane's money for a stack of poker chips and set them down in front of him. "Good luck, sir."

“Thank ye,” Rane said with a polite nod of his head and then placed a minimum bet on the table.

After winning his sixth hand in a row, Rane greedily rubbed his hands together and raked in the pot. Now feeling like a king, he lifted his proud chin, boasting to the dealer, “Is this me lucky day or what?”

Although Rane had started out winning, the tables suddenly turned. Losing numerous hands in a row, he began to believe he was down on his luck. Frantic to get his money back, he decided to press his luck by doubling up his bets; but the second he placed the wager, he saw one of the ugly, green locusts appear on top of his anteed chips. When the insect flapped its wings and disappeared, the word of warning spoken to him by his wife echoed through his soul. *“Rane, don't put your trust in money, for it can make itself wings an' fly away . . . fly away . . . fly away.”*

Rane’s meditation was cut short when the dealer said to him, “Sir, do you want another card?”

“Oh . . . um . . . ”

While Rane was thinking it over, the waitress walked up, set his glass of applejack down on the table, and then headed back to the bar.

Rane peeked at his two cards, which consisted of a six of spades and a nine of clubs, and sighed in disappointment. Hoping to improve his hand, he took a sip of his brandy and signaled the dealer for another card. Soon as Tom dealt him a Jack of Clubs, he angrily slammed his cards down on the table. “Curse that blasted Jack! He’s always bringing me bad luck.”

Dirty Jack overheard his complaint and said, “Sir, I can see you’re having a run of bad luck.”

Rane lowered his gloomy head toward the table, nodding it several times. “Aye.”

Dirty Jack reached inside his pant’s pocket and pulled out a coin. “I lost me lucky penny today, but I still got me lucky nickel. If ye’d like, ye can rub it for luck.”

Desperate to get his money back, Rane threw caution to the wind and held out a willing hand. "Sure, I could use a stroke o'luck."

Dirty Jack was glad to help out with the incantation and readily dropped the coin onto his palm. "Don't forget t'cross yer fingers."

Rane was just about to rub the nickel when he saw the image of the buffalo seemingly leap at him from off the coin. Picturing the man to be some sort of wizard, he threw his coin back at him.

Upset over what he had done, Dirty Jack scowled at him. "Are ye trying t'pick a fight with me, laddie?"

Rane dragged his stack of poker chips closer to his body and said out of fear, "No."

"Maybe ye'd like t'step outside so I can teach ye a wee bit o'manners."

Rane had a hard time taking the man seriously with all the chirping locusts hopping up and down on his head. Trying not to laugh, he replied, "Aye, ye'd like that, wouldn't ye? Then ye an' all yer little friends here could jump me at once."

Confused about the accusation, Dirty Jack scratched the back of his head and said to himself, "Me an' all me little friends?"

While the dealer was busy shuffling the cards, Rane racked his brain trying to figure out what the buffalo on the coin represented. As he slowly peered around the casino at the lucky symbols on the slot machines, he noticed all the Jacks in the house had good luck charms in their hands. "That's weird."

The very next moment Rane saw one of the gamblers smooching a dead rabbit's foot to invoke the spirit of luck before pulling down the lever on the one-armed bandit (the slot machine was formerly called that because of its ability to leave the gamblers penniless). Highly repulsed by the Jack's desire to practice sorcery, he glanced at the nickel on the table and saw the words "In God We Trust." Tears of remorse filled his eyes as he suddenly realized he, too, had been buffaloed into practicing witchcraft.

Rane touched the red coronet on his head as he stared dejectedly at his reflection in the huge mirror behind the bar. All at once his image changed into a human shadow and gave him a lustful grin. Appalled by what he saw, he looked away and caught sight of the wall clock. Noting the midnight hour and the secondhand spinning backwards, he thought how easily he had been deceived into wasting more precious time on a dead hand. He picked up his glass of brandy and smelled the stench of the brew. "Pew! I must be out o'me mind t'sit here an' drink from d'devil's cup."

At that exact moment, he heard the faint, inner voice of King Jesus speaking to his heart: "For what profit is it to a man if he gains the whole world and loses his own soul? Return to me, Rane, and I will restore the years the locust has stolen from you."

The gentle correction instantly touched Rane's heart, and he started weeping. "Ye're right, Lord. I let that stupid devil devour my life. I don't belong in this superstitious mirror. Help me t'escape this nightmare."

He blinked tearfully at the wall clock and was happy to see that the time had changed. "Six thirty? 'Tis not midnight anymore."

The very next moment he heard Haley calling out his name and quickly turned around. He was so excited to see her waving at him from the other side of the mirrored wall that he jumped out of his seat and ran back through the artificial glass.

Prosperity engaged the security shield the instant he stepped foot in the room. "Welcome back, Rane. Did you enjoy yourself?"

Rane wiped the tears off his face and complained, "No, I didn't."

Richard and his friends snickered at his misfortune.

Rane sauntered over to his wife and said, "All right, give me a swift kick in d'pants. I deserve it."

Haley peered into his sad eyes and said out of a heart of mercy, "I can only encourage you to do what's right, love. The rest is up to you."

Rane took a fleeting look at the chance takers' reflections inside the simulated glass prior to saying, "Haley, I found out there's no such thing as a lucky devil. Ye were right. I got t'quit taking gambles with me life. There's no peace there."

Haley pointed at the handkerchief wrapped around his hand. "What happened?"

He shifted his eyes onto the bandanna she referred to and wondered where the bloodstain went. Dumbfounded by the strange phenomenon, he yanked the wrap off his hand and was shocked to see the skin back to normal. "That's strange. D'cut's gone."

Rane touched his face and found out his twelve o'clock shadow had disappeared too. He then looked down at his dress attire and whispered faintly, "An' me clothes are back t'normal."

Haley was in the dark as to what he was talking about and stared at him blankly. She was just about to question his bizarre conduct when Prosperity spoke up and said, "All right, everyone, if you'll please follow me into Masterpiece Hall, you'll see some of the finest oil paintings in the world."

The sound of Prosperity's high heels striking against the marble floor echoed loudly through the long hall as the group followed her into the large, rectangular showroom. Turning around to face the audience, she extended her hands toward the pictures hanging on the two main display walls as if she was a model showing off prizes in a game show. "As you can see, ladies an' gentlemen, Masterpiece Hall houses some of Artur's finest masterpieces."

She lowered her hands, clasping them together in front of her stomach, and said further, "Although I must admit they are a bit pricey."

Haley's alert eyes roamed around the exhibit area, giving the place a brief inspection. She noticed the area in front of the walls had been sealed off by red velvet ropes chained to gold stands like in a movie theater. It was quite clear that the owner didn't want the tourists touching any of the artwork.

Rane stared at a leprechaun in one of the paintings and suddenly thought about the bot. Nudging his wife on the arm, he whispered,

"What happened t'Little Silver? I haven't heard a peep out of him in a while."

Haley made an eye-opening expression and answered, "Yeah, that is strange."

She had no sooner spoken the words than Rane heard a barely audible, snoring sound. He looked around for its origin, whispering, "What is that noise?"

Haley shifted an uneasy eye onto her jacket and queried, "Noise?"

Rane could tell something was up by the way she was fidgeting with her coat and took a peek inside her pocket. Seeing the bot lying flat on his back wheezing for air, he looked up at his wife and whispered worriedly, "D'wee fellow looks sick. What's wrong with him?"

Haley circled the tip of her index finger over the diamond chips inside the bot's belly button before whispering back, "Reddy's been in the dark too long. His energy cell must have drained."

He noted the lifeless expression in the bot's baby blue eyes. "Ye mean he has t'have light?"

She nodded her head as she continued whispering back and forth with her husband. "Uh-huh. I got to replace it right away or the snoring sound will get louder as the cell drains."

"How are ye going t'do that?"

Haley stealthily looked about to make sure none of the tourists were watching them and then pulled a small, black leather pouch out of one of the hidden pockets inside her coat. "With these."

Haley untied the drawstring on the gem bag and took out one of the luminous cells that closely resembled a miniature diamond. "I always carry them with me in case of an emergency. Sometimes I get so busy working on a case I forget to change Reddy's cell."

Rane poked his nose inside the pouch, staring intriguingly at all the glowing, sparkling gems on the bottom of the bag. "How many are there?"

Haley pushed the tiny cell through the nanobot's belly button until it disappeared out of view. "Seven. They're all coated in diamonds, which helps protect the bot's accelerator capacitor from overheating."

While watching the old cell pop out of Reddy's mouth and into her hand, Rane snickered amusingly. "Would ye look at that."

Haley dropped the dull cell into the black pouch and tightened the drawstring.

Rane momentarily shifted his peer onto her hand as she put the bag back where she originally got it. "How do ye recharge d'cells once they're drained?"

Haley gave him a bright smile and replied, "From the energy in the sun. Each one lasts about a week."

Reddy soon regained all his vigor and sprung to his feet. While leaning on the edge of the pocket, he gave his inventor a friendly wave of his fingers. "Hi, Whiz Kid."

Rane waved back and said amiably, "Hi, Little Silver, ye gave me quite a scare. I'm glad t'see ye're feeling better, buddy."

With a huge grin on his face, Reddy winked his right eye at his inventor and then replied in his adorable, cutesy voice, "Me too, buddy."

Haley scooped up the tiny bot into her hand, whispering, "Reddy, you need to stay in the light until the cell fully energizes your accelerator."

"How long will it take t'fully energize?" Rane asked.

Haley sighed as she calculated the estimated time. "He was almost completely drained of power. It will probably take about five minutes."

She put her focus back on the bot and said, "Reddy, make yourself tiny enough where no one can see you and then wait for us in the lobby."

"Okey-dokey, Haley," he replied in a raring-to-go voice and then shrank his size down to one inch.

Being extra cautious, Haley cupped her other hand over the top of the bot while scouting the area for any onlookers. Seeing the coast was clear, she released him onto the marble floor, and he took off running for the foyer.

On the other side of the hall, Prosperity was busy answering one of Walter's questions about the paintings. Just as she finished speaking with him, she saw Jillian and three British Intelligence agents heading into the conference room at the far end of the hall. Knowing she was supposed to sit in on the meeting, she looked around at the tourists and loudly announced, "Folks, I have some very important business to take care of. I'll be back in a few minutes. Please feel free to look around at all the paintings but make sure you stay behind the red ropes."

Curious about what was going on, Haley's attentive eyes trailed the tour guide down the long hall until she went inside the conference room and closed the door.

Rane stared at his wife's perplexed face and asked, "Is something wrong?"

Still partially distracted, Haley looked over at her husband and replied, "I wonder why Prosperity would be meeting with Gary Brown."

Rane's interest aroused even further when he noticed that his wife couldn't keep her meddling eyes off the conference door. "Who's Gary Brown?"

Dying to hear what they were talking about, Haley was in a world of her own and didn't answer.

Unsure whether she heard him or not, Rane waved his hand in front of her face until she gave him her undivided attention. He then raised the intensity of his voice while asking his question a second time. "Who's Gary Brown?"

Haley took the two playing cards out of her coat pocket and stared at the picture of the Jack. She shifted her gaze onto her husband and, again, spoke like she was lost in thought. "He's a British Intelligence agent. I met him about a couple of weeks ago when I went out to investigate a case."

Rane glanced at the cards in her hand and then took his notepad and pen out of his coat pocket. "Speaking of investigation, why don't we take this opportunity t'look around for more clues?"

Haley skimmed several pictures on the walls and replied, "I am. I've been looking for one in the oil paintings."

He chuckled at her seemingly ridiculous suggestion. “Ye expect t’find a clue in an oil painting?”

A clever glint unveiled in her green eyes as she openly declared, “Sure. I prayed to God to help me solve this case, an’ I feel that’s where He wants me to look.”

Rane had overheard the two police officers talking about how she had been decorated with honor twice. Since he had no other leads, he decided to succumb to his wife’s superior knowledge by motioning his hand for her to go ahead of him. “Okay, Sherlock, ye’re d’gumshoe.”

After finding no sign of a clue in any of the artworks, Rane sighed in disappointment and asked, “Now what do we do?”

Haley tapped the two cards in her hand against her lips several times before answering uncertainly, “I thought for sure I heard God telling me to check the paintings.”

Rane took another look at the oil paintings on the wall. “Well ye obviously heard wrong.”

Haley wasn’t the type to give up easily. She found her greatest victories came as a result of never giving up hope. Thinking there might be more paintings in the gallery, she turned her head toward the exit and said, “Maybe not.”

He shadowed her gaze over to the outlet and queried, “What do ye mean?”

She put the cards back into her coat pocket and replied, “There’s got to be more paintings than this.”

Rane stepped back from the long wall, sweeping his eyes across the oil paintings from left to right. “Ye really think so?”

Haley waited until several tourists passed by before nodding her head. After taking a peek around the general vicinity to make sure no one else was coming, she whispered privately in her husband’s ear, “We’ll find out everything we can on this tour an’ then sneak off to check the other rooms, okay?”

“That’s fine by me.”

CHAPTER 21

In the conference room, Prosperity had just sat down in one of the six Queen Anne chairs positioned around an oblong, cherry wood table. Sensing the tension in the room, her eyes anxiously wandered from Jillian to the three British secret service men already seated at the table in their official attire.

Gary Brown, the agent in charge, was extremely dedicated to the protection of his queen and country and saw himself of great importance. One could tell by the way he conducted himself that he had years of experience in the field.

Agent Lorrell Stratton, who had been working under Gary for the past five years, was quite good at his job but often allowed his quick temper to get in the way of his social charms.

Jamison Apalese had been with Gary only a couple of years. He was a relatively quiet young man who felt he could learn more about people through careful observation.

Jillian had shown up for the meeting dressed in black dress slacks and a black sweater that buttoned up the front. On her feet she wore black ankle boots with two-inch spike heels.

Gary, who was seated at the head of the table, made a rearward tug on the sleeve of his blue suit jacket and then checked the time on his gold watch. "I only have twenty minutes. Let's make this quick."

Lorrell, the agent sitting next to Prosperity, was highly upset that Jillian had invited a guest to their private meeting and wasted no time voicing his concerns. "Why is she here?"

Jillian looked across the table at the tour guide and countered in a superior air, "She's my attorney."

He raised his bushy black eyebrows and queried snootily, "You feel you need one, do you?"

Jillian ignored his sarcasm by turning her head to talk with Gary, who was seated in the chair to the right of hers. "Now what is it ye wanted t'see me about, Mr. Brown?"

Gary pursed his lips in disgust at the nasty scars on her face. After getting over the initial shock of seeing them, he answered her question in a deep, matured voice. "We believe Aileen's death wasn't an accident."

Jillian cocked her right ear and queried suspiciously, "Oh?"

Gary took a moment to check out the mural covering the long wall to the right of him.

Noticing his interest in her late brother's artwork, Jillian said, "That's a picture of Lucky Jack playing poker with his girlfriend. Ye can tell by d'eloquent detail in d'painting that Artur masterfully planned each stroke."

Gary nodded his head in agreement and began to unfasten the clasp on his gold wristwatch. After removing the timepiece from his wrist, he set it down on the table in front of him.

Prosperity leaned across the table to take a closer look at it. After carefully observing that its circular crystal was larger than normal size, she sat back down. "That's an unusual watch, sir. Where did you get it?"

Making sure to leave a clear print, Gary firmly pressed his right thumb on top of the watch's transparent quartz cover and then lifted it from the glass. "It's a government-issue."

Prosperity was startled when a red beam of light suddenly shot through the center of the crystal and started scanning the retina in Gary's right eye. "A secret service watch?"

He waited until the beam of light retracted into the watch before affirming her suspicion. "Yes. BIA is checking my security clearance back at the office."

Feeling uneasy about all the safety precautions, Jillian arched her back against the burgundy cushion in the chair while fondling the top pearl button on her black sweater. "Who's BIA?"

Lorrell talked back to the Irishwoman like the acronym was common knowledge. "British Intelligence Agency, what do you think?"

Gary rested his forearms on the polished table and lowered his head to speak to the home office computer through the conversational interface in the timepiece. "BIA, voice activation … Gary Povel Brown, Agent ID Number 00194385."

All at once he heard a static interference coming through the watch. It only lasted for a moment and disappeared. Directly afterward he saw a white light pulsating inside the crystal to the tempo of the audio coming through the tiny speaker within the timepiece. BIA's voice recording sounded like a highly sophisticated, British woman.

"Good afternoon, Gary Povel Brown."

Disquieted about the sudden intrusion, Gary sat erect, resting his elbow on the arm of the chair as he rubbed his cleft chin. "BIA, what was all that static interference?"

"There seems to be an overload of electrical energy in your area, sir."

Gary exchanged a bewildered look with Lorrell, who was sitting on the right side of him. He then lowered his head toward the watch as if BIA couldn't hear him from where he was positioned before. "Can you identify it?"

The colorless light inside the crystal continued flashing harmoniously to the computer's voice patterns as BIA replied, "No, sir. Whatever the outlet is, it is scrambling my ability to pin down its source."

Jillian and Prosperity grinned at each other like a couple of sly foxes as if they knew exactly where the disturbance was coming from.

Not sure what his next course of action would be, Gary sighed heavily and wiped the nervous perspiration off his forehead. After propping his other elbow on the arm of the chair, he clasped his fingers together and asked, "BIA, are you able to run motion-picture files?"

"Affirmative, Mister Brown."

"Good. Open motion-picture file on Jillian Selare Finney, Homicide Code Jsf133#65068m."

Jillian tried not to look worried as BIA replied, "Processing request, sir. You should have visual in two point five seconds."

Immediately after the allotted time, specified by BIA, the time dial inside the watch spun around to reveal a motion picture on the other side. Jillian eyed the film and soon realized the agents had videotaped her burglarizing Aileen's flat in London. While squirming apprehensively in her seat from the incriminating evidence against her, she shifted her eyes onto Prosperity, who seemed to be interested in what she was going to do next.

Gary spoke to Jillian as if he had already condemned her of the crime. "There's no use hiding your guilt behind those dark glasses, Miss Finney."

While the agent continued making accusations against her, Jillian again tilted her head to the side like she was relying more on her sense of hearing than her sight.

"We know all about how ye thwarted Aileen's plans to sell the android to British Intelligence. Why, we have enough evidence to put you away for the rest of your life."

Lorrell looked down his nose at her and snarled insultingly, "You traitor."

He pointed at the tricolor Irish flag standing proudly in the corner of the room behind Gary and added, "You're a disgrace to your motherland."

Jillian looked over at the flag while pretending to adjust her black sunglasses to fit more snugly on her nose. She didn't want the agents to know that she had just activated a pinhead camera by pressing one of the six, tiny, white diamonds in the upper-right corner of her shades. After lowering her hand onto her lap, she turned toward the accusing agents and said innocently, "I'm not hiding my guilt behind d'glasses, gentlemen."

Jamison, who was sitting at the other end of the table across from Gary, asked curiously, "Then why are you wearing them?"

Jillian crossed her legs and slowly removed her shades. "T'hide my disfigurement."

After she had exposed the upper portion of her face, Gary cringed at the massive scar tissue covering her eyelids. "Ugh! What happened to you, woman?"

Jillian put her sunglasses back on and answered sadly, "I guess ye could say a black cat crossed my path an' gave me thirteen years o'bad luck."

"I'm sorry for your misfortune, madam," Jamison said sincerely.

Jillian nodded her head once and looked back at the evidence compiled against her.

Lorrell narrowed his eyes suspiciously at Jillian as she continued viewing the video inside the watch. "If your eyes are damaged, how do you see?"

Prosperity took it upon herself to answer for Jillian. "The robot helps her."

Intrigued by this unknown phenomenon, Lorrell raised a curious brow at the tour guide and asked, "How?"

Jillian stopped Prosperity from giving him the information by cutting her off. "By forming mental pictures in my mind."

Highly interested in what they were saying, Gary swayed the flow of the conversation onto himself by asking Jillian, “You mean telepathically?”

Thinking it wise not to divulge too much information about her glasses or the microchip implanted inside her forehead, Jillian purposely gave an uneducated answer. “I’m not sure, he just does.”

Gary peered closely into the dark lenses on her shades and asked, “You can see me clearly?”

Jillian stared at his reflection inside her glasses and replied pretentiously, “Not entirely.”

Jamison genuinely desired to help the woman escape her misfortune, so he spoke up and said, “With the advanced technology we have today, there is the possibility of bionic implants.”

Loathing the idea, she didn’t hesitate for a second to shoot it down. “I don’t want anyone else’s eyes, real or synthetic, Mr. Apalese.”

Lorrell exposed his tea-stained teeth by chuckling cruelly. “Why? Are you superstitious or something?”

Jillian thought about the lucky talisman she had hidden underneath her sweater and grinned conceitedly. Choosing not to answer his question, she simply lowered her proud head and went back to watching the film.

Gary took a Jack of Diamonds playing card out of his suit pocket and laid it down on the table in front of her. “I found this in Aileen’s purse at the scene of the accident.”

Jillian picked up the card and stared with high regard at the face of her late brother.

Gary went on to say, “The only prints we found on it were hers. Any clues why she was carrying it around with her?”

Although Jillian knew more than she let on, she shook her head and gave him back the card.

Gary put the card away in his pocket and then turned on the audio button on the side of his watch. “I think you might find this interesting, Miss Finney.”

The very next moment Jillian heard a recording of her voice threatening to kill her sister if she didn't hand over the encryption code to the android's main operating system. The tape made her think back on the time Aileen caught her searching the gallery for the secret code. Although she knew her family didn't trust her after that, her sister still showed her mercy by programming the robot to aid her sight handicap.

Lorrell gloated over the fact that she had been outfoxed. "Why you haven't even been able to go to the bathroom without us knowing about it, Miss Finney."

Feeling like a helpless rat caught in a trap, Jillian pursed her crimson lips and sped up her breathing.

"How did you do it?" queried Lorrell.

Jillian glared at the agent's overconfident face and retorted touchily, "How did I do what?"

Lorrell leaned across the table and slammed his palm down on the table. "Lady, don't insult my intelligence. You know exactly what I'm talking about!"

Gary, who was sitting there habitually rubbing his chin, gave his agent a subtle shake of his head, indicating he wanted him to back off.

Lorrell got the message and reluctantly slumped back in his chair. After taking in a deep breath to calm his temper, he forced himself to lower the tone of his voice. "Aileen O'Malley Finney died in a car accident on her way to deliver the android to British Intelligence."

Jillian brushed her short, strawberry-blond hair away from her cheek and shrugged uncaringly. "So what's her death got t'do with me?"

Gary was desperate to solve the mystery behind her sister's untimely death, so he took over the lead in giving her the third degree. "Aileen left me a message on my cell phone about some swarm of locusts attacking her car. Yet when I arrived at the scene of the accident, there was no trace of any insects, nor any sign of the robot. What really happened to her, Miss Finney?"

Not wanting to be unnerved by the wary look he was giving her, Jillian turned away as she replied, "How should I know?"

Lorrell shared a confident grin with his comrades and then said to the accused, "It won't do you any good to lie."

He waited until she faced him again before motioning his hand toward Gary's watch. "As you already know, we recorded your threats against your sister."

Fed up with all their grilling, Jillian uncrossed her legs and leaned forward in her seat. With her palms pressed against the table, she raised her voice in anger. "So what! D'android wasn't Aileen's t'sell; it belongs t'Artur's son."

Gary turned off the audio switch on the side of his watch and said argumentatively, "Rane mysteriously disappeared some time ago. Since he was never seen again after the night he walked out on his wife, he's presumed to be dead. That left Aileen as the sole beneficiary, an' she signed the robot over to us. Without the boy to contest the deal, the project became the sole property of the British government."

When Jillian just sat back in her chair without saying a word. Prosperity came to her defense by declaring, "But, gentlemen, according to Artur's will, his son still has until noon tomorrow to claim his rights to the cybernetic research."

Put on the spot, Gary went back to massaging his chin while trying to come up with a loophole. He knew the British government had to gain possession of that android before it fell into enemy hands. But after careful deliberation, he knew there was no way he could infringe upon the stipulations in the ironclad will without risking a lawsuit, and he finally heaved a breath of surrender. "All right, Miss Finney, your nephew has until then."

Resentful that Artur left her sister as the executor of his will and not her, Jillian said in protest, "Aileen only wanted t'sell d'android 'cause she was afraid of it."

Jamison, who had been sitting there quietly taking everything in, gave her a fishy look and queried, "An' just how would you know that, Miss Finney?"

Jillian's body tensed up as a guilty look overshadowed her face. With all eyes in the room fixed on her, she started fidgeting with her sunglasses. Feeling like her back was against the wall, she decided to make a deal with Gary. "If I turn over d'prototype, ye promise t'clear my record?"

Knowing he had the upper hand, Gary made a quick tug on the edge of his sleeves and said arrogantly, "I'll see what I can do."

Lorrell tweaked his nose and said to Jillian, "Aileen swore the project would save the government a lot of money. Is this true?"

Although Jillian was burning to get even with these men for forcing her hand to release her brother's life's work, she decided to feign passivity. "Aye, replicas from d'prototype will make both military an' police personnel obsolete."

"How?" asked Jamison.

Once more Prosperity took it upon herself to answer for Jillian. "Unlike humans, robots don't get sick. They don't require any food or sleep to function properly, an' you can work them as much as you like—for nothing."

Not a bit impressed, Lorrell crossed his arms and said, "Tell us something we don't already know."

Prosperity stared at the agents' unsmiling faces and then picked up where she left off before. "Besides all the money the replicas will save the government in housing, food, clothing, medical bills, an' payroll expenses, they could also be used to stop violence on the streets."

Lorrell's voice dripped with worry as he mulled over the potential danger in his mind. "Allow androids to police the cities?"

Jillian played with the top button on her black sweater as she replied high and mightily, "Why not? D'Locust 52257 is far superior in intellect than any robotics yer engineers have come up with thus far."

Jamison looked apprehensively at his commanding officer and said, “Gary, I don’t know, that sounds awful risky.”

Gary tapped his fingertips together and lowered his head, contemplating the matter. He was still troubled about what might happen if the project fell into enemy hands. Drawing his concentration back onto the original topic, he said to Jillian, “What defense does it have?”

“D’robot can communicate t’any weaponry an’ make it inoperable. He can also manipulate an environment so well his enemies can’t tell what is real or not.”

“That’s interesting. Can the robot fool people into believing it is human like Aileen said?”

Jillian crossed her legs and continued toying with the button on her sweater. “Aye, d’android’s circuitry is hidden underneath an’ artificial casing o’tissue that looks an’ feels like real skin. He can mimick human behavior perfectly.”

He narrowed his curious eyes and went back to rubbing his chin. “Mimick human behavior, how?”

Jillian shrugged like the answer was perfectly obvious. “Ye know, like smoking a cigarette, drinking a glass o’brandy, or playing a simple game o’poker.”

Jamison interrupted to ask, “So it can fool anybody?”

As Jillian continued disclosing top-secret information about the Locust 52257, she deliberately left out the fact that the robot could alter its molecular structure to impersonate any human at will. “I assure ye, gentlemen, d’android is a master at hoodwinking d’human brain’s neural system. Its microprocessor responds t’our negative emotions systematically an’ uses those weaknesses to its advantage.”

Eager to learn more, Jamison hunched forward in his chair to ask, “Negative emotions? You mean like … fear?”

Jillian let go of the button on her sweater and answered in her usual, snooty tone, “Isn’t that d’root cause of all negative emotions, Mr. Apalese?”

“So what happens if I can harness my fears?” Lorrell queried.

She placed her elbows on the arms of the chair and cupped her hands. "Then d'android would have no control over ye."

Prosperity observed the troubled look on the agents' faces and said, "I wouldn't worry if I were you, gentlemen. How many people do you know walk in that kind of power?"

Jamison thought about it for a moment and then shook his head slightly. "None, I guess."

Fatigued from getting only a few hours sleep the night before, Lorrell yawned and started rubbing the stiffness out of the back of his neck. "She's got a point. I don't know anyone who is completely positive."

Considering the technical aspects, Jamison pitched another question at Jillian. "How long can it run before losing power?"

"No need t'worry about that, Mr. Apalese. D'android will keep itself fully charged."

Doubting her word, he promptly asked, "How?"

"D'transmitter inside d'master computer fills d'space around it with an electromagnetic field. D'robot resonates with d'field an' asorbs d'energy through d'receiver attached t'his left earlobe."

Suspecting there was a catch, Gary asked, "Nothing is infallible. What weakness does the android have?"

"During d'early testing stages of d'Locust 52257, Artur discovered that high levels of positive energy could countermand d'negative energy used t'run d'holograms."

Lorrel's overbearing personality remained unchanged as he leaned back in his chair. "That's not suprising. The current VRVs being marketed today are not that impressive."

Jillian grinned conceitedly at Lorrel and looked over at the tour guide. "Prosperity, shake d'agent's hand."

"Yes, ma'am."

Prosperity shifted her upper torso toward Lorrell and forcibly shook his hand.

Questioning Jillian's motives, Lorrel lowered his bushy eyebrows and asked, "Why did your lawyer shake my hand?"

"Merely t'show ye how realistic d'images are."

He looked back at Prosperity for a brief moment and then said to Jillian, "I don't get it."

Jillian flashed him another one of her aloof smirks before saying, "Prosperity is a holographic image."

Stunned by the discovery, Lorrel widened his eyes at the tour guide and gasped, "What?"

Gary and Jamison stared open-mouthed at the virtual image, too shocked for the moment to speak.

After giving the tour guide a thorough inspection, Lorrell shook a skeptical head. "No way... she can't be. I felt her warm hand when she shook mine."

Jillian's haughty tone remained unchanged. "No, ye didn't. D'Locust 52257 manipulated yer neural senses into believing Prosperity is real."

Jamison thought she was playing a practical joke and started laughing. "Come on, Jillian, quit playing games."

"All right, I'll prove it t'ye." Jillian pushed some strands of her hair behind her left ear to expose her lobe and said, "See this red, diamond-shaped earring?"

Gary leaned closer to examine it. "Yes."

"It has a tiny, two-way transmitter hidden inside. I can call d'robot whenever I need him."

"Where is the android?" Lorrell asked pushily.

While replying to his question, Jillian pinched her earring to turn on the intercom. "Not far."

She then summoned the android by saying, "Locust 52257, this is Jillian Selare Finney. Come in, please."

Without delay, a perky, Irish voice came through the loud speaker inside her earring. "Top o' d'day t'ye, sis. How are ye?"

Gary whispered questionably to Lorrell, "Sis?"

Letting the robot know she was in danger, Jillian cunningly put a cloak-and-dagger message in her reply. "A little under d'weather, Jack, but thanks for asking."

Curious about the name, Lorrell mouthed it quietly to Gary. "Jack?"

The robot picked up on Jillian's clandestine distress call and said, "How is Shadow?"

Again, Jillian pretended to adjust the sunglasses on her nose while secretly pressing another one of the small, white diamonds in the corner of her shades. "She found three blind mice in d'gallery that need t'be exterminated."

After quickly reviewing the footage of the three agents that Jillian had just sent him, the android replied, "I think I get d'picture."

Suspicious over what they were talking about, Lorrell squinted at Jillian and asked, "Who's Shadow?"

Jillian reverted back to her normal high-and-mighty speech as she replied, "My late sister's cat, Mr. Pearson."

The robot broke up the agent's little interrogation by speaking loudly to Jillian. "Now what can I do for ye, sis?"

She looked around the room and noticed that all the agents were hanging on the edge of their seats, anxious to hear her reply. "Activate partial override for Prosperity tour guide."

After about two seconds, the robot replied, "Partial override completed."

All at once the secret service men heard loud static as Prosperity's virtual image began to fade in and out.

Shocked that the tour guide was in fact only a projection, Jamison gasped loudly. "I don't believe it!"

Lorrell, who was sitting there with his mouth gaped open, shook his head in amazement. "If the holograms are that real, it would be virtually impossible for anyone to see the truth."

Considering the robot's weakness to positive energy, Jillian whispered anxiously under her breath, "Not entirely impossible."

Gary gripped his hands around the arms of his chair and chuckled, "Who would have ever thought the ultimate escape from reality would be in our own imagination?"

Lorrell and Jamison joined in, laughing along with him.

All at once Lorrell thought about the death of Jillian's sister and stopped all the gaiety by saying, "Wait a minute, what are we laughing at? That android obviously created a fantasy out of Aileen's mind that was real enough to kill her."

Jillian went back to fondling the top button on her black sweater as she replied, "I didn't say there wouldn't be risks, gentlemen."

Lorrell scowled at her. "So what do we do about those risks, Miss Finney?"

Jillian crossed her leg and pretended to wipe a smudge off the toe of her boot. At that precise moment, she eyed three locusts, like the one Bob had seen, crawling under the table. Knowing what the robot was about to do, she grinned impishly at the virtual images and then sat upright in her chair. "Nothing, unless o'course ye can figure out a way t'remove d'bugs from d'human mind."

Lorrell wasted no time mocking her sinister laughter. He then eyed the red diamond in her earlobe and suggested to his comrades, "I say we take the communication device from her an' contact the robot ourselves."

Just as Lorrell reached out his hand to take it forcibly, the three winged locusts sprung off the marble floor and flew at the agents' faces. Caught off guard by their unexpected attack, the men shrieked nosily and started swatting at the false images appearing to be real.

While the men were mentally caught up in the hologram, Jillian pressed another one of the white diamonds in the corner of her sunglasses. Immediately afterward a ray of light shot out of the gem and started scanning Gary's thumbprint, which he had left on the crystal portion of his watch. A second later, the beam disappeared. Jillian laughed in her heart at the agents' helplessness and decided to have a bit of fun with them. "What are ye afraid of, gentlemen? 'Tis only a hologram."

Trying not to get stung on the face by a charge of electricity ejecting out of the locust's tail, Lorrell accidentally banged his head on the back of his chair. Pretending like he and his comrades were still in control, he shouted in a bitter tongue, "We're not afraid of anything, lady!"

Jilllian sniggered mischievously at Lorrell's hair, which was now standing on end as if he had stuck his finger in a light socket. "Then ye have nothing t'worry about. Do ye?"

All at once the green locusts vanished into thin air as Jack spoke to Jillian on a frequency only she could hear. "Finished retina an' thumbprint facsimile—now imaging skin texture—will infiltrate d'bureau by this evening. Oh, an' one more thing: Lorrell placed a tracking device underneath d'front bumper on yer limousine."

After receiving the message from Jack, Jillian spoke pretentiously to Lorrell, who had just sat up in his chair. "As ye can see, Mr. Stratton, d'robot will not allow ye t'harm me."

Breathing heavily from the vicious attack, Lorrell gave her a drop-dead look. He then wiped his palms across his head to reflatten all the black hairs on his head.

With a lethargic look on their faces, Gary and Jamison repositioned themselves in their chairs.

Prosperity eyed Jamison, who had just begun to readjust his ruffled clothing, and then stared complacently at the other two agents. "I suggest you make the gift exchange with her, gentlemen."

Still slightly winded, Gary straightened out his tie while nodding his head in defeat. "All right. Where?"

Lorrell hit the heel of his hand on the arm of his chair and bellowed, "No, Gary! You can't make a deal with her. She can't be trusted."

Jillian scowled at the agent for his petty comment and then spoke to Gary as if she had the upper hand. "If ye don't, Mister Brown, I promise ye'll never find that android."

Gary eyed Prosperity's virtual image fading in and out and replied, "Don't worry, Miss Finney, we'll be there. You just tell us when an' where."

Lorrell was so mad about the exchange, his face turned beet red.

Jillian sniggered in her heart at his indifference toward her deal and then carried on with her conversation to Gary. "Destroy all top secret files containing evidence against me."

Stunned that his superior officer would even agree to such a thing, Lorrell protested boisterously. "You can't do that, Gary. We would all be guilty of treason."

Gary held up his hand to silence him and continued listening to Jillian's proposal.

"Meet me at d'Christmas tree in d'open square at midnight. Bring a signed an' sealed document declaring me innocent of all charges, an' I'll give ye d'android. Oh, an' one more thing, make sure there's no night watchmen. I warn ye, if there's any armed police in d'area, d'robot will know, an' d'deal is off."

Gary sat in silence mulling over her terms and then finally replied, "All right, done."

He offered her a friendly handshake and said, "You just made yourself a contract, Miss Finney, Merry Christmas."

Lorrell waited until Jillian had finished shaking Gary's hand before grabbing her firmly by the wrist. "Make sure that robot's delivered in a padlocked box, lady. We wouldn't want him to hurt anybody, now would we."

Jillian scowled at his insinuation and jerked her arm out of his grip.

Gary picked up his gold watch off the table and put it back around his wrist. He then held the timepiece close to his mouth as he spoke to the home office. "BIA, erase my activation code an' send me a new one."

BIA's computerized, feminine voice promptly replied, "Confirmed, Mr. Brown. Will have it to you shortly."

Prosperity interrupted Gary's train of thought by speaking to Jillian in a robotic voice that sounded like it was breaking up. "Maaa'am, maay, I giiiit baaack to my tour grrroup?"

Jillian at once addressed the problem to the android. "Locust 52257, override last directive an' then deactivate voice command."

"Voice command deactivated," the robot answered.

Once Prosperity's image and voice became clear again, she asked, "May I go now, Jillian?"

Jillian nodded her head once and answered, "Ye may go."

As soon as Prosperity left the conference room, she wasted no time rounding up the tour group. After making her apologies for being detained so long, she led them over to the opposite side of the room from where she originally started and picked up on her oration.

"These beautiful masterpieces are some of Artur's finest works in oil painting. He really captured the spirit of Ireland in each of them. Don't you think?"

While examining one of the art pieces, Haley was the first to speak up and give a critique. "His brush technique is mind-boggling. The landscapes are so lifelike and incredibly detailed."

"Artur truly was a man before his time. His vast knowledge of neuroscience in correlation to thermogenetic graphics is still a mystery today."

Haley whispered into her husband's ear, "Write his skills down, too, okay?"

Rane started to jot down the information but then thought, *Write 'em down? I don't even know what she just said.*

Haley closely studied the tour guide for several moments and felt like there was something not quite right about her. Pointing out one of her suspicions to her husband, she said in a barely audible voice, "Rane, did you notice the soulless expression in her pale blue eyes?"

He looked around at the other women in the group and asked, "Who are ye talking about?"

"Prosperity," she replied as if he should have known exactly who she meant.

Rane inconspicuously checked out the tour guide's eyeballs and said, "Strung out on crack no doubt."

"Why would you think that?"

"'Cause I've seen d'same look in me own eyes when I used t'do it."

Haley gave him a funny look and then raised her hand to get the tour guide's attention.

Prosperity lifted her chin toward the detective and queried, "Yes?"

Haley lowered her hand to her side and answered, "Why didn't Artur share his computer knowledge with other engineers?"

While Prosperity was answering her question, she kept a discreet, watchful eye on Richard and his two friends, who were roughhousing near the red ropes. "After Artur's fiancée had publicly humiliated him by breaking off their engagement and lying to the press about him having ESP, he trusted no one but Aileen. In fact, there are no armed security officers on the grounds. The gallery is completely protected by the Locust 52257."

"What about Jillian?"

Highly suspicious that the female sleuth was asking more off-the-wall questions, Prosperity cocked her head slightly and said, "What about her?"

"Didn't Artur trust her?"

Prosperity stared expressionless at the detective for about five seconds and finally answered, "Haven't you ever heard that curiosity killed the cat?"

Sensing the woman's indifference toward her, Haley said to be funny, "But satisfaction brought her back."

Not knowing how to respond to her quick wit, Prosperity checked to see what Richard and his two friends were doing. When she saw them about to step over one of the red ropes, she hollered out, "Gentlemen, please stay out of the sealed-off areas! No one is allowed to touch the oil paintings."

Richard scoffed at her authority by deliberately making the bottom of his tennis shoe squeak across the marble floor. "And what happens if we don't?"

Prosperity sighed tiresomely at his rebellious attitude and muttered under her breath, "There's always one in every crowd."

She ambled over to a nearby door and opened it. Before anyone could bat a lash, one-hundred electronic eyeballs swiftly flew into the room looking around for any troublemakers. Each eye was two-inches in diameter and had long, curly black eyelashes. "If you or your two friends so much as raise one finger toward one of these exceptional masterpieces, you'll receive electrical shocks from these private eyes in a matter of microseconds."

Fearful of their menacing blue eyes, Walter blurted out in his own defense, "Richard's the one who told us to do it."

Feeling a need to cover himself, Richard snapped back, "I did not!"

Prosperity put her hands on her waist and said, "You an' Carter do have a mind of your own. Don't you, Walter?"

Walter heard several people in the tour group snickering at him as he humbly nodded his head.

The tour guide strolled over to where Walter was standing. "Then I suggest you use it."

"Yes, ma'am."

Rane was completely mesmerized as he watched one of the glossy eyeballs zoom up to his nose and stop only a foot away. "Whoa!"

He pointed at the private eye's curly lashes that were flapping up and down like a wing and said, "That is so cool. Looks like it is winking at me."

Prosperity stared at the eyeball hovering in front of him and replied, "Actually, the private eyes are busy taking pictures for security precautions."

Rane meticulously looked over the design of the eyeball. From what he could tell, the lens was made out of crystal, and the socket out of shiny, white plastic. "Ye don't say."

Haley smiled at the private eye that had just flown up to her face. Being careful not to show any signs of hostility, she extended the tip of her index finger toward its eyelashes and felt its soft fibers brush against her skin. The eyeball shrank back after she touched it and darted over to Richard.

Richard, who was already surrounded by ten of them, slapped at the new arrival and said to the tour guide, "You mean to tell me that every time one of these eyeballs blinks at me it's taking my picture?"

Prosperity grinned and said teasingly, "Yes. Each private eye has its own high-powered camera lens so remember to say, 'Cheese.'"

Richard snubbed his nose at her humor and then made a cheesy face at the eyeballs.

Rane gaped at all the private eyes flying around Richard's head. Thinking back on what the tour guide said earlier, he became fretful and asked, "Prosperity, can d'electricity from these mechanical eyes kill us?"

"No. The computer merely tells the private eyes to release mild electrical charges at the hooligans until they're rendered unconscious."

Rane placed his hand over his heart as he whispered to his wife, "Whew! 'Tis a good thing for us we're not hooligans."

Richard stuck his tongue out at the watchful eyes and raised his leg in pretense of stepping over the rope. "I bet these eyeballs aren't even real."

Prosperity creased her brow at the preppy's accusation. "I'm not lying, Richard. But if you would like to find out firsthand, feel free to overstep your bounds."

Rane rolled his eyes in exasperation at Richard's defiant behavior and whispered to his wife, "I'll lay ye ten pounds that hooligan gets zapped before d'tour is over."

Pretending to have the upper hand in front of his friends, Richard smirked at Prosperity and lowered his leg. The second she turned around to answer a question, he flicked a couple of the eyeballs, snickering, "Quit making eyes at me."

When the private eyes suddenly turned an evil eye onto Richard, he felt scared and stopped laughing.

"Why are they looking at you like that, Richard?" Walter asked apprehensively.

"I-I-I don't know," Richard stammered.

All at once the two private eyes he had assaulted started thumping themselves against the right side of his head.

Richard covered his hand over the area they were striking and hollered out, "Hey, quit that!"

Out of the corner of his eye, Richard saw his two friends slowly backing away. "Where are you going, you cowards? Get over here and help me!"

Carter and Walter shook their heads and made a hasty retreat behind the tour guide.

"Some friends you are," Richard barked heatedly and then used the palm of his hand to whack the two eyeballs into the wall.

While Richard was busy laughing at the eyeballs' misfortune, more private eyes snuck up behind him and rammed the back of his head. "Ow!"

He was so shaken up by their devious attack that he whirled around in all directions, swatting at anything that moved. "Leave me alone. Go away!"

Richard's anxieties intensified when one of the private eyes zapped him on the buttocks with a stream of electricity emitted from its pupil. "Ouch! That hurt!"

To prove his point about what he had said earlier, Rane whispered into his wife's ear, "I tol' ye he'd get zapped."

Haley loathed the fact that her husband was actually enjoying the boy's misery. Making a firm stand for clemency, she whispered back, "Rane, go help him."

Shocked that she would even suggest such a thing, Rane raised his voice slightly. "Ye expect me t'help that gumby?"

Not willing to take no for an answer, Haley insisted, "Yes, now go on."

His private argument with his wife was interrupted when he heard Richard squealing sharply from another jolt to his fanny.

"Yeeeeeeoooow!"

While watching Richard cradle both hands over his buttocks to keep from getting stung, Rane whispered to his wife, "But d'chap seems t'be a bit busy right now."

She nudged her husband on the arm. "Go help him, Rane."

He heaved a huge sigh of unwilling surrender and said, "Oh, all right, but remind me later t'tape my big mouth shut. It keeps getting me into trouble."

Happy to help, Haley patted him on the back and answered jokingly, "No problem, we can use some of the duct tape off your car."

Rane rolled his eyes at her jesting and then crept over to where Richard was standing. With a fake grin on his face, he said coyly, "Hello, Richard."

Richard was busy slapping at an eyeball attacking his face and accidentally hit himself in the eye instead. "Ow!"

He was so upset he took his anger out on Rane. "Look at what you made me do!"

Rane flinched from his unforeseen hostility and apologized. "Sorry about that. I just came over t'offer my help."

Richard's aggressive tone remained unchanged as he hollered at him a second time. "Even if you were the last person on earth, I wouldn't receive help from you. Now get out of here!"

"Okay, I just thought I'd ask," he replied as if it was no big deal and then scampered back to his wife.

Haley wondered why the tour guide was just standing there watching Richard get pulverized by the private eyes. "Aren't you going to call somebody?"

Prosperity looked over at the distressed preppy and shouted, "Richard, don't make another move!"

Without question, Richard halted his body movements, and the eyeballs instantly pulled back.

Rane felt uneasy when he saw a change in the eyeballs as several of them darted past his head. "Prosperity, why are their pupils dilating like that?"

The tour guide stared uncertainly at the private eyes flying around the room and replied, "I don't know. They're not supposed to."

Rane whispered to his wife, "I think we're in big trouble."

Considering the possibility that the tourists might be in real danger, Prosperity tried to figure a way out of their predicament. After a long moment of silence, she said carelessly, "There must be some sort of malfunction in the android's microprocessor. I'll have to contact the Locust 52257 an' see if he knows anything about it."

Staring wide-eyed at the numerous private eyes giving him the evil eye, Richard asked in a shaky voice, "Prosperity, they can't kill me, right? That's what you said."

Dumbfounded by the paranormal behavior of the eyeballs, she shook her head and said, "I'm not sure of anything right now, Richard."

Petrified to move a muscle, Richard pinned his arms to his side and said in a high-pitch tongue, "What?"

Giving some thought to the things Prosperity said, Haley huddled closer to her husband to whisper in private. "I didn't know the Locust 52257 was linked to a robot. Did you?"

Rane stared at the pensive gaze in his wife's green eyes and shook his head. "No."

"I wonder what the robot looks like."

All at once the private eyes started randomly butting themselves against the tourists' heads, causing pandemonium to break out in the room.

Prosperity immediately stepped up to bring peace by hollering out, "Everyone, calm down! You'll only make things worse!"

Once she got everyone to stand perfectly still, she said further, "Nobody move until I get back."

Walter, who was standing still like a statue, queried in a worried voice, "Where are you going?"

Prosperity glanced toward the way out and replied half truthfully, "I'm, um, going to the front desk to contact the Locust 52257. Don't worry, I'll be right back."

She then hurried out the exit.

Prosperity walked fast down the corridor until she got to the surveillance equipment. After double-checking to make sure no one was around to listen in on her conversation, she faced the security camera, knowing the computer would pick her up, and whispered, loud enough to be heard, "Locust 52257, this is Prosperity Image 54599275pi, need emergency override. Private eyes in Masterpiece Hall are going haywire. Over."

Back in Masterpiece Hall, Haley was busy slapping at several private eyes trying to thump her on the back of the head. "Get off me, you little pests."

Rane wholeheartedly agreed, considering that one of the eyeballs had just spiraled out of control and slammed into his cheek. "Ow!"

He pressed his three middle fingers against the spot where he was hit, wiggling his jaw with his mouth open. Before he had a chance to fully recover from the first strike, the same private eye circled back around and darted at his face a second time. When the rapidly blinking eye stopped short from colliding with his nose, he frowned at it for toying with him and said, "Get away from me . . . ye . . . ye . . . Winker."

Rane stared down the prankster eyeball until it flew away and then turned around to see what his wife was doing. Catching sight of a private eye sneaking up on her, he hollered out, "Haley, look out! There's one behind ye!"

When Haley whirled around to stop it from attacking her, Rane noticed that two of the eyeballs had somehow gotten tangled up in the back of her curly, red hair. As he observed them wriggling around trying to break free, he couldn't help but snicker at how ridiculous they looked.

Hearing her husband cracking up with laughter, Haley spun back around and queried readily, "What is so funny?"

Rane pointed in her general direction and doubled over laughing.

Trying to find out what she had on her that was amusing him, Haley held her arms out to the side while giving her body a quick inspection. "Me?"

He lifted his trunk to nod his head and kept on guffawing. "D'next time ye go shopping for makeup, ye might want t'pick up some extra mascara."

Not a clue what he was talking about, Haley put her hands on her hips and said out of frustration, "What is that supposed to mean?"

Toning his laughter down to speak more clearly, Rane straightened up, pointing at her long red tresses. "I hate t'be d'one t'tell it t'ye straight, lassie, but ye now have an extra pair o'eyes in d'back o'yer head."

Haley smoothed her hand down the back of her hair in a vainglorious manner and felt the two eyeballs wiggling around. Extremely grossed out that they were attached to her head, she started screaming to the top of her lungs while frantically trying to shake them out of her hair. "Aaaaaagh! Rane, get them off me! Get them off! Get these critters off me!"

Noticing his wife's hysteria had drawn the interest of everyone in the room, Rane's chuckling died down. Feeling embarrassed about the situation, he simultaneously gave them a frozen smile while speaking to his wife like he was a ventriloquist. "Haley, all these nice people are watching ye."

Realizing she had made a public spectacle of herself, Haley immediately got quiet. She was so upset she crossed her arms and whispered to her husband, "You wouldn't be so calm if you had eyes in the back of your head."

Rane stared awkwardly at all the nosy tourists and thought up a hilarious excuse for his wife's adolescent behavior. "Uuuh, sh-sh-she was just rehearsing for d'part of a hysterical woman, that's all."

Haley sniggered at the tinge of truth in his jesting and playfully smacked him on the arm. "I was not."

After the silliness had died down, she turned the back of her head toward her husband and said entreatingly, "Now would you please get these little critters off me?"

Rane chortled slightly at what she called them and then began untangling the eyeballs out of her curls. "All right, critters, take yer eyes off her. She claims t'be a married woman."

"I don't think that's very funny, Rane," she replied in an indignant manner.

Rane knew her patience was wearing thin by the tone of her voice and decided it would be best to clear the gaiety out of his throat. "Okay, I'll quit laughing."

Haley quivered her body repugnantly. "Ugh! Hurry, Rane, I can feel them squirming around in the back of my head."

Joking around, Rane winked back at the two blinking eyeballs and then fought a strong urge to laugh out loud at his actions.

Haley took another deep breath to calm her anxieties and started reciting part of a scripture out of Psalm 23 in the Holy Bible. "I will fear no evil for the Lord is with me. I will fear no evil for the Lord is with me."

While still unraveling the eyeballs out of her hair, Rane cut in on her quotation by asking, "What are ye doing?"

"I'm exercising my faith. I don't want to go through life playing the part of a hysterical woman."

He stopped untangling her curly locks long enough to say, "Good, 'cause she gets on my last nerve."

Soon as Rane finished untying one of the private eyes out of the strands of her hair, he tried to grab it with his hand. When his fingers passed right through it like it was only a projected image, his eyes bulged. After the initial alarm wore off, he rubbed his eyelids as if it were only a hallucination and then stared back at it.

Haley didn't feel her husband messing with her hair anymore and asked hopefully, "Did you get them out?"

When the eyeball Rane had untangled got up and flew away, he nervously bit the skin around his thumbnail and replied, "Um … I'm still working on it."

"Well, hurry, will you?" she whined inconsiderately.

Rane nodded and went back to work. The instant he finished separating the other private eye from her hair, he snatched it before it had a chance to fly away. After feeling its glossy, plastic socket in the palm of his hand, he was certain his peepers had played tricks on him earlier and tossed the eyeball into the air.

"Did you get them out yet?" Haley reiterated in the same, selfish tone.

Gaping in the direction the eyeball flew, he replied distractedly, "Get who out?"

Tired of standing still, she raised her voice impatiently. "The eyeballs."

Rane looked down at the back of her head and replied, "Aye, I got 'em out. Ye can turn around now."

Haley twisted her body around and smiled gratefully at her hero. While using her fingertips to fluff up the back of her curly locks, she giggled, "I acted pretty childish, huh?"

Rane smiled back at her, finding her girlish innocence attractive. He brushed an eyelash off her right cheek, noticing her skin was remarkably soft. He stared at her pretty face for a long moment, desiring to kiss her. Just when he was about to make a move on her, he saw the tour guide heading back into the room. Wondering what she found out, he took his wife by the hand and hurried over to her.

Prosperity saw the other tourists heading over, too, so she shouted, "Stay where you are!"

The group instantly halted their movements as numerous private eyes circled around them.

The tour guide's strident tone transitioned into a sharp rebuke. "If you don't want to get stunned, stay perfectly still. The computer is working on the problem."

Feeling guilty that he had led his wife into disobeying her request, Rane gulped before asking, "Um, Prosperity, what exactly is d'problem?"

Prosperity answered like she was in a daze. "An audio file was recently unzipped inside the android's neural net."

Rane exchanged a confounded glimpse with his wife before asking, "Why?"

Continuing to talk like she was miles away, Prosperity looked across the room and saw several eyeballs spinning out of control. "To wipe out our memory."

Unsure what she was talking about, Rane turned up the corner of his mouth as he replied, "Huh?"

After watching the spiraling eyeballs crash into the wall, she swiveled her head in his direction and stated further, "According to the signature card, the archive was installed fourteen years ago."

Haley swatted away one of the private eyes hovering beside her as she queried, "By whom?"

The tour guide peered into Rane's teal blue eyes as if she knew who he was and then looked back at Haley. "Young Finney."

Haley flinched when the same eyeball flew at her head a second time and shooed it away. "Who's Young Finney?"

Prosperity, again, diverted her gaze onto Rane for a brief moment before replying, "Artur's son."

Totally stunned by her disclosure, Rane widened his eyes at the tour guide and started nervously folding and unfolding his arms. "I did? I mean, he did?"

Prosperity stood silent for several moments, grinning at his jittery movements.

Haley wondered in the back of her mind why they were both acting strange as she said to Prosperity, "Artur had a son?"

Looking around the room to make sure the other tourists were okay, Prosperity's reply sounded a bit distracted. "Yes."

"Where is he?"

Prosperity held out her hand to let one of the private eyes rest on her palm. After the eyeball blinked at her several times, she blew on it until it flew away. "No one knows for sure. He mysteriously disappeared from the gallery one night an' was never seen again."

Rane didn't like the new direction of the conversation, so he quickly changed the topic back to the original subject. "Go on, how would a seven-year-old know how t'timetable a file?"

Prosperity made a suspicious face at him and asked, "How did you know how old he was?"

Wasting no time in commencing with a tag question, Haley lowered her eyebrows and said, "Yeah, how did you know how old he was?"

Squirming restlessly, Rane replied, "Uuuuh, lucky guess."

Prosperity grinned in her heart at the doubtful look Haley was giving him and then said to Rane, "To answer your question about the child: Aileen tested young Finney's aptitude in the field of cybernetic engineering an' found out he was a genius like his father."

Rane made a dubious face and thought, *Then this whiz kid definitely has amnesia; 'cause 'tis sure hard t'picture me as being anything but a gumby.*

Prosperity helped Haley fan a couple of the pesky eyeballs away from her face and then went on to say, "The lad must have loaded the audio file during one of the android's diagnostic tests."

Haley inquired earnestly, "Can't Jillian override the activation sequence?"

She sighed and replied, "No. The only person Artur trusted with the encryption code other than Aileen was his son."

"Why would Aileen let the child put the file in there in the first place?"

"That's a good question. Unfortunately, it is one we'll never find out."

All at once the same pesky eyeballs that Rane had plucked out of Haley's hair came back and thumped him on the back of the head. "Ow!"

Rane shook his fist at the little rascals as they took off in the opposite direction and then resumed his conversation with the girls. "Prosperity, what happens if ye can't find young Finney?"

"The android is programmed to protect himself at all costs. If the Locust 52257 can't stop the archive from erasing his memory, his self-destruct mechanism will automatically activate."

"What will happen then?"

With a vacant look on her face, Prosperity's answer was slow upon reply. "The robot's neural net will explode like a nuclear bomb."

Rane felt his legs go limp with distress as he cupped his hand over his mouth. "Oh my goodness."

Haley asked out of deep concern for the public, "How long before you think that will happen?"

"I'm not sure. The android is doing everything he can to slow down the installation process. It could be days or merely hours."

Prosperity peered knowingly into Rane's troubled eyes and said, "I wouldn't worry though. The android will find young Finney."

Rane was intimidated by the way she was looking at him and made a nervous cough. "A lot o'years have passed. Even if d'robot did find him, he's probably forgotten d'code by now."

"I don't think so. Young Finney had a photographic memory."

Stunned by what he heard, Rane blinked his eyes speedily and said, "Oh, well, uh, what if he got amnesia or something?"

"Fortunately, the Locust 52257 was able to retrieve a small portion of an audio file from the trash bin inside his internal system. Aileen deleted the folder during one of the android's memory tests an' must have forgotten to empty the bin."

"What was in it?"

"A private conversation between Aileen an' young Finney."

"What did they say?"

"Aileen told the lad that she would conceal the key to the master code inside his password an' hide it inside the gallery in case something ever happened to her."

Haley asked pryingly, "Where?"

"The robot doesn't know. Aileen shut off his recording device in the middle of their conversation. She definitely didn't trust him."

Still frozen in place, Richard hollered out, "Prosperity, how much longer? My legs are getting tired!"

"Calm down, Richard. The android is working on the problem."

Jillian had recently adjourned from her meeting with the three agents and was now sitting upstairs in the security room in one of the three black leather chairs. Against the back wall was the Locust 52257, a large cryogenic, zettabyte processor. It had several small, flashing red lights on the front of it and was sealed inside an explosive-resistant chamber. Branching off the main processor was an energy transmitter. It made a humming noise as it condensed the particle field for reenergizing the robot.

After watching all the mayhem in Masterpiece Hall from the top-right observation screen, Jillian immediately contacted the robot by turning on the two-way radio inside her earring. "We have a virus alert. Come in, Jack. Over."

When she didn't hear anything from his end, she repeated the distress call. "I repeat: we have a virus alert. Come in, Jack. Over."

All at once a projection of the robot's face appeared inside one of the monitors. "Hello, sis."

Jillian acknowledged that she could see his image on the screen by saying, "Hello, Jack. How long before British Intelligence picks up on this frequency?"

"Approximately three minutes, ten seconds."

She pushed up her sunglasses after they had slipped down her nose and queried, "Have ye detected anymore hidden listening devices in d'gallery?"

"I found two bugs in d'lobby after d'agents left. I deactivated 'em both."

"Good. We have t'be careful, or British Intelligence will know we're on t'them."

Jack's image on the screen faded in and out for a moment as he shared more private information with Jillian. "I received a distress message from one of my imaging files."

She arched her shoulders as she leaned closer to the monitor. "An'?"

"Unfortunately, I was unable t'save d'folder containing Prosperity's holographic image."

"How long before disintegration?"

"I estimate within d'hour."

She shook her head and sighed frustratingly. "I don't understand. Yer advanced programming should have protected you from d'virus."

"'Tis not a virus."

Jillian sat back in her seat and queried curiously, "Then what exactly is causing all d'disturbance in d'holograms?"

"An' audio version of d'New Testament Bible, spoken through d'heart of an Irishman named Caleb Rivers."

She wrinkled her brow in a state of confusion and asked, "Why would these sound energy waves affect yer programming?"

"Unknown, but d'fact is they are overpowering me."

Feeling helpless to change the situation, Jillian's voice escalated. "But that can't be. How did d'audio tracks get inside yer neural net?"

"When d'archive unzipped, it revealed young Finney's name on d'signature card. He must have installed it an' d'new memory card when Aileen's back was turned. She would never knowingly betray her own brother."

Jillian gnashed her teeth out of irritation and subsequently slammed her fists down on the security board. "Why, that little brat! I curse d'day he was born!"

After calming down a bit, she stared suspiciously at Rane's face on the monitor from the camera in Masterpiece Hall and considered the plot she had set up earlier. "Jack, we've got t'find out for sure if that young man is him. Yer life depends upon it. Did ye scan d'real bar glass I planted inside d'casino hologram?"

"Aye, I'm running a fingerprint check on it now."

"How long will it take?"

"I'll have d'results t'ye shortly."

"What about d'imaging file on Gary?"

"Completed."

"Good. Ye know what t'do."

He nodded his head once.

Afraid of what might happen to her if the robot suddenly shut down, Jillian queried, "How much damage has been done t'yer memory?"

"At present, minimal damage."

"Do ye think that's why d'security system went haywire earlier?"

"What do ye mean, 'haywire'?"

Jillian motioned her hand toward the surveillance equipment and answered, "'Twas playing d'same security footage from yesterday. Carol noticed it on her monitor an' called me about it."

"Strange that I was unaware of it."

"I had Carol replace all d'film in d'cameras. D'security system seems t'be functioning properly now, but ye better run a full diagnostic check just t'make sure."

"Will start on it right away."

Still feeling apprehensive over their present circumstances, Jillian asked, "D'computer will be able t'abort d'uploading process, right, Jack?"

When he didn't answer, the anxious tone in her voice intensified. "Right, Jack?"

"Don't worry, sis. If for some reason d'Locust 52257 can't stop it, my self-destruct mechanism will automatically activate t'make sure I don't fall into enemy hands."

"Do we have any more time left?"

"No. D'agents are tapping into this frequency now. Don't call me any more. 'Tis not safe. I'll find a frequency they dunno about an' let ye know d'test results."

"But how will I talk t'ye?"

"Use former method of communication. Transmission out."

When the robot's image vanished off the security monitor, Jillian called out, "Jack, wait!"

Disappointed that she lost communication with the android, Jillian sighed heavily. "I didn't get a chance t'tell ye where we're supposed t'meet the agents tonight."

Back in Masterpiece Hall, Prosperity was busy reprimanding three women for banging on the exit door. "Ladies, please, that's not going to do you any good. The Locust 52257 has locked the doors for security reasons. If you'll just stand still, the private eyes won't attack you."

Carter was tired of posing like a mannequin and hollered out to the tour guide, "We can't stay like this forever. Can't you do something?"

Prosperity saw the pupils in the private eyes returning to normal and said, "Oh good, we're in luck, the computer has fixed the problem."

Still anxious about what the tour guide had said earlier, Rane exchanged a brief look with his wife before asking, "Did it fix d'android's blowing-up problem too?"

Prosperity didn't want anything to distract Rane from finding the master code, so she acted like everything was all right. "Yes. It seems the Locust 52257 figured out a way to stop the audio files from uploading after all."

Rane looked over at his wife and said in a voice of relief, "That's good."

Prosperity looked around the room at all the angry faces staring at her and decided it would be a good time to apologize. "Folks, I'm awfully sorry about this. I promise you'll get a full refund at the ticket counter."

Richard glanced toward the exit door when it suddenly opened and then scoffed at the tour guide's proposal. "All we get is a lousy refund? After all we've been through?"

He turned toward his two friends and said, "Come on, you guys, let's get out of this dump."

Haley looked toward the outlet and whispered, "Rane, let's go search the rest of the gallery now."

As Rane followed her out of the room, the pen he had attached to the small tablet in his jacket pocket slipped off and fell onto the marble floor. While he was walking down the corridor, he discovered it was missing and hurried back into Masterpiece Hall. After finding the place where it had dropped, he picked it up and noticed the tour guide was gone. What he didn't know was that right before he stepped back into the room, Prosperity's virtual image had disintegrated and completely vanished into thin air.

Thinking she might be at the other end of the hall, Rane strolled down to the conference room and saw the light on from underneath the closed door. He knocked on the door several times and said loudly, "Prosperity, are ye in there?"

When there was no answer, he scratched the back of his head and said, "Humph, that's strange. I didn't see her pass me in d'hall."

Rane went to find Haley and found her patiently waiting for him at the front desk.

She smiled at him as he walked up and said, "Did you find your pen?"

He swatted away three pesky eyeballs that had followed him out of Masterpiece Hall and replied, "Aye, I found it."

Rane glanced bewilderedly toward the direction he just came from and asked, "Haley, did ye see Prosperity leave the hall?"

She shook her head and replied, "No. Why? Wasn't she in there?"

Acting like he was lost in thought, Rane bit the skin around his thumbnail and replied, "Uh-uh."

Haley gave him a comforting pat on the arm and said, "Well, don't worry about it. I'm sure she'll turn up."

Rane eyed the water trickling down the leprechaun fountain and then looked around the lobby. "Where is everybody?"

"They left after Carol handed them each a free tour voucher an' a souvenir."

Thinking he might have missed out on something good, he queried, "What was d'souvenir?"

She pulled the keepsake out her coat pocket and giggled softly, "A book of matches."

He frowned at the token, which looked exactly like the one in his pocket, and then noticed the clerk wasn't at her station. "Where is Carol?"

Haley shrugged and then glued her eyes on the three, blinking eyeballs darting around Rane's head like busy bees. "I don't know. I went into the bathroom, and when I came out, she was gone. She must have stepped away for a moment."

She was suddenly startled when the private eyes zoomed over to her. As they hovered around her head like they were studying her every move, she whispered, "Rane, this is going to sound crazy, but I think Richard was right. I don't think these mechanical eyeballs are real."

Rane glanced occasionally at the said party while whispering back and forth with his wife. "Why would ye think that?"

"I thought I saw one of them fade earlier when Richard was laughing at it."

Rane reflected on what she said before replying, "Now that ye mentioned it, when I tried t'pluck one o' d'little eye flappers out o'yer hair, me fingers went right through it. I thought me eyes were just playing tricks on me."

Haley squinted at the eyeballs as they floated over to the desk. "I bet those critters are nothing but projected images."

Rane shook his head and said in a skeptical tongue, "But that can't be. I held one in me hand."

"Well, there's one sure way to find out."

She peered around the lobby for the bot, whistling the tune to summon him.

Rane skimmed his eyes across the marble floor in search of the bot but didn't see any sign of him. "So where is he?"

Haley turned her back on her husband for a moment to look in the opposite direction. "I don't know."

Rane tapped his wife on the shoulder until she turned back around. Motioning his head toward the desk, he said, "While we're on d'subject of missing persons, where's Carol an' Prosperity?"

She looked briefly toward the reception area and then checked the time on the wall clock, noting it was almost seven thirty. "You don't suppose they both went home for the day. Do you?"

Rane made a worried face and replied, "I sure hope not."

He walked over to the double glass doors and pushed down on the silver handle several times. "They locked us in."

"Oh dear," she replied in a let down tone.

He peered out the door at the cars parked on the street and then looked back at his wife. "I got more bad news for ye. D'black Cadillac is gone too."

Trying to figure out what to do next, Haley stroked the front of her long, slender neck and then felt something moving around inside her coat. Presuming it was the bot she peeked inside her pocket and was pleased to see his cheerful face. "Oh, there you are."

Reddy cupped his tiny hands around the sides of his mouth, whispering covertly, "I ran a check on that car for ye, Haley."

Haley watched her husband stroll back over to where she was standing as she whispered back to the bot, "What did you find out?"

"'Tis an old company car, purchased new by Artur in 2002. D'registration was transferred over t'Aileen in 2003."

Believing his aunt had given the suspect one of the keys to the car, Rane said to his wife, "Then d'kidnapper must have known Aileen."

Haley nodded to agree and then took a fleeting look in the general vicinity of the private eyes. Keeping her voice low, she whistled a new jingle into the air.

Rane, too, made sure the eyeballs weren't close by before asking in a hushed tone, "What's that tune mean?"

She whispered into his ear, "That I want the smart gun."

Shocked at her answer, he elevated his voice slightly. "Ye mean that bot can turn itself into a gun, too?"

Haley promptly directed her husband to secrecy by pressing her index finger firmly against her lips. Before disclosing the weapon to him, she glanced over her shoulder at the eyeball resting on top of the rose marble countertop. She slipped her hand inside her coat pocket and pulled out a shiny, silver pistol. Making sure to keep her voice low, she said, "I call it a smart gun, but it is actually called a laser neural wave disruptor."

"So if ye shoot someone with that thing ye'll scramble his brain?" he whispered back worriedly.

She grinned at his response and then spoke as if it were no big deal. "No. It only knocks the target out for ten minutes. Afterward the victim wakes up feeling disoriented."

"Disoriented?" he said in alarm.

Her lackadaisical attitude remained unchanged as she replied, "Sure, but the effect wears off rather quickly."

Rane stared uneasily at the weapon in her hand as she turned on the light switch on the side of the barrel. "What are ye going t'do?"

She motioned the gun toward the blinking eye, which was still sitting on top of the countertop, and replied, "I'm going to aim the laser sight at that little critter over there."

He stared at the intended target and asked, "Why?"

"If we're right about them not being real, the red beam will distort the eyeball's projected image as it passes through an' hits the wall."

He grinned widely. "Hey, that's brilliant."

Haley gripped both hands around the gun and held it out in front of her. She carefully aligned the red beam on the eyeball, and the light distorted its image before hitting the wall. "See, we were right. They're nothing but projections."

Thinking back on all the pandemonium in Masterpiece Hall, Rane pushed his tongue against the tender spot inside his mouth and said, "I don't get it. If those eyeballs aren't real, how come I felt 'em pelting me on d'cheek?"

Haley turned the light switch off on her gun and put it back into her coat pocket. Staring back at the private eye, she replied, "The negative energy in this hologram must be affecting our senses somehow."

He rolled his eyes upward at the eyeball that had just perched itself on the crown of his head and said annoyingly, "D'last thing I need is more false signals t'me brain."

Thinking how ridiculous her husband looked with a winking eye nestled in his hair, she giggled slightly.

Haley dropped her smile and said, "It definitely proves how easily our human mind can be deceived. Don't it?"

"Aye."

Haley fished the eyeball out of his wavy, blond hair. After closely examining it, she said in a voice of astonishment, "It's only a false image appearing to be real, yet I believe I can feel it."

She slowly opened her hand like a blooming flower and allowed the private eye to fly away.

All at once the rest of the flying eyeballs came zipping around the corner from the far end of the hallway. Seeing the hateful sneer in their eyes, Rane said in a shaky, humorous tone, "Uuuuh, Haley, ye know how ye're always trying t'get me t'run with ye?"

Haley had her back turned to that side of the corridor and didn't know what he was talking about. "Yes?"

Rane stared wide-eyed at the fastly approaching eyeballs. "I decided now would be a good time."

He grabbed his wife by the hand and took off running with her down the hall. He was running so fast she could hardly keep up with him.

Haley turned her head to see what was chasing them and saw the eyeballs closing in. "Aagh!"

After running into a dead end in the hallway, she looked over at her husband, who was breathing heavily from the chase, and said, "Now what?"

Hearing the flapping sound of their batting eyelashes directly behind him, Rane started trembling all over as he slowly turned around to face his stalkers. Not wanting his wife to get shocked by their electricity, he stood in front of her. Although he was scared out of his wits, he tried to make light of the situation by speaking comically to the eyeballs. "Look, boys, haven't ye ever heard of d'expression, 'an eye for an eye'? Since ye've only got one, I'd say ye were at a bit of a disadvantage."

Haley sniggered under her breath at his remark.

Rane turned his head to look back at his giggling wife, and a couple of the angry eyeballs rammed themselves into his tummy. Caught off guard by the unexpected attack, he sucked in his abdominal muscles and shrieked frightfully.

Haley caught sight of something strange and queried, "Rane, did you see that?"

With a fearful look still on his face, Rane shook his head and replied, "No. I had me eyes closed."

While continuing to whisper back and forth with her husband, Haley pointed discreetly over his shoulder in the general direction of the private eyes and said, "When I was laughing at your joke, I saw one of the eyeballs break apart into tiny pieces and then disappear."

Keeping one eye on his attackers for any sudden moves, he replied, "Ye did?"

Haley nodded her head and answered in a helpful tone, "Here, do what I do."

Without hesitation, she commenced in putting on quite a show by rapidly blinking her eyelids at the private eyes. Feeling humorous about her pantomime, she started sniggering at herself.

Intimidated by the unfriendly look in their eyes, Rane clung to his old habits and began cracking his knuckles. "Uh, Haley, I don't think d'eyeball gang finds that very funny. I don't hear 'em laughing."

Haley widened her smile at her husband and kept on giggling. "They can't laugh, Rane. They don't have a mouth."

Thinking how foolish he must have sounded a moment ago, Rane muttered weakly under his breath, "Oh yeah."

All at once Haley recalled something the tour guide had said earlier. Thinking it was important, she stifled her gaiety and whispered, "Rane, remember what Prosperity said right before we left Masterpiece Hall?"

Intimidated by the way the eyeball gang was scowling at him, Rane wiped the sweat off his brow and whispered back in a high-strung voice, "No, I don't remember what she said. I can barely remember my own name right now."

While glancing intermittently at the scowling eyes, Haley placed her hand on her husband's shoulder and began sharing the information with him. "She said that extremely-high levels of positive energy could interfere with the computer's transmissions."

"Really?"

She nodded her head and then spoke to her husband like she was in deep thought. "The human brain responds to sensory input, right?"

Rane shrugged while keeping his gaze fixed on the sneering eyeballs, which were still hovering around them.

Haley took her small Bible out of her coat pocket and said in a low tone, "Then joy should increase the positive energy in our hearts."

"Sounds logical," he replied, still on edge.

Haley quickly thumbed to Psalm 126:2. Placing her index finger below the specific passage, she said with a smile, "Look, Chappy, God can fill our mouth with laughter."

Rane skimmed the scripture she was pointing at until he got startled by one of the private eyes thumping him on the cheek. "Ouch!"

He anxiously watched the eyeball fall back to join the others while whining, "But I don't feel like laughing right now, Haley."

She stuffed her Bible back into her coat pocket and whispered further, "Do it anyway, by faith."

"I can't."

All at once the same private eye, which had just attacked him, shot a volt of electricity out of its pupil that just missed Rane's head. He was so alarmed by the sudden hostility, he squealed to the top of his lungs, "Yiiiiigh!"

He then lowered the tone of his voice and whimpered to his wife, "I changed me mind. I can."

Haley looked down at the passage of scripture again and prayed aloud, "Heavenly Father, your Word is our wings. Each passage we take to heart fills us with joy an' makes us feel light as a feather. So tickle us with your Word until we get drunk with laughter. We ask you, in Jesus's name."

Rane took a step of faith and followed Haley's lead in laughing at the holograms. It wasn't long before the Holy Spirit flooded their hearts with laughter, and it came easy for them. They were laughing so hard they doubled over onto the floor. As the positive energy in their joy inundated the hall, the virtual images slowly began to disintegrate and then vanished into thin air.

After several minutes of giggling childishly, Haley picked herself up off the floor. "That was fun, my whole body felt light as a feather. Thank you, God."

Still chuckling like a little boy, Rane followed suit by getting up off the floor. "Aye, that it was. I haven't had a good laugh like that in a long time."

Once the excitement had died down, Haley cautiously looked around the corridor for any signs of the eyeballs and then whispered to her husband, "I think they're all gone."

"Good, now with nobody here, we can search d'entire gallery for clues," he said in a low tone of voice.

"Rane, to save time, why don't you check the rooms, an' I'll go have a look in the magazines on the table."

"All right," he replied and then watched his wife saunter off in the opposite direction.

CHAPTER 26

Rane tiptoed down the shadowy hall, checking room after room. Not finding anything that looked like a clue, he crept down to the next door with a gold-plated plaque on it that read *Adult Virtual Realities*. Aroused with curiosity, he opened the door and peeked inside. The second he saw the pornographic hologram, he screamed in horror and slammed the door closed.

Hearing his outcry from the lobby, Haley instinctively pulled her silver pistol and ran back to see what was wrong. Soon as she saw her husband with his head pinned against the door, breathing hard from the shock to his heart, she queried out of concern, "Chappy, are you all right?"

Rane lifted his head to make eye contact with his wife and then answered in a highly stressed state of mind, "No, Chappy is not all right."

He pointed a quivering thumb toward the door he was resting against and intensified the tone of his voice. "I don't think I'm ever going t'be all right after seeing what I just saw."

Haley noted the traumatized look on her husband's face and then eyed the words on the door. "What did ye see?"

Rane cupped his hands over his eyes, whimpering melodramatically, "Oh, it was horrible, Haley. Now me virgin eyes are tarnished."

"By what?"

"Pictures from Sodom an' Gomorrah."

She giggled at his theatrical performance while pulling his hands down from his eyes. "You don't actually expect me to believe that do you, Rane?"

He pouted his lips at her for doubting his word. "'Tis d'truth. Sodom an' Gomorrah is in there."

Feeling a sudden, chilly breeze come out of nowhere, Rane warmed his hands inside his coat pockets and peered guardedly down the hallway. "Let's get out of here. This place gives me d'creeps."

Driven by a strong desire to find her suspect, Haley crossed her arms and said adamantly, "Not until we check all the rooms."

Rane wiped the nervous perspiration off his forehead and replied, "I don't want to."

"Why not?"

He pointed his thumb toward the door a second time and whispered in a taxed voice, "If ye had seen what I just saw ye wouldn't want t'check 'em either."

She sniggered at his boyish behavior and headed down the hall. Still upset that she didn't believe his story, Rane heaved a tiresome sigh and reluctantly tagged after her.

Haley walked up to the next room and saw another gold-plated sign on the outside of the door. Reading the engraved words aloud, she said, "Private. Keep out!"

She turned toward her husband and stated, "I wonder what's in there."

Rane anxiously eyed the outside of the door and then looked down the corridor to see if anyone was coming. "Who cares? Come on, Haley. Let's go."

Haley ignored his request and reached for the doorknob. At that precise moment, Jillian opened the door from the other side and almost scared her half to death. "Aaagh!"

Rane looked back at Haley to see what had frightened her and was surprised to see his aunt standing in the doorway. He hadn't seen her in fourteen years and hoped she wouldn't recognize him.

Jillian stared hard at Rane's face until he ducked behind his wife. She then eyed the gun in Haley's hand and said in her Irish brogue, "Are ye blind, miss?"

Haley put her weapon away in her coat pocket to avoid any trouble and then humbled herself to the Irishwoman by being courteous. "No, ma'am. May I ask who you are?"

Jillian adjusted the dark sunglasses on her nose and answered snootily, "Jillian Finney, proprietor of this establishment."

She pointed at the gold plate on the door. "Didn't ye read d'sign? Ye can't come in here. No one is allowed t'see Lucky Jack's private collection but me."

Rane was a bundle of nerves as he tried to deter his wife from staying in the gallery. "She looks really mad, Haley. We better go."

He looked up at Jillian and discovered she had overheard him. Acting like a shy boy, he waved his fingers at her and chuckled, "Hello."

After listening intently to the sound of his voice, Jillian wrinkled her brow and asked suspiciously, "Do I know ye, laddie?"

Rane pointed to his chest and replied innocently, "Who? Me?"

"Yer face looks familiar."

Rane glanced over at his wife and saw the bewildered expression on her face. Hoping to draw the attention away from himself, he decided to laugh it off. "Oh that happens t'me all d'time, people thinking they know me. I guess I just got one o'them faces."

Haley removed her detective's badge out of her inside pocket and showed it to the woman. "Miss Finney, we didn't mean to cause any trouble. We came here looking for a kidnapper who bears a remarkable resemblance to your late brother. He goes by the name of Jack."

She put her badge away and then handed the woman the two playing cards out of her coat pocket. "You wouldn't happen to know of anyone who fits that description?"

Without even bothering to check, Jillian handed the cards right back to her and said coldly, "No, I wouldn't. Now we're closed, so ye two will have t'run along."

Rane motioned his hand toward the lobby and replied, "We can't. D'front door's locked."

With a callous expression on her face, Jillian said, "Then go out d'back door."

When she started to walk away, Haley dug her ink pen out of her husband's coat pocket and called out, "Miss Finney, wait!"

She quickly jotted down her cell phone number on the back of her free tour voucher and handed it to the woman.

Rane watched Jillian brush some of her strawberry-blond hair back from her face and inadvertently caught sight of the red earring in her left earlobe. Jumping to the conclusion that it was the kidnapper in disguise, he raised an arrogant voice. "Didn't think we'd find ye, eh, 'Napper?"

Totally in the dark as to what was going on, Haley exchanged a confused look with Jillian, thinking, *'Napper?*

Rane pinched Jillian hard on the cheek and said crossly, "Take that hideous-looking mask off. I know that's ye in disguise."

Aspired to stop him from offending the Irishwoman any further, Haley queried in a high-pitch, stressful tongue, "Rane, what are you doing?"

Jillian gnashed her teeth at Rane as she slapped his hand off her cheek. "How dare ye talk t'me like that?"

Unsure what to do next, Haley slipped her pen back into her husband's pocket and said uneasily to Jillian, "Um … if you happen to see anyone who fits the description on the cards, you will call us, right?"

Not a bit interested in helping her solve her case, Jillian cast a vengeful eye on Rane and replied, "D'only Jack I see is this wee grasshopper, an' I'm going t'plant his disrespectful tail out in d'snow."

Straight away, she grabbed Rane tightly around the throat and hoisted him high into the air.

Crying out for mercy on his behalf, Haley whimpered, "No, don't hurt him."

Rane tried to peel his aunt's long, bony fingers off his throat, but her grip was too strong for him. Out of desperation he clutched onto the gold chain around her neck and unintentionally flung the talisman into view, which was formerly hidden underneath her black sweater.

Watching her husband's eyes protrude out of their sockets from being strangled, Haley suddenly felt cold, raw fear clamping down on her heart like a vice, causing it to pound faster. Her mouth was dry, and she couldn't seem to focus her brain on what to do next. She didn't know why she was feeling this way. She was a well-trained detective and had been in much tougher spots than this.

Rane gasped for air as Jillian squeezed harder on his neck. Turning blue in the face from a lack of oxygen to his brain, he looked down at his wife and wheezed in a barely audible voice, "Haley, help me."

Haley managed to suppress her fears and pulled her smart gun. Praying earnestly in her mind, she thought, *Please, Lord, I need your help.*

Holding the neural wave disruptor with both hands, she aimed the laser sight's red dot at Jillian's forehead and demanded, "Let him go, Miss Finney."

At that exact moment, Jillian received a message from the android on a frequency only she could hear. "Don't kill him. D'fingerprints checked out."

Jillian grinned at Rane while whispering to the robot under her breath, "I knew it."

Haley increased the power in the tone of her voice. "I said, 'Let him go!'"

With a smug look on her face, Jillian replied in a feigned, compliant tone, "Why I'd be happy to, Detective."

Still holding poor Rane by the neck, Jillian took off down the hall heading for the back door.

Fearing for her husband's life, Haley tried to shoot the woman in the back of the head with the disruptor. When the weapon wouldn't fire, she smacked the heel of her hand against the barrel and tried again. Still not receiving any help from the bot, she hit the gun a couple more times and said frustratingly, "Come on, Reddy, what's the matter with ye? Engage!"

Haley finally gave up on the idea and chased after Rane. Just as she caught up with him, she saw Jillian hurl him out the back door.

CHAPTER 27

Jillian watched the sensor security lights kick on in the backyard as Rane bounced end-over-end across the snow. When he plowed face-first into a pile of fresh powder under an old, leafless tree, she snickered cruelly, "Come back t'see me when ye're all grown up, grasshopper."

Rane sat upright on his buttocks, sneering at his aunt while wiping cold flakes of snow off his nose and mouth. Seeing her scowl back at him, he gave her a raspberry and then mocked her feminine accent by saying, "Come back t'see me when ye're all grown up."

Haley dashed out the back door in hot pursuit of her husband and saw him sitting in the snow, spitting bits of bloody ice out of his mouth. She put her pistol away in her pocket and hurried over to his side. "Rane, are you hurt?"

Rane spit more blood on the ground before answering in a sarcastic tone, "No, couldn't be better."

He gently touched his bruised mouth and added, "'Cause o'ye, I now have a busted lip t'go with d'broken foot ye gave me."

Haley cleared her throat uncomfortably at his accusation and said nothing in her defense.

Jillian got distracted from Rane's discomfiture when she suddenly heard another high frequency message from the robot. "Be careful, sis. Agents Lorrell and Jamison just drove up in a white van in d'alley across d'street."

While keeping her ear glued on every word the android was saying, Jillian went back inside the gallery and closed the door. "Let Rane an' d'detective search d'gallery, but not until after nine. I want t'run some more tests on d'security system first. 'Tis imperative we know every move she an' d'boy makes. Before allowing 'em in, make sure ye lead d'agents away from d'building. We don't want any interference from British Intelligence. Transmission out."

Haley was secretly relieved that Jillian had left them alone and tried pulling her husband to his feet.

Rane was still humiliated over what his aunt had done to him and took it out on his wife by pushing her away. "I don't need yer help. I can get up by myself, thank ye."

He slowly picked himself up off the ground and looked over at the back door. Expressing his hatred for Jillian aloud, he snarled, "What a witch! Boy, I'd love t'get even with her."

Hoping to turn his thoughts away from the ill-bred speech, Haley said in a soft tone, "You can't. The King told us to pray for our enemies."

He spit more blood out of his mouth. "Fine, I'll put d'old battle-ax on me prayer list. Goodness knows she needs it."

"Rane, we're not warring with flesh an' blood but with wicked spirits that influence the human mind to do evil acts."

"Oh she's under d'influence all right."

Haley tried to reason with him as she watched him brush the flakes of snow off the front of his pants. "Rane, you pinched her cheek. What did you think she was going to do, jump for joy?"

Rane mulled over his previous actions and then chuckled, "No, I guess not."

Using the handkerchief she had just taken out of her coat pocket, Haley wiped some blood off his chin and asked, "Why did you pinch her anyway?"

"I thought she was d'kidnapper in disguise."

Rane felt stupid when she started sniggering at him and tried not to let it show in his reply. "She could be. She was wearing d'same earring as Lucky Jack's."

Haley smiled at his handsome mug and started picking bits of snowy ice out of his hair. "Not likely."

An eyebrow went up as he queried out of pride, "An' just why not, Sherlock?"

"Well, unless our suspect is a fantastic illusionist, there are a couple of things a top-heavy woman can't hide."

Rane's face flushed red with embarrassment. "Oops!"

Haley took the bloodstained handkerchief out of his hand and then threw it into a nearby receptacle. After looking around at the ten-foot privacy wall that surrounded the premises, she drew her eyes onto the eight, colorful fairies sculptured out of marble. The female pixies stood about a foot tall and were displayed in different areas around the grounds. Although they had flakes of snow on them, she could still see the shiny gold speckles on their cheeks. Their sparkling wings and long hair were painted to match the specific color of their dress.

Haley frowned at the idea of anyone putting their faith in the spirit of magic instead of God and then strolled back over to her husband.

Rane shook the snow off the bottom of his black turtleneck sweater as Haley walked up to him. Still bitter over what his aunt did to him, he said, "Being nice t'that witch is going t'take a miracle. She is definitely demon-possessed. No woman has strength like that. I tried loosing her grip from me neck with both hands an' couldn't do it."

Mulling over the confrontation in the back of her mind, Haley stated in an uplifted voice of relief, "I'm just grateful to God I didn't have to shoot her."

Rane felt his swollen lips and cringed. Agreeing with his wife in an insincere tone of voice, he replied, "Oh me too."

Staring in the direction of the gallery, Haley's analytical nature caused her to question Jillian's behavior. "Who was she talking to anyway?"

Rane grumbled derisively under his breath, "I imagine d'devil himself."

Haley looked vacantly at her husband and said, "An' why was she wearing sunglasses? The sun is not out, an' she's obviously not blind."

Rane cradled his badly bruised neck and answered, "Aye, she had no problem finding my throat, that's for sure."

Haley stood quietly for several moments and then pulled the silver pistol out of her coat pocket. Letting the bot know she disapproved of his insubordination, she questioned him in a reprimanding tone, "Reddy, why didn't you engage when I told you to?"

A red bead of light pulsated inside the small, round diamond in the top-center portion of the gun as the bot replied in a serious, British voice, "Could not comply. The Locust 52257 distorted your sound waves so they could not be understood by my translator."

Haley sighed heavily at the bot's defense. She didn't like the fact that Reddy had been outsmarted by another robot. But she was pleased that he would not fire without identifying her voice command. Rane set it up that way for her protection in case a suspect managed to pull her gun. "Were you at least able to get an energy reading on Jillian's sunglasses?"

"Affirmative."

"What did you find?"

"The object is photosynthetic an' has the capability to record an' send phonemes directly to the android's neural net by use of the satellite. It works in correlation with a microchip implanted underneath the skin on her forehead."

"Can she see without the glasses?"

"Not very well, Detective."

"If she's using the android's neural net to produce visual impressions, where is the video camera?"

"Hidden inside her glasses."

"How does it work?"

"Processing unit translates visual images into sounds, which are then fed through the hearing device in her left earlobe."

"You mean like synesthsia?"

"Affirmative. Jillian's central nervous system has been retrained to accept auditory data as a surrogate for visual data."

Haley reconsidered the bot's analysis and asked, "Reddy, is the android using the microchip to influence Jillian?"

"Affirmative. The robot is forming pictures inside her mind through the words he speaks."

Rane decided to test the bot's theory by meditating on the word "candy." When a picture of cherry jellybeans suddenly popped up inside his mind's eye, he licked his lips as if he could actually taste them and thought, *Hey, it really works.*

Haley decided to question the smart gun to find out the secret behind Jillian's incredible strength. "How strong is she?"

The flashing red bead of light continued to keep time with Reddy's sound waves as he replied, "She can easily lift several hundred pounds."

"How?" she queried curiously.

"She has neural arm implants that are wired to respond to her brain waves."

Shocked by the disclosure, Rane raised his voice. "Her arms are synthetic?"

"Affirmative."

Thinking back on the incident in the gallery where Jillian easily lifted him into the air with one hand, Rane said to Haley, "That explains a lot."

Haley nodded her head to agree and then threw another question at the bot. "Reddy, did Jillian's analysis show any signs of burn marks on her shoulders?"

"Affirmative. Tissue scan showed severe scarring on both shoulders."

Rane looked puzzlingly at Haley and asked, "Why did ye ask him that?"

"I remember Prosperity telling us that Jillian saved the Locust 52257 from being destroyed in the fire."

"Ye think that's how she lost her arms?"

Haley nodded her head.

She put her weapon back inside her coat pocket, recalling something she had seen earlier. "Rane, did you notice the gold charm Jillian was wearing around her neck?"

Rane wiped some snow off the shoulder of his jacket while expressing more of his bitterness toward his aunt. "O'course I did. I was thinking about choking her with it."

She picked bits of ice out of his hair as she queried, "Rane, why do people wear amulets?"

He eyed one of the marble, fairy statues on the ground and replied, "'Cause they believe once a charm is inscribed with a magic spell, it has d'power t'protect 'em from being cursed."

Rane paused briefly to think about his aunt's nasty disposition and said, "O'course in Jillian's case, I think she's a wee late for that one."

Haley shook her head to show she disapproved of his slanderous remark. "Oh, Chappy."

Seeing she was displeased with him, Rane tried to justify his carnal character. "I can't help it. I didn't ask t'be cursed with this bad, Irish temperament."

"You forget you're a blessed king now," she said encouragingly.

"Aye," he answered in a revelatory tone. "I'll keep trying t'remember that."

Haley continued removing the fragments of ice out of his hair, not knowing that her husband was secretly enjoying the sensation of her gentle touch. In fact he was enjoying it so much he began to imagine himself kissing her. When she saw the euphoric look in his eyes, she became curious and asked, "What are you thinking about, Rane?"

Under pressure by her unexpected inquiry, his eyes darted about as he answered in an almost sopranic tone. "What am I thinking about?"

She removed a tube of cherry-flavored lip balm from her coat pocket and replied, "Uh-huh."

Rane's speech stammered slightly as he began cracking his knuckles. "I, uh . . . "

Afraid she might rag on him if he told her about his romantic fantasy, Rane decided to change the subject. "So what did ye find out in d'magazines?"

Haley considered all the write-ups she had browsed through and weighed the information against what she had heard while inside the gallery. "Nothing that they hadn't told us about already."

After smearing the lip balm over her lips, she put it back into her coat pocket and took out her cell phone.

Watching her open the lid on the phone, he asked, "Who are ye calling?"

Haley pushed the automatic dial on her cell phone and replied, "My dad. I'm going to see if I can get a search warrant out here."

Rane held up his hands in strong protest and said in a jittery tongue, "Uh-huh, count me out. I'm not going back in there."

Haley giggled at his cowardness. "Don't worry, I'll hold your hand."

She then stepped away for a moment to talk in private with her dad. When she returned, she put her cell phone back inside her coat pocket and sighed unhappily.

Seeing the disappointment written all over her face, Rane queried, "What's wrong?"

"My dad told me that my reasonable suspicion isn't enough to get me a search warrant. He said unless you want to press charges against Jillian for battery, there's nothing he can do to help us."

Rane pointed toward the back door of the gallery and said, "Believe me, my carnal mind would love nothing more than t'see her evil bum rot in prison, but on d'other hand, d'King inside me would have a problem with that."

All at once Haley felt her cell phone vibrating inside her coat and retrieved it out of her pocket. "Oh good, maybe my dad changed his mind about getting me that search warrant."

After checking the view window to see who was calling, she shook her head at her husband and said, "No, it is not him."

She opened the lid on the phone and held the receiver up to her mouth. Giving a friendly greeting to the caller, she said, "Hello."

The second she heard the Irishwoman's voice on the other end of the line, she widened her eyes in surprise and mouthed her name to her husband. "It's Jillian."

Rane, too, was shocked when he heard who it was and promptly mouthed back the woman's name. "Jillian?"

Haley nodded her head at her husband and then continued talking on the phone. "May I ask why you changed your mind, ma'am?"

Hoping to hear some of their conversation, Rane cocked his ear to the phone and said quietly, "What does she want?"

Haley covered her left hand over the receiver and whispered back, "She said she feels bad for the way she treated us."

Doubting his aunt's word, Rane crossed his arms and said, "Oh sure."

"So she's going to allow us to search the gallery for our suspect."

He chuckled condescendingly. "Like we can trust her."

Haley lifted her hand from the receiver and carried on with her conversation with Jillian. When she had finished talking to her, she closed the lid on her cell phone and said to her husband, "We can come back in, but not until after nine."

Highly suspicious, he queried, "An' just why do we have t'wait until then?"

"She claims she has to get ready to go out tonight for an important meeting with one of her clients."

He shifted his gaze toward the gallery for a moment and asked, "How are we supposed t'get in?"

"She said she would leave the back door open."

"Uh-huh," he said with a great deal of cynicism in his voice. "I bet we're walking right into a trap."

Haley checked the time on her cell phone and then put it back inside her coat pocket. "That gives us about an hour. While we're waiting, why don't we go grab a quick bite to eat?"

Rane shook his head and said, "I can't."

"Why not?"

He touched his sore, bottom lip as he replied, "'Cause I'm broke, that's why."

Haley placed her hand inside his coat pocket and said, "Since it is your birthday, it will be my treat."

Rane gave her annoyed look. "Would ye please get yer hand out o'me pocket?"

She slipped her free hand inside his other coat pocket and giggled teasingly, "My hands are cold."

"Why can't ye warm 'em in yer own pockets?"

She drew her tempting cherry lips closer to his and said fervently, "'Cause I like your's better."

Feeling timid from the desire in her emerald eyes, Rane pulled his head back from hers and said, "Take yer hands out o'me pockets, an' I'll go with ye ... on one condition."

"What's that?"

He lifted his chin in a smug manner and replied, "Let me borrow some money for candy."

She removed her hands from his pockets and said eagerly, "All right, it is a date."

After driving clear across town, Jack parked his black Cadillac across the street from the British Intelligence Agency. The bureau offices were housed inside a clean, white, three-story building. There were twelve stairs that led up to two huge columns on opposite ends of the main entrance. Embedded on the outside of the structure was the agency's emblem. The large round seal was trimmed in gold with the acronym B.I.A. in the center, also in gold. On the right side of the building was a parking lot for government officials. Visitors had to park around back. The grounds were well kept, bushes and naked trees regularly pruned by a professional landscaper.

Working to carry out Jillian's plan of espionage, Jack quickly altered his face to look exactly like Lorrell's. He then called Gary from his private car phone. He had prerecorded the agent's restricted number when he called Aileen at the gallery.

Gary saw the agent's face on his mobile phone and thought it was really him. "What's up, Lorrell?"

Making sure to keep his left earlobe out of the view of the camera inside his phone, Jack disguised his voice to sound like Lorrell's. "Gary, we need you to come down to the gallery at once."

"Is there any trouble?"

"I can't risk talking to you about it over the phone. Jamison an' I will be waiting for you in the van across the street."

"Okay, I'll be there quick as I can."

About five minutes after his conversation with the charlatan, Gary came hurrying out of the bureau with his brown brief case in hand, heading for the parking lot. After climbing into his beige sedan, which was parked in one of the government official slots, he started his car and drove out of the lot.

Pleased that his plan was working perfectly, Jack grinned as Gary drove off down the main street. Once the agent was out of sight, he hid his lucky talisman underneath his shirt and placed a Band-aid over his left earlobe. After altering his appearance and clothing to look like Gary's, he got out of his car and ran across the street.

Upon entering the building through one of the side, glass doors, Jack noticed the security checkpoint and the two armed guards standing by the x-ray machine. The night guard on the right quit chatting with his partner to acknowledge who he believed to be Gary. "Did you forget something, Mr. Brown?"

Not wanting the guard to get suspicious, Jack placed his hand over the Band-aid and pretended like he was rubbing an itch. "Yes. I left my cell phone back in my office."

The night guard nodded as if he understood and then let him go by without being searched.

Jack walked fast around the corner to escape the guard's view and got on the nearest elevator. After checking the map on the wall to find out where Gary's office was located, he got off on the third floor. Once he had made his way down the hall to the agency, he opened the glass door and went inside.

Gary's secretary was working late and hung up the phone as he walked into the room. "Is there a problem, sir?"

While answering her question, Jack scanned the place and discovered there were quite a few office cubicles with big glass windows. "I forgot I had to send some very important documents to parliament this afternoon."

"Is there anything I can do to help?"

Since Jack didn't know that Gary's office was the one closest to his secretary, he decided to trick the woman into showing him. Seeing a teapot sitting on a white table in the left corner of the room, he replied, "Bring a cup of tea into my office."

With a confused look on her face, the woman asked, "Tea, sir?"

His voice became stern when she hesitated to reply to his request. "Yes. I would like some tea brought into my office if that's not too much trouble."

Not wanting to offend him, his secretary humbled herself by saying, "No, sir. I'll get it for you right away."

She got up out of her chair and hurried over to where the teapot was located. After pouring him a cup of hot tea, she turned around and caught sight of the Band-aid wrapped around his left earlobe. Voicing a heartfelt concern for his well-being, she queried, "What happened to your ear, Mr. Brown?"

Jack touched the ear she indicated and answered eye-openingly, "Oh, the Band-aid."

He quickly sifted through the human responses in his database and picked one as his excuse. "I put it there to stop the bleeding. I scratched an itch an' accidentally cut it with my fingernail."

She set the teapot back down on the table and replied, "I see."

The secretary carried the cup and a saucer into Gary's office, which was the first office down the hall, and set them on his chestnut wood desk.

Jack followed her into the room and closed the white blinds so no one could see in. "Hold all my calls. I don't want to be disturbed."

"As you wish, sir," she replied courteously and then left the room, closing the door behind her.

After she had gone, Jack locked the door. He sat down in Gary's brown leather swivel chair and proceeded to scope out the office.

When Jack had finished snooping around inside Gary's desk drawers, he picked up his cup of tea and walked over to inspect the government computer. After discovering that the operating system was run completely by voice commands, he faced the giant screen and said, "Good afternoon, BIA."

A dim light pulsated on the screen as BIA responded to his greeting in a friendly, feminine, British voice. "Good afternoon, Gary Povel Brown. I see you're wearing a Band-aid. Did you hurt yourself, sir?"

He touched his earlobe and replied, "No. I merely scratched it, that's all."

"What can I do for you, Gary?"

"Commence scan for top-secret clearance."

Immediately after his demand was made, BIA changed the picture of the government emblem on the screen to a huge eyeball. "Position right eye in front of scanner."

Jack moved closer to the screen and allowed BIA to scan his eye.

After the ray of light disappeared, BIA replied, "Retina scan completed."

The view on the screen changed to show a picture of a giant palm.

"Place right hand on screen," BIA requested in a gentle but firm voice.

Jack shifted his cup of tea over to his opposite hand and placed his palm against the monitor.

Once he had complied, BIA gave it a thorough examination and said, "Fingerprint check completed. Gary Povel Brown, Agent Identification Number 00194385, you are cleared for top secret information."

Pleased that he had fooled the computer into believing he was the real deal, Jack spread a conceited smirk across his face and then proceeded to give orders to the government computer. "BIA, search for all archives on Jillian Selare Finney, Homicide Code Jsf133#65068m."

"Processing request, sir."

After several moments went by, miniature icons that looked like silver disks appeared on the screen. "Search completed. Six archives were found. Would you like me to open these files, Mr. Brown?"

He gripped the handle on his teacup and said, "No. Destroy all records, including any back-up files."

"Warning, archives will be permanently erased from the government net."

"Understood."

"Do you still wish me to proceed?"

"Yes. How long will it take?"

"Approximately thirty seconds."

Jack took a sip of tea from his cup before answering, "Very good, commence abolition now."

"Is that tea you're drinking, Gary?"

Suspicious why BIA had asked him that question, he hesitated to answer. "Yes. Why?"

"Just curious, sir."

The silver disks on the screen started flashing rapidly as BIA stated, "Destruction of archives in process."

Jack grinned naughtily and polished off the rest of the tea. Once he had completed his venture, he opened back up the blinds, grabbed the saucer off Gary's desk, and came out of his office. After putting the dirty cup and saucer back on the white table, he walked over to the secretary and said, "I'm going to my meeting with Lorrell now. I should be back within a couple of hours."

"Very good, sir."

About thirty minutes later, the real Gary Brown walked back into the room with a confused look on his face.

His secretary watched him scratch the back of his head and asked, "Is something wrong, Mr. Brown?"

Upset that he had been sent on a wild goose chase, Gary didn't answer her. He just stormed into his office and slammed the door behind him.

She looked toward the outside of his door and said coolly, "I'll take that as a yes."

CHAPTER 29

Rane and Haley got a quick bite to eat downtown and subsequently stopped into a candy shop afterward. While browsing the four glass cases filled with tempting treats, Rane said, "I feel like I died an' went t'heaven."

After taking careful thought to what he wanted, he finally selected a bag of cherry jellybeans and a pack of grape-flavored bubble gum and paid for it out of the cash he had borrowed from his wife. Following her out of the store, he eagerly tore open the top of the plastic wrap and scooped out a handful of the candied beans. Cramming them all into his mouth, he moaned pleasurably, "Mmm."

While they were strolling down the snow-covered sidewalk looking at the Christmas lights and decorations, Haley spotted a couple of sweethearts throwing snowballs at each other from across the street. Still wishing for romance back into her own life, she stopped to watch them, giggling at their jollity.

Rane swallowed the glob of sugar in his mouth before asking, "What's so funny?"

Haley inhaled the cool fresh air through her nose and let it out through her mouth. Enjoying the ambience all around her, she said spiritedly, "Chappy, don't you just feel the love in the air?"

He gazed up at the dark sky, noting the snowfall had slackened somewhat, and answered, "No."

As they were busy talking, the bot climbed out of Haley's pocket and jumped into a pile of snow below.

Haley inadvertently glanced at the ground and was surprised to see Reddy playing in the snow.

Reddy looked up at her with a big grin on his face and said, "Look, Haley, I'm building a snowman."

She smiled back at his cute, little face and then got a gleam in her eyes. Hoping to bring out the playful boy in the heart of her husband, she grabbed him by the arm and said, "Hey, Chappy, I've got a great idea."

Imagining the worst, he whined under his breath, "Oh no, not again."

"While we're waiting to go back inside the gallery, why don't we build a snowman?"

Shocked by her suggestion, he chuckled, "Are ye daft? 'Tis freezing cold out here."

"Oh come on, let's have some fun."

Haley crouched down on the ground and picked up a pile of snow. After forming it into a snowball, she threw it at her husband's mug and giggled, "Got ye last."

While groaning under his breath to keep his cool, Rane wiped the snow crystals off his chin and mouth.

Continuing to act childish, Haley scooped up another pile of snow off the ground and powdered him in the face with it. "Got ye last, again." She sniggered a second time.

He brushed the flakes of snow off his nose, trying hard not to laugh at her silliness. He had to admit he found her zeal for life quite humorous.

Reddy decided to get in on the excitement too. He took the head off his snowman and hurled it at his inventor's face, chuckling goofily, "Got ye last."

Rane pursed his lips and slowly wiped the bits of ice off his cheek. Tired of being picked on, he stuffed his bag of candy inside his coat pocket and said, "All right, ye two, three can play at this game."

When he knelt down on the ground and started gathering a heap of snow, Haley picked up the bot from off the ground and said, "Uh-oh."

Reddy widened his eyes at what his inventor was doing and said worriedly, "I think a snowstorm's coming our way, Haley. We better take cover."

He then leaped out of her hand and into her coat pocket.

Haley looked down at the bot and replied, "Don't worry, Reddy, I'll zip you up until the storm blows over."

Haley had barely got the zipper down on her pocket when she saw her husband coming after her with a huge pile of snow in his hands. She squealed like an excited toddler and took off running down the street.

It didn't take long before Rane caught up with his wife and pelted her in the back of the head with snow. Enjoying being a little boy again, he said teasingly, "Got ye last, haha … hahaha."

Right away she mimicked his childish game by retaliating with a big chunk of snow and saying, "Got ye last, haha … hahaha."

Rane threw numerous snowballs in Haley's direction, but his aim was not as good as hers. Feeling like he was losing the snowball war, he grabbed his giggling wife around the waist and wrestled her to the ground. Being winded, he tripped over her leg and landed on top of her. While staring uncertainly into her captivating green eyes, he heard the clock tower gong the half-hour and suddenly recalled the night he walked out on his wife.

It was around midnight when Rane stormed out to his old beater of a car that he had parked out front of their flat. The faded blue paint on his coupe had rusted away in quite a few places. He sighed unhappily at his corroded hubcaps that he had duct-taped to the tires to keep them from falling off and opened the squeaky door. He threw his luggage onto the passenger seat and heard a couple of cats fighting. When he looked up and down the street and couldn't see them anywhere, he climbed inside his vehicle and slammed the door closed. The night air was quite nippy so he pressed his fist against his cold lips and blew his warm breath on it several times. Unable to see out of his windshield from it being covered in snow, he put his key into the ignition and turned on the wipers. After the blades cleared most of the flurries off the glass, he tried to start up the engine. When it failed to turn over after several attempts, he pounded the heel of his hand against the steering wheel, squealing out of frustration, "Ugh! Ye lousy, piece o'junk!"

To make matters worse, his palm got stuck to one of the pieces of duct tape that was holding his steering wheel together. He ripped the adhesive strip off his hand and wound up getting it caught on his left thumb. While trying to shake it off, he threw a big, hissy fit. "Ye gumby! I hate ye, I hate ye, I hate ye!"

Rane finally managed to get the tape off his thumb and back onto the steering wheel. He was so mad, it took several moments for him just to calm down. Desiring his emotional pacifier, he opened his suitcase and took out the jar of cherry jellybeans. After unscrewing the lid, he dumped a pile of the candied beans into his mouth. Munching contentedly on the glazed sugar, he replaced the lid on the jar and put it back inside his luggage. All at once he thought about his new time travel device and the blueprints he had put inside his coat pocket earlier in the day. He pulled them out of his jacket and started admiring the craftsmanship he had put into designing the mechanism. The gadget looked like a shiny gold sphere with twelve flashing red lights around the center. It also had a small, crystal window embedded in the top-portion of the ball for displaying the date and time. While considering the possibility of time travel, he grinned and said, "Ye're going t'be my ticket out o'here."

He adjusted the two levers on the right side of the crystal window to reset the date to December 1, 2018, and the time to noon. He thought about the fight he just had with his wife and felt guilty about leaving her. Peering out the windshield at their Christmas wreath on the front door, he said tearfully, "Maybe in d'future, I can forget d'past."

Rane sequentially tapped the red lights around the middle of the globe to unlock the upper half of the sphere. Once he had it opened, he took a small screwdriver out of his glove box and started fiddling around with the wires inside. While connecting a red and blue one, he had more gloomy thoughts about abandoning his wife. He was so distracted he crossed the wrong wires. All at once a strong current of electricity shot out of the center of the device and started shaking him violently. Immediately afterward, he and his car vanished into thin air.

The next thing Rane remembered was waking up at noon in his vehicle. He peered out the window at his neighborhood but didn't recognize the place. "How did I get here?"

He stared curiously at the time travel device, still in his hand, and said, "An' where did this thingamabob come from?"

He noticed the date and time flashing inside the view screen and said, "December first twenty eighteen? Must be some sort of alarm clock or something."

Rane turned the gold sphere as he examined it more closely and then looked down at the blueprints on his lap. "I think some gumby's playing a little joke on me."

Not recollecting what the items were, he saw a garbage truck driving down the street and tossed the blueprints and the globe into the back of it. He then brushed his hands together like he was wiping off dirt and said in a resentful voice, "People always dumping their garbage on me, they have absolutely no respect for d'poor."

Rane started his car and then drove off down the street.

Haley heard the beeper going off on her cell phone and said in disappointment, "Oh, is our time up already?"

Rane snapped out of his dreamlike state and helped his wife to her feet. "Time sure flies when ye're having fun."

She smiled at his comment and then walked with him to the bus stop at the end of the street.

The bus dropped Rane and Haley off at the closest bus stop to the gallery and then sped away in a loud whir, leaving a trail of smoke behind.

Carrying on with their conversation they started before climbing off the bus, Haley said in a voice of shock, "You threw your project for Parliament in the trash?"

Rane let a couple of pedestrians pass by them before answering in a forlornly tone, "Aye, an' d'blueprints too."

Wondering how she was going to pay back the money he had already spent from his government grant, she queried in a stressful tone, "Don't you remember any of it?"

Rane wracked his brain for several moments and finally shook his head. "No. Not a stitch."

Haley followed her husband down the sidewalk and said glumly under her breath, "A scientific breakthrough, tossed out with the garbage."

Overhearing what she said, Rane raised a defensive voice. "I didn't know what it was at d'time, or I wouldn't have thrown it away."

Haley waited until he quieted down before bringing up the night he walked out on her. She just had to know how he could vanish from her life without a trace. "So where have you been for the past year?"

"In some time warp, I think."

She thought about his dream he had told her about earlier and said, "Time warp?"

Rane nodded, wracking his brain to recall every detail of the mishap. "Apparently, I couldn't enter time that didn't exist yet, so the time device suspended my particles in animation until December first twenty eighteen. The last thing I remember is waking up in my car. Me life with ye was a total blank, like that part never existed."

Haley was a bit hurt that he had somehow blocked her out of his memory and tried not to let it show.

"So how did ye know where t'find me?" he asked out of sheer curiosity.

Thinking about the voice mail her dad had left on her cell phone around eight o'clock in the morning, she bit her lip nervously before giving him an answer. "I, um, filed a missing persons report on you. The department called me when they located your new address."

"Oh."

Feeling the wind's chill numbing his lips, Rane pulled his black turtleneck collar over his nose like he was a bank robber and said, "Is it time t'go in yet? Me face is starting t'freeze."

Haley checked the time on her cell phone and answered, "Yes, but we should give her another ten minutes just to be sure."

Yanking his sweater down from his face, he said in a disconcerted, boisterous tongue, "Another ten minutes?"

She gave him a sympathetic look as she slipped her phone back inside her pocket.

Rane lowered the tone of his voice to a grumble. "If I stay out here another ten minutes, ye won't have t'bother building that snowman."

"Why?" she queried while unzipping her coat pocket to check on Reddy.

Brushing flakes of snow off his shoulders, he answered, “Ye can stick a corn pipe in my mouth an’ admire me.”

Haley giggled faintly at his pun. “Admire you. You make me laugh, Chappy.”

Feeling his mood dropping, Rane dug into his candy bag and took out a handful of jellybeans.

Reddy lifted his head out of the pocket and saw his inventor popping the colored beans into his mouth, one by one. With a longing look in his eyes, he extended his palm toward Rane and asked, “Can I have a jellybean, Whiz Kid?”

Rane tossed the last jellybean he had left in his hand into his mouth and said, “No. Ye don’t have any teeth.”

The tiny bot widened his baby blue eyes and replied fretfully, “Oh no, Reddy boy’s got bugs an’ no teeth?”

Haley giggled at the bot as he felt around inside his mouth. She then eyed the spiral notepad her husband had just taken out of his pocket and said, “Rane, let me see that for a minute. I want to go over the clues.”

“Sure,” he replied in a pleasant voice and handed her the booklet.

Haley skimmed over the notes he had written down, turning the pages as she read. “How could the suspect have no blood or fingerprints?”

“I dunno.”

“The only way that could be possible is if he or she is an android.”

Rane snickered at her suggestion before bringing her thoughts back down to earth. “Ye forget, lassie, robots don’t smoke, an’ they don’t have human skin.”

She handed him back the notepad, sighing in surrender to his better judgment. “You’re right. Well, we better head back to the gallery before Jillian changes her mind.”

Just as Rane and Haley turned the corner to stake out the gallery, she spotted a black limousine parked out front. Afraid the chauffeur might see them, she pushed her husband back and ducked with him behind a brick building.

Rane queried in a low tone, "What's d'matter?"

Haley peeked around the side of the structure they were hiding behind and saw the driver helping Jillian into the rear of the car. Looking back at her husband, she motioned her head toward the gallery and whispered, "Check it out. It's Jillian an' her chauffeur."

Rane took a quick glimpse across the street at the man climbing into the driver's seat of the limousine and asked, "Do ye think they saw ye?"

Haley shook her head and kept a vigilant eye on the limo as the chauffeur drove off down the street. When a white van suddenly drove out of a nearby alley and started following the limo at a distance, Haley questioned it in the back of her mind. She waited until both vehicles had turned right at the stoplight and then came out of hiding.

"Rane, didn't it look like that van was following Jillian?" Haley queried.

Rane huddled close to his wife and whispered in jest, "So ye think she's being tailed by secret agents?"

"Quit making fun of me, Rane. I'm being serious."

He snickered at her some more. "I think ye've been watching too many detective movies, Hal."

The instant she heard her nickname, Haley put a delighted smile on her face.

Uncomfortable about the way she was looking at him, Rane asked, "What?"

"You haven't called me Hal in a long time."

Not quite sure what to say, Rane made a nervous tug on the front of his turtleneck sweater and picked another topic. "Are ye ready t'go in now?"

She glanced down the street at the stoplight and replied, "No. We better wait a few more minutes to make sure they don't come back for anything."

Rane rubbed his cold hands together and suggested, "While we're waiting, why don't we go get that hot tea?"

Haley watched several cars pass by before replying, "You go. I'm going to stay here an' keep an eye on things."

Noting the serious expression as she stared at the front of the gallery, Rane queried uneasily, "Do ye think d'kidnapper might show back up here tonight?"

"If he does, we've got to be real careful. I'm not trying to scare you, but the man that pushed me down had incredible strength. I don't think he's going to let us haul him off to jail without a fight."

Pretending as if he wasn't afraid, Rane lifted his chin and boasted, "No problem. I can take him. I'll put some fancy karate moves on him that I learned from me dojo master."

Immediately after the bragging words spewed off his tongue, Rane started showing off for his wife by imitating the sounds and techniques of a karate master. "Whoooa! Eeeeya! Eiya!"

While watching her husband make karate chops and kicks into the air, she giggled. "You look ridiculous."

Rane's puffed up ego remained unchanged as he replied, "I bet ye didn't know I had a black belt in karate. Pretty impressive, eh?"

Haley kept on sniggering at his arrogance.

Rane didn't like the fact that she wasn't taking him seriously. Thinking he could intimidate her, he used his right hand to make a quick karate chop motion toward her nose and shouted in an energetic tone, "Yeeeeah!"

The second she flinched, he gave her a conceited smirk and said, "Scared ye, eh?"

Feeling like he needed to be taught a lesson, Haley grabbed Rane by the same hand he used to almost hit her in the face and hollered boisterously, "Kiiiyah!"

She then swiftly used a judo technique on him, called the *Tai otoshi* or body drop, and flipped him onto his back.

Rane was completely caught off guard by her offensive maneuver and crashed hard onto a pile of snow on the ground. Lifting his dazed head, he peered up at her with his eyes crossed, groaning as if he was in misery, "Ooh, I think ye broke me back."

Haley looked down at her husband and said in a feisty tone, "I bet you didn't know I had a black belt in judo. Pretty impressive, huh?"

He rolled his bemused eyes at her and let the back of his head thunk against the snow.

She put her hands on her hips and continued giving him a piece of her mind. "No matter how good you think you are, Rane, there's always someone better."

"Ooh, Lord, out of all d'lassies ye could have picked for me, why her?" Rane complained.

He slowly got up off the ground and pouted his lips at Haley. "Ye big bully."

"You should be grateful the only thing damaged was your pride."

Rane rubbed his aching back while raising a disagreeble voice. "Grateful?"

Haley spoke with conviction into his face, "Yes, grateful."

She looked toward the gallery and lowered the intensity of her voice. "All the black belts in the world are no match for a gun."

Rane's body tensed up with worry as he queried, "A gun?"

She put her eyes back on her husband and nodded her head.

He slapped his hand to his heart. "I didn't even think about that."

Haley took her hands off her hips and shrugged uncaringly. "So what if he does? You don't have anything to worry about. You have an entire regiment of angelic soldiers at your disposal."

Rane blinked his eyes in surprise. "I do?"

She replied back with a clever answer, "Yes, but you don't need that many. One angel can easily defeat a brigade."

Looking around the general area, he said, "I don't see any angels."

"Take my word for it. There are at least two royal guards with you right now."

He gave her a foreboding look. "These invisible angels ye're talking about, they don't watch me all d'time. Do they?"

Knowing why he was asking the question, Haley put on a playful grin and answered, "Uh-huh."

"Even when I'm getting undressed?"

"Sure. You're one of God's sons, Rane. Royalty is never left unguarded."

Rane widened his eyes fretfully and replied, "Go on, ye mean t'tell me that these angelic soldiers have seen me bum naked?"

Seeing a perfect opportunity to tease him, Haley got nose to nose with him and whispered, "That's right. An' they know all about that cute, little four-leaf clover tattooed on your left cheek."

Cupping his hands over his blushing face, Rane lowered his head and whimpered, "How embarrassing. I don't think I'm ever going t'get undressed again."

Haley squeezed her lips together to keep from laughing at his modesty and wound up sniggering through her nose. She razzed him some more by saying, "Shouldn't you be covering the other end?" Tickled by her pun, Haley threw her head back, laughing harder.

Highly annoyed by her tomfoolery, Rane took his hands down from his face and pouted his lips at his wife. "Never ye mind. I'm going t'get us that tea now."

He stormed off in the direction of the tavern, brushing the flakes of snow off his clothes while griping about the tattoo. "If me dad was still alive, I'd punch him right in d'nose for that."

Soon as he turned the corner, Haley reached into her coat pocket and pulled out her cell phone. Keeping a vigilant eye out for her husband's return, she opened the lid on the phone and dialed her voicemail. After retrieving the private message from her dad that had helped her find her long, lost husband, she held the phone up to her ear and listened to the voice recording again.

"Hi, Haley. I know you wanted me to respect your husband's privacy, but I took the liberty of running a background check on him anyway. I was unable to locate his whereabouts until recently when he applied for a job in the city. Where he has been for the past year remains a mystery. In case you wanted to ask him yourself, the address he put on the application is One Hundred Ukine Street, London, UK. I warn you, it is in the slum area. I told you not to marry that loser. If you ask me, the man has too many skeletons in his closet. I'm doing this investigation for your own good. You're far too trusting. Like it or not, your dad is going to look out for you. I'll call you when I come up with anything else."

Haley knew her husband would be furious if he found out her dad was snooping around in his private life and decided to delete the message to avoid another fight. She was just about to put her cell phone back in her pocket when she felt it vibrating in her hand. After checking the number of the incoming caller, she lifted the lid on the phone and said expectantly, "Margaree, what did you find out?"

"There was one case filed against Lucky Jack back in two thousand eight by a man named William Isaac, a reporter for the *London Times*."

"In two thousand eight? Are you sure?"

"That's the date on the report."

"But that can't be right. Lucky Jack committed suicide in two thousand three."

"I know. The journalist claimed Lucky Jack's ghost came back to haunt him for printing that article about him having ESP."

Haley called to mind Jake's testimony, which was similar in nature, and then queried, "An' the reporter actually believed that?"

Margaree replied, "Yes. That's why his case never went to court."

"So whatever happened to Sir Isaac?"

"William swore he saw his ghost everywhere he went and eventually had a complete nervous breakdown. He was institutionalized for his mental illness and died of a heart attack a year later."

Before asking her next question, Haley ruminated briefly on the similarity between Aileen's mental collapse and the reporter's. "Margaree, is there anything in the police report about Lucky Jack giving William a calling card?"

She paused for a moment to go over the facts she had written down and answered, "Yes, a Jack of Spades."

Haley took a moment to examine the two playing cards that were in her coat pocket and then asked, "Did it have a hologram on the back?"

Growing more suspicious by the moments from all Haley's target questions, Margaree said unhurriedly, "Yes, a clock tower. How did you know that?"

Haley saw Rane heading back in her direction and rushed to get off the phone. "Just a hunch. Well, I got to go now, Margaree. Thanks for all your help."

Haley quickly hung up the phone as her husband walked up. Seeing the downcast expression on his face, she drew her eyes onto his empty hands and queried, "Where's the tea?"

"They ran out."

Haley put her phone and the cards away in her pocket and replied in disappointment, "Oooh, that's too bad."

Rane ambled over to the edge of the sidewalk and watched the cars go up and down the street. "'Tis a bit nippy out here, ain't it?"

Haley shivered all over from the cold wind and said, "Yes. I think we've waited long enough. Let's go in now."

"Okay."

"An' while we're in there, we're going to find out where Aileen hid that code."

Haley shined the beam from the flashlight down the snow-covered sidewalk as they snuck around to the rear of the building to enter through the back gate.

All at once Rane saw his shadow moving along the privacy wall and jumped backwards out of fright. "Yiiigh!"

Tickled by his theatrics, Haley sniggered, "It is only your shadow."

Rane placed his hand on his pounding chest and sighed in relief. "Oooh, be still me heart. For a moment I thought it was d'Boogeyman."

She opened the back gate and queried, "The Boogeyman? What's a Boogeyman?"

Acting like it was going to jump out at any moment, Rane looked fearfully around the grounds before whispering his answer. "An imaginary thing that comes out at night an' scares ye. Haven't ye ever seen d'movie *Boogeyman*?"

Haley made a repulsed face and replied, "Why would I want to?"

Hearing a spooky noise as they stepped into the backyard, Rane shifted his eyes back and forth, whispering in a slight stutter, "Wha-what was that?"

Not hearing anything strange, Haley creased her brow at her husband and queried, "What was what?"

Rane homed in his hearing on the area around him before answering, "It sounded like a bunch o'crickets."

Haley giggled at his timidity, "It's not crickets."

"What makes ye so sure?"

She patted him on the back and replied, "Field crickets can't survive in cold temperatures, love."

His fears were calmed somewhat upon hearing her answer. "Oh, then it was probably just me bones creaking again."

Just as her husband was about to sneak past the tree, Haley grabbed him by the coattail and whispered loudly, "Rane, wait!"

Being careful not to trip over the fairy statue in front of him, Rane whispered back, "What is it?"

Lowering the tone of her voice, Haley pointed toward the surveillance equipment by the back door and said, "Keep to the left. We don't want to trigger the sensor on the security lights."

Rane noted the security equipment and the camera above the back door and whispered, "I thought ye said we had an open invitation."

"We do," she replied as if she wasn't quite sure.

"Ye don't trust Jillian either. Do ye?"

Haley stared at her husband's face for a long moment and then finally shook her head. "No."

She looked down at the flashlight in her hand and said, "Reddy, is the footage on the security cameras still looping?"

"No. The Locust 52257 discovered the problem an' reworked the security access."

"Can't you reset it?"

"No, Detective."

"Why not?"

"The android has locked-out the system with an encrypted code."

She looked up at her husband's face and sighed woefully, "Oh dear."

Rane reached into his coat pocket and pulled out the pack of grape-flavored bubble gum. "Hey, I got an idea."

Watching him remove one of the pieces of gum from the pack, she queried, "What?"

Rane took off the wrapper on the gum and crammed the piece into his mouth. "We'll stick a wad o'gum over d'camera lens."

Haley glanced up at the camera and said to her husband in a voice of surprise, "I didn't know you knew about those things."

He blew a big bubble out of his mouth and popped it. After peeling the sticky gum off his lips, he replied conceitedly, "Who do ye think ye're dealing with, an' amateur?"

Rane looked up at the surveillance equipment and continued whispering back and forth with his wife. "D'camera's too high for me t'reach. I'll tell ye what, I'll boost ye up on me shoulders, an' ye cover d'lens."

Having strong moral conviction about tinkering with other people's property, Haley reluctantly followed him over to the camera. "Okay, but only if you promise to let me clean the lens when we're done."

Rane thought over her proposal and decided to agree. "I promise."

While Haley was busy stuffing the flashlight inside her coat pocket, Rane playfully cupped his hands under the seat of her pants and hoisted her into the air. Stunned that he had made a pass at her, she squealed and looked down at him. Scolding him for his actions, she said, "Hey, watch where you're putting those hands."

Rane lowered her to the ground and said in a frisky, mischievous tone, "Remember, dear, we're married. What's yer's is mine, an' what's mine is yer's."

She crossed her arms and gave him a suspicious squint. "I thought you said you didn't remember me."

He stuck another piece of bubble gum into his mouth before replying in a remorseful tone, "I didn't until I made ye cry at d'gallery."

Satisfied with his answer, Haley replied softly, "Oh."

Rane hunched over at the waist, patting his fingers on his shoulders. "All right, lassie, climb on."

Haley straddled her legs around his neck like she was mounting a sawhorse. She held onto his forehead for dear life as he slowly stood upright.

Rane chewed rapidly on the wad of bubble gum in his mouth and then offered his hands for her to hang onto. "Now stand on my shoulders."

She widened her eyes at the possibility of falling from the acrobatic stunt and whispered in a high-pitch tone, "Stand on your shoulders?"

"Aye, 'tis d'only way ye're going t'reach d'camera," he replied as if the solution was quite obvious.

Haley peered up at the camera with a sick look on her face and then heaved a huge sigh of dread. "Okay."

She grabbed onto his hands for support and slowly but surely stood up on his shoulders. While wobbling from side to side, she looked down at the ground with a scared look on her face and said, "Don't drop me, Chappy."

Annoyed that she didn't trust him, he replied, "Would ye stop worrying? Yer Chappy is not going t'drop ye."

Rane waited until she had safely gripped the neck of the camera before handing her the huge wad of bubble gum from his mouth. "Haley, make sure ye keep yer hand away from d'camera. Don't let 'em see ye."

Haley turned up her lip at the slobbery gum as she gripped it between her thumb and index finger. "Okay."

Rane wrapped his arms tightly around her legs to keep her from falling as she covered the sticky gum over the lens. "'Tis a good thing for me ye don't weigh much."

Haley kept her concentration on her work as she queried in a hopeful voice, "So do you remember making Reddy now?"

Worried he might accidentally drop her on the ground when he felt his legs starting to buckle, Rane answered distractedly, "No."

Haley made one last push against the lens to make sure the gum was securely attached. "Not at all?"

He sighed at his lack of recall. "No."

Trying to remove the gummy residue, Haley wiped her palm on her hip several times and said, "Okay, you can put me down now."

Once Rane had safely lowered his wife to the ground, he eyed the security box attached to the right of the door. "Looks like this place is guarded by a silent alarm system."

Haley took her flashlight out of her pocket and shined it on the panel. "Jillian knew we were coming, I wonder why she didn't deactivate it."

Rane cracked a smirk out of the corner of his mouth and said, "I tol' ye she couldn't be trusted."

He put his eyes back on the box. "I'll have t'disarm it."

Haley raised her eyebrows in shock. "You know how to disarm an alarm?"

Rane blew his warm breath on his cold hands and then cracked his knuckles. "Aye, I learned a few things on d'streets."

Haley felt a bit nervous when her husband started randomly pushing buttons on the security panel. "Rane, are you sure you know what you're doing? I see a lot of lights flashing."

He kept on trying to decode the alarm as he replied, "Don't worry. 'Tis a fail-proof system. I learned it from Stinky Mahooligan."

Haley looked around the grounds to make sure no one was coming as she queried, "Who is he?"

"One of d'hooligans I ran with in Ireland." He chuckled jokingly.

Haley didn't like hearing about his former carousing and promptly cut him off by suggesting, "Rane, why don't we have Reddy disarm it?"

Insulted by her proposal, he raised a prideful tongue. "No. I don't need Little Silver's help. I can do it myself, thank ye."

After five minutes of standing in the cold waiting for her husband to crack the code, Haley decided to take matters into her own hands. Making sure her husband couldn't hear her, she whistled the tune for the teleportation device in a barely audible tone. Soon as the flashlight in her hand had transformed into the watch, she pushed the accelerator button and disappeared in the blink of an eye.

Rane was so busy toying with the machine he didn't see his wife vanish into thin air. Now having trouble seeing in the dark, he said, "Hey, what did ye do with that flashlight?"

Not hearing her answer, Rane turned around and noticed she was gone. Unsure where she went, he called out to her in a loud whisper, "Haley? Haley? Where are ye?"

Rane didn't know what to do. He just leaned his head back against the door and closed his eyes, praying that somehow she would miraculously reappear.

All at once the back door opened and startled him. "Aaaaagh!"

Losing his balance, he stumbled backwards onto the gallery floor and landed hard on his derriere. Groaning from the pain, he said, "Oooh, my aching bum!"

Haley shined the beam from the flashlight onto her husband's face. "Oh, Rane, I'm so sorry."

Rane squinted from the bright light shining into his eyes and clasped his hands to his sore buttocks. "I think ye broke d'thing."

She was so tickled by his assessment of his injury, she started giggling. "I didn't know you were leaning against the door when I opened it."

Rane gradually picked himself up off the floor and replied, "Ha-ha, sure ye didn't."

She closed the back door and kept on giggling. "I didn't. Honest."

He rubbed his hands up and down his bruised bottom and grumbled, "Oh fine, now I won't be able t'sit down for a week."

Haley made light of the situation by continuing to snigger at him. "Don't be such a baby."

Rane frowned at her insensitivity toward his current predicament and said, "That's easy for ye t'say. Ye didn't fall on yer bum."

He shifted his gaze onto the back door and asked, "Wait a minute. How did ye get inside d'building?"

She smiled at him and answered, "The door was open."

He made a skeptical face at her. "But I was standing in front of d'door. How did ye get past me without me seeing ye?"

"I played a little trick on you. I used the teleportation device."

Rane widened his eyes at her and said in a voice of shock, "Ye let Little Silver play around with yer molecules again? Are ye out o'yer mind?"

She completely ignored his concerns for her safety by glancing down the corridor. "Are you ready to search the gallery now?"

He took a moment to calm down before motioning his hand for her to go first. "Sure. Lead on, Sherlock."

Haley shined the light down the hall to see what was up ahead and spotted another security camera just below the vaulted ceiling. "Looks like we won't be able to cover that one. It is too high for me to reach even with me standing on your shoulders."

Feeling frustrated that they couldn't go any further without being seen, Rane said in a tetchy tone, "So what do we do now?"

Haley bit her lower lip and said, "Don't worry. I'll think of something."

Hearing her whistling a jingle into the air, Rane asked curiously, "What are ye telling Reddy t'do?"

Haley smiled at him as the flashlight in her hand suddenly transformed into the watch. After opening the silver lid, she held it toward her husband and whispered, "We'll use this teleportation device to speed up our particles. That way, when they review the footage, we'll be moving so fast they won't be able to see us."

Rane held up both hands as an act of protest and backed away from his wife, whispering anxiously, "No way. Ye keep that contraption away from me. I don't want that bot messing around with me particles."

Haley overlooked his qualms and spoke into the speaker inside the watch. "Reddy, besides me an' Rane, are there anymore human beings inside the gallery?"

"No, Detective, there are no other lifeforms currently in the building."

Rane cracked his knuckles and said, "Good."

Haley made sure her husband wasn't looking and then secretly pressed the accelerator switch on the side of the watch. The instant the green light started flashing rapidly, she knew the bot had changed the speed of their particles and started whistling the tune for the flashlight.

After the bot had changed himself back into a flashlight, Rane saw a funny look in his wife's eyes and queried suspiciously, "What did ye do?"

She made an innocent face and walked on down the hall.

Her unwillingness to answer only intensified Rane's uncertainties. "Haley, what did ye do?"

He watched her nonchalantly pass in front of the security camera and then knew for sure what she had done. "Ye had Reddy speed up our particles, didn't ye?"

Rane followed her around the corner, repeating himself. "Didn't ye?"

She stopped underneath a dim, security light and turned off the flashlight. "You know, you'd make a great detective, Rane."

Rane was so upset he lost his Irish temper and started shouting at her. "I don't believe ye did that after I tol' ye not to!" He snatched the flashlight out of her hand. "Give me that thing!"

"I don't know what you're so upset about. You didn't get hurt."

Rane took the King of Hearts playing card out of his coat pocket and angrily shook it in front of her face. "That's not d'point, Haley. D'man is supposed t'be d'king. Ye might have a wee more respect for me if ye try letting me sit on d'throne for a change."

She stared forlornly at the face card in his hand and then humbled herself by declaring, "You're right, Rane, I shouldn't have disobeyed you."

Rane was touched by his wife's repentant heart and didn't know quite what to say. "Oh ... then I guess ye're forgiven, my queen."

Upon hearing the memorable address, Haley spread a smile across her face and opened the silver, heart-shaped locket around her neck. "You remember giving this to me?"

Rane stared recognizably at the three-dimensional locket in her hand and nodded his head.

She pressed the tiny switch inside the silver ornament to show him their faces on a King and Queen of Hearts. They had bought the photos as souvenirs when they were on a date at a renaissance fair. "You put your king's picture inside one half of the heart an' my queen's in the other."

After taking a moment to reflect back on their wedding day, he replied, "Aye, then I closed d'locket an' gave it t'ye."

She stared favorably at their pictures and then closed the ornament to make one heart. "Do you remember what you said afterwards?"

Rane eyed the silver heart in her hand and found it difficult to answer from a guilty conscience.

Haley's eyes pooled with tears as she reminded him of his vows held dearly in her mind. "You said, 'We'd always be one heart.'"

Rane felt convicted for breaking his half of the promise and swallowed awkwardly. "I'm sorry I broke yer heart, lassie. I guess I've been pretty selfish."

Haley wiped the tears off the sides of her cheeks and grinned. "You're forgiven, your highness."

Rane gently stroked his fingertips down the side of her cheek. After admiring her gorgeous face for a long moment, he drew his mouth close to her lips and whispered, "I love ye, Hal."

Haley embraced the hand he was using to stroke her cheek and said passionately, "I love you too, Chappy."

Rane was just about to kiss her but then felt the gallery wasn't the best place for romance. It brought back too many bad memories. "We better get going. Jillian may be back soon."

Haley was disappointed that he didn't kiss her. She found it difficult to hide her emotions as he walked on down the corridor. "Sure."

Rane put the playing card into his pocket and looked back over his shoulder. Upon discovering that his wife was still standing in the same spot he had left her, he said, "What are ye doing? Come on."

She sighed and followed him down the long corridor to the door that read, *Private. Keep out.*

The instant Rane saw the gold sign on the door, another unpleasant memory shot through his mind. The nostalgia of fourteen years earlier was a little foggy; but nonetheless, it still rewound to reveal a nightmare locked inside his soul.

Rane was about seven and a half years old then and still in the custody of his aunt Jillian. One night while she was working late at the gallery, he snuck into the private room to take a peek at her crystal ball. He just had to find out why she sought her future from such an insignificant object. After all it was only manmade, and he had learned from his Christian nanny that divination was forbidden by God.

Throwing all caution to the wind, he tiptoed over to the table where the ball was displayed and peered into its empty reflection. Hearing the clock tower gonging the midnight hour, he reached out his hand and picked up the sphere. All of a sudden he felt an uncanny presence creeping up behind him. Trembling with fright, he held his breath and turned his head to see who it was. When he didn't see anyone there, he shrugged off the anxiety as a figment of his imagination. After setting the globe down, he spotted a Jack of Diamonds tarot card on the table that symbolized a harbinger of bad news. He picked up the fortune-telling card and felt a huge weight of depression come over the top of him. Hating the sensation, he ripped the face card into tiny pieces and tossed the fragments all over the floor. Believing the crystal ball had somehow cast a spell on him, he started bashing it against the wall, shouting, "Die! Die! Die!"

Jillian heard all the commotion her nephew was making from the down the hall and ran into the room. Soon as she saw him trying to break her globe, she grabbed him by the scruff of his neck and bellowed in a voice of panic, "Are ye mad, laddie?"

He tried to wriggle out of her grasp as he shouted back, "Let me go, ye evil witch! I have t'break this evil eye!"

"No! Ye could hex us all."

Rane couldn't seem to break free from her hold on him, so he spiked the crystal ball hard as he could against the marble floor.

Jillian bulged her eyes in horror as the ball shattered into a millions pieces. Flying into a rage, she screamed, "Nooo!"

Directing all her negative energy onto her nephew, she gripped him tighter around the throat and hissed vengefully, "Ye little brat! I'm going t'kill ye for that."

Terrified she might actually do it in the state of mind she was in, young Rane called out to the Lord for help in a frail voice, "Jesus, help me!"

Jillian shook him by the neck and snarled, "Yer invisible King won't save ye, boy."

Young Rane knew he had to figure out a way to break free from her hold before she strangled him to death. As he began to lose consciousness from near suffocation, he wondered why Aileen's black cat suddenly ran into the room. *Raven?*

The feline was wearing a beautiful, red leather choker with ten, tiny, white diamonds set in a row. Hanging from the metal hook on her collar was a round, gold identification tag.

To young Rane's surprise, Raven peered up at him with her big, yellow eyes like she knew somehow from all his coughing and choking that his life was in danger. Springing to his defense, she leaped up off the floor, spitting and growling, and started clawing at his aunt's face.

Jillian was so frightened by the unexpected attack that she started screaming hysterically. She released her grip on her nephew's throat to throw off the frenzied feline, and he fell into a heap on the floor. Rolling over on his side, he clutched his badly bruised neck while wheezing air back into his lungs.

Raven landed safely on her feet after being thrown down by Jillian and ran over to Rane. She purred and meowed like she was glad he was all right and then rubbed her cheek several times against his face.

Young Rane wasn't fully cognizant of where he was until he heard his aunt groaning. Curious what happened to her, he directed his blurry eyes over in that direction. When his focus became clearer, he saw her hands cupped over her eyes with blood dripping down her face. Appalled by what Raven had done to her, he leaped to his feet and bolted out of the gallery, never intending to return again.

Haley tapped her entranced husband on the shoulder to get his attention and said, "Rane ... "

Befuddled where he was at, Rane's reply was slow and uncertain. "Huh?"

Haley waited until he made eye contact with her and queried, "Are you ready to go inside?"

Rane answered, yawning, "I'm sorry. My mind must have wandered off. What did ye say again?"

She picked up the flashlight he had dropped on the floor and replied, "I said, 'Are you ready to go inside?'"

He stared uncertainly at the private door and took a couple of steps backward. "No. I'll-I'll wait for ye out here."

Haley gave him a funny look and queried, "Why?"

He replied in a jittery voice, "I-I dunno why. I just don't want t'go in there, that's all."

Haley grabbed him by the arm as he turned to walk away. "Oh no you're not, Rane Rivers. You're going in with me."

Tugging nervously on the collar of his turtleneck sweater, he replied, "I am?"

Haley kept her grasp on her husband's arm as she turned the knob. "Yes."

Rane started trembling all over as Haley slowly pushed open the creaky door. Not feeling like he could face up to what was on the other side, he squeezed his eyes shut.

Haley shined the beam from the flashlight around the dark, dusty room, revealing a round oak table, an old armchair, a black trunk, and a couple of wooden bookcases filled with art books. After a subtle cough from the musty odor in the room, she saw a daddy longlegs spider scurrying across the hardwood floor. She looked over at her husband's tensed up face and giggled. "Chappy, open your eyes."

Rane raised his nose into the air and said haughtily, "I like 'em better closed, thank ye."

Haley bit on her lower lip, wondering what little trick she could play on her husband to get him to open his eyes. When the joke came to mind, she sniggered in her heart at the idea and said in a voice of alarm, "Rane, is that a rat on your foot?"

Rane popped open his eyes and started screaming psychotically as he looked down at his feet. Even though it wasn't really there, he had such a fear of vermin that he went through the motions of shaking it off his boots. "Aaaaagh! A rat? Where is it? Where is it?"

Tickled that he was actually freaking out over an imaginary rodent, Haley threw her head back, laughing at her ploy.

Realizing she had just played a little practical joke on him, Rane stopped jumping around and gave her a perturbed look. "Very funny."

Haley sniggered a little more and then squeezed her lips together to keep from laughing.

Rane took the flashlight away from her and pointed a firm finger at her lips. "I'm warning ye, lassie. I better not so much as hear one more snigger out o'yer mouth."

Although still giggling on the inside, she humbly replied, "Yes sir."

Rane shook his head at her for making him look like a fool and then anxiously shined the flashlight around the room like a rat might be lurking in the darkness.

Haley patted her husband on the back to reassure him that everything would be all right. "See, your fears were only imagined. There's nothing scary in here."

He gulped hard before replying in an unconfident tone, "Aye, nothing scary."

With a trembling hand, Rane swept the beam from the flashlight over to the left side of the room, exposing a box of oil paintings on the floor.

Haley got excited when she saw the stack of canvases. "Hey, that must be Jack's private collection Jillian was talking about."

Searching the room for another source of light, she spotted a kerosene lantern on the oak table. "Rane, turn on that paraffin lamp over there, will ye?"

Still shaking from fright, he shined the flashlight toward the table she mentioned and replied, "All right."

While tiptoeing over to the lantern, Rane almost tripped over the trunk by the bookcase. "Yeesh! Creeping around in here makes me feel like a cat burglar."

The very next moment he heard a floorboard creaking as if someone was following him. He instantly froze with fear, the hairs on his arms standing on end. In a subdued, mousy tone, he whispered, "Haley, is that ye?" Not hearing a response from his wife, his anxieties increased. "Please tell me that's ye."

The quiet made his skin crawl and set the stage for his imagination to run wild. Was the kidnapper stalking him, or was it Haley masterminding another prank? He just had to know. To appease his curiosity, he slowly turned around. At that precise moment, a black cat leaped past his face and frightened him out of his wits. "Aaaaagh!"

Rane slapped his hand over his racing heart and then shined the flashlight toward the dusty table where the cat had landed. After seeing the feline's squinting, green eyes, he groaned a breath of relief. "Oooh, be still me heart. Kitty, ye scared me half t'death."

He dug into his coat pocket and pulled out the book of matches his wife had given to him earlier.

Hearing him talking to the feline as he lit the wick on the kerosene lamp, Haley queried, "Rane, you weren't scared by the cat, were ye?"

Rane blew out the match in his hand and refuted defensively, "Oh, ye're one t'talk, Miss Eyes in the Back o'yer Head."

He altered his voice to reenact her girlish hysteria in Masterpiece Hall. "Eeeeeeeek! Get 'em off me, Rane. Get these nasty critters out o'me hair."

She giggled at his theatrical portrayal of herself. "I did make a fool out of myself, didn't I?"

Rane dropped the burnt match on the table and put the glass cover back on the kerosene lamp. "That's an understatement."

"I imagine I gave my royal guards quite a show while they were sitting around with nothing to do."

Rane turned off the flashlight and put it and the book of matches inside his jacket pocket. "What do ye mean, 'They were sitting around with nothing t'do'?"

Haley made her way across the room to join him by the table. "The angels don't hearken to the voice of fear."

She took the small Bible out of her coat pocket and handed it to Rane. "They only respond to the voice of faith. So unless I'm speaking in the King's regal authority, what could they possibly have to do?"

Rane thumbed through the pages in the book and thought about the time his aunt almost killed him. Muttering under his breath, he said to be humorous, "An' if yer angels are out on a tea break, he might just send ye a cat instead."

He closed the Bible and stuffed it back inside her coat pocket.

Haley picked up the feline off the table and started scratching under her chin. "You're a sweet kitty. Aren't you?"

The contented cat meowed as if answering her question and graciously rubbed her head against Haley's cheek.

Rane shot an irritated sneer at the purring feline and said to his wife, "Go on, lassie, there ain't nothing sweet about a dangerous killer."

Haley looked over at her husband and sniggered softly, "You think cats are dangerous killers?"

"Aye, haven't ye ever seen that horror picture *Catatonic*?"

"Cata what?"

He spoke like she had already seen the film. "*Catatonic.* Ye know where all d'cats turn schizo an' gang up on all d'humans."

Haley rolled her eyes at his choice of pictures and said indignantly under her breath, "*Catatonic*, indeed, I can see why you're having nightmares."

Overhearing her mumbling to herself, he asked, "What did ye say?"

Haley quickly changed the tone of her voice to sound more pleasant. "Nothing, I was just thinking aloud."

"Oh."

Curious to find out the cat's name, Haley silently read the engraving on the round, gold, identification tag that was attached to a red leather collar around the animal's neck. After discovering who she was, she stroked her palm down the feline's arched back and said, "Hello, Shadow."

Rane frowned at the animal as it meowed a second time and said to his wife, “D’cat’s name is Shadow?”

Haley smiled, nodding her head a couple of times. “Uh-huh.”

He smacked the heel of his hand against his forehead and said to himself, “I don’t believe this. I must be dreaming.”

Haley silently read the owner’s name on the other side of the gold medallion and then shared the information with her husband. “According to the identification tag, she belongs to Aileen.”

She offered the cat to her husband. “Would you like to hold her?”

Holding up his hands in strong protest, he stepped back from the feline and almost knocked a gray ceramic vase off the table. While steadying the vase to keep it from tipping over, he said, “Not on yer life, ye keep that man-eating leopard away from me.”

Haley sniggered at her husband’s comment as she put the cat back on the table. “A man-eating leopard.”

Rane gulped hard when he saw the feline sharpening her claws on the edge of the oak table. He kept imagining Raven’s vicious attack on his aunt’s face and was afraid that might happen to him. Expressing his fears to his wife, he said, “Aye, an’ ye better get rid o’her before she scratches out yer eyes.”

Haley rubbed the top of the cat’s head and said, “Aw, Chappy, how could you possibly think that about this sweet kitty?”

Rane looked uneasily at Shadow as she finished sharpening her claws. “Easy, I hate cats.”

Haley went back to petting the feline’s back as she replied, “I don’t know why. God made them. What’s not to like?”

Rane watched the cat lie down on the table and heaved an unenthusiastic sigh of surrender. “Fine, if it will make ye feel better, I’ll pet d’gumby.”

Highly repulsed that he had to actually touch the cat, Rane turned his head away while giving Shadow a couple of quick pats on the head. He looked back at his wife like he had just done her a huge favor and said, “There, are ye happy now?”

Haley giggled at his theatrical performance. "I can't wait till you get all your memory back."

Rane creased his brow and queried, "What do ye mean?"

Her sniggering died down to speak in an aristocratic tone. "You own a cat, Chappy."

With a revolted expression on his face, Rane peered into the feline's slanted, green eyes and had another flashback of Raven attacking his aunt. Not wanting to face up to the fears of his past, he replied, "Ye're making that up. Chappy would never own a cat. A dog maybe, but a cat, never."

Her superior tone remained unchanged as she replied, "Never say 'never,' I always say."

Bored with the topic of their conversation, Rane redirected his interest onto the ten, tiny gems embedded across the cat's collar. He was disturbed by the fact that Raven wore a collar just like it but didn't let it show on his face as he said to his wife, "Ye think these diamonds are real?"

Haley eyed the sparkling stones and replied, "There's one way to find out."

She puckered her lips and started whistling the tune for the bot.

Reddy appeared in her coat pocket and said, "Ye need me, Haley?"

With a dumbfounded look on his face, Rane peeked inside his jacket and found out the flashlight was gone.

Haley nodded at the bot and replied, "Reddy, are these genuine diamonds?"

Reddy used his magnifying glass to make a quick analysis of the gems before replying, "Aye, rare, flawless stones—worth about a million pounds."

Rane whistled at the high price and said, "One could feed a lot of orphans with that kind o'money."

While pondering in the back of his mind why Aileen would do such a crazy thing, Rane felt the cat pawing at his elbow. Thinking she was trying to attack him, he swiftly retracted his arm and scolded her. "Kitty, get away from me!"

Haley sniggered in her heart at him fussing at the cat and then strolled casually across the room to examine the box of paintings on the floor. Kneeling down on the area rug, she flipped through the pile of pictures and queried, "Rane, why do you suppose Jillian is hiding these portraits back here?"

Rane walked over to the box and turned up his nose at the artwork. "'Cause no one in their right mind would buy those worthless things, that's why."

She stood to her feet and replied, "It must have been some of Artur's earlier pieces when he lived in Ireland."

Haley looked down at the paintings in the box and said, "My art professor said a picture paints a thousand words."

"If that's true, how come I can only think of one t'describe these?"

"An' what's that?"

He looked over at his wife's interested face and replied, "Trust me, ye really don't want t'know what I'm thinking right now."

While Rane was busy chatting with his wife about the paintings, Shadow jumped off the table and ran over to him. Feeling her purring body brush up against the front of his pant legs, he looked down at her. "Kitty, go away, shoo."

Haley grinned a smidgen at the cat's fondness toward her husband and said, "She likes you."

"D'feeling isn't mutual, okay."

Rane pushed the feline back from his legs and said out of frustration, "Kitty, go away! Ye're getting yer black hairs all over me jeans."

Reddy probed Rane's fear of the animal and decided to come to his rescue. After diving off the edge of Haley's pocket, he landed feet first on the floorboard next to the cat. He quickly sized up the feline before boasting, "No problem, Whiz Kid, I can take her. I'll put some o'me fancy karate moves on her that I learned from ye."

The bot straight away began to imitate his inventor's actions by making karate chops at the cat's face. "Whoooah! Eeeeyah! Eiyah!"

Haley giggled at the bot's antics.

When the cat slowly began to back away from him, Reddy got tickled pink. With a goofy grin on his face, he said, "Scared ye, huh, kitty? I bet ye didn't know I had a black belt in karate."

Rane made a puzzled face at the bot and queried, "Reddy, what do ye think ye're doing?"

Reddy looked up at his inventor and said, "I'm saving ye, Whiz Kid."

Rane gave the bot a perturbed smirk and asked, "From what?"

Reddy lifted the cat's muzzle to expose her white fangs and replied, "From this man-eating leopard."

Shadow spit and growled at the tiny bot for tugging on her whiskers and then swiped her paw at his face.

Reddy widened his fearful eyes at the cat's sharp teeth and shrieked loudly, "Aaaaagh! Don't eat me, kitty. I'm not a rat."

Rane pursed his angry lips at the bot as it leaped into Haley's coat pocket for safety. "Reddy, I'm warning ye, if that cat bites me, ye're going t'get it."

Acting like he was scared, Reddy squealed at his inventor's threat and then ducked down out of sight. "No spank."

Rane sighed in relief when Shadow suddenly walked away. After several moments of studying the feline's unusual behavior, he said to his wife, "What's with that crazy cat?"

Haley took a fleeting glance at Shadow and queried, "What do you mean?"

"She keeps jumping up an' down on top of that trunk over there."

Haley shrugged her shoulders. "Maybe she's trying to tell you there's something in it."

Rane chuckled, "Go on, lassie. I'm not going t'look in that barmy trunk."

"Why not?"

“’Cause there’s probably nothing in it but a bunch of rats.”

“It couldn’t hurt to look.”

He spoke firmly into her face, “No.”

Rane cleared the musty air out of his throat and started cracking his knuckles. “I’m not wasting time playing cat an’ mouse games with d’likes of her. We came in here t’look for a clue. Remember?”

Although his advice was against her gut feeling, Haley put her hands on her hips and sighed submissively for his sake. “Okay, you’re the boss.”

Rane walked away in search of a clue, and Shadow ran after him. Sensing her presence, he turned around and said, “Kitty, stop following me.”

Hearing the stress in his inventor’s voice, Reddy poked his head out of Haley’s coat pocket and secretly scolded the cat by whispering, “Ye heard him, kitty, off with ye. Cheerio!”

Haley watched the cat trail Rane around the room. “Now you know why Aileen named her Shadow.”

He shook his head at the feline and chuckled feebly, “Ain’t that d’truth. She’s a persistent little devil, I’ll give her that.”

Rane bent over at the waist to pick up one of the paintings out of the box, and Shadow brushed her furry cheek against his face. “Kitty, quit it! Ye’re tickling me nose.”

Tired of trying to stop the pushy feline from bothering him, Rane picked up the cat and held her in his arms. “Oh great, she’s got something stuck in her mouth.”

“What is it?” Haley queried.

He stared at the object closely and replied, “Looks like a piece o’paper.”

Rane watched the feline inhale it. “Correction, she had a piece o’paper stuck in her mouth.”

Haley raised her voice out of concern. “She swallowed it?”

He nodded and secretly whispered to himself, “An’ I seriously hope it wasn’t my password.”

"Do you think it might hurt her?"

Rane shook his head at her genuine concern for the cat. "I can't believe ye're worried about her swallowing a wee piece o'paper when I've seen one o'these vicious killers gulp down an entire rat with one bite."

Haley grinned at him and said, "You have not."

Rane put the cat down and raised a proud chin. "I have too."

Acting afraid, Reddy widened his eyes at the cat and whispered under his breath, "With one bite?"

Still doubting her husband's story, Haley giggled at him as she ambled to the other side of the room. "Gulp down a rat with one bite."

Rane rummaged through all the desk and cabinet drawers, hoping to find his access code. Not hearing anything out of his wife for a while, he looked across the room and saw her snooping around inside a small office. Curious to see what she was up to, he stepped in that direction without watching where he was going and accidentally knocked over one of the paintings. As soon as the picture slammed against the floor, the cat started hissing and spitting at him.

Rane reached down to retrieve the picture, grumbling under his breath, "Crazy cat! If it wasn't for bad luck, I wouldn't have any luck at all."

Haley heard the loud racket and came running out of the room. "Rane, what was that noise?"

He threw the painting into the box and looked over at her. "Oh I knocked over one of d'pictures, that's all."

"Oh."

She walked over to him and heard the voice of God speaking softly to her heart. Desiring to share what she heard, she said, "Rane…"

Seeing the strange, euphoric look in her green eyes, Rane was almost afraid to ask her what she wanted. "What?"

"I think I just heard the Lord telling me to check the paintings in Masterpiece Hall again."

Highly skeptical after what happened the last time, Rane replied leisurely, "Sure ye did."

"No. I'm serious. I think I really heard him this time."

Although he had his misgivings, Rane decided to give in for her sake. "All right, we'll have another go at it."

After whistling the tune to turn Reddy back into a flashlight, Haley shined the beam down the shadowy corridor as she and Rane made their way back to Masterpiece Hall. Upon entering the quiet showroom, they heard wind whistling against the French window.

Rane stopped dead in his tracks and stared wide-eyed at the snow flurries outside the window. "Kind o'spooky in here, ain't it?"

Haley didn't feel the least bit afraid and calmly shined the flashlight along the wall. "There's got to be a light switch around here someplace."

Upon finding the lever, she turned on the lights and put the flashlight in her pocket. Drawing her attention over to the oil paintings on display, she suggested, "Rane, why don't I check these, an' you check the ones over there."

"Okay."

Haley began her inspection of the oil paintings and caught sight of a picture she hadn't seen before. Excited about her new discovery, she immediately called out to her husband. "Rane, come here."

Hearing the exhilaration in her voice, Rane ran over to his wife and queried a bit windedly, "What is it?"

Haley pointed at a picture of a black cat sneaking up behind three blind mice dressed up like the secret service men and said, "I don't remember this painting being here before. Do you?"

Rane looked over the forlornly trio of gray rodents sitting on top of a black trunk and replied, "No. I don't think it was."

Haley closely studied the artistic detail in the depiction and replied, "It's definitely not Artur's modus operandi. I wonder why Jillian put it here among his other masterpieces."

Rane frowned distastefully at the painting. "Knowing her, she probably painted d'eyesore an' tried t'pass it off as her brother's."

Haley pulled her cell phone out of her coat pocket and started taking snapshots of the picture. "It's not bad, but any art expert could tell it was painted by an amateur."

She took a couple more pictures of the mysterious painting and then put her cell phone back into her pocket. Drawing her probing eyes onto the green-eyed feline in the painting, she said, "The cat looks like Shadow."

He squinted at the name tag attached to the red collar and started cracking his knuckles. "Aye, her name's on d'collar."

Haley leaned over the red rope to get a closer inspection of the painting. "That mouse on the right looks like Gary."

"Ye mean d'agent that was in here earlier?"

Haley stopped leaning over the rope and nodded her head at her husband. "Uh-huh."

Rane took a closer gander at the features on the rodent in question and then shrugged uncertainly at his wife. "Kind of."

Haley pointed at the large object behind the trunk and said, "I think that's supposed to be a picture of the Christmas tree over at the Ritz Mall."

He agreed by nodding his head and then diverted his wife's attention onto the left wrist of the same mouse they were talking about earlier. "Haley, look, d'time on his gold watch is set at midnight."

Haley checked the time on the rodent's wristwatch and said jokingly, "Maybe the mice have a blind date with the cat at midnight."

"Those three rascals would have t'be blind t'keep an' appointment with a vicious killer."

She sniggered at him for being silly. "Would you quit? Cats are not vicious killers."

"Try convincing d'mice."

Gluing her eyes back on the painting, Haley pointed at the right side of the chest and whispered, "Rane, see that tiny bit of red fabric sticking out of the back end of the trunk?"

Rane nodded once and replied, "Aye."

Haley lowered her hand as she made eye contact with her husband. "What do you think it means?"

He shrugged and answered, "That someone slammed d'lid closed before they got all of it inside."

Haley stared back at the trunk. "I don't think so."

Rane anxiously bit the skin around his thumbnail. "Ye think this might be a clue?"

"Possibly."

Rane strained his eyes to see if there was an autograph on the canvas. "I can't quite make out d'signature from here. I'll have t'hop over d'rope."

He climbed over the red cord and smelt a faint odor.

Puzzled why he was sniffing the canvas, Haley asked, "What are you doing?"

He wriggled his nose a couple more times before replying, "Do ye smell wet paint?"

Haley sniffed the air and then nodded her head. "Uh-huh."

Rane swiped his index finger down the area on the canvas where the cat was painted and came up with black residue on his fingertip.

With a baffled expression on his face, he showed the smear to his wife and said, "D'picture's wet."

Highly suspicious, he took the painting off the wall and handed it to his wife. "Something weird is going on around here."

Haley gave the canvas and the frame a thorough inspection and handed it back to her husband. "It's signed in Artur's name, but he definitely didn't do it."

Rane hung the picture back on the wall and climbed over the rope. "It had t'be Jillian."

She got closer to her husband to whisper in secret. "I think you're right, because I found an easel an' some tubes of oil paint in that back room. Also, when we ran into Jillian earlier, I noticed she had a tiny smudge of black paint on the end of her pinky."

Rane gaped at his shrewd wife and said, "Ye got quite a sharp eye, Detective."

Haley believed the objects in the picture stood for something and stared inquisitively at the painting. "I bet we'll find a clue in that trunk."

Rane's voice permeated with disbelief as he glanced at the alleged item in the picture. "In the trunk?"

"Yes."

While disagreeing with his wife, Rane tried to remove the black residue off his finger by rubbing it up and down the side of his jeans. "That's crazy."

"It couldn't hurt to look, you know," she uttered persistently.

Tired of being coerced, Rane threw his hands into the air and said, "Fine, if ye want t'waste yer time chasing shadows, that's yer business. I'll wait here."

Being obstinate, he sat down on the marble floor and crossed his arms. Leaning his head back against the wall, he looked up at her and said to be arrogant, "When ye get back, ye can tell me I was right."

When he closed his eyes like he was taking a siesta, Haley sighed at his foolish pride and then listened to the wind whistling outside the window. Feeling a sudden draft inside the room, she shivered all over and started rubbing her hands up and down her arms. Looking toward the other end of the hall, she noticed the conference door was slightly ajar and decided to go down and investigate.

Haley stepped quietly into the conference room and caught sight of the huge mural on the wall. Believing it was the very painting that God had told her about, she hollered out to her husband, "Rane, come here! I think I found it."

Startled by the tone of her voice from nodding off, he sprang to his feet and called out worriedly, "Haley? Where are ye?"

"I'm in the conference room!" she shouted back.

Running all the way, it didn't take Rane long to get there. Upon entering the room, he saw the picture his wife was talking about and gasped in horror. He couldn't believe he was standing there staring at a painting of his Irish mother, sitting in the lobby at a poker table across from Lucky Jack. With her shoulder-length, curly, blond hair, slightly freckled face, and piercing sea blue eyes, she looked exactly like he remembered her.

"I'm not sure who the young lady is," said Haley, "but that's definitely a picture of Lucky Jack. Look at the big diamond rings on all his fingers."

Desperate to keep his past a secret, Rane uplifted his downtrodden expression, pretending not to recognize the woman in the painting. "That's him all right. Did ye see those ugly, green locusts painted on top of his red coronet?"

Haley turned up her lip in distaste as she examined the three, winged insects. "Yes. They look exactly like the Chandlers described."

She roved her eyes over the rest of the painting and then touched the glossy wall. "Artur must have put some sort of sealant over the mural to keep it from fading."

"Probably."

Paying close attention to some of the details in the picture, Haley commented, "The Queen Anne furniture looks like the ones in the lobby."

"Aye," he replied in a barely audible voice.

Haley stared at the little boy asleep in the chair next to Kathryn's and said, "Aw, he's cute, isn't he?"

He stared sadly at the child's innocent face and chose not to comment.

Haley pointed at the amulet on the end of the gold chain around Artur's neck and said, "That looks like the same talisman Jillian was wearing."

Rane nodded his head as he read the name of the ornament aloud, "Abracadabra."

Haley drew her husband's attention onto the painting of the woman by saying, "She's lovely."

Rane gazed hypnotically at the picture of his mother while depressing thoughts from his past bubbled up inside his mind. He wished more than anything that he could forget her, like she obviously had done him. Not being able to keep up the idyllic charade, he swallowed hard on a huge lump of sorrow and replied, "Aye, she's beautiful."

Hearing the unhappiness in his voice, Haley looked over at him and queried, "Are you okay?"

He answered her question with a slow nod of his head.

Haley stared closely at the mystery woman's visage when she noted a resemblance between her and her husband. "She has your eyes. Don't you think?"

Rane shrugged unfeelingly and remained silent.

Haley eyed the French-style, porcelain telephone sitting on the edge of the poker table by Artur. She noticed the black phone was an antique and that the handset, rotary dial, and base had gold accents. Upon taking a closer look at it, she saw Kathryn's face carved inside the gold circle on the dial. Excited to share the new detection with her husband, she looked over at him and said, "Rane … "

He reluctantly gave her his full attention by asking, "What?"

Making sure he could see it clearly, she pointed at the circle inside the dial on the phone and said, "There's an etching of the woman's face."

She took a step back from the mural and said, "I bet that's Kathryn."

"Does it matter?" he replied uninterestedly and then turned away to look at the Irish flag in the corner of the room.

Unsure why her husband was acting so strange, Haley gave him a perplexed look and then put her eyes back on the painting. After staring at the teardrops painted on the Irishwoman's cheeks, she diverted her attention onto the five cards in her hand and said, "Aw, she lost. Her poker hand wasn't good enough to beat Artur's three Jacks."

Rane just stood there staring off into space, thinking how heartless his mother was for gambling him away. He thought he had forgiven her when he cried out to God, but his heart had deceived him.

Haley eyed the playing card lying on the table in front of the woman and said, "She discarded the Jack of Hearts."

Rane gaped at the throwaway card like he and Artur were the unwanted Jack and thought resentfully, *Discarding hearts seems t'be my mum's specialty.*

Haley's inquisitive eyes wandered onto the *Fame* periodical, lying open on the cushion in the empty chair. "Rane, look. That magazine might have an article about Lucky Jack."

Desiring to know more about Artur's personal life, Rane's blue mood perked up slightly as he moved closer to the mural. "Where?"

She pointed at its general location and replied, "In the chair."

Although he was wondering why he hadn't noticed it before, he replied, "Oh, now I see it."

Haley leaned closer to the wall, straining to see the words in the magazine. "Artur must have painted a write-up about himself, but the words are too tiny to read."

Blown away by the artist's finely tuned eye for detail, she looked over at her husband and said, "That's incredible. I wish I knew how he did that."

Rane thought about the bot in his wife's coat pocket and asked, "Ye think Reddy could read it?"

She nodded her head and then whistled the jingle for the bot.

All at once Reddy sprung up out of her pocket with his tiny magnifying glass held in front of his eye and said eagerly, "I can read it for ye guys."

Haley picked up the bot and sat him down on the edge of her palm. "Reddy, you can quit with that little charade too."

Peering at her face through the lens, he asked, "What charade is that, Haley?"

"You don't need the magnifying glass. You have high-powered lenses in both eyes."

He lowered the round glass from his face and pouted his lips as if he was going to cry. "But ye said I could play Sherlock."

Rane whispered into his wife's ear, "Ye better let him. D'little fella's hair is turning blue."

Remembering her promise, she sighed deeply and said in a voice of surrender, "You're right. Reddy, go ahead."

Thrilled that he could help her solve the case, Reddy raised the magnifying glass into the air and shouted, "Yipee! I get t'play Sherlock."

The bot's hair turned back to its original color as he held the magnifying glass in front of his right eye. While happily swinging his legs, he leaned nearer to the magazine in the painting and started reading the words aloud. "Artur Jack Finney, also known as Dirty Jack, was one of d'top high rollers in Las Vegas ..."

Rane recalled the dirty-minded gentleman he had met inside the hologram and interrupted the bot's narration to say, "Dirty Jack? Don't tell me d'chap had more than one alter ego?"

Reddy lowered the magnifying glass from his eye and said, "It sure looks that way, Whiz Kid."

The bot repositioned the lens in front of his eye and continued reading the biography. "D'handsome Irishman got his nickname Dirty Jack by showing up one night for a poker tournament dressed up like a Jack of diamonds. He was so drunk he winked his eye at all d'pretty cocktail waitresses, shouting, 'Down an' dirty!' What started out as a joke on his twenty-first birthday soon became a headliner in all d'scandal magazines. Loving all d'attention he was receiving from d'press, Artur decided t'never appear in d'public eye again without wearing his costume, boasting that 'Jacks are better.'"

Recalling what Prosperity said about Artur being turned down for the Hope Diamond, Rane looked at the winning poker hand in the painting and said under his breath, "Jacks are better?"

Reddy took a quick peep at his inventor through his magnifying lens, wondering what was troubling him. Not being able to figure him out, he shrugged unwittingly and pressed on with reading the article. "Instead, Artur wisely used d'exposure of his Lucky Jack shadow or alter ego t'promote his artwork. Shortly after his image change and d'birth of his illegitimate son ..."

While Haley and the bot were absorbed in the article, Rane squinted at the painting of Artur and thought worriedly, *Illegitimate son?*

He then snuck a peek at the photo in his coat pocket. After comparing the picture with the man's face on the wall, he stuffed the snapshot back inside his jacket. He was so afraid his pious wife might find out about his parents' immoral lifestyle that he screamed alarmingly in his heart, *Noooooo!*

Seeing Haley glance over in his direction, Rane shunned his hurt emotions and pretended to be wrapped up in what the bot was saying.

"Artur started winning big at all d'major casinos, stripping his opponents' o'vast fortunes, an' before long, d'struggling artist sky-rocketed to world-renown fame. Since he was lauded in d'public eye as d'luckiest man in d'world with both money an' voluptuous showgirls, d'press decided t'change his pseudonym to 'Lucky Jack, d'Stripping Locust.'"

Haley was appalled at the way the Irishman treated women and said to her husband, "Then the insects in the mural represent stripping locusts. That would explain the dirty wink of his right eye. But the article only mentions two alter egos. Why are there three locusts on his crown?"

Rane gnashed his teeth at his dad's promiscuous ways. He was so upset he started cracking his knuckles. "Who cares?"

The bot, again, spied on Rane through the magnifying glass as if he was still trying to figure out what was bothering him.

Wanting to hear the rest of the article, Haley gently tapped the bot on his shoulder to get his attention and said, "Okay, Reddy, continue."

Reddy shifted the magnifying glass over to his opposite hand and held it in front of his left eye this time. He picked up where he left off by reading the next page. "D'tabloids accredited Artur's lucky streak t'his inscrutable poker face, which made him tough t'beat. However, his highly superstitious nature accredited his good luck t'his son an' d'gold talisman he wore around his neck. He believed its magical powers protected him from bad luck."

Haley cut in on the bot's recital by asking, "Reddy, does the article mention the name of Artur's son?"

Fearing rejection, Rane's eyes bulged at the thought of his wife discovering who he really was. His heart was beating so fast he thought he was going to pass out. *Please, God, she just can't find out. She'll tell her self-righteous dad, an' he'll judge me. He already thinks I'm a loser—always making fun o'me.*

Reddy scanned the article with his magnifying glass and replied, "Nope, sorry, Haley."

Haley sighed disappointedly and asked, "Does it say anything about Artur's girlfriend?"

Reddy quickly scanned the rest of the editorial before answering, "Aye, it says, 'Artur hung up his cloak in 2002 after Kathryn publicly exposed that he had extrasensory perception. His gambling streak ended after only five years."

"How much did she get for d'story?" Rane asked in a resentful tongue.

The bot lowered the magnifying glass from his eye and said sadly, "One million pounds. Poor Lucky Jack, all d'gamblers started calling him a Wizard an' wouldn't play poker with him anymore."

Rane fixed a resentful eye on his wife and stated indirectly, "That's what he gets for trusting a lassie."

Knowing he still had unrepentant prejudice in his heart toward women, Haley mercifully shrugged off Rane's biased opinion. "Reddy, is there anything more on Artur's girlfriend?"

Reddy gave her a brisk bob of his head to indicate there was and retrieved the information he had previously read from his memory chip. "Uh-huh. It says Kathryn was d'only high roller Lucky Jack never beat."

Stirred up with interest after hearing more of Artur's life story, Haley tilted her head slightly to the side and said, "Really?"

Reddy nodded a second time before replying, "He swore she had cast a love spell on him that made him lose his concentration."

"How many times did Kathryn beat him?"

"Twenty-one times."

Rane raised his voice in surprise. "She beat him twenty-one times?"

Reddy grinned at his inventor and answered, "Yep! She boasted to d'press that she had cleaned him out for six million pounds."

Finding the account hard to swallow from Artur being clairvoyant, Haley trailed off their conversation by asking the bot, "You mean to tell me that in all the times Lucky Jack played her, he never beat her once?"

"Not according to d'article."

Upon hearing the last tidbit of the write-up, Haley took a moment of quiet deliberation and afterward said to her husband in a voice of conjecture, "Artur signed an' dated the mural in December 2002, a year before he died. If he had already hung up his cloak earlier in the same year, then this must have been a private poker game he conducted at the gallery."

Still feeling sorry for himself, Rane stared resentfully at the picture of his mother, thinking, *I guess he found someone daft enough t'play him after all.*

Haley put the bot inside her coat pocket and went right back to examining the mural. After several moments of concentrated study, she said, "That's strange."

Rane drew his eyes onto the picture of the ruby, diamond-shaped earring in his dad's left earlobe before asking, "What?"

"In the mural Artur is reaching across the table to take the prize from the woman, but she doesn't have any poker stakes. All the chips are stacked in his favor."

Reddy leaned over the edge of Haley's pocket with the magnifying glass held in front of his eye. After probing the total monetary value of each of the colored chips, he disclosed the findings by giving a poor impersonation of Sherlock. "Well, what do ye know, his chips just happen t'total up t'six million pounds. I suspect foul play, Detective."

Haley wasn't listening to the bot's parody. She was too busy talking to her husband about the sleeping child in the chair next to the mystery woman. "The only thing she's holding is her cards an' the little boy's hand."

When they just kept on chitchatting like he wasn't even there, the bot decided to give himself a pat on the back. "Good show, Reddy. I see a promotion in yer future."

Not a bit interested in the topic of their discussion, Rane said listlessly to his wife, "So?"

Haley peered into her husband's teal blue eyes and replied, "I was just wondering what she lost, that's all."

Choked up from what his mother did to him as a child, Rane found it difficult to answer. "I'm sure it wasn't anything important."

Not understanding the abrupt change in her husband's demeanor, Haley queried, "Why do you say that?"

He eyed the open pack of Lucky Strike III cigarettes on Artur's side of the poker table and shrugged indifferently.

Haley redirected her attention on the mural and said, "The little boy looks like he's about five, huh?"

Rane took a quick glance at the picture of the lad and replied coldly, "I guess."

After receiving another callous answer, Haley turned toward Rane and queried, "Is something wrong?"

"No," he retorted insincerely.

Haley stared at her husband's face for a long moment, hoping he would come clean with her. When he refused to say anything further, she put her concentration back on the painting. "Rane, did you notice the black cat on the boy's lap?"

Reddy knew they weren't paying any attention to him but decided to voice his opinion anyway. "That's not a cat—that's a man-eating leopard."

Knowing the feline was Raven, Rane replied in an anxious tone to his wife, "I . . . I saw it."

While meticulously going over the fine points of the picture, Haley stated, "The part that has me puzzled is the cat has yellow eyes yet the red collar looks exactly the same as Shadow's, except of course for the gold, identification tag."

Although Rane had a pretty good idea that Shadow's choker formerly belonged to Raven, he went through the charade of moving closer to the painting to check it out anyway. "It does, huh?"

Feeling like he couldn't stand to be around the mural another moment, Rane eyed the door for a way of escape. Nervously cracking his knuckles, he looked back at his wife and said in a rushed tone, "I think we've wasted enough time here. Let's go."

He then took off toward the outlet like his pants were on fire.

Haley turned to follow him out of the room until her eye caught sight of a small inscription at the bottom of the mural. "Rane, wait!"

Stopping abruptly underneath the doorway, he turned around and asked uninterestedly, "What?"

With her eyes still glued on the inscription, she replied, "Look at the dedication. It says, 'In memory of my beloved Kathryn.'"

Haley made a baffled expression at her husband and said, "That is a picture of Artur's girlfriend."

He stared coldly at the painting of his mother and queried, "So what's yer point?"

"I was just curious why a woman would be playing poker with a man she betrayed."

Rane propped his hand on the doorway as he answered in a cynical tone, "For money, what else? Ye heard it yerself, he never beat her."

Haley glanced at the losing hand the woman was holding in the painting and then stared forlornly at her husband. "But the reporters were wrong. Weren't they, Rane? The Jack somehow got his revenge an' wound up stripping her of something she prized highly."

She paused to look back at the pool of tears painted in Kathryn's eyes and said further, "An' left her with a broken heart."

He gaped painfully at the picture of his mother and walked away.

Haley found her husband back in the private room checking for the code inside the art books on the shelf. "Why did you take off like that?"

He slowly looked up at her confused face, shrugging without interest.

She eyed the small pile of books he had thrown on the floor. "Are you all right?"

Rane tried to mask his blue mood by saying, "Why wouldn't I be?"

He picked up the last book off the shelf and blew dust off the cover. After sticking another piece of grape-flavored bubble gum into his mouth, he rummaged through the pages in the book and then tossed it in the pile with all the others.

Listening to him smack on his gum, she queried, "Rane, did you know that woman in the painting?"

He chewed on the wad of bubble gum as he looked around the room for more books. "I don't want t'talk about paintings right now, Haley. I got more important things t'do like finding that code."

Haley dismissed his touchiness as she turned to watch Shadow play with her toy mouse. "Rane, look."

Rane turned toward her, not watching where he was going, and accidentally rammed the front of his left kneecap into the trunk. Crying out from the severe pain, he clutched both hands around the injury and started hopping around on one foot. "Ow! Oooh, that hurt!"

Haley hastened to his side. "Chappy, are you all right?"

He lowered his throbbing leg to the floor and said angrily, "Does Chappy look all right t'ye?"

Watching him limp around on one foot, she queried, "What happened?"

After calming down somewhat, Rane motioned his hand toward the item he ran into and said, "Oh, I banged me knee on that stupid trunk an' accidentally swallowed me bubble gum."

Feeling a strong urge to laugh at his comment about the gum, she squeezed her lips together.

Rane tightened his jaw to fight back his discomfort and then started kicking the chest with the toe of his right boot.

While trying not to giggle, Haley asked, "Why are you kicking the trunk?"

He plopped down on the edge of the chest, cringing from the bruises on his buttocks, and replied short-temperedly, "'Cause it makes me feel better, all right."

Reddy, who had been secretly spying on them, snickered goofily, "Makes me feel better. Whiz Kid, ye crazy guy."

Haley made a puzzled face at her husband. "I don't understand how kicking a trunk can make you feel better."

Rolling up his pant leg to examine his hurt knee, he replied, "I don't understand some of d'things ye do either, so I guess we're in d'same boat."

She hooked some strands of her curly, red hair behind her ear and said, "Well, at least we're in the same boat."

Rane rolled his eyes at her wacky response and then visibly flinched after touching the tender spot on his kneecap.

Haley placed her hand on his shoulder. "Ugh! That's a nasty bruise."

He slowly looked up at his wife. "I suspect it will match all d'other ones, wouldn't ye say?"

Rane lowered his head and went back to nursing his kneecap. "Now what was it ye wanted?"

Knowing he was probably going to get upset with her, Haley giggled nervously before giving her answer. "I thought you might want to see Shadow playing with her toy mouse."

Rane glanced toward the area where the cat was playing and replied, "Now why on earth would I want t'see her do that?"

Haley shrugged her shoulders nonchalantly and, again, tried to hide the fact that she was sniggering on the inside. "I just thought you might like to see her doing something cute."

Rane shook his head at her and began rolling down his pant leg. Just as he finished smoothing the wrinkles out of his jeans, Shadow leaped up on the chest and dropped her motorized toy mouse in his lap. The plaything had fake brown fir, pink ears, and a pink tail. It was so lifelike it was hard to tell it wasn't real.

The instant Rane saw the vibrating mouse wiggling around on his thighs, he widened his eyes in horror and started screaming to the top of his lungs.

Haley giggled at her husband's petrified reaction to the toy.

Finding it hard to talk out of fear, Rane pointed a shaky finger at the rodent on his pants and stuttered breathlessly, "She-sh-sh-she, she dropped a ra-ra-rat on me."

Reddy took a peek at the small, mechanical mouse that was causing all the ruckus and then chuckled to himself. "Whiz Kid, ye're one funny guy."

Haley grabbed the mouse by the tail and tossed it across the room, sniggering, "Rane, it's only a toy mouse."

After turning red in the face from embarrassment, he said, "I knew that. I was just playing around. I wasn't really scared."

She smiled like she didn't believe him and then inadvertently caught sight of a tag on the front of the trunk. "Hey, Rane …"

While flexing his injured knee, Rane queried, "What?"

Pointing at the front of the chest, she answered back right away, "Look at this sticker."

Rane stood unstably on his right foot. Trying to keep his weight off the injured knee, he slowly crouched down to read the tag. "Date o'delivery … December 24th … midnight."

He looked up at his wife as if he was in deep thought and said, "Midnight? That's d'time set in d'painting of d'mice."

Haley bit her lower lip, deeply contemplating the matter. "Rane, does it say who's picking up the trunk or where they're delivering it to?"

He smoothed out the crinkled label to find the information she requested and replied, "I dunno. That part of d'tag has been torn off."

Shadow jumped off the trunk and started chewing on the sticker.

Rane pushed the cat away from the tag and said in an aggravated tone, "Kitty, quit it!"

Standing upright, he put his hands in his coat pockets and stated to his wife, "Now we know where the rest of the tag went."

"Rane, open the trunk an' see what's inside."

With a fretful look plastered all over his face, Rane shook his head and said, "Not me."

"Why not?"

He took several steps back from the trunk and replied, "There might be rats in there."

Haley rolled her eyes at his cowardice and opened the lid herself. Soon as she saw what was inside, she made a confounded expression and said, "Toys?"

Rane moseyed back over to the chest when he saw that it was safe and peeked into the box. "Aye, 'tis a bunch of toys all right."

Haley got down on her knees and started feeling along the front panel inside the trunk.

Observing her every move, Rane queried, "What are ye doing?"

"I'm looking for a release mechanism."

"A release mechanism? For what?"

She ran her fingertips along the back panel inside the chest as she replied, "A secret compartment."

"Ye think this might be a magic trunk?"

Haley nodded her head and replied confidently, "The toys are just a decoy. A person could easily hide in the bottom of this trunk."

He thought about the dangers of actually doing that and joined her on his knees. "But wouldn't they suffocate t'death in there?"

"Not if they weren't in there for very long."

"That's true."

All at once Rane heard a well-known jingle and the sound of a Jack-in-the-box springing up out of its compartment. Scared by the mysterious noises he heard, he held his breath and peered around the dark room. "Who's there?"

Seeing the distressed look in his eyes, Haley whispered out of concern, "What is it, Rane?"

He laid his index finger against his lips and whispered, "Sh."

After doing a double take of the room, he lowered his finger from his mouth and said in a barely audible tone, "Didn't ye hear that?"

Although Haley knew exactly what it was that had frightened him, she played along by querying in a covert fashion, "Hear what?"

Rane swallowed hard at the thought of confronting a dangerous criminal and slowly turned his head to look behind him. "I think there's somebody in here with us."

While his back was still turned, Haley saw a perfect opportunity to play another joke on him. Using the spur of the moment, she grabbed the Jack-in-the-box toy out of the chest, shoved its head down inside the compartment, and closed the lid. Trying hard not to laugh out loud, she kept on with her little charade by whispering, "Do you think it might be Jack?"

Keeping his gaze in the opposite direction, he replied shakily, "I think so."

Haley held the box out in front of her, waiting for her husband to turn back around. The second he did, she pressed the lever on the side of the toy and released the spring. When the Jack's head popped up out of the compartment and almost hit Rane in the face, he started screaming hysterically.

Amused by what she had done, Haley laid back on the floor, laughing her head off.

Reddy, too, thought her prank was funny and snickered under his breath.

After realizing his wife had played another gag on him, Rane placed a protective hand over his chest and scolded, "Would ye quit it? I almost had a heart attack for goodness sake."

He snatched the toy out of her hand and tossed it on the floor.

Haley sat up giggling and pointed at her husband's face. "You should have seen the look on your face."

Acting as if his pride had been pricked, Rane pursed his lips at his wife and crossed his arms. "Can we get back t'work now?"

Haley guffawed, nodding her head, and then joined him in taking all the toys out of the trunk.

After they had removed all the playthings from the box, Haley felt along the back, left corner of the tray and felt a push button, the size of a pinhead. "Rane, I think I found it."

"Ye did?" he said excitedly.

Haley nodded and pressed the switch. All at once the top tray retracted, revealing a hidden compartment underneath. She ran her hands over the entire cubicle but didn't find anything. Deeply disappointed, she said, "There's nothing here. I thought for sure we'd find a clue, a code, or something that would help us with this case."

Rane comforted his wife by saying, "Don't let it get ye down, Hal. At least ye were right about it being a magic trunk."

She smiled at his encouraging words and then pressed the button again to close the tray.

Rane helped his wife put all the toys back inside the trunk and then said, "Let's go downstairs into the lobby. I'm tired of this cat pestering me."

She smiled at Shadow rubbing her furry body along his pant legs before replying, "Okay."

CHAPTER 38

Haley followed Rane into the foyer and took a peek out the front door to see if the Cadillac was parked back on the street. Unable to spot it, she sighed disappointedly and then joined her husband on the Queen Anne sofa.

While they were busy trying to figure out where Aileen hid the code, Haley saw the cat run into the room and giggled, "Our Shadow seems to follow us everywhere we go."

Rane watched the cat jump on his lap as he replied, "That's 'cause we're so irresistible."

He petted the purring feline and then gazed at the sparkling, white diamonds in her choker, thinking, *Now why would Aileen put rare gems in Raven's collar an' then pass it down t'Shadow? That doesn't make any sense.*

Just when Rane was feeling like he had come to a dead-end, he remembered something from his past. *Wait a minute. Aileen implanted a microchip into Raven's neck right before she put this collar on him. I bet she hid me password inside d'collar.*

Acting upon his gut feeling, he removed the choker from around Shadow's neck and said, "Reddy, come here."

Haley stroked her hand along the cat's back and queried hopefully, "Rane, did you come up with something?"

Rane flexed his leg a couple of times to work out the sore kink in his kneecap as he replied, "'Tis just a hunch, but I think Aileen might have hidden young Finney's password inside this collar."

With his magnifying glass still in hand, Reddy hopped out of Haley's pocket and landed on the arm of the sofa. "Ye need me, Whiz Kid?"

Rane handed the red choker to the bot. "Aye, scan d'cat an' this collar with yer x-ray vision an' tell me if ye find any microchips."

Eager to help, Reddy rubbed his hands together and said, "Okey-dokey, Whiz Kid, I'm on d'case."

Hoping her husband would let her in on what he knew, Haley queried, "Microchips?"

Rane couldn't give her any specific details and merely nodded his head.

Reddy finished his examination and handed Rane back the collar. "Aye, there's one in d'back of d'kitty's neck about d'size of an ink dot."

"An' d'collar?"

"No microchip detected."

While pulling out his pen and notepad from his jacket pocket, Rane said, "Good job, Reddy. Now give me yer analysis on d'microchip's primary function."

The bot put on an intelligent face and replied, "D'chip is sending out some sort of secret code."

Rane wrinkled his brow and queried earnestly, "Where to?"

Acting like the answer was plain as the nose on his face, Reddy pointed at the collar in his hand and snickered, "Into d'gems, ye funny guy."

Shocked at the bot's report, Haley looked down at the collar and whispered to herself, "Into the gems?"

Rane held the collar closer to his nose as he peered into each of the tiny, white diamonds. After careful scrutiny, he handed the choker back to the bot and said, "I don't see anything."

Reddy held his magnifying glass in front of his eye while meticulously inspecting the gems. "That's 'cause d'cryptographer designed d'code t'be read in a high magnification. I can barely make out d'symbols even with me super-duper, high-powered, detective lens."

Rane rolled his eyes at the bot and replied, "Reddy, just tell me what ye see, okay?"

With the glass lens still positioned over his eye, the bot flashed his inventor one of his silly grins and said, "Okey-dokey, Whiz Kid, ye're d'boss."

The bot let down his head and squinted at the diamond on the far left. "I see a lowercase *a*."

Rane scribbled down the letter and said, "All right, read me d'next one."

Reddy gazed into the subsequent diamond and replied, "Looks like d'number five."

He jotted down the numerical symbol and queried, "Okay, what's next?"

The bot shifted the magnifying glass over to his other eye and answered, "A lowercase *r*."

Soon as Reddy finished reading him all the symbols, Rane tapped the end of his pen against the tablet in his hand. "*A* … five … *r* … two … *b* … two … *e* … five … *h* … seven? What is that?"

Haley looked at the mysterious cryptogram and shook her head. "It has the computer's digits in it, but I don't know what the rest means."

After several moments of unprofitable study, Rane felt irritated by his own ignorance and smacked the tablet with his pen. "I'm going t'decipher this thing if it kills me."

Without considering what it might do to his ego, Haley said, "That language code is going to be tough to crack, Rane. You better ask the bot to help you."

Thinking she was implying he was stupid, Rane frowned at the bot and then looked up at his wife like he was offended. "I don't need his help. I can figure it out for myself, thank ye."

Haley could tell by the tone in his voice that she had insulted him. Trying to make amends, she whistled the tune for the bot to turn into a watch and put his changed form into her coat pocket. She then gave her husband an encouraging pat on the hand and said, "You're right. You don't need his help. You're a genius. You can figure it out for yourself."

Believing her compliment was insincere, Rane responded sarcastically, "Oh sure, a regular Einstein. Now how in d'world am I supposed t'get d'master code to d'robot if I can't even figure out what young Finney's password is?"

Haley got up off the couch and said to encourage him, "You'll get it."

Pacing back and forth, she thought about the hidden code inside the collar. Coming up with an idea, she stopped abruptly and said, "Rane … "

"What?"

"Reddy said, 'the cryptographer designed the code to be read in a high magnification,' right?"

Rane nodded and replied, "Aye."

"Do you think Aileen did that so the android couldn't read it?"

He looked down at the code he had written on the tablet as he answered his wife. "Probably, Prosperity said she didn't trust the robot."

Haley reseated herself on the sofa while her husband studied the cryptogram.

Rane couldn't come up with any solution and laid his head back against the couch. Closing his eyes, he pleaded prayerfully, "Lord, we need some help here. Anything ye give us will be greatly appreciated."

Soon as he had finished praying, he put all his concentration back on the alpha and numerical sequence in the code. "Five two

two five seven? Let's see now, if I take away the series of numbers that leaves me with … *a* … *r* … *b* … *e* … *h*."

Haley halted his train of thought by saying, "Arbeh is not an English word."

Rane calmly shrugged off her correction and replied, "Okay, maybe if I unscramble d'letters, it will make sense."

Haley looked down at what he was writing. "Rabeh is not an English word either."

Rane jotted down two different arrangements of the letters and asked, "How about, hearb or hareb?"

She crossed her leg and shook her head. "No."

He reshuffled the letters in his mind and then scribbled them down on the tablet. "Bearh?"

Haley shrugged, giving him a blank look. "They all look like foreign words to me."

Rane stared curiously at the original layout of the letters, muttering to himself, "Arbeh? Now where have I heard that before?"

While he was deeply contemplating the matter, Haley felt her cell phone quivering in her coat pocket. After discovering it was her dad who was calling, she quietly slipped around the corner to find out what he wanted. By the time she had lifted the lid on her phone, he was in the process of leaving her a message. She waited until he had finished it and then dialed her voice mail.

Rane was so busy trying to figure out the code he didn't see her leave. "Ar … beh … arb … eh … arbe … h … arbeh?"

Haley cocked her ear to her cell phone, listening intently to the voice recording left by her dad.

"Hi, Haley, I told you I'd call back when I finished my investigation. I hope you're sitting down. Rane's late dad was the legendary Lucky Jack, a man known for being a womanizer."

Haley's eyes bulged in shock as she pushed the stop button on the recording. "Lucky Jack is his dad?"

She peeked around the corner at Rane and saw him scribbling on his tablet. Upset that he had deceived her, she shook her head and then played the rest of the message.

"His mother is Kathryn O'Malley. She's a compulsive gambler an' often prostitutes herself to get the money to pay off her poker debts. Some family tree, huh? I knew Rane was a loser from the first day I laid eyes on him. Sign the divorce papers he sent you an' be done with him. I told you he couldn't be trusted. If I were you, I would stay far away from him. If you need a shoulder to cry on, I'm here for daddy's little girl."

After Haley had finished listening to the message left by her dad, she laid her head back against the wall, stunned by the fact that her husband had betrayed her. Sharing her pain with God, she sobbed, "Rane's been lying to me the whole time, Lord. I didn't want to believe it. I wanted to trust him. How can I stay married to a man I can't trust?" With a stream of tears trickling down her face, Haley stared numbly across the hall, feeling like nothing mattered. After several moments of drowning her heart in thoughts of divorce, she remembered her wedding vows. Not thrilled about keeping them, she said hurtfully, "If I hadn't made that promise to Rane, I'd walk out on him right now an' never come back."

She had no sooner spewed out her self-righteous words when she heard the Holy Spirit convicting her heart. *Haley, see your marriage vows as sacred, an' my everlasting life will rest upon your heart.*

Tears filled her eyes as she humbly replied, "Yes, my Lord. Help me an' Rane to be a blessing to one another an' not a curse."

Rane looked up from the notepad and noticed his wife was gone. Standing to his feet, he hollered out uneasily, "Haley?"

Hearing him calling her, she quickly straightened up her face and walked around the corner. "Yes?"

He sat back down on the couch and replied, "Come here an' see if ye can help me figure this thing out."

Haley found it extremely difficult to mask the pain she was feeling in her heart as she ambled over to husband.

Rane eyed the cell phone in her hand and noticed she wasn't her usual perky self. Her eyes were puffy and red from crying, and she was sniffing her nose. "Is something wrong?"

Haley did what she usually did when she felt like she couldn't talk to her husband; she changed the subject. "Um, you come up with anything yet?"

Distracted from his original thought by her new inquiry, Rane drew his attention onto the tablet and said wearily, "No."

While staring at the code he had written down on the small, spiral notebook, she wiped away a teardrop that had escaped out of the corner of her eye and said, "Maybe 'arbeh' is a foreign word."

Upon hearing her suggestion, Rane had a flashback of something his nanny had taught him as a child. Snapping his fingers like he had just got a revelation, he blurted out excitedly, "That's it!"

"What?"

"*Arbeh* is a Hebrew word for locust. Locust 52257 is young Finney's password. He used d'name of d'master computer."

Haley peered at Rane distrustfully and asked, "How did you know that?"

Intimidated by the look she was giving him, Rane slumped in his seat, answering shyly, "Uuuuh … lucky guess?"

Tired of his deceptive games, Haley glared at her husband for several moments before playing back the voice recording left by her dad. "Lucky guess, huh?"

Not sure what she meant, Rane listened to the entire message. After finding out she knew the truth about him, he swallowed hard.

Haley placed her cell phone back in her coat pocket, giving her husband a smug look. "What say you now … Finney?"

Rane's heart was pounding so hard he could hear it inside his head. He didn't like having his back up against the wall, so he got up off the sofa and said angrily, "If ye knew the truth, why let me go through that whole charade?"

Haley's eyes pooled with tears as she replied, "I didn't till I got this message from my dad."

Rane's cross tone remained unchanged as he threw the writing pad down on the couch. "Oh fine, Chase McConaley, Mr. Eye Spy himself. I guess snooping around in people's affairs runs in d'family, eh?"

She replied in a slighted tongue, "It was my dad's idea to run a background check on you, not mine. I believe a marriage should be built on trust."

Feeling convicted that he had betrayed hers, Rane got quiet and lowered his head. After staring emptily at the scuffmarks on his black boots, he at last worked up enough courage to apologize. "I'm sorry I lied t'ye, Hal. I-I seem t'have a problem trusting women."

Tears flowed down her face as she queried, "Have I ever hurt you, Chappy?"

He dropped his head again and replied out of remorse, "No."

"Then why didn't you tell me the truth?"

Bitter from the past, Rane pursed his lips and then answered, "I thought ye would judge me like yer dad if ye found out. People have been poking fun at me my whole life, like I have no feelings."

"I'm not my dad, Rane. I make my own choices in life, an' I choose to love you."

Rane stood quiet for several moments, taking in everything she said. Believing her word to be sincere, he smiled at her and said, "Ye're a special lady, Hal."

She used the back of her hands to wipe the tears off her cheeks and then thought about the five-year-old boy in the mural. "The toys in the trunk were yours?"

"Aye. Aileen bought d'toys for me in memory of me dad."

Rane took the photo of Artur out of his coat pocket and handed it to his wife. "My mum gave me this picture of him when I was just a wee laddie."

Haley eyed the man's face in the photo and handed the picture back to her husband. "Your parents were gambling over you. Weren't they, Rane?"

Rane squeezed his eyes shut to fight back the painful memory and shortly afterward nodded his head. Feeling numb inside, he sat back down on the couch and picked up the tablet.

Haley took a seat beside him. Showing him that she sympathized with the emotional pain he was experiencing, she caressed his hand and said, "When you're ready to talk about it, I'll be here for you."

Rane slowly looked up at his wife and saw mercy in her eyes. He stared at her without blinking for several moments, wondering why she chose to forgive him. Not being able to fully understand the love she had for him in her heart, he cleared his throat and put his attention back on the cryptogram.

Haley prayed in her heart for their marriage and then looked at the notepad on her husband's lap. "So Hebrew is the other language your nanny taught you that you couldn't remember before?"

He eyed the code on the pad of paper and answered, "Aye."

While strolling down memory lane, Rane said, "I remember Jillian used t'get mad at me every time I called d'robot *Arbeh*."

"Why?"

He shrugged and replied, "I dunno. It just bugged her, an' boy how I liked t'bug her."

"How long did you live with Jillian?"

Rane thought about the time he broke his aunt's crystal ball and grumbled, "One year, an' that was way too long."

He leaned back on the couch, still reminiscing about the past. All at once his head filled with scientific equations and star charts. The knowledge was like a breath of fresh air to him. Eager to share the good news with his wife, he said high spiritedly, "Hey, Hal . . . "

"What?"

"I remember making Little Silver."

Thrilled to hear some good news, Haley got nose to nose with her husband and said, "You do?"

His enthusiasm died down somewhat as he replied, "Well, parts of him anyway. I recall giving him a large-capacity, zeta-zenith memory storage for accelerated space travel."

"Do you remember how you designed his particle communicator?"

Rane shook his head out of disappointment. "No."

Thinking back on some of the things he had shared with her about the top-secret project, Haley filled in some of the missing gaps. "Evidently, Reddy can communicate with things through their sound waves."

His tone lifted as if he was suddenly recalling the concept from the past. "Through their sound waves?"

"Yes. He can tell an asteroid belt to move out of the way long before the spacecraft reaches that point in space."

Rane's eyes darted about excitedly as more of his genius returned to him. "Or he can simply dilate its particles, an' d'spaceship will pass right through d'asteroids."

Haley smiled at his intellect. "Rane, that's fantastic. All your memories are coming back."

Tapping his ink pen against the tablet in his hand, he replied, "Aye, I even remember loading d'Bible archive into d'android's mainframe."

Rane's jovial mood was suddenly choked out by a frightening thought from his past. With his eyes bulging like a frog's, he groaned in a hard to hear voice, "Oh no."

"What is it?"

Without changing his expression, he slapped his hand to the side of his cheek and said louder, "We're in big trouble."

Deeply concerned over the way he was acting, Haley queried with great interest, "Why? What's wrong?"

Distant in thought, he answered slowly, "D'android ..."

"What about it?"

Rane lowered his hand from his face and continued talking as if he was miles away. "He's d'kidnapper."

Stunned by his disclosure, Haley elevated her voice. "The robot is the man we're looking for?"

Thinking about the android's deceptive abilities, he nodded his head and said, "Aye, that's why Reddy didn't find any blood or fingerprints. Yer assumptions were right, Hal."

She wondered how in the world she was going to explain all this to her dad and giggled faintly. "How do you arrest a mechanical man for a crime? He doesn't have any rights."

He grinned at her and shrugged. "I dunno."

"What does the robot really look like?"

Rane's photographic memory began to kick in as he recalled a conversation he once had with Aileen when he was a little boy. "In his original form, he looks exactly like Lucky Jack. But he has d'ability t'alter his molecular structure t'take on d'identity of anyone he chooses."

The stress in her voice mounted as she visualized the robot shape-shifting his appearance to look like Mr. Chandler's. "He can actually do that?"

Rane nervously twisted his wife's ink pen back and forth as he continued to reflect on the past. "Aye, an' he's quite good at it. That's why I secretly loaded d'archive into d'robot's neural net during one of Aileen's experimental tests."

"Did Aileen know about it?"

He froze the pen in his hand as he replied, "No way. I waited until she left d'room. Although me aunt hated her family's practice of magic, she made it quite clear t'me she wanted no part of our King. Aileen believed science was d'answer for everything."

"Why didn't she just remove the file?"

Rane thought about his little scheme and chuckled mischievously. "She couldn't. The biblical archive was electrically charged."

With a dense expression on her face, Haley lowered her eyebrows and asked, "Electrically charged?"

He kept on snickering, "Uh-huh, each time she tried t'remove d'archive without my access code, she short-circuited d'robot's neural net."

"So why timetable the file to open fourteen years later?"

Rane stopped snickering and replied, "I didn't have much choice. My dad set up d'mainframe t'prohibit me from opening any files until I was twenty-one."

"Why?"

He shrugged his shoulders and said, "I dunno. That was d'legal age he stipulated in his will when I would inherit his entire estate."

"How did you know he willed everything to you?"

"Aileen tol' me. She was d'executor of his will."

Haley glanced at the notepad in his hand and asked, "But she didn't tell you how to decipher the master code hidden inside your password?"

He shook his head and replied, "Nope, she refused t'give me d'key until I turned twenty-one. An' now that she's dead, we have no way of finding out what it is."

Haley rested her head against the sofa and said, "I'm sure God will help us figure it out. In the meantime, that robot is bound to show up here eventually. An' when he does, I'll put the cuffs on him. We're just going to have to wait him out."

Rane chuckled faintly at the idea of his wife handcuffing a robot and then stared back at his password. "These set of numbers must mean something."

Not being able to come up with anything, Haley got bored and inadvertently looked down at the French-style black telephone on the round, white marble table top next to her. After careful observation of it, she pulled the two playing cards out of her coat pocket and stared at the face of the Jack. All at once she remembered something the perpetrator had said to all his target victims and put her attentive eyes back on the phone, whispering to herself, "One of my calling cards."

Rane saw the strange fixation in his wife's eyes as she picked up the telephone. "What is it?"

Haley put the porcelain telephone on her lap and pointed at the etching of Kathryn's face inside the gold dial. "This looks like the phone in the painting."

She showed him the two cards in her hand and added, "I think the telephone an' the cards are somehow connected together."

Believing she was leading him to another dead-end, Rane shook his head at her suggestion and went back to trying to decipher the code. "I don't think so."

Haley sighed at his lack of interest and then drew her eyes onto the set of letters on the right side of each number on the phone. Coming up with an idea, she leaned toward her husband and whispered, "Rane, maybe there is a secret word hidden inside the numbers in your password. If we can figure it out, we might be able to decipher the master code."

Rane glanced at the phone on his wife's lap and queried, "Secret word?"

She nodded and continued the secrecy by keeping her voice low. "I saw it done in an old mystery movie once."

Feeling like it was a waste of time, he replied, "I dunno."

Before he could completely throw out her proposal, Haley shook his arm and said, "Come on, Rane. I bet you'll change your mind if I tell you the name of the movie."

"What was the name of the movie?"

She put on a superior air as she replied, "Every Man Jack."

Rane mulled over her pitch and took the book of matches out of his coat pocket. After staring at the icons of the three Jacks, he decided to give in. "Why not? I'm so desperate, I'll try anything."

Haley smiled at him for giving her the go ahead and repositioned the telephone on her lap to easily see the dial. "You want me to start reading you the letters for the number five?"

Rane rested the tip of his ballpoint pen on his notepad and nodded his head.

She looked down at the gold dial and began reciting the correlating letters off the phone. "*J… K… L.*"

Rane put the matches back in his pocket and then jotted down the information above the first digit. "All right, give me d'letters for d'number two."

Haley used the tip of her index finger to help guide her eyes to the area he requested and replied, "*A… B… C.*"

After scribbling down the letters, Rane looked up at his wife and queried, "How about seven?"

She found the corresponding set and said, "*P… Q… R… S.*"

Rane circled the number five and wrote the first letter she gave him under the digit. "Okay, let's start with the letter *J.*"

Haley set the black phone back on the table and gawked at what her husband was writing.

Rane circled the next digit in the code and said, "We need a vowel, so I'll put d'letter *A* under d'number two, which gives us *J…A.*"

With Haley's astute eye for detail, it didn't take long for her to figure it out. "Rane, the secret word is *JACKS.*"

He gave her an unsure look and queried, "It is?"

"Yes. Check the rest of the letters."

After verifying it for himself, Rane grinned at his wife. "Hey, ye're right."

Haley thought about the write-up in the magazine and asked, "Do you suppose this has anything to do with Artur's alter egos?"

"Ye mean Lucky Jack an' Dirty Jack?"

Haley nodded her head. "Uh-huh."

Rane stared suspiciously at the name he had spelled out on his tablet and said, "Knowing my dad's obsession with gambling, it probably has something to do with cards."

Haley pointed at the circled numbers on his notepad and said, "Then the pair of deuces an' the pair of fives could be a poker hand?"

Rane tapped the pen against his cheek, thinking aloud, "But why two of a kind?"

"Maybe it had something to do with the game he was playing."

He stared back at the code written on the tablet and suddenly had a flashback of the mural in the conference room. Seeing Artur's poker hand in the back of his mind, he jumped up out of his chair and said jubilantly, "I think that's it!"

Rane pulled the matches out of his coat pocket and glanced in the direction of Masterpiece Hall. "Artur was playing Jacks or better."

"He was?"

Still hyped up over his discovery, Rane shook his notepad in the air and replied, "I bet this is d'losing hand my mum is holding in that picture."

Making sure she understood him correctly, Haley queried, "So you believe the master code is Jacks or better?"

Thinking back on what Lucky Jack boasted in the article the bot had read to them, Rane didn't hesitate before answering, "No. Jacks are better."

Unsure what he was talking about, Haley lowered her eyebrows and asked, "Jacks are better?"

Rane nodded his head as he stuffed the matches, pen, and tablet into his coat pocket. "Aye, remember that's what Lucky Jack boasted in d'magazine write-up in d'mural. He must have said it t'me mum after he dethroned her."

Haley's sharp knowing eyes glistened. "You know that makes sense. Kathryn was the reigning queen."

Taking his wife by the hand, he said in an eager tone, "Come on, Hal. Let's go see if I'm right about her cards."

After running all the way into the conference room, Rane discovered his suspicions were correct. Panting hard from the fast sprint, he raised his fist into the air, shouting victoriously, "Yes!"

He pointed at his mother's poker hand and said, "See. I was right. She's holding a pair of deuces an' a pair of fives."

Thrilled that he had figured it out, Haley kissed her winded husband on the cheek. "Like I said before, Rane, you'd make a great detective."

He grinned at her and said, "I can't take any credit for it. God is d'one who helped me figure it out."

All at once Rane heard a beeping noise and looked toward his wife's ski jacket. "Sounds like Reddy's expending too much energy."

Haley pulled the teleportation device out of her coat pocket and sighed wearily when she saw the red warning light flashing inside the small crystal. "Oh dear, the accelerator overheated again. I'll have to turn our velocity back to normal."

"I'm not sure why that keeps happening. 'Tis one of d'bugs I haven't quite worked out yet."

She turned off the accelerator switch on the side of the mechanism and said, "It will take at least ten minutes to cool it down before I can reset it."

Rane took a seat at the conference table to rest his aching knee. Leaning his forearm on the table, he looked around the room and said, "Lucky for us, there are no security cameras in here. Speaking o'cameras, we don't have t'worry about cleaning d'gum off d'one outside. It now belongs t'us, an' we'll pay someone t'do it."

Haley smiled at him and replied, "Yeah, that's right. You're the rightful heir now. Artur willed everything to you."

He chuckled to himself, "Jillian's probably not going t'be too happy when I serve her an eviction notice."

Haley laid the watch down on the table and pulled her cell phone out of her other pocket. Once she had engaged the high-powered camera feature inside her phone, she aimed the view screen at the mural on the wall and started taking pictures.

Rane looked over at what his wife was doing and asked, "What are d'pictures for?"

While continuing to photograph the mural on the wall, she replied, "In case I need them later."

"Oh," he replied.

Haley finished taking pictures of the painting and put her cell phone away. After shifting her eyes back and forth from Artur's face to his winning poker hand on the table, she said suspiciously, "Rane…"

"What?"

"Artur had only two alter egos, right?"

"Aye."

"Well don't ye think it is strange that he won with three Jacks?"

Rane noted Artur's poker hand and then looked over at his mothers. In his dad's defense, he said, "He sure couldn't beat her with two."

Picking up on a theory, Haley wrinkled her brow at the pack of Lucky Strike III cigarettes on the poker table and whispered under her breath, "He couldn't beat her with two."

Seeing his wife was lost in thought over the painting, Rane queried, "What is it?"

Haley pointed at the winning hand in the painting. "Look at the three Jacks lying on the table in front of him."

Rane eyed the Jack of Diamonds, the Jack of Spades, and the Jack of Clubs and queried, "What about 'em?"

She stared at the three stripping locusts on top of Lucky Jack's coronet before answering, "I think Artur had a third shadow the media didn't know about."

"Ye mean d'robot?" he replied as if he wasn't sure.

Staying with her gut feeling, Haley nodded her head and replied, "Prosperity said that Artur was known for hiding secret things about himself in his artwork. If I'm correct, the Jacks in his poker hand are supposed to represent three different characters."

"How so?"

Haley referenced the cards on the table by saying, "Don't you see—the Jack of Diamonds stands for Lucky Jack, the Jack of Spades for Dirty Jack…"

Rane interrupted her to say, "D'diamonds I can see, but how does spades tie in for Dirty Jack?"

She crossed her arms and gave him a smart answer. "From an old idiom 'call a spade a spade.'"

Rane thought about how the Dirty Jack treated the cocktail waitress in the hologram and said, "Aye, he was known for speaking bluntly to d'lassies an' not sparing their feelings."

Haley directed her husband's attention onto the next card by saying, "An' the Jack of Clubs…"

She paused to look up at the mischievous wink on the Jack's face and then replied in a leisurely, melodramatic tone, "The Locust 52257 Jack… his secret weapon."

"How do ye figure that?"

Haley pointed at the symbol on the card and replied, "Club means beat."

"But what about d'Jack o' Hearts?"

She drew her green eyes onto the discarded face card on the table and then looked up at the picture of the android's face. "Evidently he didn't have one."

Not wanting to believe her assumption that it was the robot in the painting and not his dad, Rane snickered, "Do ye know how crazy that sounds, Hal?"

Haley made it quite clear that she was serious by the look on her face. "It may sound crazy, but I think that's how he beat her."

To prove her hunch, she motioned her hand toward the mural and stated further, "He even boasted about it in the concealed message in her cards."

After giving what she said a second thought, Rane replied, "Aye, d'numbers in me mum's cards spelled out 'Jacks.'"

She thought about the license plate on the black Cadillac and added, "An' if I'm not mistaken, the numbers also total up to three sevens or twenty-one. Now how did Artur know the Jacks would get lucky beforehand unless he had the third one stack the deck?"

Rane looked back at the Jack of Hearts card his mom had discarded on the table and, again, thought about the three icons on the matches in his coat pocket. "Ye know ye may be right."

Haley picked up the teleportation device off the table to check the heat sensor, and it started changing its molecular structure into a weapon. Baffled why the bot had altered his form without her permission, she queried, "Reddy, what are you doing? I didn't ask for the gun."

Picking up on Jack parking his car across the street, Reddy warned, "Danger! Android approaching."

Rane jumped up out of his seat and stared uneasily toward the open door. "Where, Reddy?"

"Android is 0.03048 kilometers away an' is heading in this direction."

Haley quickly shut off the lights.

Rane joined his wife over by the door and whispered, "Haley, that won't do any good."

"Why?"

"That robot has both night vision an' high frequency hearing. If he gets close enough, he'll be able t'hear us breathing."

She aimed her silver pistol toward the entranceway and gave her husband a look of concern. "So what do we do?"

He thought up a plan and whispered in her ear, "I got an idea."

Fixing his eyes on the gun in his wife's hand, Rane asked in a hushed tone, "Reddy, can d'robot's transmitter be accessed externally?"

"Affirmative."

"What transmitter?" Haley queried to her husband as they continued whispering back and forth.

"D'robot's power source is located inside a ruby, diamond-shaped earring attached t'his left earlobe."

Thinking back on when she first saw the kidnapper, Haley looked up at the earring Lucky Jack was wearing in the mural and stated in a revelatory tone, "Oooh, so he did wear the Band-aid to cover up his lobe."

"Aye, he couldn't remove his earring, or he'd automatically set off his built-in defense mechanism an' be blown t'kingdom come."

Shocked by the end result, Haley widened her eyes and muttered under her breath, "Blown to kingdom come."

Directing his attention back on the smart gun in her hand, Rane maintained secrecy by asking in a barely audible voice, "Reddy, can ye change d'android's hearing range without him knowing about it?"

"Affirmative."

"Good, adjust d'megahertz t'below a whisper."

"Frequency change to android's synthetic, tympanic membrane will be completed in three point five seconds."

Hearing the android's heavy footsteps echoing from down the hall, Rane said in a fretful, pushy tone, "Hurry, Reddy."

"Transformation completed, sir."

Rane and Haley held their breath as the robot entered Masterpiece Hall.

Jack slowly walked down the showroom looking for a secret message in one of the oil paintings. When he spotted the picture of the three mice, he was certain that Jillian had placed it there and removed it from the wall. While deciphering the pictorial communication in the artwork, he noticed the smudge mark. Highly suspicious of how it got there, he did a quick fingerprint check by scanning the imprint with a beam of white light shooting out of his right eye. When he found out the print was Rane's, he put on a clever grin and hollered into the air, "I know ye're here, boy! I heard ye whispering t'yer lassie when I came in."

Rane's heart was pounding so hard he was afraid the android might hear it.

Haley knew the robot was deliberately baiting her husband into giving away their position, so she pantomimed someone zipping his lips.

Letting his wife know that her hand signal came in loud and clear, Rane nodded his head and remained silent.

Jack stood quietly, listening hard for several moments before going on to say, "Strange, I don't hear ye now. I know ye're looking for that code."

When the robot finally gave up and left the hall, Haley heaved a huge sigh of relief and asked, "What was he looking for in Masterpiece Hall?"

Rane shrugged, indicating he didn't' have a clue.

Jack carried the painting up to the security room on the second floor. After melting the picture with a red laser beam from each eye, he laid it on the floor. He then sat down in one of the two black leather chairs behind the gray metal security counter. Hoping to spy on Rane, he rewound the video recording from the camera in the showroom and played it back on fast-forward speed. When he didn't see Rane's face anywhere on the tape, he leaned back in his seat with a mystified look on his face. "What sort of magic is this, young Finney? How are ye able t'walk about in d'gallery without being seen by any of d'cameras? An' what is that faint humming noise in d'audio? It sounds like d'buzzing of a bee."

After about thirty seconds of sitting in silence, the android decided to rewind the footage and play it back on a reduced speed. When he still didn't see any sign of Rane, he rewound the tape again and played it back on the slowest possible speed. This time, he saw Rane and Haley's image flash across the screen like lightning. "I think I just found my two busy bees. I see your knowledge of physics surpasses mine, Finney. We can't have that, now can we?"

Jack contacted Jillian through the transmitter in his ear and discreetly let her know what was going on. "Got yer message—can't risk talking t'ye over d'transmitter so I'll paint a picture for ye. We'll need t'set some more traps. I found a couple of rats hiding in d'gallery. Transmission out."

Rane and Haley came out of the conference room and tiptoed down Masterpiece Hall. Seeing the empty space on the wall where the picture of the mice used to be hanging, she whispered to her husband like the android was still in the room, "He took the painting."

She aimed her gun toward the outlet and said further, "I'm going to find out what he's up to."

The instant she turned to leave, Rane took a hold of her coattail and whispered assuredly, "I'm coming with ye."

She nodded, and they went off together to find Jack. While sneaking down the corridor, Haley saw the robot leaving out the front entrance. Taking no chances, she tightened her grip on her pistol and raced down the hall to see where he was going.

Rane chased his wife to the double glass doors and said windedly, "Do ye see him?"

Haley continued spying on the robot as she replied, "Yeah, he's headed toward the black Cadillac across the street."

Hoping to find out the connection between Jillian and the British Intelligence, she pushed down on the silver handle and said, "I'm going to follow him to see what they're up to."

Rane grabbed his wife by the arm to stop her and snickered, "Ye an' what army?"

Confused what he was talking about, Haley queried, "What do you mean?"

He pointed at Jack climbing into the car and said, "That android has d'strength of ten men, ye know."

Not the least bit intimidated, she answered assertively, "If he finds out I'm tailing him, I'll just shoot him with the disruptor."

He shook his head, whispering in a stern voice, "No! You can't rely on Reddy. He's got too many bugs in him. You tried t'use d'gun before an' it wouldn't engage, remember? Call for a backup. I'm sure with your influence ye can get d'entire police force out here."

"I can't do that. I'm working undercover."

Feeling the helplessness rising up within her as she watched her suspect drive off down the street, Haley stamped her foot on the floor and whined, "Oh no, he's getting away."

She pushed the front door open and hurried outside to see what direction his car was headed.

Rane followed his wife out to the sidewalk and stared down the street. When he saw the Cadillac turn right at the traffic light, he looked back at his wife and asked, "Now what do we do?"

"We follow him."

Peering around the street at the parked cars, he replied, "There's a slight problem with that, Hal."

Haley lowered her eyebrows and asked, "What do you mean?"

"I don't think we can run fast enough t'catch him."

Upon hearing what he said, Haley smiled, releasing a diminutive giggle. "That's right. We came here on foot, didn't we?"

He nodded his head and turned his gaze back down the street.

While he wasn't looking, Haley cupped her hand over mouth, quietly whistling the tune for the teleportation device.

Soon as Rane turned around and saw her whispering into the silver pocket watch, he opened his mouth to question her secrecy but, instead, found himself sitting behind Jack in the backseat of his car.

Rane looked up at the rearview mirror and saw the robot's cold blue eyes staring back at him. Believing his life was in danger, he flooded the compartment of the car with repeated, loud shrieks.

Haley suddenly materialized in the seat next to her husband. Watching him go to pieces over nothing, she got tickled and started sniggering. "He can't see you, Rane. I used the teleportation device to speed up our particles."

She reassured him some more by waving her fingers in front of the robot's face. "See."

Breathing sporadically from the shock to his system, Rane placed his trembling hand to his chest and said in a frazzled tone, "Oh, be still me heart."

Haley giggled at the motionless android and then glanced out the window. "Where do you suppose he's driving us?"

Capping off his wife's comment, Rane got up in his wife's face and whispered upsettingly, "I dunno about him, but ye're driving me up the wall! Would ye quit using that teleportation device to pop me in an' out o'places? I feel like a Jack in d'box."

Haley gave him a pining smile and whispered back, "You really are sexy, you know that?"

Rane didn't like her coming on to him and shrunk back in the corner of his seat. When she started giggling at his bashfulness, he pouted his lips at her and looked out the side window. After seeing something disturbing, he turned toward his wife and said, "Hey, we're not moving."

Haley let him know he didn't have anything to worry about. "The car's moving. It's just that our particles are moving so much faster that it doesn't seem like it's moving."

Rane took the open watch out of his wife's hand and said, "Then I'll tell d'teleportation device t'switch us back t'normal."

"All right, but then Jack will be able to see us."

He glanced at the back of the robot's head and said, "We'll just duck down in d'backseat."

"Okay, you're the boss."

After Rane and Haley knelt down on the floor, he pushed the particle deceleration button on the side of the watch and the speed of their atoms returned to normal. Hearing the striking sound of a match, he peeked around the side of the backseat and saw Jack lighting up a cigarette. He watched the robot puff out smoke from his mouth and turned up his nose in distaste. *Yuk!*

Smelling tobacco smoke as her husband ducked back down to her level, Haley queried in a low whisper, "Is he smoking a cigarette?"

Rane hacked mutely a couple of times on the smoke fumes filling the car before answering in a barely audible voice, "Aye, d'thing's trying t'get lung cancer."

Haley whispered in her husband's ear, "He's a robot. How is he supposed to get lung cancer?"

Rane watched the robot drive the car onto a bridge and then continued whispering back and forth with his wife. "I dunno. I figured if d'thing could smoke it could get lung cancer."

Haley coughed under her breath, fanning the stench out of the air. When Jack finally tossed the cigarette out the window, she sighed in relief. "Oh praise God."

Highly annoyed that he couldn't even hear himself think, Rane stuck his index fingers into his ears and said, "I wish he'd turn that radio off. He's got d'music blasting so loud me eardrums are starting t'bleed."

Haley giggled a smidgen. "Reddy turned the android's hearing down so low he's practically deaf."

All at once Jack sped up the car and swerved into the left lane of the bridge, causing Rane to tumble onto Haley.

Rane picked himself up off his wife and queried, "What's this gumby doing now?"

Haley glanced toward the robotic driver and shook her head. "I don't know."

Dying to find out, Rane raised his head a bit and snuck a peek out the windshield. When he saw headlights coming at him from a distance, he widened his eyes out of fear and started whining to God. "Oh, Lord, please tell me we're not going t'hit head on with that lorry."

Hearing the truck driver blasting his horn for Jack to get out of the way, Haley peered out the windshield and said, "Uh-oh. It looks like he's playing a little game of chicken."

Rane made a desperate face at his wife and whimpered, "I know how that game works, Hal. If d'chap in d'truck is not a chicken, we're dead."

Haley tried to remain calm as she took the shiny, silver pocket watch out of his hand. "No, we're not. We'll just use the teleportation device an' transport ourselves out of here."

"Oh, good idea."

Haley opened the lid on the watch and whispered their previous coordinates into the tiny speaker inside, "Jack's Masterpieces, London."

Not seeing herself dematerializing, she smacked the teleportation device a couple of times and repeated the command in a more frantic tone. "Jack's Masterpieces, London!"

Rane could feel the anxiety rising up in his heart as he queried in a rushed tone, "Why are we still here?"

Haley repeatedly pressed the activation switch on the side of the watch and said in a fretful tone, "I don't know. I can't get it to work."

Hearing the truck driver make a continuous blast of his horn, Rane stared without blinking at the oncoming headlights and grabbed onto his wife. "We're going t'get pulverized!"

She un-pried his fingers off her leg and replied, "No, we're not. God will save us. He promised he would have his angels keep watch over us."

Rane could feel his whole body stiffening up with fright as he whimpered, "But what happens if mine are out on a tea break?"

He peered back out the windshield and saw the truck getting dangerously close. "Ugh! What a horrible way t'go. I can't bear t'look."

Rane cupped his hands over his eyes to avoid seeing the inevitable and cried out to God, "Open d'pearly gates, Lord, yer laddie's coming home."

The stress of the moment caused Haley to become overemotional. She slapped her husband on the shoulder for having a doubting heart and hastened her speech. "Oh no, you're not, Rane Rivers. You're not leaving me to raise that baby all by myself."

Jack suddenly swung back into the right lane and almost jackknifed with another vehicle.

Grateful to be alive, Haley laid the side of her head against the rear passenger seat, whispering prayerfully, "Thank you, Heavenly Father, I knew you'd save us."

Hearing tires squealing across the pavement, Rane opened his eyes and looked out the window. Seeing he was out of immediate danger, he placed his hand over his rapidly beating heart and sighed, "Oooh, thank God."

After Jack had driven off down the highway, Rane leaned toward his wife and whispered to be funny, "Haley, I need a jumper cable."

She lifted her head up off the seat to make eye contact with her husband and asked, "For what?"

Although Rane's nerves were still frazzled, he laughed off the situation to prove he could. "T'jump-start me heart."

Haley smiled at his joke and then rested her head back against the front seat. The long hours were beginning to take their toll on her body from not getting enough sleep the night before.

Rane kissed his wife on the cheek and then flinched when he saw her dematerializing.

All at once Rane appeared on the sidewalk next to his wife. After discovering he was outside the front of the gallery, he threw his hands into the air and hollered out of frustration, "Oh that's just great. Now we're right back t'where we started."

Haley sighed at the silver watch in her hand. "Sorry, Rane, the particle transporter must have come back on an' processed my last request."

She let him know the situation wasn't hopeless by saying, "We'll just wait here until he gets back."

Recalling a way to defeat the robot, Rane gave his wife a mischievous smirk and said, "An' when he does, ye're going t'take his picture."

Unsure what he meant, Haley queried, "What for?"

"I just remembered something else about that robot. He's highly superstitious."

"He is?"

"Uh-huh. Aileen loaded all sorts of silly nonsense into his memory banks."

"Why?"

"T'give herself d'upper hand, I imagine."

"So what happens after I take his picture?"

Rane cracked his knuckles and chuckled, "That thing is going t'totally freak out."

Not liking the idea, she replied hesitantly, "It is?"

"Sure. He's programmed t'believe that if ye take his picture, ye freeze frame a moment in time an' capture a part of his soul."

She looked at her husband like that was the most ridiculous thing she had ever heard in her life. "But androids don't have a soul."

"Try telling him that."

Haley replied in a joking manner, "Okay, I'll take his picture, but don't expect him to be smiling."

He laughed at her comment. "Aye."

"While we're waiting for the android to return, let's go recheck all the paintings in Masterpiece Hall."

"Why?"

"Just in case we've overlooked anything."

"All right," he replied and then followed her into the gallery.

Upon entering the hall, Haley noticed the lights were still on. She walked over to the wall where the painting of the mice used to be and found another picture in its place. Sharing the detection with her husband, who was busy looking at another painting on the opposite end, she called out, "Rane, come here."

Concerned by the shrill tone in her voice, Rane darted over to her and asked, "What is it?"

Haley pointed at the new painting and replied, "I think those two rats with their tails caught in a trap are supposed to be us."

Rane gaped at the picture like he couldn't believe his eyes. He removed the picture from the wall and gave it a short critique. "Aye, she has yer green eyes an' curly, red hair."

She countered his appraisal by saying, "An' he definitely has your teal blue eyes an' blond hair."

Haley checked the signature on the painting and said in surprise, "Artur sure get's around for a dead man."

Rane shook his head at the obvious forgery and declared, "It had t'be d'robot."

She nodded and responded with a clever answer. "I agree. No human could be that precise in duplicating Artur's modus operandi."

Rane stared hard at the painting and then gave his wife a perplexed look. "But why would d'android paint our tails into a trap?"

Haley bit her lower lip while studying the traps and other symbolisms in the picture. "I wish I knew."

After several moments of close observation, she decided to take some photos of the painting and activated the picture-taking device in her cell phone.

Rane lowered his eyebrows as he closely studied the painting. "That's strange."

She took a couple of pictures of the painting before asking, "What?"

"D'time set on d'silver pocket watch in yer rat's hand is exactly d'same as d'time set on d'gold watch in d'other painting."

Haley put her cell phone away in her pocket as she leaned closer to the picture. "I noticed that too. Why midnight?"

Rane thought about something he learned from his dad and shared it with his wife. "Caleb said midnight represents d'time of death."

She recalled her husband's dream about the clocks and then thought of what it would be like if the people were on the forward side of time. *An' noon the time of life.*

Rane looked toward his wife's jacket and asked, "Haley, what time is it?"

Haley pulled the silver watch out of her pocket and flipped open the lid. "It is after ten thirty."

She was just about to put the teleportation device away when she felt it transforming into the smart gun. Startled by the quivering sensation in her hand, she raised her voice slightly. "Reddy, what's going on?"

"Danger! Android approaching."

Rane tilted his head, listening to the heavy footsteps from down the corridor. "He's right, Hal, it is definitely d'robot."

Haley tightened her grip on the pistol as she spoke quietly with her husband. "How can you tell it is him?"

Rane hung the painting back on the wall as he replied, "His steps are weighted from the metal in his shoes."

"Metal?"

"Aye, so he won't ground out."

"Oooh," she replied in a revelatory tone.

Haley whispered into the voice mechanism inside the gun. "Reddy, load dead-eye laser an' engage disruptor."

After a red bead of light started flashing inside the small, circular diamond in the center of the barrel, Reddy said, "Dead-eye laser loaded, an' disruptor engaged, Detective."

"On my signal, fire on d'android."

"Affirmative."

Rane took his small notepad out of his pocket and tore off several sheets of paper.

Haley lifted up the bottom of her evergreen sweater and slid the gun barrel down the front of her pants. After concealing the weapon under her cashmere pullover, she looked over at her husband and saw him stuffing the papers into his mouth. Baffled at his peculiar actions, she asked, "What are you doing?"

Rane's answer was a bit muffled from chewing on the wad of paper. "We can't afford t'let Jack get this code, it is our ace in d'hole."

Haley was temporarily distracted when she noticed the robot's footsteps had stopped. "Rane, I don't hear anything."

Rane made a distasteful face as he swallowed the chomped paper in his mouth. "Me neither."

Haley listened hard for a noise but still heard nothing. Motioning her head toward the entranceway, she whispered to her husband, "Come on."

They crept down the corridor and didn't see Jack anywhere in sight. Not the type to give up easily, Haley rummaged around the ticket counter a second time and said in a barely audible tone, "The footsteps disappeared about here."

Rane leaned on the ticket counter beside his wife and stated, "He can't just vanish into thin air. He must have snuck out somehow without us hearing him."

While they were trying to figure out where Jack went, his reflection suddenly appeared inside the large mirror behind the ticket counter. Rane and Haley had their backs turned to the wall and didn't see him.

Haley looked toward the double glass doors as she replied to her husband's statement, "He couldn't have, or we would have heard him."

"Then where is he?"

Jack grinned mischievously as he listened in on their private conversation and then stepped out of the simulated glass. Standing close behind them, he said, "Hello, young Finney. I see ye're right on time."

Startled from the sound of his voice, Rane and Haley both spun around and cringed at the sight of the android. When the mechnical menace started ambling toward them, Rane grabbed his wife by the hand and took several steps backwards.

Jack sneered at both of them and said, "If ye're wondering how I found out about my hearing, I stopped at d'store t'buy a pack of cigarettes, an' d'clerk asked me if I was deaf."

Rane and Haley snickered amongst themselves.

Jack sneered at them for laughing at him. He then held out his palm and feigned a gesture of friendship by saying, "I didn't come here t'hurt ye, laddie. I just want ye t'give me d'code."

Rane put his hands behind his back and covertly signaled his wife to take the robot's photo. "Sure, I'll give it t'ye, if ye let me take yer picture."

Aroused with anger by the mere suggestion of it, Jack held a psychotic fixation on Rane as he bellowed into his face, "Nobody takes my picture, boy!"

While Jack was busy focusing all his negative energy on Rane, Haley managed to sneak around to the side of the android. After turning on the camera feature on her cell phone, she aimed the viewscreen at the robot's face and said in a taunting tone, "Say, 'cheese,' Jack."

Hearing the clicking sound of the camera, the robot turned his head in her direction and discovered she had taken his picture. Reacting out of superstition, he cupped his hands over his eyes in a blind attempt to protect his soul from evil and screeched like a loud horde of locusts.

Not sure what the robot might do next, Haley instinctively pulled her silver pistol and shouted, "Rane, get behind me!"

Shaking with fright, Rane watched the robot lower his hands from his face and immediately got behind his wife.

When the android came toward her, Haley aimed her gun at his head and said heatedly, "Stay back, or I'll shoot!"

With a frenzied look in his eyes, Jack growled, "Ye hexed me, witch! I'm going t'kill ye for that."

Feeling a need to protect his wife, Rane yelled at the robot. "Stay away from my wife, gumby!"

Haley knew Jack was extremely dangerous at this point and hollered out for the signal. "Reddy, now!"

Without hesitation, Reddy responded to her request by saying, "Cannot comply, Detective."

The alarm could clearly be heard in her voice as she replied, "What do you mean, 'you can't comply'?"

"Robot jammed my release mechanism back in Masterpiece Hall."

Rane whispered anxiously into his wife's ear, "I think now would be a good time t'call for a backup."

Jack slapped the gun out of Haley's hand, snickering at her vulnerability. "Yer insignificant weaponry won't work on me, Detective."

The robot turned all his attention back on Rane by saying, "I want that code, boy. Ye see, my life depends upon it."

Unsure what he meant, Haley thought, *His life depends upon it?*

Rane put on a naughty grin and replied to the robot, "Sorry, I can't give it t'ye."

Jack leaned toward him and snarled in his face. "Why not?"

Tickled that he had outsmarted the robot, Rane lifted his shoulders and chuckled. "I ate it."

Jack was not amused and punched him hard in the stomach. "Then ye better pray it comes back up."

Upon receiving the hard blow to his tummy, Rane doubled over, wheezing and coughing like he was about to throw up.

Haley sized up the robot and mused, *Jack's joints seem to be the weakest area on his body. I'll have to attack him there.*

She then came to her husband's defense by judo kicking the android on the back of his right kneecap. "Eeeeeeeyah!"

Seeing him lose his balance, she swept the same leg to cause him to fall.

Jack hollered as he crashed hard onto the marble floor. He was shocked that she had outmaneuvered him. He then got back up and sneered at his attacker. "Don't get in over yer head, Detective."

Taking his anger out on Rane, he clutched onto the front of his sweater and hoisted him high into the air. "Give me that code!"

Rane shrieked with pain while trying to pry the android's fingers off his chest. "Ow! Watch it will ye, chum. I think ye got some chest hairs in there."

Out of the corner of his eye, Jack caught Haley going for her gun and backhanded her across the room. Dazed from the blow to her head, she staggered to her feet.

Rane saw the blood dripping from her nose and hollered out worriedly, "No, Haley, run! Get out d'gallery!"

More concerned about her husband's safety than her own, Haley ran at the android and judo kicked him on the opposite leg. "Aiiiiiyah!"

The robot lost his balance and stumbled backward. When she straight away attacked him a second time, he grabbed her by the arm and slammed her body into the wall.

Fearing for her life, Rane shouted even louder, "Haley, no!"

With the adrenaline surging through her body, Haley quickly picked herself up off the floor. Shouting her judo attack lingo, she kicked Jack on the back of his right kneecap and on the elbow of the arm he was using to pin her husband. "Aiiiiiyah! Eeeeyiiigh!"

Feeling the jar to his body, Jack hit head on into the wall and almost dropped Rane on the floor. Regaining his bearings, he turned toward Haley with a crazed look of vengeance in his eyes and snarled, "Ye're pushing yer luck, Detective!"

Terrified that the robot might kill her, Rane pleaded with his wife to withdraw. "Please, lassie, for me. Go! Get out of here!"

But Haley wouldn't listen. She wiped the blood off her nose and came at Jack yet again. Unfortunately, by that time, the robot had figured out her attack maneuvers and easily tossed her across the counter like she was nothing but a rag doll.

Rane's eyes filled with tears as he watched his wife's body fall lifeless onto the floor. Seeing all the blood dripping down from her head, he assumed the worst and sniveled under his breath, "Oh noooo. Please, God, she can't be dead."

Jack couldn't care less about his grief and shook Rane violently in the air. "Now, are ye ready t'give me that code, or would ye like t'play some more cat an' mouse games?"

Rane mournfully eyed his wife's body on the floor and then said to the robot in a voice of disgust, "Ye actually think I would give it t'ye after what ye did t'her?"

Infuriated that he couldn't get his way, Jack yanked out several strands of Rane's blond hair and then threw him squealing toward the double glass doors.

Rane hit hard on the marble floor. He felt a dull heaviness in his arms and legs, but then it quickly disappeared. After discovering he hadn't broken anything, he leaped to his feet and fled the gallery.

CHAPTER 43

Hoping he could find someone to help him, Rane ran nonstop to the tavern he had gone to earlier. When he got there, he flung open the front door, and to his horror, found Jack standing there waiting for him.

The android stepped outside the pub and demanded, "Give me that code! No human is going t'have control over me."

Frightened by the robot's presence, Rane slowly stepped back from the entranceway, still winded from the fast run. "No!"

Jack sneered at him and then hurled him across the parking lot.

Rane squealed from soaring several feet through the air and then plowed hands-first into a pile of snow. Momentarily dazed from the fall, he blinked the blur out of his eyes while lifting his wobbling head. He pushed his belly against the snow on the ground and arched his stiff neck, moaning low in his throat, "Ooooh, my aching back."

Rane rose stiffly from off his stomach. He staggered a few steps and then collapsed back on the ground. When he saw Jack heading in his direction, fear rose up inside him and supplanted any thoughts of soreness. Scrambling to his feet, he took off sprinting in the opposite direction like he was competing in a fifty-yard dash. He kept on running until a huge fog bank swept in front of his path. Not being able to see the danger that lurked inside, he stopped dead in his tracks and backed away from it.

All at once Jack stepped out of the fog and gave him a wicked smirk. "There's nowhere ye can run, boy."

Trembling all over, Rane stared into the robot's eyes that were now glowing in the dark and stuttered a breathless response. "Ye-ye-ye stay away from me."

Jack bared his synthetic white teeth and said in a ruthless tone, "I'm going t'get that code if I have t'take ye apart piece by piece."

The robot gripped Rane around his throat, lifted him high into the air, and then threw him across the car park a second time.

After landing on a soft bed of snow, Rane felt a painful throb across the front of his neck. When he touched the tender area, he flinched. It was even more bruised than it was before. He groaned at his discomfort until he saw Jack coming toward him.

"Oh no, not again," he whined tiresomely and then took off like a shot.

Enjoying the cat-and-mouse game, Jack snickered at his opponent as he chased after him.

Rane ran fast as he could for about a half-mile down the street and then stopped to rest in a nearby alley. Laying his tired head against the brick wall, he panted hard. After wiping the beads of perspiration from his brow, he closed his eyes with nothing to comfort him but the loud pounding of his heart. Just when he was getting his wind back, he heard footsteps, far away at first, but then getting much closer. He was so scared he didn't dare move a muscle, fearing he might give away his position to the robot.

The long, eerie, dead silence that followed made the seconds seem like hours. Rane felt like his heart was going to explode out of his chest as he stood there motionless. While trying to mask his heavy breathing by holding in his breath, he thought about his beautiful wife. In his mind's eyes, he could see her lifeless body lying on the gallery floor.

The picture of her being gone from his life brought tears to his eyes. She was a gift from God that he had taken for granted, and now, more than anything, he wished he could have her back. The sadness seemed unbearable as he faintly whimpered out her name, "Haley."

All at once Rane's adrenaline spiked when he felt a cold hand clutching him around the throat. He instinctively looked out the corner of his eye to see who it was while trying to pry the strong grip off his neck. When he saw the android's vengeful face staring back at him, his muscles tensed up, and he shrieked in terror.

Jack squeezed dangerously hard on Rane's throat and said, "Say your prayers, boy."

Rane started wheezing. He wondered how in the world he wound up in another superstitious mess like he had fourteen years earlier. Just when things appeared the darkest, a positive thought flashed through his mind. He realized he had been so scared he had forgotten to call upon the only power that could release him from the enemy's grip. "Jesus, please, send an angel t'help me."

Like an answer to his prayer, Haley came running up with her cell phone in her hand and took Jack's picture.

Hearing the clicking sound of her camera, the android instantly let go of his grip on Rane to cover his eyes and started screeching like a horde of locusts.

Rane collapsed on the ground, not quite sure what had just happened. Caressing his badly bruised neck, he coughed and choked a couple more times and then looked up, expecting to see the robot. When he saw his lovely wife standing there instead, he gasped a breath of shock. "Hal?"

Haley took her husband by the hand and helped him to his feet. "You sound surprised to see me."

He stared affectionately into her bright green eyes and answered, confused, "I am—I mean—I thought I'd lost ye."

Haley smiled at him and replied, "Do you honestly think I'd leave you to raise that baby all by yourself, Rane Rivers?"

Rane grinned back at her until he considered the robot. While looking around for his whereabouts, he cleared his hoarse throat and said in apprehension, "Where did Jack go?"

She skimmed her eyes over the parking lot before answering facetiously, "To lick his wounds, I imagine."

Rane scanned the area one more time before looking back at his wife. Noticing the dark purple hues on her forehead, he said, "That's a nasty bruise, lassie."

She eyed the black and blue marks on his throat and made light of what he said about her by replying, "I hope it doesn't look as bad as the ones around your neck."

Rane laughed. "We look a mess. Don't we?"

She grinned from ear to ear and nodded her head. "Uh-huh."

Rane cleared his throat again and then stopped when he saw some blood dripping from a small cut in the upper portion of his wife's forehead. Eager to help her, he pulled his handkerchief out of his pocket. He knew at that moment he could trust her, and it felt good. After all, she had risked her own life to save his.

When he started dabbing the blood from the wound on her head, Haley winced from the pain. "Ouch!"

He swiftly retracted the handkerchief from her face. "Aw, poor baby has a booboo."

Rane pulled her closer to him and said further, "Here, let me kiss it an' make it better."

After he had kissed her forehead, Haley smiled and said, "I love your medicine, Doctor. I'm feeling better already."

He stared vulnerably at her angelic face for a long moment before saying, "Don't ye ever scare me like that again."

Rane peered into his wife's enchanting green eyes, and before he knew it, he was kissing her on the mouth, enjoying the sweet sensation of her lips, his body burning with desire. Then, nuzzling his cheek against the side of her face, he whispered fervently, "I love ye, Hal. I must have been out of my mind t'let ye go."

Haley's eyes pooled with tears as she stroked the soft blond hair on the back of his head. "I love you, too, Chappy."

Rane stopped cuddling his wife and went back to cleaning the blood off her head. "Haley, why didn't ye call out for God t'help ye?"

She wiped the tears off her face and sighed glumly. "I guess I've been so dependent upon human weaponry, I didn't even give it a second thought. An' here I gave you a lecture on not trusting God when I should have been giving it to myself."

When she lowered her head in regret, Rane lifted her chin with his fingers and said, "We all make mistakes, Hal."

Haley reflected back on her dumb stunt at the gallery and nodded her head. "I'm just grateful to God I didn't break my neck."

Rane gave her a peck on the side of her throat and replied, "Me too. It is such a pretty neck."

Haley giggled shyly at the touch of his cold lips and then looked in the general direction where she last saw Jack. "Rane, how did Aileen run her tests on the robot? He seems pretty headstrong about anyone messing with him."

Without even hesitating, Rane shook his head and replied, "I dunno."

Haley made a gentle squeeze on his hand and said coaxingly, "Please, love, try an' remember. It is very important."

He heaved a deep sigh and proceeded to crack his knuckles while wracking his brain for the answer. After taxing himself for several moments, he unexpectedly had an epiphany, his eyes widening as he remembered. "Wait, I know how she did it."

"How?" she queried in great interest.

Rane motioned his head in the general direction of the gallery and answered, "She used d'Locust 52257 in d'security room."

"Oh, that's right. His neural net is linked to the master computer."

Rane nodded and then looked down at the blood on his hands from the soiled handkerchief. "After I go to d'loo an' clean up a bit, I'll show ye where it is."

On their way back to the gallery, Rane and Haley spotted a black cab parked out in front of the gallery. To avoid being seen by the driver, they quickly ducked behind the brick building across the street.

Haley peeped around the corner from where she was hiding and took a closer look at the car. "What's that taxi doing here?"

Rane stood on his tiptoes to see over the top of his wife's head and then answered in a tone of distrust. "I bet Jack an' Jill are up t'something."

Haley pulled her smart gun out of her coat pocket, which she had retrieved off the gallery floor when she came to, and said, "Reddy, are you fully functional?"

All at once she heard loud static coming through the voice mechanism inside the weapon. It quickly cleared up right before Reddy answered.

"Affirmative, Detective."

Haley watched the mystery cab take off down the street as she replied, "Good. Now read me the license plate on that vehicle."

While the bot was disclosing the information she requested, Haley again heard static coming through the gun. Casting a suspicious eye onto the pistol in her hand, she queried, "Reddy, where is that interference coming from?"

"Unknown, Detective."

Rane mulled over the possibilities in his head and stated to his wife, "D'gun's audio chip might have been damaged when it hit d'marble floor."

"Do you think you can ye fix it?"

He elevated his voice emotionally. "Fix it? I still don't recall entirely how I built that thingamabob."

Haley gave her husband a comforting pat on the back and said, "I'm sure it will all come back to you eventually, love."

Rane looked down the street at the taxi turning right at the green light. "I wonder what they're up to?"

Haley motioned her gun hand toward the main entrance of the gallery and said, "Let's go see if we can find out."

Without further delay, they darted across the street and went inside the building.

Rane made sure no one was in the lobby before whispering to his wife, "Follow me."

He then vigilantly led his wife down to the east wing and up the back stairwell. When they got to the security room, he turned on the lights and pointed toward the giant, high-tech computer on the other side of the room. "See that massive beast?"

Haley gave it a quick once over and nodded her head. "Uh-huh."

"That's d'Locust 52257. That's where Jack gets all his power."

Haley marveled at the size of the equipment. "It is big, isn't it?"

"Aye, that it is," he replied and then headed toward the unit.

Haley took a moment to case the rest of the place and just happen to catch sight of the painting Jack had left on the floor. Curious why it was there, she strolled over to the picture and picked it up. After giving it a quick inspection, she called out to her husband who was busy fiddling around with the computer. "Rane, come here an' look at this."

She waited until he came up to her and then showed him the canvas in her hand. "The paint's been melted."

Rane stared at the smeared colors while agreeing with his wife. "Aye, d'picture's all distorted. Ye can't tell what it was."

Haley turned the canvas over to check the other side and whispered confidentially, "Rane, this is the painting of the agents."

Following her covert actions, he lowered the tone of his voice. "How can ye tell?"

Haley pointed her index finger at the lower, right corner of the chestnut frame and answered, "From the two tiny nicks on the back. I saw them earlier when I was examining the picture."

Rane eyed the small scratches. "Pretty clever. I never would have thought o'that."

She smiled at his flattering remark and directed her attention back on the painting. "The robot must have left it here."

He took the ruined artwork out of his wife's hand and continued speaking in a cagey tone just above a whisper. "Do ye think they found out d'agents were on to 'em?"

Haley eyed the painting in his hand and answered, "That would be my guess."

"It is a good thing ye used yer cell phone t'take a picture of it."

"Yeah, in case we need it later."

Haley sat down in one of the chairs behind the gray security table and carefully eyed the pictures on the six camera monitors mounted to the panel. She didn't see anything out of the ordinary until Jillian's image appeared inside the top-center screen. The camera from the lobby had filmed her coming into the gallery. Keyed up by her new detection, she whispered, "Rane, is that who I think it is?"

He stared hard at the woman's face as she passed by the fountain in the vestibule and nodded his head. "That's auntie all right."

Haley diligently observed Jillian's every move on the monitor until she left the view of the camera. "Looks like she's on her way to Masterpiece Hall."

A few moments later, Rane saw his aunt walk into the hall from the camera in the display room. Drawing his wife's attention over to the top-right monitor, he tapped on the glass and said, "There she is."

While watching Jillian search through the oil paintings on the wall, Haley queried suspiciously, "What's she doing?"

Rane gawked at his aunt's strange behavior and shrugged his shoulders. "Admiring d'artwork? Who knows."

When Jillian suddenly turned around and walked out of the hall, Haley made a baffled face at her husband and said, "What she just did made no sense at all."

"Believe me, common sense has never run in our family."

Haley glued her eyes back on her suspect as the cameras filmed Jillian walking back down the corridor and out the front door. "She's leaving."

"Good," he said in a firm voice of relief.

Rane watched his wife rewind the footage where Jillian first entered Masterpiece Hall and queried, "What are ye doing?"

"I want to check something."

While playing the recording back on slow speed, Haley closely studied Jillian's prior steps. As soon as she spotted what she was searching for, she freeze-framed the motion picture and said, "Rane, look..."

He leaned against the metal table and queried uncertainly, "What?"

Haley tapped the glass monitor with her index finger and replied, "Jillian smirked at the picture of the rats as she passed by it."

"Maybe she has thing for rats."

She exaggerated the tone in her voice to get her point across. "No. Don't you see? She didn't get upset when she saw the counterfeit picture there among the other masterpieces."

Finally sinking into his brain, Rane slowly spread a grin across his face and said, "She didn't, did she?"

Haley leaned back in her chair with a wary gleam in her eyes. "I bet they're secretly communicating to each other through the paintings."

Rane glanced at the ruined artwork in his hand and said, "Talking t'each other through pictures—slick cloak an' dagger idea."

Haley crossed her arms and replied, "That way the agents can't listen in on their conversation."

Rane set the painting back on the floor and said, "Makes me wonder what Jack tol' Jillian about us."

She nodded and began rewinding the security footage from each camera. "Hopefully there's more on the tapes that can help us figure out what they're up to."

While waiting for the video to finish rewinding, Haley suddenly heard more static. Reacting on her instinct, she pulled her smart gun out of her coat pocket. Turning toward her husband to warn him, she held her index finger over her mouth and whispered, "Sh."

Rane stood perfectly still and mouthed the words, "What is it?"

When she just stood there listening intently to the sound of the static, Rane's curiosity stirred him to question her secrecy again. "What?"

Haley held up a firm hand to indicate she wanted him to remain silent while peering guardedly around the room. She had a hunch that someone was listening in on their private conversation. Not hearing any static other than in their general location, she reduced the audio level on the gun and whispered, "Reddy, scan the area for bugs."

The red light on top of the gun started flashing rapidly as Reddy answered in a volume she could barely hear. "Bug scan commencing, Detective."

Rane whispered anxiously in his wife's ear, "Ye think we're bugged?"

She nodded her head and whispered back, "I think that's what's causing the interference."

The static cleared up as Reddy announced, "Scan completed."

"How many did you find, Reddy?" Haley queried.

"One."

"Where?"

Knowing they wouldn't like the answer, the bot was hesitant to reply.

"Reddy, did you hear me? I said, 'Where?'"

After a long moment of silence, the bot finally replied, "Inside the barrell of the gun."

Shocked by the news, Haley unconsciously mouthed the bad report to her husband. "Inside the gun?"

Concerned for his wife's safety, Rane whispered a direct order to the bot. "Reddy, it is imperative that ye deactivate that bug."

"Affirmative."

Without delay, Reddy short-wired the device and announced, "Bug deactivated."

Haley sat quietly while trying to figure out how it got there in the first place. Believing she had come up with an answer, she wasted no time in sharing the inkling with her husband. "Jack must have planted it there while I was knocked unconscious."

Rane got upset and started cracking his knuckles. "Why that little sneak. He was hoping I'd reveal d'code."

She countered in a voice of respite, "It is a good thing for us you didn't."

Their conversation about the code made Haley ponder a second time on what Jack meant when he said, *"My life depends upon it."*

Rane glanced at the painting on the floor and thought about the agent who had come into the gallery. "Haley…"

She came out of her deep meditation and said, "Yes?"

"Ye said ye met Gary when ye went out t'investigate a case."

"That's right."

"What case were ye working on?"

Feeling awkward about disclosing the information to him, Haley shilly-shallied in giving him a straight answer. "I, uh, um, let's see now, which case was that?"

Seeing that he was getting upset with her, she finally lowered her head in submission and divulged the truth. "It was the one involving Aileen."

"My aunt?" he responded in a loud voice of surprise.

Haley looked up at him and nodded her head. "Uh-huh."

"Why didn't ye tell me?"

"I didn't want to upset you."

Rane leaned on the security table as he went on to say, "I don't understand. Why would homicide or British Intelligence be interested in a car accident?"

While wishing she was off the hook, Haley shrugged and answered like it was merely routine police work. "I heard the call on the radio an' happened to be in the area."

Rane knew she was hiding something by the evasive look in her eyes. "Come on, Hal. I know ye better than that. Give it t'me straight."

She bit down her lower lip, reluctant to speak. "I don't think it was an accident, Rane."

He thought back on the account made by the tour guide and replied, "But Prosperity said ..."

Haley abruptly cut him off with a defensive tongue. "I don't care what Prosperity said. I believe it was foul play."

Rane raised his eyebrows and queried, "Then ye did find locusts on her car?"

She shook her head a little and started talking quietly with her husband as if someone might be listening in. "No. But I did find one of Jack's calling cards in her purse an' a cigarette butt burning in the ashtray."

Rane put his hands inside his coat pockets and shrugged like it was no big deal. "So she was smoking a cigarette. That doesn't prove anything."

Haley huddled closer to her husband. "Aileen was wearing red lipstick that day, yet there was no stain on the butt."

"Are ye sure?"

She nodded her head. "Positive. I even had Reddy scan the cigarette for human saliva just to make sure."

"An' there wasn't any?"

Haley shook her head a couple of times and replied, "Not a trace."

Rane appeared to be miles away in thought as his wife continued revealing the evidence.

"I also checked Aileen's cell phone an' found out she had recently called Gary. Before I had a chance to investigate any further, he showed up at the scene of the accident an' took the calling card away from me. When I showed him my credentials, he told me the case belonged to secret service an' to leave it alone."

"Maybe it was a different Gary Brown she called. The name's pretty common, ye know."

"I thought of that. That's why I snuck a peek at his caller identification when he phoned the agency."

"His cell number matched the one Aileen called?"

"Yes."

"What do ye think is going on?"

Haley turned back up the volume on the smart gun and replied, "My guess is British Intelligence is after the robot, an' the only thing standing in their way is the beneficiary."

Rane pointed his thumb at his chest and answered, "Namely me."

"Yes, which could explain why Gary had my dad send him a copy of the missing persons report I filed on you."

He nodded his head to agree with her assumptions and replied, "He must have shown it t'Aileen an' convinced her that I was dead."

"Do you think she signed the robot over to British Intelligence?"

Rane recalled a previous conversation he had with his aunt and answered, "Aye, she tol' me she would gladly give it away if something ever happened t'me. She was afraid of d'thing. I can't say that I blame her."

"I bet the robot was in the car with Aileen at the time of the accident."

"If that's true, how did Jack get out of d'car before it crashed?"

"She must have stopped somewhere along the way, an' he snuck out of the car without her knowing about it."

"How?"

"I believe the android slipped a virtual reality disk into the back of her cell phone when she wasn't looking."

"She had one o'them new cell phones Prosperity tol' us about?"

Haley nodded. "I saw broken pieces of a miniature disk in the front of her car. It had fallen out of the back of her phone."

"So ye think after Aileen got back in d'car, she was only seeing a virtual image an' not d'real robot?"

She nodded and replied, "That way she'd never suspect a thing."

Haley was right. The robot had snuck the virtual disk into Aileen's cell phone when she wasn't looking. On their way to British Intelligence, he had her stop at a local store to buy him a pack of Lucky Strike III cigarettes as a going away gift. The second she went inside the shop, he communicated to her cell phone and told it to activate the program. He then altered his appearance, got out of the car, and hid in the men's restroom until she drove away.

Haley laid her silver pistol on the security table and proceeded to check the timer on the tapes. "Looks like the android covered all his tracks."

"What do ye mean 'covered his tracks'?"

"He not only destroyed the picture Jillian left for him, but he also erased all the security tapes with him on it. The automatic timers on all the cameras were set to come back on at eleven o'clock."

Rane narrowed his eyes uncertainly at the counter on the security panel and asked, "Eleven? Why?"

She rested her elbow on the arm of the chair while placing her index finger on her lower lip. "I wish I knew."

Haley picked up the smart gun off the counter and pushed a tiny button on the belly of the barrel. "We'll use the bot's particle communicator to run the control panel. It will be much faster."

"Good idea."

Haley sat the weapon back down on the metal table in front of her and said, "Reddy, integrate the system's computer language to make it respond to your commands. Then tell it to run all the footage recorded after eleven o'clock."

Without delay, a red beam of light shot out of the diamond eye on the gun and penetrated the security system's central processing unit. "Commencing, Detective, override will be completed in ten point five seconds."

While waiting for the bot to finish the job, Haley revealed her plan of attack. "Rane, you watch the film on the bottom three monitors, an' I'll watch the ones on the top, okay?"

"That's fine by me," he replied agreeably.

When the integration process was fully completed, Reddy announced his next course of action. "Prior footage on screen, Detective."

Rane and Haley directed all their concentration onto their assigned monitors and carefully eyeballed the videotapes being played back.

It didn't take long before Rane got tired of looking at what seemed to be a bunch of still pictures and said, "Reddy, we're a little short on time. Can ye speed up the tapes a bit?"

"Affirmative," the bot replied and then sped up the footage.

Haley's keen eyes stared intently at the fast-moving pictures until a man's face flashed by on the top-center monitor. "Reddy, stop motion picture on camera two."

Reddy relayed the commands to the computer, and the video recording instantly froze on the screen.

Rane squinted curiously at the still picture and looked over at his wife. "What is it?"

"I thought I saw something."

Haley gave another command to the smart gun by saying, "Reddy, tell the camcorder to rewind the footage that was recorded after eleven an' play it back at regular speed."

After Reddy had complied with her request, Rane waited to see something out of the ordinary come into view. Just when he was about to tell his wife she had obviously made a mistake, he saw a clone of himself entering the gallery from the lobby. Alarmed that someone else had his face, he gaped at the monitor and said, "Am I seeing what I think I'm seeing?"

Haley stared at the security screen as if she couldn't believe her eyes. "Rane, that man looks like you. He's even dressed up like you, except for the black wool beanie on his head."

Rane couldn't seem to take his eyes off the screen as he watched the imposter's every move. "What am I doing with that dolly?"

She bit her lower lip as the stranger left the view of the camera to head down the corridor. "My hunch is you're here to pick up the trunk."

"What?" he asked in a befuddled tone.

Haley didn't bother to explain her gut feeling to her husband. She was too busy concentrating on what she was going to do next. "Reddy, tell the computer to stop the footage on camera two an' then rewind the film recorded after eleven o'clock on camera six. When you finish that, have the cam play back the film at regular speed."

"Commencing, Detective," replied the bot and promptly obeyed each request.

Rane lowered his gaze onto the bottom-right screen, expecting to see more footage of the imposter. When he saw the suspect entering the private room, he whispered to his wife, "Ye're right, there he is."

Haley watched attentively as the man picked up the magic chest with the dolly and carted it out of the room.

Highly upset over what he was seeing on the monitor, Rane's voice turned shrill. "Where am I going with that trunk? I don't remember telling me I could do that."

Haley kept a sharp eye on the impersonator as he bent over to reposition the trunk on the dolly. "A better question would be ... why do you have a silencer gun in your back pocket?"

Eyeing the weapon sticking out of the rear of the perpetrator's pants, Rane's heart sped up at the thought of someone setting him up. "I don't like d'looks of this, Hal."

Haley, again, drew her interest onto the black wool cap on the suspect's head as he left the view of camera six. "Me neither. Jack is definitely up to something. He deliberately covered up his ears to make sure the camera couldn't film his earring."

She looked up at the still picture on the top-center monitor and said, "Reddy, continue playing the footage on camera two."

"Video running on screen, Detective."

After several moments of monitoring nothing but the lobby, Rane suddenly saw a picture of the charlatan heading toward the double glass doors. "Jack, ye sly devil! What are ye up to?"

Feeling on edge by what she just witnessed on the footage, Haley said, "This doesn't look good, Rane. He made sure the camera in the lobby could see his face clearly before he went out the front door."

Rane started cracking the knuckles on his right hand while replying in a fearful, irritated voice, "Ye think I dunno that. It was my mug he flaunted."

Haley looked down at the smart gun and said, "Reddy, have the cam rewind the last bit of footage an' then zoom in on the picture before playing it back in slow motion."

After the bot complied with her request, she spotted the back of the taxi through the double glass doors. Tapping her index fingernail against the glass screen to point out the object, she said, "Look, Rane, that's the cab we saw parked out front earlier. It has the same license plate number."

He lowered his eyebrows questionably. "Why would Jack call a cab when he has d'Cadillac?"

Haley took her gaze off the monitor and put it on her husband. "My guess is he wanted the cabbie to be an eyewitness."

Rane's face began to turn pale. "I have a sick feeling about this, Hal."

Haley picked up her gun off the security table and queried, "Reddy, how long can the robot hold his new appearance before having to change back to his original identity?"

"Two hours before sensors overheat, Detective."

"Scan the gallery an' see if the android is in the building."

The red light in the center of the barrel on the gun began to pulsate faster as Reddy replied, "Commencing scan."

After several moments of accelerated inspection of particles, the bot declared his findings. "High energy readings reveal one hundred androids in the gallery."

Stunned by the findings, Rane practically shouted at the smart gun. "One hundred?"

Haley, too, had her misgivings about the report. "Reddy, are you sure you're reading it correctly?"

"Affirmative, Detective."

"Where are they?" she queried pushily.

"In the lobby."

Rane glanced toward the door and said fearfully, "We got t'get out of here, Hal."

Haley jumped up out of her seat. "I'm with you."

Rane and Haley tiptoed along the corridor, hoping to sneak out the front door without being seen. Right before coming into view of the camera in the lobby, they leaned back against the wall, listening carefully to see if there was anyone in the reception area.

Haley heard her husband breathing hard from fright and gave him a reassuring smile. She then gripped both hands around her pistol and held it out in front of her.

Reddy picked up that she was about to step out in the foyer and said, "Warning, scanner reveals one hundred clones in your area, Detective."

Haley was a bit apprehensive about confronting that many robots. After all her last encounter with one wasn't a pleasant experience. Realizing she couldn't stay in hiding forever, she looked over at her husband and said, "Rane, I don't hear anything. Do ye?"

He shook his head and whispered back, "No."

Afraid of laying her husband's life on the line, Haley prayed in her heart to the Lord to help her overcome her imaginary fears and then inhaled a deep breath to calm her nerves. After feeling more relaxed, she whispered to the gun, "Reddy, load the disruptor."

"Disruptor loaded, Detective."

Haley stared back at Rane and said in a barely audible tone, "On the count of three, we make a run for it, okay?"

With his eyes filled with dread, he nodded his head in a brisk way and whispered back, "Okay."

Haley's heart beat faster as she slowly began to give the countdown. "One . . . two . . . three."

She then jumped out from where she was hiding and aimed the gun's laser sight toward the lobby. Not seeing an android anywhere in sight, she exchanged a puzzled look with her husband and queried, "Where are the androids?"

Rane glanced around the lobby a second time to make sure they weren't there and said in a bothersome tone, "Reddy, are ye sure ye're reading it correctly?"

"Scanner reveals one hundred clones in your area."

"Where?"

"Automaton entities are 0.004572 kilometers in front of you."

Rane and Haley looked toward the ticket counter where Reddy had indicated and then treaded softly in that direction. After taking a cautious peek behind the desk, he heaved a tiresome sigh and said, "I think Reddy's microchip is malfunctioning again. There's nothing here."

Haley turned her head in the direction of the double glass doors. "Reddy, where are the androids?"

"Composite readings show one hundred entities directly behind you."

She widened her eyes and turned around to face her reflection in the huge mirror behind the counter. While staring at the virtual glass, the Battle of Armageddon hologram began to play. "Reddy, those clones aren't real."

"Understood, Detective."

Tired of running around in circles, Rane raised his voice at Reddy. "Then what clones are ye talking about?"

"The automatons in front of you, sir."

Remembering how Jack seemingly appeared out of nowhere, Haley whispered in an eye-opening tone, "Ooooh, they must be behind the mirror."

Not seeing any immediate danger, Haley turned off the laser sight switch on her gun and stuffed the pistol inside the front of her pants. Pressing hard against the artificial glass, she said, "There's got to be a way to get past this energy shield."

Rane ambled over to where she was standing. "Ye think this is a secret passageway into another room?"

She nodded her head and continued pushing against the mirror. "That's why we stopped hearing Jack's footsteps about here."

He watched the army of Lucky Jacks march down the road as he piggybacked off her statement. "An' how he was able t'sneak up on us earlier."

After several moments of joining his wife in pressing against different areas on the computer-generated glass, Rane stepped back from the mirror and said, "As long as our brain thinks this virtual image is real, we can't get past it."

Haley lowered her hands from the fake glass and sighed in frustration. "There's got to be a way to shut it off."

Rane watched the Battle of Armageddon hologram vanish after its short run and then thought about the smart gun. "Hal, do ye think d'disruptor could scramble d'computer's signal?"

Haley pulled her pistol. "We're about to find out."

She aimed her weapon at the mirror and squeezed the trigger.

Rane heard a loud static drain and thought the virtual glass would disappear. When it didn't, he looked over at his wife. "'Tis still there."

Haley lowered her gun hand to her side. Choosing to keep an optimistic attitude, she uttered, "Let me try again."

She extended her weapon toward the mirror and pressed the trigger.

Rane made a disappointed face at the simulated glass. "It didn't work."

Haley stared warily at her image in the mirror. "Maybe it did an' our human shadow is deceiving us."

He gave her a curious look. "How?"

She held up her gun hand to give an illustration. "Look at my reflection in the mirror."

Rane fixed his eyes on her mirrored image as she continued talking.

"My smart gun is in my right hand, yet my shadow has it in my left."

He turned his body in the direction her reflection was facing. "Hey, ye're right."

"I bet the disruptor disabled it an'… "

Rane chimed in like he was on the same wavelength. "D'Locust 52257 is hoodwinking us into believing d'mirror is still there?"

She nodded her head and replied, "Exactly. Now let me see if my theory is correct."

Haley slowly extended her left hand toward the mirror. When her fingers glided right through it, she got so excited she leaped into the air, shouting, "Yes!"

He smiled at her happy reflection in the simulated glass. "Ye did it, Hal. Ye outsmarted Jack."

Taking extra precautions, Haley aimed her pistol at the mirror while taking her husband by the hand. "Come on, love."

After they both stepped through the virtual reality projection, they discovered a room filled with one hundred replicas that looked exactly like the robot.

Rane gaped open his mouth in astonishment at the ten-wide, ten-deep formation of the androids. "Whoa!"

He lowered his voice as if the clones could hear him and said to his wife, "Look at all d'dummies."

Haley stared wided-eyed at all the electrodes and flashing lights inside the robots' open skullcaps. Noting the comatose look in their eyes, she whispered in her husband's ear, "Do you think they can hear us?"

Acting silly, Rane knocked on one of the robots' foreheads and shouted into its ear, "Can ye hear me, chum?"

When all he got was a blank look, he turned toward his wife and chuckled, "Guess not."

Haley smiled at her husband for clowning around and then decided to get some information from the smart gun. "Reddy, are these androids functional?"

"Affirmative, Detective."

Rane didn't like the vacant look in their eyes and slapped one of the robots on the face. "Then why doesn't this dummy respond t'me?"

"Clones are designed to operate collectively, sir," Reddy replied.

"Collectively?"

"Affirmative, all modules will be controlled by the Locust 52257."

"So what's d'problem?"

"Mainframe is requesting master code in order to load memory cards."

Rane put on an impish grin and snickered to his wife, "Isn't that great? Jack's completely helpless without that code."

Haley roved her eyes over the small army of robots and asked, "So what do we do with them? We can't just leave them here."

He shrugged an uncaring shoulder. "We'll shoot 'em."

Shocked at his suggestion, she looked at the frozen stare in the clone's eyes and said, "Shoot them?"

Rane took the pistol out of his wife's hand and gave a direct order to the smart gun. "Reddy, load dead-eye laser an' run a domino pass."

After a red bead of light started flashing inside the small diamond in the top-center portion of the barrel on the gun, Reddy replied, "Specify target."

Rane aimed the gun at the android's forehead in the front-center line and replied, "Memory cards in all d'replicas in this row."

"Domino pattern commencing, sir."

Without hesitation the laser shot out of the diamond and penetrated the circuits inside the heads of all ten clones in that line. With their memory cards melted, the robots started twitching violently and then began to topple backwards onto each other like a bunch of dominos.

Seeing the robots fall onto the floor, Rane laughed idiotically.

Haley shook her head at his sick way of amusing himself and then drew her eyes onto the blueprints covering the walls. Curious why they were there in the first place, she walked over to the wall and started looking them over. "Hey, Rane ... "

He quit laughing at the clones and sauntered over to his wife. "Aye?"

She pointed at one of the many sketches of androids in the plans. "From what I can tell from these blueprints, Artur planned on placing a robot in every major city in the world."

Rane carefully studied the details in the blueprints and said, "An' he planned on using all his diamonds t'make diamond lasers."

Haley thought about the mount of gems in the Battle of Armageddon hologram and queried, "Diamond lasers?"

He roamed his eyes across the sketches and replied, "Aye, diamonds have a very high thermal conductivity that can be used for thermal management like electronic devices. With more powerful lasers, it would be easy t'shoot down missiles."

She smiled in her heart at his returning wit and then looked back at the blueprints. "Artur obviously spent years of careful planning on this project. It doesn't make sense that he would go through all this trouble an' not finish it."

Rane got quiet for a moment, wondering if the robot killed his dad over the diamonds. "No matter what happens, we can't let Jack get that code."

Haley nodded to agree and went right back to reading the blueprints on the wall.

Rane looked around the room and said, "I wonder where Artur stashed all those diamonds."

Haley stepped back from the wall. "I don't know."

She was just about to give up on the idea when she saw something strange in the blueprints. "Rane, look at this."

He drew his attention onto the sketch as his wife pointed at the wall.

"The drawing of the robot in London is the only one with red glitter on his earring," Haley stated.

Rane leaned closer to the wall to check it out. "Ye're right. All d'other ruby, diamond-shaped earrings don't sparkle."

He rubbed the glitter with his index finger, and the wall to the right of the one he touched began to lift up. Unsure what he had done, he quickly withdrew his hand and stepped back from the blueprints. "Uh-oh, I think I just triggered a booby trap."

Once the blueprinted board had retracted enough to see what was behind it, Haley widened her eyes in surprise and gasped. "It's a giant safe."

Presuming the missing diamonds were inside, he grinned at his wife and said, "Hal, I think we found 'em."

She stared at the combination lock on the front of the metal safe and asked, "Did your friend Stinky teach you how to open one of these too?"

He rubbed his thumb along his fingertips like he was a safecracking pro and replied, "Aye, but I'm going t'let Reddy do it."

Rane aimed the gun at the safe. "Reddy, can ye tell us what d'combination is?"

"Affirmative."

All at once a baby blue ray of light shot out of the end of the barrel and started scanning the numbers on the turn dial. After the bot had finished his inspection, the beam retracted inside the weapon. "The combination is 52257."

Eager to open the safe, Rane handed his wife back the gun and placed his fingers on the dial. "In what order, Reddy?"

"Five right..."

Rane speedily dialed the knob to the number indicated and then cocked his ear to hear more of what the bot had to say.

"Two left ... two right ..."

Rane twirled the dial as instructed and then listened for the final set of numbers.

"Five left ... seven right."

After hearing a faint click, Rane pulled down on the silver handle and opened the safe. The instant he saw the pile of shimmering white diamonds, he gasped in awe. "I think we just hit d'jackpot, Hal."

Haley put her gun into her left hand and then picked up a handful of gems with her right. "There's a king's fortune in here."

Rane used his hands like a shovel and scooped up a huge pile of the gems. "An' it is all ours, lassie. It is our inheritance," he said joyfully.

Haley closed the door and locked it after they had put all the diamonds back inside. She then pressed the glittered earring on the blueprint that her husband had touched earlier, and the panel in the wall lowered to its original position. "Rane, you'll have to come downtown with me to the police department an' sign papers declaring you legally alive, or you'll lose everything."

After a long moment of silence, he said, "Ye know what Caleb said t'me once?"

Her eyes lit up with interest. "What?"

"He said, 'True wealth is not measured in how many things we have but in how rich we are in d'love of God.'"

She smiled. "Your dad was a very wise man."

Rane nodded, thinking warmheartedly about Caleb. "Aye, that he was."

Before leaving the room, Haley glanced over at the clones still twitching on the floor and suddenly remembered she had left the incriminating evidence against her husband in the security room. "Uh-oh."

Hearing the alarm in her voice, Rane queried, "What's wrong?"

"I left the tape in the security room."

Afraid of going to jail over a crime he didn't commit, he raised the tone of his voice. "Ye left it?"

Haley nodded. "We have to go back an' get it before anyone else has a chance to see it."

Upon reentering the security room, Haley ejected the recording of the imposter and destroyed it. While feeling pleased with herself over what she had done, she tossed the remains into the trashcan and heard a loud crash from down below. She pulled her pistol and whispered, "Rane, I'm going to go check it out, wait here."

Rane stopped her from walking away by clutching onto the back of her jacket. "Not without me."

With her gun still held out in front of her, Haley turned around and said in a hushed tone, "Okay, but be real quiet."

Rane agreed by nodding his head and then quietly followed her down the stairs. When he had reached the bottom floor, he heard another noise and whispered, "Sounds like it is coming from d'private room."

Haley took off in that direction with her husband running close behind. When she got there, she held her pistol into the air, ready to fire if she had to, and slowly pushed open the creaky door. After discovering the cat had broken the vase by knocking it off the table, she put her gun away and heaved a sigh of relief. "Ooooh, it was only Shadow."

Rane made a perturbed face at the meowing feline and then looked over to where the chest used to be. "Jack took d'trunk all right."

Haley took a quick glimpse at the vacant spot on the floor while taking her cell phone out of her coat pocket. After retrieving one of the stored pictures of the painting of the three mice, she made a puzzled face and said, "Rane, come here."

He walked up to her and asked, "What is it?"

She pointed her index finger at the red piece of fabric sticking out of the chest in the picture of the painting and replied, "This must mean something."

Rane bit on the skin around his thumbnail while staring at the material. He didn't have a clue and shook his head at his wife to let her know.

Haley eyed the gold watch in the picture and queried, "Why would Jillian tell Jack to deliver a trunk with toys to the mall at midnight?"

Rane rested his elbow on his wife's shoulder while staring at the three mice in the painting. "Maybe she's having a blue-light special on my toys an' d'agents get first dibs."

"A blue-light special, huh?" she replied as if his suggestion was the dumbest thing she had ever heard in her life.

He grinned goofily at her response. "I could be wrong."

Haley prayed in her mind to God for the answer and then shifted her eyes back and forth from the gold watch to the piece of fabric stuck in the trunk. After a minute of deliberation, she stroked the front of her long, slender neck. "This is a cloak an' dagger message, right?"

"It appears that way."

"Then all these things in the painting are supposed to symbolize something."

"Right," he replied without hesitation.

Haley held the view screen on her cell phone up in front of her husband's face so he could get a clear look at the picture. "So if ye were Jack, what would the cloth be saying to you?"

Nervous about giving her another stupid answer, Rane started cracking his knuckles. "Uh, get inside d'trunk?"

Haley's eyes widened with excitement. "Inside the trunk."

She paused to give him a big smooch on the cheek before saying further, "I said it before, Rane Rivers. You'd make a great detective."

A grin spread across his face as he touched the area she kissed. He was happy he had somehow pleased his wife. "What did I say?"

"Jillian told Jack to hide inside the magic trunk. The toys are just a decoy."

Rane stared at the picture of Shadow sneaking up on the mice and whispered his thoughts aloud, "A surprise attack, eh?—clever scheme—like a cat going after its prey."

All at once Haley felt a vibration in her coat and looked down at her pocket, whining tediously under her breath, "Oh, Reddy, you little toot. What are you up to now?"

After shape-shifting into his original form, Reddy jumped out of her pocket and landed on the floor next to the cat. Holding his tiny magnifying glass over his right eye, he ineffectually tried to make his cutesy, Irish voice sound tough. "Ye're not going t'surprise attack my friends, kitty. Not on my watch."

Upon hearing what the bot said, Haley giggled, "Reddy, we weren't talking about that cat."

Emulating a human, he drew his mind away from the embarrassment by batting his palm against the side of the round, identification tag dangling from Shadow's collar. "Ye weren't?"

Rane answered for his wife. "No."

Haley stopped sniggering at the bot when she saw a miniature, silver disk eject out of the side of the cat's gold medallion.

Rane knelt down beside the cat and patted the bot on the head. "Good boy, Reddy."

Reddy watched his inventor remove the compact disk from the hidden compartment inside the gold tag and queried, "Reddy, good boy?"

Haley picked up the bot from off the floor and put him back inside her coat. "Yes, an' like all good boys, he stays in his pocket."

Reddy peered at her face through his magnifying glass and sniggered goofily, "Stays in his pocket."

Rane stood back up and handed the object he had fished out of the gold medallion to his wife. "Now why would Aileen hide a miniature disk inside Shadow's identification tag?"

Haley looked at both sides of the CD and shook her head unknowingly. "Why don't we go find out what's on it. I saw a miniature disk player in the security room."

Haley walked over to the player in the surveillance room and inserted the compact, silver disk. She then pushed the play button and a tiny hologram of Aileen beamed out of the projector and onto the table.

Rane dropped open his mouth in shock at what he saw and moved closer to the projection. "Look, Hal, it is Aileen."

Haley nodded and then focused all her attention on what the hologram was saying.

"Hello, Rane. If ye are listening t'this prerecorded message, then most likely I, Aileen O'Malley Finney, have died. I didn't want t'depart this world without leaving ye with d'truth. I felt I owed ye that much. Ye see ... Artur an' I built d'Locust 52257 t'get revenge on yer mum for ruining his life."

Rane gave his wife a brief, concerned look. "Revenge?"

"But my sister, Jillian, wasn't satisfied with just her. She wanted my brother t'get back at everyone who had done him wrong. 'An eye for an' eye,' she vowed. T'throw off d'police, we planned d'strikes several years apart. I never should have agreed t'this. It became a nightmare. D'robot easily assimilated d'human behavior an' started making attacks on his own. I was so afraid we would get caught.

T'make matters worse, Jillian found yer dad dead in Masterpiece Hall an' went mad. She couldn't accept d'fact that he was gone, so she hoodwinked herself into believing Lucky Jack had somehow put his soul inside d'robot. She became obsessed with d'android an' threatened t'kill me if I didn't hand over d'master code. Although I can't prove it, I believe d'robot killed yer dad. D'machine is a menace an' must be destroyed. Now ye know d'truth, Rane. I'm truly sorry. Ye were so heartbroken after yer mum walked out of yer life. I found that one life touches so many other lives. My love goes with ye in spirit, nephew. For d'protection of my sister, I have set up this disk to self-destruct in two seconds. Good-bye, young Finney."

Immediately after the hologram ended, the disk started smoldering. Haley pushed the eject button and stared at the melted CD. She sighed heavily. "Well, that evidence just went up in smoke."

Rane raised an eyebrow and nodded. "Aye."

Haley started to walk out of the room and suddenly thought about the time. After checking the clock on her cell phone, she widened her eyes and said, "Oh no, it is fifteen minutes before midnight. I've got to call Gary an' warn him, just in case."

After dialing the agent's number several times, Haley said, "Rane, the computer must be interfering with my cell phone. I can't get a signal. We're going to have to go outside."

"Okay."

Once Rane and Haley were outside the front of the gallery, she tried calling Gary again. When she still couldn't get a signal on her cell phone, she took off down the sidewalk.

Rane was a bit confused why she left without him and hollered from behind her, "Where are ye going?"

She turned around and answered as if it was perfectly obvious, "To the mall of course."

He ambled over to where she was standing, whining selfishly, "But that's over a mile from here. Why don't ye use the teleportation device?"

She took the silver pocket watch out of her coat pocket. "I tried. It appears when I whistle for it, but I still can't get it to work."

"Then let's call a cab."

Haley dropped the watch back inside her pocket and sniggered slightly, "On a Friday night? A cab will take too long to get here. We can get there faster if we run."

Just the thought of more exercise caused him to raise the tone of his voice. "Run?"

Haley glanced in the general direction of the mall. "Sure, the exercise will be good for us."

"I hate t'exercise. My philosophy is 'Why run when I can ride?'"

Haley kissed him. "Then I'll see you when I get back."

When she took off running down the sidewalk, Rane was dumbfounded. He couldn't believe she was actually leaving him behind. Not knowing what else to do, he chased after her, shouting, "All right, Haley, ye win. Wait up!"

Haley slowed up her pace to let him catch up with her. "The run will be good for your heart, Chappy."

Jogging down the street alongside his wife, Rane said, panting, "If it is so good for me, why do I feel like I'm about ready t'have a heart attack?"

Not a bit winded, she patted him on the back. "'Cause you're out of shape, sweetie."

Feeling like his lungs were going to explode at any moment, Rane stopped to catch his breath. Placing his hand over his heart, he said almost breathlessly, "Hal, hold up for a second, will ye? I-I can hardly breathe."

Haley quit running and pushed the redial on her cell phone. After several rings with no answer, she finally heard a man's voice on the other end of the line.

"Hello."

Haley saw the agent's face appear inside her cell phone and got excited that she had finally reached him. "Gary?"

The agent made a puzzled face at her image as it appeared inside his view screen. "Do I know you?"

"We met briefly about a couple of weeks ago."

While trying hard to recognize her face, Gary leaned back against his beige sedan, which was parked in the back lot outside the mall. "Oh now I remember you. You're that detective lady. How did you get my private number?"

"Never mind that. I called to warn you," she said in a desperate, concerned voice.

Anticipating the arrival of Jillian's limousine, Gary took a brief moment to glance over the parking lot and then carried on with his conversation. "Warn me? About what?"

"You're walking into a trap, sir."

"What are you talking about?"

"I know all about your meeting with Jillian tonight."

Gary saw a black limousine drive into the parking lot. Taking precautions, he reached underneath the side of his black wool overcoat and unsnapped his brown leather, concealment holster. While pulling out his .357 magnum revolver, he asked, "Who told you about that?"

"I don't have time to explain, sir. You have to trust me."

"Why should I trust you?"

"Please, Mr. Brown, you've got to get out of there before it is too late."

Gary aimed the gun's stainless steel barrel at the limousine as it came to a stop alongside his car. Allowing his prominent position to fill him with pride, he foolishly brushed off Haley's warning. "I think we can handle it from our end, Detective."

He closed the lid on his cell phone and put it back inside his coat pocket.

When Rane saw the disturbed look in Haley's eyes, he queried, "What's d'matter?"

She blinked sadly. "He didn't believe me."

"Oh that's too bad."

Haley stared expressionless down the dark street. She wasn't quite sure what to do next and prayed in her mind for God to help her. All at once a gleam came into her eye when she thought of an idea. Acting upon it, she pushed a button on her cell phone that automatically dialed a stored number.

Not sure what she was up to, Rane asked, "Who ye calling?"

She held her phone up to her ear and answered, "My dad, hopefully he can get there before we do."

Gary opened the car door on the limousine and was surprised to see Jamison in the driver's seat. "Where's the chauffeur?"

Jamison climbed out of the car before answering, "We knocked him out an' put him in the trunk."

Lorrell got out of the back seat of the car on the driver's side with his gun held tightly in his hand. "Yeah."

Thinking their act of aggression was unjustified, Gary frowned at his two agents and queried, "What did you do that for?"

Lorrell, who was the guilty party, glanced nervously at Jamison and then spoke up in his defense. "He, uh, went for his gun."

Gary gave him a dubious look and then peered through the car at Jillian sitting in the backseat. After motioning his gun toward the side she was sitting on, he said to Lorrell, "Let her out."

Lorrell opened the car door and forcibly grabbed Jillian by the arm.

Gary held his gun on her as Lorrell dragged her out of the car. "Where's the trunk, Miss Finney?"

With a hateful sneer on her face, Jillian yanked her arm out of Lorrell's grasp and motioned her head toward the open square. "By d'Christmas tree where I said it would be. Now where's d'documents I asked for?"

Before his commanding officer had a chance to give a reply, Lorrell gave her an arrogant smirk and queried, "You didn't actually think we'd betray our own kingdom an' queen, did you, lady?"

Not wanting to waste any more time on small talk, Gary motioned his revolver in the direction of the exchange and asserted his authority. "Let's go."

The moment they all arrived at the Christmas tree, Lorrell pushed Jillian toward the locked trunk and demanded in a harsh tone, "Open it! An' no tricks."

Jillian glared at the agent's face and dialed the combination on the silver padlock. Once she had removed the lock, she layed it on the ground and opened the lid on the trunk.

After seeing all the playthings inside, Gary raised his voice in surprise. "Toys?"

Lorrell made a careful search through the items in the chest and slammed the lid closed. "What are you trying to pull, lady?"

Jillian merely spread a wicked grin across her face, saying nothing in her defense.

Lorrell looked toward Gary and said, "I told you she couldn't be trusted."

Jillian watched the agents whisper privately amongst themselves. "Don't worry, gentlemen, Jack is in his box."

Lorrell eyed the chest. "He is, huh?" he replied in a voice of mistrust.

"Aye, d'magic trunk played tricks on yer eyes, check it again."

He aimed his pistol at her head. "No. You do it," he insisted.

Jillian grinned as if she had the upper hand. "All right."

Just as she hunched over to comply with his order, Gary, and his agents, heard a familiar tune coming from inside the trunk. He pulled Jillian back from the chest and signaled Lorrell to open it instead. The second he did, Jack popped up out of the trunk with the Jack-in-the-box toy in his hand and startled him.

Jamison acted like he had just seen a ghost as he spoke out the dead gambler's nickname, "Lucky Jack?"

While turning the crank-handle on the side of the box to keep the music playing, Jack greeted the onlooking agents with a playful wink of his right eye. "Abracadabera."

At that precise moment, the lid on the toy sprung open and a swarm of virtual image locusts flew out of the box. With no time to take cover, the three men held up their arms to protect their faces, shrieking at the top of their lungs.

The robot removed the blond wig from his head, dropped it and the toy box into the trunk, and stepped out of the hidden compartment. He then reached inside his cloak and pulled out a gun with a silencer attached to the barrel. After making the agents believe that the electricity discharging out of the locusts' tails had stung their eyes to blindness, he made the hologram disappear.

Jillian unmercifully teased the men as they felt around in the dark. "Look, Jack, three blind mice." She laughed in an unfeeling manner.

Infuriated that she was mocking them, Lorrell blindly swung his gun at her and wound up stumbling over the trunk. "You just wait until I get my hands on you, lady!"

The robot had made all their weapons inoperable. So while Jillian was busy taunting his partner, Gary sightlessly felt around for the silent alarm switch on the side of his watch and secretly contacted BIA. She got the distress message back at the homebase and at once activated the visual and audio recording device inside his watch.

Hearing Big Ben commence in gonging the midnight hour, Jillian put on a pompous smirk and said to Lorrell, "I suspect after tonight, ye won't be getting yer hands on anyone ever again."

Gary was afraid his covert actions might be discovered at any moment. With a shaky hand, he ripped the watch off his wrist and flung it into the Christmas tree, hoping a branch would stop it from falling into the snow on the ground.

Jillian checked the time on her watch and said to the robot, "Exterminate these vermin for me, will ye, Jack."

She cleverly walked out of the view of the surveillance camera right before it turned back on.

Jack made sure his left earlobe was kept out of the view of the security camera as he brutally pelted the three agents on the back of the head with the steel barrel of his silenced pistol. After they collapsed onto the ground, he kicked them over onto their bellies and aimed the gun at the back of their heads. He made sure he spoke loud enough in Rane's voice so that the mic in the surveillance equipment could hear him. "Ye played yer last card, gentlemen. But I'm afraid ye wound up with a dead hand. Nobody beats Lucky Jack."

After coldheartedly shooting all three agents, the robot hid the murder weapon inside his cloak and walked out of the view of the camera. At that moment the clock finished the twelfth chime, and the life of the three men had been stripped away by the Locust.

By the time Rane and Haley arrived at the mall, the police and SWAT team were already there and had sealed off the area. Hearing the loud sound of two helicopters circling overhead, Rane looked up at them and said, "Looks like d'entire police force is here."

Haley watched the choppers' searchlights penetrate the night sky as she replied, "It sure does. I wonder what's going on."

Dying to find out, Haley took her husband by the hand and hurried him over to the police officer guarding the crime scene. Although the officer knew who she was, she routinely showed him her badge, and he allowed them onto the grounds. After walking only a few feet from the blockade, Officer Todd came running up and bumped into Rane.

Curious why he didn't stop to say hello, Haley hollered after him, "Todd!"

When he kept on running, Haley made a puzzled face at her husband and said, "Humph, I guess he didn't hear me."

Rane kept his eyes glued on the officer's black hat until he disappeared around the corner of the building. "Looks liked he's headed toward d'open square. Ye want t'follow him?"

She nodded, and they both tailed the police officer into the open square.

Haley looked farther down the way and saw her father standing by the Christmas tree with several other police officers. Hoping to hear that they had apprehended the suspect, she darted toward them. When she arrived at the tree, she couldn't help but notice the three dead bodies lying on the ground in a pool of blood. "Dad, what happened?"

Chief Officer Chase McConaley bent over and pulled back the bloody drop cloth on the center victim. "All three agents were shot in the back of the head at close range."

Upon discovering that the body he uncovered was Gary's, Haley stood rigid as her eyes glossed over with tears. Her line of work never seemed to get any easier. Unable to turn off the heartfelt pain she was experiencing at that moment, she groaned pitiably, "Oh no."

Seeing how upset she was, her dad covered the body. "I'm sorry, Haley. I know you tried to warn him."

Just then, Rane walked up and saw the blood splattered all over the white snow. Feeling both faint and sick to his stomach from the sight of it, he cupped his hand to his mouth and turned away.

Haley wiped the tears out of her eyes and looked around the open square to see if they had arrested anyone for the crime. "Dad, did you catch the killer?"

He sighed glumly as he watched one of his men drop the blond hairpiece, which Jack had purposely left for them to find, into an evidence bag. "No. He was gone by the time we got here."

Chief McConaley shifted his attention onto Rane long enough to give him a nasty look. He was still resentful over the fact that his son-in-law had walked out on his daughter. Speaking about him as if he wasn't even there, he said to Haley, "What's he doing here?"

Haley glanced at her husband, who was biting the skin around his thumbnail. "Dad, please don't start."

Feeling intimidated by the hateful glare in his father-in-law's eyes, Rane tried to sneak off and accidentally bumped into the Christmas tree. The jolt to the branches shook Gary's watch loose, and it fell to the ground. Thinking he had broken one of the silver bulbs, he said in an uneasy tone, "Oops!"

Chief McConaley frowned at Rane's clumsiness and then pulled his black flashlight out of his jacket pocket. He turned on the light and then stooped down on the ground to see what had fallen. After spotting the gold watch lying in the snow, he took a pen out of his shirt pocket and tried to fish it out.

Haley nosily peeked around the side of his body to see what he was doing. "What is it, Dad?"

Instead of answering her question, he stuck the writing end on the pen through one of the holes on the watchband and carefully lifted the watch into the air. He stood back up and looked around for the crime scene investigator. Seeing him across the way, he hollered out, "Detective Hanson, come here!"

Without hesitation, the officer scurried over to him and said, "Yes, sir?"

Chief McConaley extended the pen in his hand toward the officer. "Take this down to the lab along with the wig an' have it analyzed."

Dectective Hanson opened his evidence kit and pulled out a paper collection bag. Chief McConaley gently lowered the watch into the container.

Haley leaned over to her husband and whispered in secret, "If I'm not mistaken, that looks like the same watch Gary was wearing."

Rane gave the branches a quick once over and whispered back, "What was it doing up in d'tree?"

"That's a good question."

Detective Hanson sealed the bag with red evidence collection tape. He then logged the item's description, time, date, and location on the evidence log before documenting the same information on the outside of their respective collection bags. Once he had finished, he printed and signed each item and took off in the direction of his police car.

After he had gone, another police officer walked up to Chief McConaley and spoke privately into his ear.

Chief McConaley turned off his flashlight while looking toward his daughter. "Haley, I'll be back in a minute."

Fifteen minutes later, he and two apprehending officers returned to the scene of the crime. With an angry look on his face, Chief McConaley pointed in Rane's direction. "Arrest him!" he bellowed.

The words struck a chord in Haley's ear like a badly tuned instrument. "What do you mean, 'arrest him'?"

When Rane tried to run, the two policemen grabbed him by the arms and pinned them behind his back.

"Let him go. He didn't do anything!" Haley insisted.

Rane foolishly tried to resist arrest while the men were putting the cuffs on him. "Get yer hands off me, gumbies!"

After watching one of the policemen, use his nightstick to knock the wind out of her husband by hitting him hard on the diaphragm, Haley shouted in a voice of panic, "What are you doing?"

Rane instantly doubled over from the pain, wheezing hard to get air back into his lungs. When his legs started to buckle, the two arresting officers helped keep him on his feet.

Chief McConaley held up the camera footage from the mall and replied, "We got it all on tape, Haley."

Uncertain what he was talking about since she had previously destroyed the false evidence on her husband, she lowered her eyebrows and queried, "You got what on tape?"

While watching one of his arresting officers remove the silenced pistol and the deck of cards out of Rane's coat pockets, Chief McConaley replied in an accusing tone, "He murdered those three agents in cold blood."

Swallowing hard out fear, Rane widened his eyes at the murder weapon and said, "How did that gun get into me jacket?"

Knowing the robot had somehow put it there, Haley's heart sped up faster as she began defending her husband. "No. Rane couldn't have done it. He was with me the whole time."

Chief McConaley pointed toward the pistol in the police officer's hand and said in a tone of disbelief, "Didn't do it, huh?"

Haley knew her husband was in big trouble and tried to think of a way to prove his innocence. "Dad, can't you see? He was set up."

Chief McConaley took the deck of cards out of his officer's hand. After removing the Jack of Diamonds from the pile, he held it up in front of his son-in-law's face and said in arrogance, "Looks like you played your last card, Rane. Or should I call you, Lucky Jack, Junior?"

He put the card back in the deck and added, "Like father like son, I always say."

Rane swallowed hard at the mention of his dad's alter ego. He knew there was nothing he could say in his defense.

Chief McConaley looked at the two arresting officers standing on each side of Rane and said, "Read him his rights, and then take him downtown and book him."

"No, Dad, please!" Haley begged with tears in her eyes.

Rane gave his wife a forlornly look as the two police officers hauled him away.

Feeling helpless to change the situation, Haley cupped her hands over her face and started sobbing heavily. "No. Please, God, help us."

CHAPTER 50

Several hours later, Haley walked into her dad's office at the police station and asked hopefully, "Did you find them?"

Chief McConaley spun around in his brown swivel chair to face his daughter. "Close the door."

After Haley had complied with his request, he gripped the padded arms of his chair and replied, "No. We didn't find any androids."

Haley took off her black ski jacket and hung it up on the silver coat rack by the door. "Did you check the simulated mirror behind the ticket counter?"

"Yes, an' there was no mirror. All we found was a wall."

Totally stunned by his disclosure, she gasped, "What?"

"In fact, we searched the entire building an' didn't find any of the holograms you told us about."

With a let down look on her face, she queried, "You didn't?"

Chief McConaley hunched forward in his seat and started chewing her out. "I stuck my neck out for you, an' you made me look like a fool in front of my men."

He slowly leaned back in his vinyl chair. "Now Jillian is threatening to sue the department."

Haley sat down in the beige chair on the other side of his desk and said glumly, "But they were there, Dad, honest. Rane and I both saw them."

He pushed the play button on his computer to playback the film recorded at the mall. "Your ex-husband is in big trouble."

Haley crossed her legs and answered in her husband's defense, "We're not divorced yet, an' Rane didn't murder those three agents."

"Then how do you explain the lab report?"

Not being able to deny the undisputable facts compiled against Rane, Haley raised her voice excitably. "I don't know how some of his hairs got inside that blond wig. All I know is he didn't do it."

He pointed at the costumed gunman on his monitor. "That sure looks like him to me."

She swallowed hard at the incriminating evidence. "That isn't Rane shooting those men, Dad. It is an android that can alter its molecular structure to look like anyone he chooses."

Disbelieving her testimony, he answered in a stern voice, "Oh come on, Haley. We don't have technology like that today."

Haley thought about the bot in her pocket. "I can prove it."

"How?"

Haley bit her lower lip out of nervousness and looked over at her coat hanging on the rack. She knew Rane would be furious if she exposed his top-secret project, but she was desperate to save him. Against her better judgment, she started whistling into the air for Reddy.

Questioning his daughter's strange behavior, he asked, "Why are ye whistling that tune?"

By the time Haley had finished the short jingle, she had a change of heart. Seeing Reddy poke his head out of her pocket, she widened her eyes apprehensively and put her index finger to her mouth. This was her way of telling the bot not to give away his position.

Reddy imitated her gesture, nodded that he understood, and then lowered his head.

Haley waited until the bot was safely out of sight and then shifted her uneasiness back on her dad. "Uh, why am I whistling the tune?"

Chief McConaley nodded his head.

Haley shot him an innocent smile and then said like she wasn't sure, "I like the sound of it?"

When he gave her a funny look, she squirmed in her seat, picking at her fingernails. To get the attention off of herself, she said, "Um, Dad, why don't you check the imposter's left earlobe in the footage."

"Why?"

"It will prove he's not Rane. The android is wearing a pierced earring."

While rewinding the video to check out her story, he asked, "If the robot was disguising himself as your husband, why didn't he just remove it?"

"He can't, it is his power source."

Chief McConaley played back the entire film, fast-forwarding certain parts as he watched. "You can't see it."

Highly upset that the android had outfoxed them, Haley stamped her foot on the floor. "Ugh! Jack deliberately kept his ear out of the view of the camera."

Thinking about his own reputation, Chief McConaley shook his head at his daughter and said worriedly, "If this leaks out to the press, it is not going to make us look good."

Haley leaned closer to her dad, clasping her hands between her legs. She couldn't believe how callous he was being at that moment. "Make us look good? What about Rane, Dad?"

At the mere mention of his son-in-law's name, Chief McConaley tensed up his jaw and snarled, "Forget him! You got my granddaughter to think about now."

Tears filled her eyes as she cried, "I am thinking about her, an' she needs her daddy."

Rane was sitting in the interrogation room at the police department with his head facedown on the table, feeling like his life was over. "Lord, please tell me this is just a bad dream, an' I'm going t'wake up at any moment."

While he was busy feeling sorry for himself, the police officer standing guard outside the cross-examination room pushed the buzzer and allowed a French lawyer into the room to speak with Rane privately. The classy, tall gentleman with gauze badges wrapped tightly around his head carried a black leather attaché case over to the table. He placed the thick case on the floor and then pulled out one of the four wooden chairs.

Rane lifted his head to see who had just sat down next to him. When he didn't recognize the attorney's clean-shaven face, he queried, "Who are ye?"

The Frenchman adjusted the knot on his blue silk tie and smoothed out a wrinkle on the sleeve of his black suit. "My name is Felone Ferarsh."

Not wanting the gentleman to know that he secretly thought his cologne reeked, Rane released a couple of subtle coughs. It was quite obvious from the smell that the man did a poor job of masking the fact that he smoked. "Ye're French?"

"Oui," he answered back in his native accent. "I'll be representing you as your attorney."

Rane blinked his eyelids rapidly as he pondered what the man said. "But I didn't hire an attorney."

"Your wife procured me, monsieur."

Rane looked down at the black attaché case on the floor beside the Frenchman and queried in a voice of surprise, "Haley hired ye?"

He nodded his head once. "Oui."

Rane worked up enough nerve to ask the man about the bandages. "What happened t'yer head?"

Felone felt the white bandages on his person. "I had several malignant tumors removed."

Rane turned up his lip and thought, *Ugh, ye poor thing.*

Turning his attention back on representation, Felone said, "Your wife has disclosed to me all z'details on z'case, including z'secret code."

Rane was surprised that his wife would actually do that without checking with him first. "She told ye about d'code?"

"Oui," he replied resolutely.

Rane lowered his head and muttered under his breath, "I can't believe it."

Felone took a note out of his white, dress shirt pocket and handed it to Rane. "Read it for yourself, monsieur."

Rane read the permission slip written in his wife's handwriting and said in a voice of shock, "Haley wants me t'give ye d'code?"

"Oui. You can save z'lives of many innocent people by handing it over to z'proper authorities. With you locked away in here, you can't help anybody."

Rane thought it over carefully and finally sighed in concession. "I guess she's right."

The French attorney pulled his fancy ink pen out of his shirt pocket and handed it to him. "Here, use zis."

Rane started to write down the code on the paper Felone had given him but then noticed the same lifeless look in his eyes that he had seen in the tour guide's. Bearing in mind what his wife said about the eyes being a gateway to the soul, Rane thought, *Wait a minute. Prosperity mysteriously vanished after d'computer went haywire. I bet she was nothing but a hologram. That would explain d'empty expression in her eyes an' her sudden disappearance in Masterpiece Hall.*

The Frenchman could clearly see him studying his face and asked, "Is there something wrong, monsieur?"

Rane didn't answer and continued staring unblinking at Felone's blue eyes. The expression in them was slightly different than what he had seen in Prosperity's. His were more mechanical like Reddy's. He had a gut feeling that he was really Jack in disguise. If he was right, his reaction time would be faster than a human's. To test his theory, he tried to slap the man on the nose while pretending to ward off an insect. "Get out o'there, grasshopper!"

Taking the bait, Felone used his lightning-fast reflexes and blocked the strike to his face. After his palm smacked hard against Rane's, he lowered his hand onto the table and said warily, "I didn't see any locust, monsieur."

Rane was totally flabbergasted at how fast Felone could move. He was now almost certain this imposter was the robot. Knowing he was taking a big gamble, he threw the pen on the floor to distract Felone and then ripped the bandage off the left side of his head. Responding to the sudden hostility, Felone quickly cupped his hand over the exposed earring on his left lobe while screeching like an angry swarm of locusts.

After Jack's cover had been blown, Rane gave him a haughty smirk and said in reply to the robot's last statement, "I do."

With an overconfident look on his face, Jack pulled a deck of cards out of his suit pocket and started shuffling them. He then dealt Rane a Jack of Clubs off the top of the pile and went back to speaking in his original Irish brogue. "Welcome to d'club, laddie."

Rane eyed the face card on the table in front of him and said, "So my wife was right. Ye're d'third Jack—Artur's secret weapon."

"If ye're wondering if I was d'one who beat yer mum at cards, d'answer is a resounding yes. D'queen had t'be dethroned. After all, Jacks are better." Jack replied in the same haughty tone.

Rane tossed the torn gauze into the android's face and said bitterly, "Artur couldn't beat her, so he built ye t'do his dirty work, eh?"

Jack stuffed the cards inside his pocket and rewrapped the bandage around his head to cover his earring. "Aye, she never suspected a thing."

He showed him the pack of cigarettes in his pocket and said further, "Artur programmed me t'simulate every one of Lucky Jack's bad habits."

"Did ye kill me dad?" Rane queried bluntly.

Jack stared coldly at him for a long moment before giving him the answer. "Aye."

"Why? He built ye."

With no heart to care, Jack simply performed another magic trick by making it look like he pulled a Jack of Diamonds out of thin air. "True, but then everyone knows there can only be one Lucky Jack."

Rane scowled at the robot as he spun the Jack of Diamonds playing card on the tip of his finger.

Jack made the card vanish into thin air and then held out his palm to Rane. "Now give me d'code."

Rane picked up the Jack of Clubs card off the table and snickered, "Give it up, gumby. Ye're holding a losing hand."

He ripped up the playing card and threw it in the android's face. "Ye'll never beat me. Kings are better."

Jack scowled at him and then picked up the black leather briefcase off the floor. After laying it down on the table, he released the gold latch on each side of the container and said in a smart-alecky tone, "A losing hand?"

He opened the lid on the case that was full of bundled money and turned it toward Rane. "I think not."

Rane gasped in awe at the sparkling diamond tiara resting proudly on top of the cash. "Would ye look at that, a crown fit for a queen. 'Tis beautiful."

The robot nodded once and began to sweeten the deal. "Including d'tiara, there's over fifty million pounds in here—enough for yer family t'live like kings."

Jack turned up his lip at Rane. "While ye rot in prison."

Desiring to do something nice for Haley for once in his life, Rane picked up the gorgeous crown and began to imagine how great it would look on her head.

Seeing he was tempted, Jack pressured him some more by stating, "D'gems will go nicely with yer queen's pretty face, eh, laddie?"

Rane continued to admire the shimmering diamonds as he nodded his head. He knew he wasn't going to get out of a life sentence without a miracle from God anyway. Just when he was about to take Jack up on his offer, he saw the same phantom locust appear on top of the crown. Remembering what his wife told him about not putting his trust in riches to save him, he slowly looked up at the android's face. "Did ye know that a locust has no king?"

Jack was puzzled why he would ask him that out of the blue, but he answered his question anyway. "Aye."

Rane set the tiara back inside the attaché case. "Then how could ye possibly know how one lives?"

Jack was so insulted by his statement that he slammed the lid closed on the case and growled vengefully, "Why ye ..."

Rane snickered at the android as he locked the case.

Jack angrily pushed his chair back and got up out of his seat. "We'll see if ye're still laughing after d'last card is played."

The robot pinned the briefcase under his armpit and then buzzed the police guard to let him out of the room.

Back on the other side of the police department, Haley was still trying to convince Chief McConaley of her husband's innocence. "Dad, you've got to believe me. Rane, didn't do it, he was set up."

Chief McConaley picked up his blue hat off the desk and stood to his feet. "It will take a miracle to get him out of this one, hon."

Haley's eyes filled with tears as she looked up at her dad. "Then I trust God will give us one."

Chief McConaley put his hat on his head and headed for the closed door. "I sure hope so, for his sake."

"Where are you going?"

"I'm going to have a little chat with him."

Eager to see her husband, Haley queried in a desperate tone, "Dad, please take me with you."

Opening the door to his office, he answered firmly, "No. I don't want you anywhere near him."

Haley wiped off a teardrop that had trickled down her cheek as she queried, "Where is he?"

"In the interrogation room."

Chief McConaley went out the door and closed it behind him.

Haley was so overwhelmed with grief that she felt the strength leave her body. Squeezing her eyes shut, tears streamed down her face as she blubbered prayerfully, "Heavenly Father, please help me. I'm scared. I don't know what to do. Show me a way out of this."

She laid her forearms down on the desk, resting her head on top of them, and broke down sobbing.

Hearing her crying her heart out, Reddy discreetly poked his head out of her coat pocket and whispered in a compassionate tone, "Aw."

The tiny bot made sure it was safe to come out and then leaped out of the pocket with his magnifying glass in hand. After running across the floor, he sprung onto the desk, grabbed a tissue out of the box, and brought it to her. "Here, Haley."

She slowly lifted her head and forced herself to smile at the bot as she took the tissue out of his hand.

Reddy watched her grin fade as she wiped the tears off her face. Hoping to cheer her up, he patted her on the hand and said in an optimistic voice, "Don't cry, everything will be all right."

Haley nodded her head as she took another tissue out of the box to wipe her nose.

The bot held his magnifying glass in front of his eye while taking a quick look around the room. "We just got t'find some proof that will clear Whiz Kid, that's all."

Haley sniffed her runny nose a couple of times and then got up out of her chair with a confident look on her face. "You're right, Reddy, an' we're going to find it."

She walked over to the trashcan and threw the wet tissues away.

Reddy raised his hand into the air and said in a hyperactive tone, "Can I play Sherlock again, Haley?"

Haley gave him a casual shrug of her shoulder and sat down in her dad's chair. "Sure, why not."

Reddy leaped into the air and shouted happily, "Goodie!"

"An' what would be our first move, Sherlock?"

The bot repositioned the magnifying glass in front of his eye and said in a superior, British voice, "Elementary, my dear, I believe we'll find what we're looking for in d'video recorded at d'mall."

Haley thought Reddy's off-the-wall suggestion was a waste of time since she had already gone over it with her dad. Having nothing to lose, she decided to take the bot's advice and rewound the incriminating footage against her husband. While rewatching the tape, she found nothing that would help her case. She sighed in a breath of disappointment and then suddenly thought about the pictures of the paintings that she had taken with her cell phone. *Oh, I forgot all about them.*

She got up out of her seat and went over to where her coat was hanging on the rack. After digging her cell phone out of her coat pocket, she opened the picture files and started browsing through them.

Reddy observed her actions as he sat down on the edge of the desk. A couple of minutes went by before he asked in a hopeful voice, "Did ye find something in d'pictures yet, Haley?"

Haley shook her head and replied unhappily, "No."

She ambled over to where the bot was sitting and handed him her cell phone. "Reddy, use your magnification optics an' tell me if you see anything strange in the picture of the mice."

Reddy held his magnifying glass over his eye as he carefully examined every detail in the painting. When he had finished looking at it, he gave her one of his famous, goofy grins and started snorting chuckles through his nose. "D'painter made a booboo."

Haley smiled at the bot's good humor and asked interestedly, "A booboo?"

Reddy's snickering died down as he pointed at the picture of the silver bulb on the lower branch of the Christmas tree. "D'artist forgot t'put d'Gary mouse's reflection in d'Christmas ornament."

Haley peered closely at the blind rodent on the right and noticed that the bulb was in fact near the left side of his head. All at once a clever gleam shot through her eyes when she thought about where the robot was standing at the scene of the crime. "You're right, Sherlock. His profile should be there. Now that's what I would call a booboo."

Haley picked up her cell phone from off the desk. "Reddy, rewind the tape again."

"Okey-dokey, Haley," he replied in his usual perky voice and then straight away played back the video for her to watch a second time.

Haley studied the tape intently until she saw an image appear in one of the large, silver bulbs on the Christmas tree. Curious what it was, she looked over at the bot and said, "Reddy, I need you to infiltrate the system."

The bot nodded and then shrunk himself down until he disappeared out of her sight.

A few moments later, a message from Reddy appeared across the computer monitor that read, "Need access code."

Haley watched the prompt appear on the screen and immediately typed in her code. *Daddy's little girl,* *13359209.

Reddy wrote back by displaying the word, *Secured.*

Once the bot had penetrated the policing system, Haley spoke to him through the intercom. "Reddy, run motion picture on slow speed, will you?"

Reddy's voice came through the speaker on the computer in his serious, British tone, "Affirmative."

Haley gaped at the footage on the monitor like she was looking for something specific. "Reddy, freeze-frame motion picture."

After the bot had complied with her request, Haley gave her next command. "Now slowly pan back."

Watching the still picture shift gradually to the left, Haley said further, "Stop, an' zoom in on the center, silver bulb on the far right side of the Christmas tree."

"Increasing magnification, Detective."

The instant the image was enlarged, Haley saw the side of her husband's face in the reflection on the bulb. Seeing the red earring in his left ear, she giggled under her breath. "We got you, Jack."

Haley hopped up out of her chair, threw her hands into the air, and shouted joyfully, "Yes! Thank you, Jesus. I knew the King would come through for me."

She printed a copy of the picture. "Reddy, reset the system an' dispatch."

"Dispatching policing system."

Haley was so eager to get the information to her dad that she forgot all about the bot and left without him.

While walking down the corridor in the women's jail, Rane stopped and shared his heart with his wife. "I got t'tell ye, Haley, I was really scared. If God hadn't come through for me, I dunno what I would have done."

Haley kissed him on the cheek to comfort him. "I'm sorry it took so long. My dad didn't want to release you until they apprehended Jillian."

Extremely tired from the long day, Rane yawned, answering, "That's all right. I was just glad t'get out o'there."

Haley motioned her head toward the other end of the hall. "Jillian's in the last cell on the right. The police brought her in about an hour ago."

While following his wife down the confinement area, Rane glanced up at the clock on the wall and noted the time was 4:00 a.m.

Haley watched her husband crack his knuckles. She could tell he was nervous about seeing Jillian again. "Are you sure you want to talk to your aunt? She's in a really bad mood."

"When isn't she?" Rane replied grimly.

"My dad said the picture BIA took of her won't hold up in court."

"Why not?"

"It was too dark. You couldn't tell for sure if it was her."

"Great, without any evidence she'll walk scot-free."

Haley lowered her voice to a whisper as she approached the cell Jillian was in. "Don't worry. We have an ace in the hole."

She peered through the bars at Jillian and saw her leaning against the back wall. "Miss Finney, your nephew is here to see you."

Rane noticed the wires sticking out of his aunt's elbow and whispered to his wife, "What happened t'her left arm?"

Haley eyed the body part in question and whispered in his ear, "They had to cut it off. She tried to kill one of our arresting officers."

While watching his nearly blind aunt feel her way over to the steel rods, Rane whispered back to his wife, "I see they removed her sunglasses an' earring too."

"That was for her protection an' ours. We didn't want her to contact the robot."

Haley pulled her husband back from the bars as Jillian walked up.

Jillian sneered at her nephew as she gripped her right hand around one of the bars. "I thought I smelt a rat."

Rane waved his fingers at her like a shy, little boy and said contritely, "Hi, Auntie, sorry I pinched yer face."

Believing his apology to be insincere, she didn't hesitate to snap at him. "Cut d'rubbish! What do ye want?"

Rane flinched at her vulgarity and answered, "I, uuuh, see ye're in need of a savior. Did I ever tell ye about Jesus?"

Thinking back when her nephew first came to live with her at the gallery, Jillian replied in an irksome tone, "At least a hundred times."

Rane grinned at his aunt, shrugging in a cavalier manner. "Okay, consider this a hundred an' one. Jesus tol' me t'tell ye that he loves ye."

Despising the taste of truth, Jillian snarled at him, "How many times do I have t'tell ye, boy? I don't want yer King. Now get out of here!"

Rane held up his hands in a surrendering gesture. "Okay, okay, just thought ye might have changed yer mind."

"When I get out of here, ye're d'one who's going t'need saving."

Haley crossed her arms and said confidently, “I suspect ye won’t be getting out of here for quite some time, ma’am.”

Hearing the assured tone in her voice, Jillian turned her head toward the detective and queried, “What do ye mean?”

“BIA didn’t destroy the top secret files on you, Jillian.”

Jillian tried not to look worried as she replied, “Ye’re lying. D’android saw her do it.”

“It was all a charade.”

Upon discovering that BIA had called their bluff, Jillian stepped back from the bars and said anxiously, “A charade?”

“Yes. BIA suspected d’android wasn’t Gary.”

“How?”

“The answer was found in an unopened message inside Gary’s watch. BIA had sent it to him right before he died.”

Rane leaned closer to his wife and asked curiously, “What did it say?”

“It said, ‘I knew you hated tea, Gary. Thanks for the verification.’”

Overcome with fear that she would spend the rest of her life behind bars, Jillian screamed into the air, “Nooo!”

Rane and Haley met her dad at the main entrance of the police station.

Chief McConaley handed his daughter her coat and said, “Officer Todd is waiting in the police car out front. He’ll give you both a ride home.”

Haley put on her black ski jacket and asked in a voice of deep concern, “Dad, did you find the robot yet?”

“No, but we got every available man out looking for him.”

Chief McConaley cupped his hand under his daughter’s chin and added, “Don’t worry. We’ll find him.”

She smiled, embracing the hand he put under her chin. “I know you will, Dad.”

He lowered his hand from her jaw and then motioned his head toward the double glass doors. “Now go home an’ get some sleep.”

Rane and Haley walked out the front entrance of the department and climbed into the back seat of the police car.

Rane peered out the window at the falling snow and then laid his head on his wife's shoulder. "I'm so glad we're fnally going home."

Haley kissed him on the forehead and said, "How does it feel to have your crown back, your highness?"

He thought about how Chase had him sign the papers to declare him legally alive before leaving the police station. That way Jillian and the government couldn't lay claim to Artur's estate. "It feels great. Now I'll be able t'do more in helping fund Christian orphanages all over d'world."

She smiled widely. "I'm sure glad I married a very generous Irishman."

Rane grinned at his wife's compliment and then went on to share more of his shopping fantasy. "Then I'm going t'make sure my daughter an' me wife has d'best of everything, including a nice home for me little girl t'grow up in an'…"

He paused briefly to smooch the wedding ring on his wife's finger. "A big, fat, diamond ring for me sweetheart, fit for a queen."

She giggled fondly. "What about something for yourself?"

He yawned before replying, "I'm going t'take yer advice an' get me that car I always wanted."

Haley was so excited her eyes lit up. "The GT-7 Panthera Sports Coupe?"

Rane nodded his head and replied, "Aye, I'm sure Reddy will help me drive it."

Haley sniggered. "I bet he will."

She hugged her cheek against her husband's face and then looked out the window to watch the snow.

During the long ride across town, Rane yawned numerous times, struggling hard to stay awake. Feeling like he couldn't keep his eyes open any longer, he laid his head back on his wife's shoulder and fell asleep.

Chief McConaley was sitting back in his office, going over the police report on Jillian. Hearing a knock on his door, he hollered out, "Come in!"

Officer Hanson walked into the office and said, "Chief, I just came in off my watch an' got a call from Todd. He told me to tell you he won't be in today."

Chief McConaley was a bit confused since Todd had just driven off in the police car not ten minutes before. "Won't be in today?"

"No. He said he had the flu."

Concerned for his daughter's safety, Chief McConaley jumped up out of his chair and hollered out her name as if she could somehow hear him. "Haley!"

Rane suddenly awoke and saw his wife asleep with her head against the window. He yawned twice and then leaned forward in his seat. While watching the windshield wipers clean the snow off the glass, he discovered that the policeman was on the wrong side of town. "Hey, Officer. Ye're going d'wrong way."

Haley was awakened by the boisterous sound of her husband's voice. Still a little groggy, she blinked several times and gazed out the window to see where they were.

Rane pointed his thumb in the opposite direction and raised the tone of his voice at the driver. "I live on d'other side of town."

The driver kept his eyes on the road and didn't answer.

Rane exchanged a confused look with Haley and then tried to get the policeman's attention by banging on the dividing, metal cage. "Hey! Did ye hear me? I said ye're going d'wrong way!"

Still not getting a response from the driver, Rane got frustrated and threw his hand up in the air. "I don't believe this. D'dude must be on crack or something."

Haley hunched forward in her seat. "Todd, you went the wrong way."

When he refused to acknowledge her, she knocked on the metal cage and raised the tone of her voice to a shout. "Todd, can you hear me? Todd!"

Unsure why he wouldn't give her a reply, Haley peered into the rearview mirror and saw a Band-aid wrapped around his left earlobe. Her eyes widened in alarm as she leaned back in her seat and looked over at her husband.

Rane saw the panicky expression on her face and whispered edgily, "What is it, Hal?"

Her response was slow and apprehensive. "Uh, Rane, I don't think that's Officer Todd."

With concern in his eyes, Rane glanced at the back of the policeman's head and replied, "What?"

She rubbed her left lobe with her thumb and index finger to signal her husband to look at the driver's ear.

Rane took a long, hard look at the man's face in the rearview mirror and saw it transforming into Jack's. Caught off guard by what he saw, he cringed unpleasantly. "Uh oh."

Jack grinned at Rane from his rearview mirror. "Relax, Finney me boy. Enjoy d'ride."

Rane frowned at the kidnapper's phony hospitality and shouted, "Where are ye taking us, Ripper?"

Jack turned right at the corner while replying, "Back to d'gallery of course. Ye're going t'give me that code if I have t'break every bone in yer body."

Haley peered into the rearview mirror to make sure Jack wasn't looking and then reached into her coat pocket. After discovering she had left Reddy back at the station, she dialed his secret cell number from the phone in her jacket and started whistling his tune.

Hearing the noise, Jack looked at her reflection in his rearview mirror and asked, "What's all that whistling about, Detective?"

Rane watched the bot appear on the floorboard and then grinned impishly at the robot. "What's d'matter, Jack? Never heard a lassie whistle a love tune to a gentleman before?"

Just to mess with him, he leaned forward in his seat and spoke into the robot's ear. "It just so happens that me wife finds me quite sexy."

Jack lost interest in what Rane was saying when he heard the shrill sound of police sirens coming up fast behind him. He peered into his rearview mirror at their flashing red lights and then floored his accelerator to try and outrun them.

Rane turned around and looked out the back window. Seeing numerous headlights on cars in hot pursuit, he whispered to his wife, "Looks like yer dad sent d'entire police force after us."

Jack swerved his car around the corner, causing a slight spin out in the snow. He was driving so fast and squirrelly that he caused Rane to topple onto Haley several times.

Tired of banging into his wife, Rane angrily pursed his lips at the back of the robot's head and shouted, "Slow down, gumby! What are ye trying t'do, kill us?"

Reddy wholeheartedly agreed as he picked himself up off the floorboard. "Aye, what are ye trying t'do, kill us?"

Thinking back on how the android had killed the agents in cold blood, Rane's eyes bulged with fear as he said to the tiny bot, "Oops! We wouldn't want t'give that Ripper any ideas."

Reddy shook his head to agree and then dove into Haley's coat pocket to hide from the robot.

Haley heard a police officer from behind them shouting at Jack through his megaphone.

"Pull over!"

Jack glanced at the driver from his side mirror and sped up faster down the street.

Rane hung on to the side of the door for dear life as Jack squealed his tires around another turn. "Yeeeesh!"

Staying right on Jack's bumper, the same police officer hollered through his megaphone a second time, "I said, 'Pull over!'"

All at once a bunch of police cars came up from the opposite end of the street and joined in on the chase. Trying to avoid being sealed in, Jack swerved off the road and wound up crashing into one of the police cars. Without hesitation, the police officers got out of their cars, took cover, and aimed their guns at the vehicle the android was driving.

Officer Peter put his microphone up to his lips and hollered, "Come out with your hands on top of your head!"

Jack slowly opened the door and climbed out of the car with his hands on top of his head.

Rane peered out the window and saw one of the policemen handcuffing the robot's hands behind his back. Disturbed by what he saw, he looked over at his wife and said, "Something's wrong. Jack's making it too easy for 'em."

The words had barely left his mouth when he heard a faint, chirping sound. "I hear crickets, or is that just me bones creaking again?"

Haley tilted her head while listening for the sound. "I hear them too."

"My bones or d'crickets?" he queried jokingly.

She giggled. "The crickets, Rane."

All at once the chirping noise got louder. When the sound reached a deafening pitch, Rane cupped his hands over his ears and peered out the window. "I can't see where it is coming from. It is too dark outside."

Haley covered her ears, groaning in anguish. "Ugh! The shrill chirping hurts my eardrums."

Reddy poked his head out of her pocket. "Don't worry, Haley, I'm working on d'problem. D'change to d'audio frequency for that hologram should take place in about three point five seconds, providing that Jack doesn't pick up on my signal."

Immediately after the specified time given by the bot, the noise diminished. Haley sighed in relief and lowered her hands from her ears. Concerned about the well-being of her fellow comrades, she looked out the window at the night sky and saw a plague of green locusts appearing out of nowhere. The winged insects flew toward their intended target and descended on all the police officers standing outside.

Feeling sharp stings on their faces from the electricity in the locusts' tails, the police officers covered their heads with their jackets and started running around in circles, screaming at the top of their lungs.

Watching the flying locusts disintegrate as they tried to set down on their windshield, Haley queried, "What's wrong? Why can't they get near our police car?"

Rane stared curiously at the screeching locusts and replied, "I dunno."

Haley fished Reddy out of her coat pocket and set him down on her thigh. "Reddy, what's stopping the virtual images from coming inside the car?"

He cupped his hands behind his buttocks and whined, "No spank."

Haley lowered the tone of her voice to make it sound gentle. "Reddy, no one is going to spank you. Now tell us what you did."

The bot nervously picked at one of the sparkly blond curls on his head as he replied, "Ye promise. No spank?"

She used her index finger to make the symbol on her heart and answered, "Cross my heart."

Reddy let go of the curl he was playing with and pointed toward the front of the car. "I cleared a channel on d'radio an' patched in yer audio file."

Totally in the dark as to what he was talking about, Haley promptly queried, "What audio file?"

The bot grinned at her as if it was going to make everything okay. "D'one I recorded of ye an' Whiz Kid laughing at d'private eyes."

Rane listened intently to the noisy static coming over the radio and said, "I don't hear us laughing."

"That's because I speeded up d'sound waves t'sound like static, so ye couldn't tell what I did."

To show he approved of what he had done, Rane patted the bot on top of his head and said, "Good boy, Reddy."

Reddy widened his eyes in surprise and queried, "Reddy good boy, Whiz Kid?"

Rane grinned at the bot and nodded. "Aye, Reddy's a good boy."

He then joined his wife in looking out the car window.

Haley sighed helplessly as she watched the locusts harass her fellow police officers. "Rane, I don't think we're going to be able to convince them to laugh."

"That's all right; I think God just gave me an idea."

Rane picked up the bot off his wife's leg and asked, "Reddy, can ye get rid of these bugs?"

Reddy batted his long, black eyelashes at his inventor and said out of concern, "Ye got bugs too?"

He heaved a snickering breath. "No, I don't have bugs. I'm talking about d'ones outside."

Reddy looked outside the window at the swarm of locusts and chuckled, "That's not bugs, ye funny guy. It is a hologram."

"I know what it is, Reddy. What I want t'know is can ye scramble the robot's linguistics signal t'shutdown d'program he's running?"

The bot glanced at the android laughing at the police officers as they tried to fight off the attacking locusts and then replied unsurely, "I can try, but his safe file might detect it an' block my signal."

"Well, have a go at it anyway."

Reddy hopped off Rane's hand and landed on the seat. "Okey-dokey, I'm on d'case."

Haley saw Chief McConaley pull up alongside of them in his police car. Trying to warn him of the impending danger, she hollered through the window, "Dad, no! Go! Get out of here!"

Alarmed by the unsightly insects descending upon his windshield, Chief McConaley dropped open his mouth and thought, *What in the world?*

Haley felt a strong need to help her comrades outside and tried to open her door. Banging on the window, she hollered, "Dad!"

Chief McConaley got out of his vehicle and opened the door on Haley's side. Before he had a chance to do anything else, the locusts descended on him. Coming to his rescue, Rane and Haley jumped out of the backseat and hurried her dad to safety inside their police car.

Unfortunately, Rane did not get into the vehicle behind Haley in time and was overcome by a swarm of locusts. "Aaagh!"

Haley stashed the bot in her coat pocket to make sure her dad couldn't see him and hollered out, "Rane, I'm coming to help you!"

Rane bellowed back at her, "No! Stay in d'car!"

Chief McConaley grabbed his daughter by the arm when she tried to go save her husband. "Haley, what are those things?"

With a helpless look on her face, Haley kept one eye on Rane as she replied, "Virtual images."

"Is this one of the holograms you were talking about?"

"Yes. If you believe they're real, they can harm you."

Chief McConaley leaned back in his seat and said, "I'm sorry I doubted your word."

Haley put all her focus back on her husband, shouting into the air, "Rane, get in the car!"

Rane headed in that direction, until a swarm of locusts cut him off at the pass. "They won't let me."

"They're not real. How can they stop you?"

Intimidated by their evil crocodile-looking eyes and the aggressive chirping sounds they were making, Rane slowly backed away from the police car. "'Cause me warped brain thinks they're real, that's how."

Haley decided to coach him from the sidelines. With her hands cupped around her mouth, she hollered into the night air, "Do what we did before! Laugh, honey! That will diffuse their negative energy!"

Before he had a chance to join her in laughing at the counterfeit pictures, several locusts snuck up behind him and stung him on the buttocks. The pain was so severe he squealed until his throat was sore and took off running.

Haley listened to the whirring sounds of the locusts' wings and shouted even louder. "Don't be scared of them, Chappy!"

Still running around in circles, trying to avoid getting shocked, he bellowed back, "I think it is a little late for that, Hal!"

"Trust me, the pictures are not real!"

After taking several more jolts of electricity on his derriere, he leaped into the air and hollered, "Ouch! Me sore bum begs t'differ with ye, lassie!"

Haley coaxed him again as she yelled back and forth with her husband. "Come on, Rane! You can do it! Laugh, like this: hahaha!"

Dodging an electrical current that came dangerously close to his face, he squealed to the top of his lungs, "Yiiiiigh!"

The horde of virtual images grabbed ahold of Rane's blue jacket and lifted him high into the air. "Haley, throw me a weapon!"

Haley leaned out the car door and tossed him the small Bible she had just taken out of her coat pocket. "Here, use this!"

Rane fumbled the book like a football and almost dropped it. After getting a good grip on it, he looked back at his wife. "Good choice!"

"Now read Psalm one-hundred-twenty-six, verse two, an' pray for God to fill your mouth with laughter!"

Rane didn't hear a word she just said. He was too busy using the Bible like a fly swatter to smack the locusts that were trying to haul him off. "Let go o'me, gumbies!"

Hanging out the window, Haley re-cupped her hands around her mouth and hollered out, "Honey, you're supposed to read it, not beat it over their heads!"

Not being able to hear her from all the racket the police officers and locusts were making, he shouted back in a voice of confusion, "What?"

Reddy was listening to the commotion and snuck a peek at Rane from over the top of Haley's coat pocket. Seeing his inventor pelting the locusts with the Bible, he snickered goofily, "Whiz Kid, ye are one funny guy."

Finally figuring out that her husband couldn't hear her no matter how loud she yelled, Haley groaned disappointedly under her breath, "Oh dear."

Reddy gave Haley a comforting pat on the hand and whispered, "No problem, Haley. I can get rid of those ugly critters for ye."

Totally surprised, a happy pitch rose in her voice. "You can?"

Reddy nodded his head and answered, "I'll just play ye an' Whiz Kid's laughing track on a very loud frequency. Here, I'll show ye."

The bot opened his mouth wide, releasing a high-pitch sound that lasted for almost a minute.

Chase cupped his hands over his ears and looked around inside the car, wondering where the noise was coming from.

Haley was overjoyed to see the images of the locusts outside breaking up into fragments. "Keep it up, Reddy. It is working."

With a confused look on his face, Chief McConaley thought, *Who's Reddy?*

All at once the virtual insects that were attacking Rane completely disappeared, and he fell to the ground.

Haley leaped out of the car and ran over to him. "Are you all right?"

Rane picked himself up off the ground and made reference to the Bible by saying, "Hey, this really works."

Haley smiled and took her book out of his hand. "That's not exactly what I had in mind when I told you to use it."

Rane chuckled at himself as he replied, "Oh."

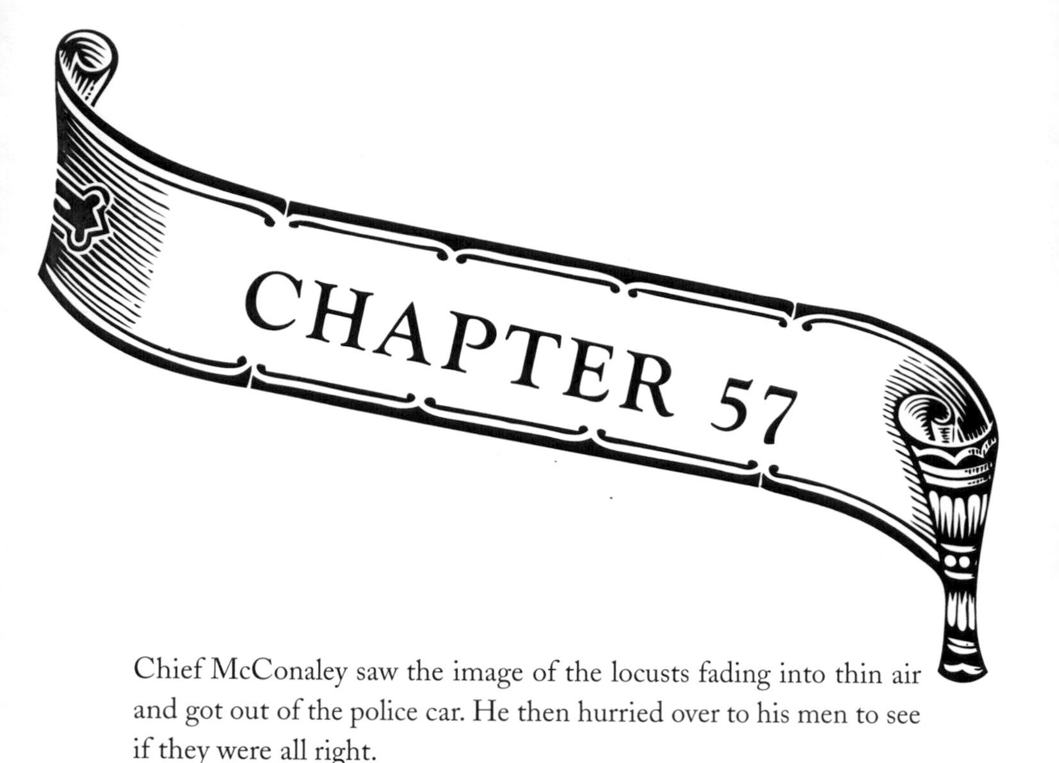

CHAPTER 57

Chief McConaley saw the image of the locusts fading into thin air and got out of the police car. He then hurried over to his men to see if they were all right.

Jack was so mad about his program being shut down he looked around at all the police officers and shouted, "Who did that?"

Reddy snickered at the robot under his breath, "Ye're about t'get trumped, Jack."

The bot knew he had successfully scrambled the android's sensors to the point where he could no longer pick up on any weaponry. Revealing this fact to the detective, he said, "Ye should be able t'use yer disruptor on him now, Haley."

Boiling mad with thoughts of revenge, Jack easily broke the handcuffs off his wrists like they were made of straw and headed toward Rane.

Rane widened his eyes as the android came toward him. "I think I'm in for it."

Haley whistled the tune for the smart gun as Jack got closer to her husband. Once the transformation was completed, she pulled the silver pistol out of her coat pocket and shot the robot in the forehead.

The disruption to Jack's memory circuits caused him to start shaking violently like he was about to explode. With a dazed look in his eyes, he reiterated in a mechanical, rushed, Irish brogue, "Destroy pictures that exalt themselves against d'knowledge of God, destroy pictures that exalt themselves against d'knowledge of God, destroy pictures that exalt themselves against d'knowledge of God!"

Haley put her gun away and whispered into her husband's ear, "D'robot looks like he's having a seizure."

Chief McConaley and his men gathered around the robot to observe his psychotic behavior.

With his head twitching from side to side, Jack continued saying the same thing over and over again. "Destroy pictures that exalt themselves against d'knowledge of God, destroy pictures that exalt themselves against d'knowledge of God, destroy pictures that exalt themselves against d'knowledge of God!"

"What's wrong with him?" asked Officer Peter.

Rane watched the android drop to his knees and replied, "I dunno."

Haley studied the mechanical man's anomaly behavior and finally figured it out. "Rane, the Bible archive you loaded into his neural net must be overpowering his memory bank. If I'm not mistaken, some of that audio coming out of the robot is from Second Corinthians, chapter ten, verse five."

Pleased that the audio files were shutting down the robot's faulty programming, Rane snickered roguishly, "Isn't it great?"

Rane stopped chuckling when he suddenly heard a prerecorded, British woman's voice coming through the audio system inside Jack's chest.

"Energy overload. Activate self-destruct mechanism."

Hearing the robot's built-in alarm sounding off as he went into a comatose state, Haley whispered anxiously, "Rane, the Locust 52257 activated his . . . "

Rane didn't give her a chance to finish as he replied jumpily, "I know, I know."

"I thought Prosperity said the computer fixed the problem."

"That's what we get for trusting a hologram."

Haley nodded, sighing heavily. "Now we know why Jack was so desperate to get the code. His life really did depend upon it."

"Why isn't the robot moving?" asked Chief McConaley.

"D'Locust 52257 has activated his self-destruct mechanism," Rane confided.

The computerized voice came through the speaker again and said, "Danger. Five minutes to detonation."

"We better get out of here," Chief McConaley said out of concern for everyone's safety.

"It won't do us any good," Rane explained. "D'android has enough fire power in him t'blow up d'entire city."

Fearing for his daughter's life, Chief McConaley raised his voice and said, "There's got to be something we can do."

Rane knelt down on the ground and ripped the smock off the android. He then looked up at his wife's hopeful face and whispered, "Haley, get me a screwdriver . . . if ye know what I mean."

Haley nodded and started whistling a new tune into the air.

Shocked at his daughter's seemingly irrational behavior in a time of crisis, Chief McConaley queried, "Haley, have you seen a doctor about that?"

Haley smiled at her dad and then pulled a shiny, silver screwdriver out of her coat pocket. Handing it to her husband, she said, "Here, love."

Rane gave his wife a secret wink of his eye and then used the screwdriver to remove the tiny screws. After removing the panel on the robot's chest, he gave his wife back the tool. "I'm going t'try t'shut down his control system."

Chief McConaley eyed all the circuits and flashing lights inside the robot's chest and asked, "You know how to do that?"

Haley came to her husband's defense by saying, "Of course he does, Dad. Rane's a genius."

Rane grinned favorably at his wife's comment and then laid the panel on the ground. After pushing a button to release the keyboard and small monitor inside the android's chest, he heard the British woman's voice say, "Four minutes to detonation."

Uneasy by the sound of the alarm, Rane wiped the sweat off his brow and quickly keyed in the password: *Jacks are better.* Immediately afterwards he saw the words *Access granted* flashing across the monitor. The words disappeared off the screen, and three Jack playing cards like the ones on the front of the matches appeared in its place. Wasting no time, he silently read the serial number for the microchip on the inside panel and proceeded to change the encryption code by speaking into the command system. "Override Jacks are better. Delete memory card 6300006104156."

The computer responded by removing the three playing cards from the screen and saying, "Deleted. Indicate new password."

Rane keyed in *Kings are better* on the keyboard and heard the femine voice recording say, "Three minutes to detonation."

Feeling on edge by the countdown, Haley put the screwdriver into her pocket as she pleaded to her husband, "Hurry, Rane."

Rane anxiously nodded his head while waiting for the system to change the password. "Come on, come on."

Chief McConaley placed his hand on his gun as he asked uncomfortably, "What's taking so long?"

Rane kept his eyes glued on the monitor as he replied, "I dunno."

The British computerized voice continued counting down. "Two minutes to detonation."

Chief McConaley allowed the nervous tension to overtake him and raised a demanding voice. "Type it in again!"

Rane nodded his head, wiping the cold sweat off his brow, and keyed in the new password a second time. When nothing happened he became agitated and smacked the circuit box, shouting, "Come on, gumby!"

Haley closed her eyes and started praying in her heart for God's help. She was praying so hard her lips were moving.

"Ninety seconds to detonation," cautioned the voice recording coming out of the robot.

Desperate to see a message appear on the screen, Rane bit the skin around his thumbnail and said impatiently under his breath, "Come on, come on."

After Haley had finished praying, she opened her eyes. Seeing how upset her husband was, she stroked his bangs with her fingertips to reassure him everything would be all right.

"One minute to detonation," the British soundtrack warned yet again.

Rane looked up at his wife's confident face and said, "I'll try it one more time."

He typed in the password and the words *Processing request* started flashing across the screen. He wiped the nervous sweat off his brow and heaved a huge sigh of relief. "Oh, good, it took it."

"You did it!" Chief McConaley shouted excitedly.

"Aye, I just hope I have enough time left t'shutdown d'self-destruct mechanism."

Rane spoke hurriedly into the audio system, "Locust 52257, Kings are better. Switch over t'new memory card 6100396954386."

With everyone on edge, the feminine computerized voice slowly began to give the final countdown. "Twenty seconds to detonation … nineteen … eighteen … "

Rane's heart was racing so fast he started talking like his tongue was on fire. "I repeat, 'Locust 52257, Kings are better. Switch over t'new memory card 6100396954386.'"

Hearing the seconds ticking away, Haley said in a voice of hope, "Lord, we're counting on you."

"Ten ... nine ... eight ..."

Pressed for time, Rane's speech sped up even faster. "I repeat, 'Locust 52257, Kings are better. Switch over t'new memory card 6100396954386.'"

"Three ... two ... one...."

Expecting the worst to happen, Chief McConaley squeezed his eyes shut and looked away.

All at once three King of Hearts playing cards appeared across the screen as the computer said, "Kings are better. Aborting termination activation sequence. Switching over to new memory card 6100396954386."

Rane and all the officers were so excited they started cheering, hooping and hollering. "Yahoo!"

With a gleeful smile on her face, Haley clapped her hands together. "I knew God would come through for us."

Filled with joy, Rane picked up his wife and spun her around once before setting her back on the ground. "Aye, that he did indeed."

He looked over at the android when he heard his keyboard and monitor retracting back inside his chest.

Jack got up off the ground and removed the coronet from his head. He then started quoting a passage of scripture from the audio Bible recorded in Caleb's voice. "A new commandment I give t'ye, that ye love one another; as I have loved ye, that ye also love one another (John 13:34, NKJV)."

Rane identified the Irish voice and smiled. "That's Caleb."

Rane stared curiously at the robot and asked, "Jack, do ye have any memories left of your old programming?"

Jack ambled over to the police car he was driving, opened the trunk, and threw his coronet inside. He then pulled out the attaché case full of money and said, "Jack is dead, sir."

The android brought the case to Rane and announced with a grin, "Long live the king."

Rane opened the case and took out the diamond tierra. After giving it a place to rest on top of his wife's head, he peered into her bright green eyes and said with passion, "An' long live d'queen."

Haley smiled at her husband and then suddenly thought about his mother. "Rane, I have a dream I would like to see come true."

Rane gently stroked his thumb across the heart-shaped beauty mark on her cheek and replied, "Ye name it, my queen, an' it is yer's."

Mustering up some courage, Haley drew in a deep breath and slowly let it out through her mouth. She knew the petition she was about to make could easily set off his Irish temper. "Let me help you find Kathryn so you can forgive her an' break free from the past."

Rane's heart filled with hate at the mention of his mother's name. "No!"

He was so mad he tightened his fists and started breathing heavily through his nose. He sounded like a snorting bull ready to charge.

Haley let him know how she felt about his decision by filling her eyes with tears. "Rane, you're dreaming the wrong dream. Hate is not part of our character in Christ. Please wake up to the King's love."

Rane pursed his lips at her face, not willing to give in no matter what she did.

All at once he heard the sound of thunder rumbling and peered up at the flashes of light in the night sky. Making sure he could be heard above the noisy wind that had just kicked up, he shouted into the air, "Looks like an electrical storm's coming in!"

Haley peered up at the purple and blue electrical veins piercing the heavens and then whistled the tune for the teleportation device.

Rane watched her take the silver pocket watch out of her coat pocket and wondered what she was up to. "Hal, we better take cover. We don't want t'get struck by lightning."

He looked over to see what Chase McConaley and the other officers were doing and discovered they weren't moving. "Hey, what's going on here?"

Haley stared at the luminous star on the lid of the watch and noticed its blue hues were pulsating. She then stepped closer to her husband and slowly roved her sad eyes over every inch of his handsome face.

Sensing something bad was about to happen by the way she was acting, he queried anxiously, "What is it, Hal? Why are ye looking at me like that?"

Haley called to mind a scripture in the Holy Bible in Philippians 3:13 and felt led to silently pray for her husband. Then, with tears in her eyes, she tried to encourage him to forgive his mother. "Don't let hate separate you from my love, Chappy. Let go of the past, so we can be together."

He thought about how hard it would be to love his mother again after all that she had done to him. "I can't do it, I can't. She ruined my life."

Haley gazed up at the radiant blue star that had just appeared in heaven. It looked exactly like the one they had come out of when they first arrived at the Ritz Mall. She wiped away a tear trickling down her cheek and then blew her husband a kiss. "I will always love you, your highness. I pray the King will help you come back to me."

Rane saw her angelic image fading away and feared he would never see her beautiful face again. Hoping to stop her, he reached out and hollered, "Noooo!"

All at once Rane found himself trapped inside a replica of the London tower. The clock was floating out in the twilight zone with a bunch of other clocks. Startled by his new surroundings, he shrieked at the top of his voice and then looked around the tower. Seeing the Bible in his left hand, he queried, "What am I doing here? An' where is Hal?"

He peered out the window at the twilight sky and thought about the dream he had shared with his wife. Staring curiously at the other clocks floating out in space, he said in a whisper, "I seem t'be stuck in some time warp. Maybe Haley was right. Maybe all this is just a dream. If it is, I pray God will wake me up out o'this nightmare."

Not knowing what else to do, he randomly opened his Bible and saw a scripture glowing on the left page. Intrigued by the strange phenomenon, he drew the book closer to his eyes and read the passage in Matthew 6:14 (NKJV): "For if you forgive men their trespasses, your heavenly Father will also forgive you."

Not wanting to forgive his mother, he flipped to the next page, but it quickly turned back. Feeling uneasy by the occurence, he stammered, "Bu-but this can't be."

Making sure it wasn't just a fluke thing, he tried it again. When the page turned right back to the same one, he widened his eyes and then recalled something his wife had said to him earlier in regards to his mother.

"You need to forgive her so ye can go on with a new page in your life."

Thinking about all the pain his mother had caused him, Rane slammed the book closed and shouted out of foolish pride, "No! I'll never forgive her for what she did t'me."

He searched around for a way of escape. When he couldn't find one, he put the Bible under his armpit and started pounding his fist on one of the glass panes. "Let me out o'here! Can anybody hear me? I'm locked in d'tower!"

Rane got tired of banging on the glass. Feeling like he would never break out of the prison he had locked himself up in, he started pleading for mercy. "Please, God, help me t'wake up to d'truth. I want t'break out of d'past. Please, I'm begging ye. I'm a broken man."

He stood silently for several minutes, hoping to hear from heaven. When he didn't hear anything, he observed the secondhand on the clock going round and round in a backwards sweep and lowered his head, crying, "I'm sorry, Hal, I dunno know how t'come back t'ye. Ye said, 'D'best dreams are d'ones we share together.' Somewhere along d'way I lost sight o'that. I forgot d'King's love."

Rane stared motionless out the window, feeling dead inside. The twinkling stars seemed so far away. Was there really one out there with his name on it? Just as he was about to put the dream out of his mind forever, he heard the beautiful melody from the watch playing inside his head. It was like the music was calling him back to love. He liked it so much he started humming the tune and then saw a vision of Jesus with an Imperial State Crown upon his head.

The King was standing in the glory of His Father. The light was so bright upon His countenance Rane couldn't make out His face.

While squinting at the Lord's radiant appearance, Rane felt a pleasurable, warm sensation come upon his heart. He looked down at his hands and was surprised to see his skin glowing like the sun. The light felt so magnificent it brought tears to his eyes. "Yer love is like a shadow on me all d'time. Is there no place I can hide from ye, yer majesty?"

King Jesus answered him by speaking in a British tongue to emphasize God's United Kingdom. "This is the masterpiece that I set before you, Rane, love one another as I have loved you."

Then the clock began to gong.

Rane was still dreaming on his king-size bed. He was so dead to the world he didn't even know his black cat had perched herself on top of his chest. Hearing the clock tower gonging the noon hour, he awoke, fluttering his eyelids. The second he saw his feline with her right eye squeezed shut, he cringed, banging the crown of his head against the headboard. "Aaagh!"

After seeing the green and purple striped curtains covering the picture window above him, he realized where he was at and sat up in bed. Looking toward his living room, he placed his hand on the bump on his noggin and hollered out to his Irish setter. "Ireland, did ye slobber in Shadow's eye again?"

Ireland loped into the bedroom with a yellow tennis ball in his mouth and dropped it on his master's bed. He licked Shadow on the face, and the cat moved to the end of the bed.

Rane patted his panting dog on the head and picked up the wet tennis ball. While eyeing it closely, he thought about the rules in the game and how the Lord wanted him to serve love to his wife. As the clock tower finished the twelfth chime, he recalled something the Lord had said in his dream. "This is the masterpiece that I set before ye, love one another as I have loved ye."

Rane put his feet on the floor and inadvertently caught sight of his reflection in the mirror on his closet. He sighed at his sad face and then saw the remnants of the Queen of Hearts playing card lying on top of their divorce papers on his nightstand. He picked up the torn pieces and said out of remorse, "Oh, Lord, what have I done t'my queen? She was a love gift from ye, an' I threw her away. I was too wrapped up in meself t'care about her, an' now she's gone."

Still beating himself up over breaking his vows to his wife, Rane angrily threw the ball toward the living room and the dog took off chasing it. He wanted to call Haley and apologize but was too afraid she might hang up on him. And for good reason, he had sent her divorce papers an' demanded that she sign them, knowing she still loved him. With tears filling his eyes, he sniveled out of guilt, "Oh, God, please forgive me. I said some hurtful things t'her. I broke me queen's heart."

He was just about to give up on the idea of ever getting back with her when he suddenly remembered some good advice from his dream. "Destroy pictures that exalt themselves against d'knowledge of God."

Rane picked up the papers off the nightstand and stared at his wife's signature. Thinking aloud, he said, "God is love. He hates divorce. D'best dreams are d'ones we share together."

Reflecting back on his dream, he considered the swarm of stripping locusts and how he had allowed the devil to strip him of everything he had ever cared about. Was he going to allow him to take away his wife too?

After hesitating for several minutes, he finally decided to stand up to his fears and destroy any pictures of divorce coming against his marriage. He knew he had to rely on the love in Jesus and trust him to save it. After all, Rane was a king, and it was high time for him to start acting like one. Swallowing his pride, he picked up his cell phone off the table and called his wife. Soon as he heard a friendly greeting on the other end of the line, he queried to be sure, "Hal, is that ye?"

Haley was surprised to hear from him. They hadn't spoken to each other in months. "Rane?"

His blue mood perked up at the sound of her voice. "Aye, 'tis me, lassie."

"It sure is great to hear from you. How have you been?"

"All right, I guess," he replied as if he didn't really agree with his answer.

"Did you get the papers?"

Rane stared tearfully at his wife's signature on the divorce papers and swallowed hard. He was so choked up with grief he barely managed to squeeze out a reply. "Uh-huh."

Hearing the sorrow in his heart, she queried, "Is something wrong? I signed the papers. Isn't that what you wanted?"

Rane cleaned the tears off his face with the bottom of his blue undershirt and tried to share the regret he was feeling in his heart. "Haley..."

"Yes?"

He looked at the card pieces in his hand and replied uneasily, "I... I..."

Rane squeezed his eyes shut and several teardrops dripped down his face. Losing control over his emotions, he broke down sobbing.

Deeply concerned for his well-being, Haley spoke up. "What's the matter?"

Although it wasn't easy for him, he lowered his masculine guard and revealed his true feelings to her. "I don't want a divorce, Hal. I'm sorry for being such a gumby. Please forgive me. I promise I'll start studying d'Bible with ye like ye want. I just want ye an' d'baby t'come home."

She widened her eyes out of shock and said, "You know about Faith?"

Rane used the back of his hand to wipe away a stream of tears flowing down his cheek and calmed himself down. "Aye, I dreamed ye tol' me about her."

Haley was so overjoyed that God had answered her prayers to save their marriage she didn't know what to say.

"Please, Hal, come back t'me."

With her heart filled with adoration, she replied, "Your queen has never stopped loving you, your highness."

"Haley..."

"Yes?"

"Ye think ye could use yer great detective skills in helping me find me mum? We have a lot o'catching up t'do."

Haley was deeply touched by his merciful heart and started crying. "You bet I will."

After hanging up the phone, Rane picked up his Bible off the nightstand and opened it to the same scripture he saw in the clock tower. He stared at the passage and then gripped the top-corner of the page with his thumb and index finger. Squeezing his eyelids shut, he said worriedly, "Please, please, please, don't turn back."

He opened his eyes, held his breath, and slowly turned the page. With his hands frozen in mid air, he waited with great anticipation to see what would happen. When the page didn't turn back, he sighed in relief. "Oh, thank God. I can go on with a new page in my life."

Rane removed the King of Hearts from the pile of playing cards on his table and used it as a bookmarker to mark the page. He didn't want to ever forget to walk in love again. Standing to his feet, he lifted the Bible into the air and said in allegiance, "Long live d'King."

He set his Bible back down where he originally got it and then flopped down on his bed. While staring toward his living room, he recalled more of the occurrences in his dream and whispered to himself, "Reddy bot? Wait a minute. If me dream for a daughter was real, then maybe..."

Rane opened the drawer on his nightstand and started digging through a pile of papers. Once he had found his set of blueprints, he pulled them out of the drawer. After unfolding the draft, he saw the words *Reddy Bot* in the upper right corner of the margin and grinned from ear to ear. "Ye know, Lord, Oi think Whiz Kid is going t'build that thingamabob after all."